THERE WAS A TIME

BY THE SAME AUTHOR

UNKNOWN TRUTH

I knew by the time I was done with the first page that I was in for a great reading experience. *Unknown Truth* is the stuff of award-winning sleuth stories, as they should be told.

—Reader's Favorite

One in four women is abused in her lifetime, and there are 4.8 million intimate-partner-related physical assaults and rapes reported each year, reports the National Violence Against Women Survey, sponsored by the National Institute of Justice and the Centers for Disease Control and Prevention. That makes domestic violence the leading cause of injury to women. On average, more than three American women are killed by their partners every day, and one-third of all women murdered in the U.S. lose their lives due to domestic abuse, say Department of Justice statistics.

This is a work of fiction. Names, characters, places and incidents either are the product of the author's imagination or are used fictitiously, and any resemblance to actual persons, living or dead, business establishments, events or locales is entirely coincidental.

ISBN-13:978-1539840831

ISBN-10:1539840832

THERE WAS A TIME

A novel by

CONNIE NELLOS

THERE WAS A TIME when she felt happy and content with her life.

That was BEFORE

THERE WAS A TIME when the circle of fate stepped in and brought them together unpredictably.

That was LOVE.

THERE WAS A TIME she regretted ever having met him.

That was EXPERIENCE

THERE WAS A TIME after him.

This is NOW

What is more astonishing *now* was how *indifferent* she felt about him.

Actually, she felt *more* than indifferent....*her soul was sick to death of him.*

CHAPTER

Friday, the first of February, was the day Wes Blair assessed his image in the bathroom mirror. His body slumped over the basin, his hands holding onto the edge of the counter, he exchanged a scorching look at this face, scrutinizing the image for clues as to who this was staring back at him. He gave a startled gasp. "That... can't be... me," he groaned as he struggled to control his quavering voice. He waved his hand and when the person waved back, he realized it *was* him.

In stunned silence, he stood for several moments, staring at this image—*his image*. Dark rings of exhaustion under his eyes, the haggardness of his face. This face belonged to an old man. He rubbed his eyes with the back of his hands and then continued to stare at himself as if waiting for something to change the shock of the moment. He blinked his eyes several times. Nothing changed.

A sudden spurt of nausea waved up from his gut and he felt the bile rise in his throat. He quickly turned on the faucet and scooped cold water on his face in an effort to avert the whale from vomiting out Jonah. He grabbed a hand towel and dried his face.

Fixed with a level stare, he again looked in the mirror. He still didn't like what he saw. *When did this happen?* When was the last time he'd looked at himself in the mirror? He rubbed his temples with his index fingers.

He felt tired. No, actually, he felt more than tired; he was weary... weary of his sorry life.

He'd never felt this way before.

Hit with a sudden stab of anxiety, he started to tremble and he tried not to think any thoughts at all. But there was no *off switch* to his brain and within seconds, his eyes darted maniacally at the collage of vivid images that zoomed through his mind. He wrapped his hands around his head in an attempt to keep out the nonsensical words and images, but like pieces of a jigsaw puzzle, they tumbled through his battered brain. Images of the worst period of his life—his childhood. The bitter remembrance of his father's verbal sarcasm and name-calling: *you'll never amount to anything. You're nothing but a dumbass and a screw-up.*

All the painful memories came back. His father—his tormentor. All the grief, the nightmares, the unimaginable suffering... everything came back.

He gave up on his father before he was twelve. The man never once showed a shred of affection. He never showed that he could laugh or have fun. Never watched or went to a baseball or football game. His life only seemed to represent the dark side of humanity.

It took him a bit longer to figure out what his mother was and was not. He always surrendered to her whims because he wanted her to love him. However, she had only to pull the strings, and he became her puppet. Although he hated himself for allowing her to treat him this way, he secretly believed that *one day* he would be in control, navigating his own ship.

Now, here he was, weary, shaken and confused, wishing he could transport the images from his private hell to an erratic comet orbiting the sun. He was certainly not in control.

He *must* calm himself down so he can think only rational thoughts. He must envision only happy thoughts. He must think only happy thoughts. He *must*.

He staggered into the living room and plopped himself on the sofa, resting his head on the leather high back, his heart, aching with nostalgia. He sat there remembering earlier days... memories of what his life had once been. His first thought was that of his oldest son Lucas, who had just learned to ride his tricycle. As soon as he got off the seat, his younger son, Adam, crawled up on the seat trying to mimic his big brother, but his feet couldn't reach the pedals. When Lucas told him to get off his bike, he didn't budge. He was a tough little guy who wouldn't let anyone push him around...

"Push him around?" he murmured. *Push him around.*

Immediately he had vivid, visceral images of Emma. His pulse quickened, his jaw clenched, his hands balled into fists. In seconds, the vein that always stood out on his forehead when he got angry started to throb.

"That's it! It's her! *She's* pushing me around," he shouted out loudly as the invidious recall raked up the past. "She's the one who stole everything from me. She is the one who won't allow me to see my sons. Why am I not allowed to spend time with my own children?"

As quickly as this torment had come, he plugged up the dam of anger that seemed to spring up every time he thought about Emma. He must calm down and think. He sat quietly, wondering how this eluded him for so long. Why hadn't he seen this problem sooner? She was the one responsible for the dark cloud over his head, and the dull, empty ache in his heart. It's all her fault. "Yes, that's what's wrong," he uttered, finally feeling good about his discovery.

After a few moments a brief flicker of hope emerged—his nerves suddenly tingled with excitement. He knew what it was he had to do now. He had to destroy her.

He must formulate a plan and put it into action—not to kill her yet—that will be another plan for another time.

Now he was beginning to feel how he should feel—*in control.*

CHAPTER

2

The windshield wipers were barely able to keep up with the relentless downpour that streamed down the glass. When he switched off his headlights as he rounded the curve into the quiet narrow street he could hear the swish of the tires turning on the wet pavement. He took the turn so sharply that the car slid sideways, jolting over the pot-holed blacktop.

He pulled over to the curb and stopped the car under the giant eucalyptus trees that lined the street. The limbs overhung the car, offering some oasis from the rain, but the winds became turbulent and sprayed raindrops that sounded like buckshot against the windows. He sat quietly in his parked car, drumming his fingers on the steering wheel as he stared at the rain without actually seeing it. After brainstorming all day, his mind kept replaying his plan to reinforce every step so it would be as vivid to him as if he had carried out every detail a hundred times before.

Suddenly, the storm sky found its voice when an elongated jagged bolt of lightning exploded like a missile to earth, electrifying the air and sending its reflection on the narrow road. Seconds later thunderclaps violently boomed from the heated air.

He looked up at the sky and smiled before he glanced down at his watch. It was nine-forty-seven: time for action. He hiked the collar of his jacket around his neck before he pulled his hood down over his head and slipped on his black gloves. He turned to grab the baseball bat that rested on the front seat before he opened the door and stepped out into the driving rain.

"*Damn it*," he muttered under his breath as soon as his feet hit the ground.

The car's interior light beamed like a gray pool across the pavement. He had forgotten to turn off the dome light. Quickly, he shut the door. No one must see him.

But he had it all planned... he doesn't make mistakes. It was perhaps because the storm dislocated his thoughts. That's why he made the first small mistake.

Dressed all in black, his tall, dark hooded figure blended in with the darkness of the night as he trampled across the wet grass. He shivered and turned his head downward as if to avoid the blustering wind and rain. He squinted against the wind as he walked unerringly down the uneven brick path that led to the side entrance of the garage.

His hand gently turned the knob on the garage door. He felt the adrenaline surge through his blood—the door was unlocked. He could hear his pulse thud in his ears as he slowly opened the door. Then, without warning, another bolt of lightning, brighter than the first, slammed out of the sky. The reflected crackle of lightning outlined his tall hooded frame that lurked outside the home. Quickly, he slid into the darkened garage, not making a sound.

Once inside, he closed the door, stood still and listened as his eyes adjusted to the darkness. He heard no sounds. He glided noiselessly through the garage, his hand closed firmly around the handle of the baseball bat. When he reached the door that led into the house, he stepped into the shadowy hall and closed the door behind him. An inky shaft of light wafted down the hallway, not enough to see clearly, but it was of some help. He heard the sound of the television in the bedroom. *Ah, she's awake. The boys must be asleep upstairs. He must be quiet so as not to wake them.*

Perfect timing. His plan hinged on her habitual behavior. Every evening at ten o'clock, Emma had her hot Chamomile tea while she listened to the nightly news. His plan was perfect.

In black, he was invisible flattened against the wall. *When she comes down the hallway to prepare her tea, she'll flip on the hall light and find him standing there like a thief in the night.*

He pitied all men who wished they could do what he was doing. They just don't have the guts. Men are chickenshit when it comes to women. They let women tell them *what* to do *when* to do it and *how* to do it, and they would rather humiliate themselves than take control and be a real man! *Well, I'm the one in total control here, and I will show that self-righteous bitch who the boss is.*

Suddenly, a noise. The saliva dried in his mouth, and his vision sharpened. He was ready to take care of the woman who had wrecked his life. Not to kill her... *yet*. Tonight is to only show her who the boss is.

She flipped the light switch. Inescapable fear caused her to jump back as the hairs on her skin stood on end. Horrified, she gasped, "Wes! What are you doing here? How did you get inside the house?"

Full of rage, he walked toward her, his eyes solely focused on her frightful face. "A restraining order!" he yelled. "Why do you continue to wreck my life? You will never, ever, take my sons from me. Didn't I tell you I'd kill you first? Didn't I, huh? Didn't I? You just won't listen. You're just like my mother, always doing something fucking stupid to screw up my life."

Emma tried to reconcile the words she had just heard with the baseball bat clenched in Wes' hand. It was at that moment she realized Wes was not angry—he was madly furious. She needed a weapon. In a split second, fear triggered her adrenaline to get to safety. Like a jackrabbit, she sprung past him in less time than it takes to blink.

He swung the bat wildly. Missed her. The loud crash echoed in the hallway when the bat smashed the floor. Fused with anger and blind with rage, he swung again.

Instantly, Emma felt the forceful blow on her back and she found herself barreling headlong into the wall. An enormous gush of air left her lungs as pain seared through her body from the impact.

She had gasped for breath before she felt the shocking flash of pain when her nose crumpled—leaving blood on the wall—she was in trouble. She dragged herself to her feet and hobbled toward the bedroom. She must get herself inside and close the door.

Just as she pushed the door closed, Wes caught it with the bat. With a rage that gave him strength much greater than that of a normal human being, he dropped the bat and kicked the door open so violently the house vibrated.

Emma frantically staggered backward when the door pushed inward. Wes was out of control. She gasped in horror when he thrashed forward and lunged at her. He grabbed her by the hair and tumbled her to the floor. Bent over her, he lifted her head upward as he breathed heavily through an open mouth. His breath was hot and foul on her face when he yelled out, "I'm going to teach you a lesson, my dear Emma. One you're not likely to forget."

Pure panic pulsed throughout Emma's body. *This can't be happening to me.* She struck back, but her blows only seemed to enrage him. She managed to grab his shirt and hold on to it when he stood up. She screamed, "Stop! Stop this!" She prayed that he would come to his senses before he killed her. He whipped her around and hurled her back up against the wall with his hand around her throat. His cold, savage-looking eyes couldn't be mistaken for anything other than hatred as he repeatedly butted her head against the wall and shouted, "You are not taking my boys away from me. Never will I allow you to do that. I'll kill you first. Do you understand me now, you bitch?"

Emma felt the blood drip down her face and mucus drip from her nose, and she tasted the coppery bite of blood in the back of her throat. He was clearly going to kill her.

"Don't you fuckin' ever think of leaving," he screamed as he held her head inches away from his face. His breath was repulsive and flecks of spittle flew from his mouth and splattered her face.

Panic welled inside her. *If he doesn't stop, he will kill me. I must fight back.* She moved beyond pain when uncontrollable rage and fear for her life and for the safety of her children suddenly exploded.

A sudden burst of terror-fueled adrenaline forced its way through every vein in her body when she surged her body forcefully upward in a frightening momentum and hit him in the nose with her head. The sickening crunch of cartilage she heard caused instant satisfaction. She knew she'd broken his nose. When he bent his head forward in pain, she slammed her fist on the back of his neck, grabbed a handful of his hair, spun him around, and slammed his head up against the wall.

"Now it's my turn," she screamed out as she took full advantage of the moment and grabbed his head and repeatedly smashed it against the wall. "How you do like it?"

Blood gushed from his nose, and for a few moments he was motionless. He stumbled sideways as if his feet didn't want to hold him. He staggered and held the wall for balance in an attempt to gain some awareness of what just happened.

He pushed her away with his arm and screamed out, "You broke my nose! You fuckin' broke my nose!" He straightened his body up and turned, grabbed her by the shoulders, spun her around and thumped her up against the wall. Just as his fist thrust toward her, she dropped her body down. His momentum transferred his fist right through the wall.

A non-human cry of pain suddenly filled the room. His bloody face, distorted with agony and rage, looked like a character in a horror film. He immediately pulled his hand to his chest. His lips, covered in blood, quivered as he moaned in pain, but his eyes were still in combative mode.

That could have been my face, Emma thought. She stood up and suddenly realized that *this was the first time in her life she'd ever had a physical battle.*

Although the phone seemed an impossible distance away, Emma knew she had to get there somehow. This was her only chance. Like a whip, she sprang across the room in a blur of anguish and grabbed it.

With adrenaline and rage pumping through him, Wes barreled toward her. He kicked her in the shins and knocked her off balance. The sound of her body when it hit the floor made a loud thud, but she still grasped the phone tightly in her hand. She hit speed dial and depressed the "1" key just before she felt his strong hand clamp around her wrist like a vise grip. He snatched the handset away.

Forcefully, he crashed down on her back. The tremendous weight of his body violently crushed her lungs and knocked the wind out of her. The power he now had over her gave him the high he craved. He rolled her over and then pressed her arms over her head and pinned her to the floor.

Emma saw menace in his eyes as beads of sweat and warm blood dripped from his nostrils onto her face. Her eyes opened wide in terror, believing it was the end. But suddenly, his body fell limp. He released her arms and stood up as he stared at her lying on the floor.

Is he finished? Emma wondered. *Is his power trip over?* She rolled her body to one side in an attempt to get up from the floor, but Wes violently kicked her on her back causing her breath to whoosh out from the blow. *He clearly wasn't finished.*

A pulse of intolerable pain throbbed on the right side of Emma's skull when she raised her head. Dizziness swept her like an incoming tide and she thought she would pass out. Her whole body felt ruptured. Bile suddenly rose in her throat.

"Please stop, Wes. I won't leave. I won't take the boys from you. Please… no more…" she begged. "I'll do whatever you want me to."

"Well, it's about time you start understanding," he barked. "If I even think you're leaving the area, I'll find you and finish the job. Do you understand me now?"

"Yes," she said as she thrust her hands out to protect her face. "Whatever you want," she moaned. She tried again to stand up. Her pain surpassed all adjectives, but she managed to get her feet placed firmly on the floor as she braced herself on a chair. She could smell blood, taste it too, when she licked her lips. She had difficulty opening her left eye because the lashes seemed stuck together by congealed blood from a gash on her head.

Wes reached over and cupped her bloody face in his hands. He saw the damage that he had done. Red welts were beginning to show on her face, and he could imagine what the bruises on her neck and body would look like tomorrow.

Without warning, Emma's body bent over and fiercely ejected the contents of her stomach. Vomit spewed out onto Wes' shirt, jeans, and shoes.

Impulsively, he jumped back. "What the hell? Look what you've done to me! You puked all over me, you stupid bitch! You just won't listen. You always have to have the last say."

He lifted her head, pulled back his fisted arm, and slugged her jaw. At once, Emma felt the room whirl around as she stumbled back a few steps.

As if in slow motion, her body crumpled in a heap to the floor, unconscious.

CHAPTER

3

"Is she breathing?" a voice yelled out.

"Barely," he said as he pressed his fingers against her neck just below her ear. "I've got a feeble pulse."

"Hook her up to O_2 and start an IV," the voice yelled out as he clamped a cervical collar around her neck. "And, let's give her some morphine. She looks to weigh about one-ten, one-twenty. I'll call Trauma at Stanford and tell them we're on our way."

The room soon filled with people who all had a specific job to do. Cameras flashed, and voices crackled over the police two-way radios, which squawked in garbled, unintelligible chattering, as investigators treated the scene as a possible homicide. They marked and documented evidence as they went through the house.

"There's blood everywhere. She's a real mess," a young police officer said. "Was anyone else in the house?"

"No, just the victim," another older officer responded. "Don't touch anything in the house without gloves on. Everything is evidence."

"Okay," the paramedic said, "let's lift her gently. On my count, one... two... three."

"Let's get her inside the squad. Easy."

"Jesus Christ. Does anyone know her name?" one of the paramedics asked.

A woman, who stood in front of the fire truck with yellow and red lights glaring from behind her, stepped forward and said, "Her name is Emma Blair. She's a professor at Stanford."

"Are you the woman who found her?" the older police officer inquired. "I'm Officer Swanson."

"Yes. Both her sons are at a sleepover at my house next door. I called Emma on the phone and when she didn't answer, I went over to her house. She was lying unconscious on the floor. I immediately called nine-one-one."

"Are her two sons in your home now?" Officer Swanson asked as he pulled out a pad and pen from his jacket pocket.

"Yes, they're asleep."

"Was anyone else in the house when you went over there?"

"No, I didn't see anyone else."

"Did you hear anything? Anyone screaming for help, perhaps?"

"No, I didn't hear any noise. With the garage on that side of the house, we don't usually hear anything from over there."

"May I have your name, please?"

"Certainly. It's Debbie Jones."

"And the names of both sons?"

"The older boy is Lucas, and he's four and a half. The younger son is Adam, and he's three and a half."

"Is there a father?"

"He doesn't live with them."

"His name?"

"Wes Blair."

"Do you know how we can reach him?"

"No, I'm afraid I don't know. However, I do know there's a restraining order out on him. They were having marital problems."

"Okay. Thank you, Miss Jones," he said as he reached into his jacket pocket and pulled out his business card. "Here's my card. Please feel free to call me if you think of anything else."

CHAPTER

Seven Years earlier – June 2, 1995
Washington, D.C.

Nervously, Emma waited on the bench in front of Professor Bradford's office. She had no idea why he had summoned her. She hadn't been late with any of her assignments, she's not missed any classes, and she couldn't come up with any reason for him to want to speak to her.

With growing dread, she tried to settle her nerves and appear calm by taking deep breaths. *I desperately need to be calm*, she kept telling herself, but she still felt a knot in her stomach.

Five minutes passed, then ten. Finally, the door opened.

"Hello, Emma. Come right in, please," Professor Bradford said, gesturing with his arm.

Emma jumped up, rushed into his office, and sat down in one of the three chairs in front of his desk. The professor closed the door, walked around his desk to his large black leather chair, and sat down. A file folder with Emma's name on it was centered on his desk.

"I asked you here today because I have a job offer for you, should you want to accept it. I was asked by one of my former classmates if there was a student I could recommend to fill an open position in his department."

Emma's mouth fell open, and for a moment she sat stunned. Her next reaction was relief; her resolve broke into overwhelming excitement. *I had no idea... here I am, just a few days left for college and there is this wide-open stretch of highway beckoning me. I never imagined.*

She blinked, grasped the arms of the chair and sat up straighter. A look of pleasure spread across her face. "Really?" Emma said, her eyes widening. "What's the position?"

"It's a laboratory research analyst position at Stanford University. You've been my first student in more than five years who's actually shown exceptional perception in your class experiments and since you completed your first year of college at Stanford, I just thought that perhaps you would be interested. Do you think you might be interested?"

"Oh, my. Yes," she said, smiling ecstatically. "I'm extremely interested. What a fantastic opportunity. I spent an incredible year at Stanford, but I never dreamed I would ever work there."

Professor Bradford managed a meager laugh and replied, "I'll set up the interview for you with Professor Stanton."

"Wow," she said, unable to find a better word at the moment. "I don't know what to say. I've been anxious to jump-start my career, but I never imagined starting with a position at Stanford. I'm completely overwhelmed."

"I'm delighted to hear you say that," the professor said with a broad, easy grin.

"But," she added, "I'll need to talk with my Uncle Ross before I commit. There's no doubt that he'll be happy for me, but I would like to speak with him first."

"That's understandable. If you can get back to me within the next few days with your decision, we'll go from there."

"Yes, I'll get back to you."

"One other thing," he said as he stood up, "If you do take the position, I would encourage you to give some serious thought about entering the biomedical informatics training program at Stanford for your graduate work."

"That is something I'm very interested in doing. Thank you so much," Emma said as she grabbed the professor's hand in an overexcited both-hand handshake. "This is a great opportunity for me."

The professor smiled and said, "You're quite welcome, Emma."

Gasping for breath in a heightened state of excitement, she dashed out the door and raced down the corridor, her shoes clicking on the tiled floor. *I can't believe this is happening,* she thought as she stopped at the pay phone and dialed her uncle's number.

"Uncle Ross, I have some wonderful news."

"What is it, darlin'? You sound really excited."

"I just came from my professor's office and he wants to recommend me for a laboratory research analyst position at Stanford. Is this too exiting? I can't believe it."

"In California?" Ross gasped.

Silence.

"I know you're excited, Emma, but you tend to make lightning-fast decisions without much thought when you get like this. You really need to give this some serious consideration. California is a long way from home."

"But this is a great opportunity and Professor Bradford wants me to get back to him in a few days so he can set up the interview."

"I realize that. Just think about it for a few days, Emma. Don't be hasty is all I'm saying. Proper decisions are the backbone for your future. I don't want you to make a mistake moving to California."

A prolonged silence on the phone.

"Ugh!" Emma said. "I was all excited, and now I'm faced with decisions, decisions and more decisions. I don't have much time to think this over."

"Calm down, Emma. Think this through before you act… give it a few days and then make your decision. I know you'll make the right decision. Have you told Hawk the news yet?" Ross asked.

"No. Not yet. I'll tell him when we meet for dinner. We'll talk it over tonight."

"You do realize he's not going to like this. You two have been inseparable all these years. He was expecting the two of you to work together somewhere."

"Oh, he's going to give me grief, I know. He had plans of us working together in a forensics lab and solving all those high-profile crimes. But the world offers just so many opportunities, and if you turn them down, you miss out of what could have been. I want to avoid missing a perceived opportunity. I don't want to miss out and be the one five years down the road saying, 'I shoulda.' He'll understand that."

"I hope so, for your sake. You know he's crazy about you."

"Yes, but we decided long ago that the timing was off. I want to work in a lab and do some serious research. He knows that. But you're right; he is not going to like this at all. We'll talk it through and work this out somehow."

"As much as I don't want to bust your bubble, darlin', I just want you to seriously think about this before you jump in. You need to calm down and think rationally."

Emma let out a big sigh. "Okay," Uncle Ross. I'll slow down and think about it."

CHAPTER

5

"This is a big step for you, darlin'. You'll do well in your interview if you just settle down and try to relax and be yourself," Uncle Ross instructed while seeing her off on the early six o'clock flight to San Francisco.

"I love you, Uncle Ross," Emma said sadly, taking a deep breath to quell the tears she felt rising to her eyes.

"Love you too, darlin'," he said with tears in his eyes. Emma turned and waved before walking through security to proceed to the gate. *She's all grown up,* he thought to himself. *She's been the best thing in my life. Her father would be bursting with pride if he were here now.*

He waved back and watched her until she was no longer visible. He had cared for her all by himself since she was ten years old. It was an arrangement that went a long way toward explaining why he had never married. He and Emma were a team, and he didn't seem to need anyone else. Now the team is split up and going in separate directions.

Emma walked toward the window where there were two gray leather benches and lowered herself onto one just as an airliner pulled in from the long runway.

After taking a deep breath, she closed her eyes for a few seconds and tried to put everything in perspective. Yesterday afternoon she had just graduated with honors and now, twenty hours later, she was on her way to California for what she hoped would be a promising career at Stanford University. Everything was happening so quickly. *Am I doing the right thing leaving D.C? Leaving Uncle Ross and Hawk?*

Within minutes, rumpled passengers began to disembark. A woman clutching the hands of two small children emerged from the Jetway, the first passengers off the plane. Several men, carrying garment bags and attaché cases, followed closely behind her. Ten minutes later, her flight was called, her boarding pass was handed over and she headed down the ramp to her seat in first class. She slipped her purse and briefcase under the seat, sat back, fastened her seat belt, and relaxed for the first time in days.

When the aircraft taxied down the bumpy runway, she could see the tip of the Washington Monument. The plane accelerated through the air into the clouds, taking her across the country to start a new life *if* she passed the interview.

During the last few days, the excitement and anticipation left her sleep deprived and as soon as the plane leveled off, Emma's eyes closed and within seconds the drone of the jet engines lulled her into a deep sleep.

She had an anxious dream that she had arrived thirty minutes too late for her interview with the professor, and she started to argue with the receptionist to let her in. She demanded that she see the professor today. For a split second, her eyes wouldn't open while she waited for her brain to connect the touch on her shoulder with the action in her dream… "Miss, please put your chair in an upright position. We'll be landing shortly."

Feeling hollow and slightly light-headed, she quickly raised her seat and looked out the window, not quite believing that she slept all the way to California.

The flight attendant's voice on the PA system announced, "The captain advises we will begin our approach into San Francisco. Please make sure your seat belt is fastened, tray tables stowed, and seat back restored to an upright position."

As the plane began its descent, Emma looked down seeing clear blue skies and the Oakland Bridge. The landing was smooth. She quickly gathered her purse and briefcase and prepared to disembark. First class seating allowed her to be one of the first to leave the plane. She stuck with the crowd losing herself in the mass of recently arrived passengers being greeted by loved ones. She hurried down the long concourse following the signs to the baggage claim area, stopping first at the restroom.

The signs directed her toward the escalator that would take her down to retrieve her luggage. Once she stacked them on the luggage cart, she went across the aisle to the car rental desk. Within minutes, she had her rental papers and was instructed to go to the car rental shuttle stop just outside the door. Someone there would take her to her car.

Emma stepped out onto the sidewalk and inhaled a deep breath. It was late morning and the air was fresh and cool. At the curb, she stopped to scan the area for the shuttle pickup area. She immediately saw the sign in the center divide and pushed her luggage cart across the street. When the shuttle driver saw her wave, he walked toward her and snatched up her suitcases to load them into the bus. She stepped aboard and took a front seat. Once all the other passengers were in their seats, the pleated doors closed, the engine whined, and the bus gave off fumes before it lurched forward and rumbled into traffic toward the rental office.

Within ten minutes, the bus groaned to a stop at the curb of the office. The driver quickly grabbed Emma's suitcases and set them next to a bench just outside the office doorway. She handed him a twenty-dollar bill and thanked him.

"May I help you?" the young attendant from the rental office asked.

"Yes," she replied, handing the paperwork to him. Within minutes, the car was at the curb. Emma smiled when she saw the white Cadillac convertible. "That's my Uncle Ross," she said to the smiling attendant as he popped the trunk to load her luggage. "Drive safely," he said as he handed her the keys.

She got in on the driver's side, fastened her seat belt, and maneuvered the car right along Airport Drive to the 101 Freeway South. The sheer volume of traffic going to Silicon Valley was congested, as usual. She was grateful she was turning off in Palo Alto. Uncle Ross had made her room reservations at the Garden Court Hotel in downtown Palo Alto with an early arrival.

Forty minutes later, she was in front of the hotel. "Will you be staying with us?" the valet attendant asked.

"Yes."

"Do you have luggage?"

"Yes." She popped the trunk.

"If you would like to have me valet your car, I would be happy to do that for you."

"Yes. That would be fine," she said as she handed him the keys.

She slipped her shoulder into her purse strap, grabbed her briefcase, and walked into the hotel. The bellman unloaded her luggage from the car and followed right behind her.

"Good morning," the perky desk clerk said cheerfully.

"Good morning. Reservations for Emma Griffin."

The clerk punched a few keys and said, "Yes, we have your reservation right here. You have an open reservation. You don't know how long you'll be staying with us?"

"No, I 'm not sure yet."

"That's fine. Your stay has been taken care of. The bellman will assist you to your suite," she replied, as she handed the bellman the keys.

"Thank you very much," Emma said as she turned to follow the bellman down the corridor. He opened the door to her room and then stepped aside, gesturing for Emma to enter.

The living area had a large, off-white sectional sofa and a large white desk and chair with an enormous flat-screen television mounted on the wall. The bellman walked over to the patio door and opened the drapes to expose a beautiful private garden interior patio. The bedroom, elegantly decorated with a king-size bed and a white goose down bed covering, had an adjoining bathroom surrounded with white marble.

"This is very lovely," she said to the bellman as she handed him a tip. "Thank you very much."

"Thank you. Enjoy your stay, Ms. Griffin," the bellman responded before he closed the door.

She unpacked all her clothes and hung them in the closet before she carried all her toiletries into the bathroom and arranged them neatly on the counter.

It wasn't until her stomach began to rumble that she realized she hadn't eaten anything.

She combed her hair, put on earrings, a little mascara and light makeup and changed from the jeans and jacket to her beige pantsuit with a hot pink blouse. She didn't want to look too drab and not too flashy.

She slipped on her shoes, grabbed her purse and left the hotel. She walked leisurely down the street to one of the favorite coffee shops she frequented when she lived here. The outside patio had wooden tables with scalloped paper placements and wooden chairs tucked under the tables. As soon she sat down, the server took her order for two crepes filled with blueberries and cream cheese along with a pot of coffee. *She desperately needed coffee.*

She relaxed and enjoyed her coffee as she watched the lunchtime crowd search the various Ethnic and American restaurants that lined both sides of the street. Palo Alto had the comfortable feel of a small town with tree-lined streets and historic buildings—a charming mixture of old and new that reflected its California heritage. She had enjoyed the year she lived here.

"Ah, this looks delicious," she said as the server placed her plate on the table in front of her.

"Is there anything else I can get for you?" the server asked.

"No. Thank you, this is perfect."

She enjoyed every bite of her fabulous lunch. The food in California seemed to taste better. She wondered if it was because of the water.

CHAPTER

6

Though she was not running late, after the dream she had on the plane, she wanted to arrive early. She retrieved her car from valet parking and drove to the university an hour before her appointment time only to make sure she found a parking spot in front of the biosciences building. She sat quietly in the car trying to relax while going over some interview notes she had written out.

Fifteen minutes before her appointment, she climbed the stairs to the building and went to the reception area only to find the room packed with prospective applicants. *Oh, I haven't a chance*, she thought as she checked in at the reception desk.

"I have an appointment with Professor Stanton," she announced to the receptionist. "My name is Emma Griffin."

"Please sign in on the log sheet and take a seat. Professor Stanton's assistant will call you."

Fifteen minutes passed. Suddenly a young professional-looking woman announced loudly, "Emma Griffin," while her eyes scanned the crowded lobby.

When Emma stood up, the woman smiled and said, "If you'd like to come with me, Professor Stanton will see you now."

Emma followed several feet behind her. Her stomach was growling. *Must be a nervous stomach*, she thought. As the woman approached the door at the end of the hallway, she opened it and stepped aside, saying, "Please, Ms. Griffin, have a seat and the professor will be with you momentarily."

The room was elegantly furnished with four burgundy leather chairs and a large ornate varnished table scattered with reading material. A middle-aged, lonely-looking man wearing black-rimmed glasses occupied one of the chairs. He slouched down so that the newspaper he was reading shielded his face. He turned the pages of the newspaper repeatedly and it crackled every time he crossed and uncrossed his legs. He seemed extremely nervous about whatever or whoever he was going to meet with.

Emma sat in the chair opposite him and picked up a *Psychology Today* magazine and casually flipped through a few pages, glancing at the various articles: *The Extrovert, Nimble Brains, Do you Remember?*

Mr. Nervous Pants kept peeking from behind the newspaper with his measuring eyes; *a quick glance between the rivals kind of thing*, she thought. He still fidgeted in his seat, anxious to end the wait.

Twenty minutes passed.

Suddenly a door opened and the professor stood in the doorway and called, "Miss Griffin?" Emma stood up and smiled at him. He welcomed her with a firm handshake. "Please, Miss Griffin, come in."

She had expected someone a bit older, or someone who looked older, since he was a classmate with her professor at GW who looked sixty. He looked to be in his forties, slim, alert and impeccably dressed in a blue shirt with a stiff white collar and navy slacks. He had graying hair and blue eyes with a round, bespectacled face. His voice was gentle and refined, exactly appropriate for his appearance.

He politely held the door open while Emma walked into his office. She sat in one of the two tan leather chairs facing his desk. Centered in the room was a large mahogany desk with the conventional computer, telephone, and pen and pencil holder. A large brown leather-bound notebook was on the center of the desk—a Mont Blanc pen placed diagonally on top of it.

The professor picked up his pen, opened the notebook, and sat in his chair, quietly tapping his pen on the notebook while he read the letter of introduction from his friend and her former professor at George Washington University.

Emma glanced around the room at the ceiling-high mahogany bookshelves filled with scholarly tomes interspersed with several impressive mahogany-framed diplomas and citations. The outer walls held an array of various photos, probably of his family.

The professor smiled, put the letter and pen on the side of the notebook and then leaned back in his chair putting his hands behind his head. "You come highly recommended from my former classmate, Professor Bradford. I see you made it through his classes with flying colors."

"Yes, Professor Bradford was very tough but fair," Emma replied.

"You must have impressed him greatly to have him recommend you for this position. He doesn't usually do this type of thing—recommend any of his students for a position at Stanford."

"I spent my first year of college at Stanford before transferring to George Washington University. Professor Bradford was aware of how well I liked Stanford and thought it would be something I would be interested in doing. He also spoke to me about entering the graduate program. Of course, I would be very interested in that program."

"Yes," he said as he straightened his chair and picked up his pen from the desk. "I have every confidence in your ability to fill this position. You'd be an excellent addition to our team."

Emma smiled but didn't quite know what to say.

"I'm not going to ask you about your academic studies for the simple reason that you wouldn't be sitting here if you weren't capable of fulfilling the job requirements. I do have one question for you. One question that won't be in any of the paperwork that Professor Bradford was kind enough to send me."

He paused a few moments and then asked, "Tell me, Emma Griffin, what would you say are your weaknesses?"

An unquiet silence lingered in the room for a few moments. Emma thought, quickly picking her words with care before she responded.

"When a baby is born into the world, he or she possesses natural gifts and talents. These areas of God-given ability, be it athletic ability, musical skill, or intelligence, develops as one grows and provides direction for one's life. God blessed me with a gift of intelligence when I was born, and I have a need to fulfill this gift and to do whatever it takes to succeed and be the best at whatever I choose to do.

"As a teenager in high school, I struggled to fit in. I was very timid and always felt disconnected from my classmates. Because of my shyness, they all treated me like an outsider. I never experienced a bond with any of my classmates… you know… the type of bond that would last forever.

"My Uncle Ross was very concerned about my inability to make friends, and he told me that I was not born to blend in. I was born to stand out. So, to overcome my shyness and hide my insecurities, I swept my social issues out of the way and excelled at whatever I attempted to do. I resorted to become a perfectionist, so everything I did, I did with passion. Winning became embedded in me and since then I've excelled at being the best of the best. So, if you're searching for someone who is genetically competitive, you've got the right person."

After several moments, mulling over Emma's response, the professor asked, "So you believe your competitive edge is a weakness?"

"I guess one could say it is if you look at it from my point of view. Through the years, I've learned good social skills that have helped me to have friends who admire my mind but then there were always others who would get jealous or envious and wouldn't have anything to do with me. It's not that I feel self-important, on the contrary. I become very shy and introverted in many situations where I feel like I don't fit in. I'm not as street smart as I would like to be. I have areas of my life that need improvement just like everyone else. My biggest challenge is not to feel like an outsider and to strive to become part of my culture.

"A diploma only proves I'm a student, but I'm still learning to love the journey. But what comes with that journey is the experience and growing process of building relationships along the way. I'm hoping the end result will be to share my passions with others by teaching."

He looked quite pleased with her perceptive response. "Okay," he said.

Emma, thrown off by the one-word answer did not know what he meant. *Did I get the job? Is he finished interviewing me?* She looked at the professor with confused silence.

"You certainly are a breath of fresh air, Ms. Griffin. I don't ordinarily make quick decisions, but because of your recommendation from Professor Bradford, I believe we've found a challenging position that you will excel in. You have the job."

Momentarily stunned, Emma felt a small thrill run
through her body. She pressed her hand to her mouth and
looked at the professor, not sure what to do or say. She
sat forward. "You mean I have the job?"

A flicker of a smile came into his eyes when he
nodded, "Yes, you have the job."

Her smile widened. "Oh, I'm going to be working
at Stanford," she announced triumphantly.

A small smile touched Professor Stanton's lips.

"Just like that?" Emma asked.

"Yes, just like that. However, don't for one
moment think that the position you're filling will be as
easy."

"Oh, I would never believe that. I'm confident that
I'll meet any challenges you throw my way."

"Wonderful. Get yourself settled in the next few
days. I had my assistant put an employment portfolio
together for you to fill out at your convenience. Bring it
with you when you return back to my office on Monday
morning at eight sharp." He handed her the portfolio,
which she held in her left hand.

"Thank you so very much, Professor Stanton. I'm
looking forward to working with your team," Emma said
as she stood with her right arm outstretched.

"We'll see you on Monday," he said as he shook her
hand and smiled before he walked around the desk to
open the door for her. "Eight o'clock sharp."

The pot of coffee she drank was catching up with
her bladder, so she immediately headed for the restroom
down the corridor. She was all smiles when she stood in
front of the mirror above the washbasin. After drying her
hands, she punched the air in a pantomime cheer. She had
worked hard for this moment and it paid off for her. She
was ecstatic. She could not have had a better interview.

She got the job!

Emma's job as a laboratory research analyst was exciting, and it kept her days full and her mind on her work. Within six months, she earned a promotion to research scientist, researching the genetics of disease, intelligence and aging.

Emma was quite happy with her life and she continued to excel in her research position feeling confident of her knowledge and her adeptness to excavate answers. It wasn't long before she was chosen to be a candidate in the graduate program in biophysics, conducting her research requirements under the guidance and sponsorship of the faculty advisor. The heavy workload kept her in the laboratory nights, days, and weekends. She was determined to get her Ph.D. degree the following year.

She found that friendships with her lab co-workers were somewhat easier than her college years because everyone had the same "brain level," and they respected each other's thoughts and ideas—unlike her college days when it was a struggle to make friends because she didn't party or belong to clubs or sororities. Other than her best friend, Hawk, she really hadn't chummed around with anyone else. Actually, with Hawk around, she hadn't *needed* anyone else around. What they had was special. A trusting, no frills, no lying to each other friendship. *Only* a friendship—never lovers.

She had weekly telephone conversations with both Hawk and Uncle Ross, usually during her lunch hour. If she wasn't talking with them, she jogged over to the Rodin sculptures to have lunch with Susan Mahoney, who was the museum director. Her husband, Jimmy, was an orthopedic surgeon at Stanford Hospital and rarely, if ever, had time to have lunch with his wife.

Susan was intrigued by Emma's extraordinary creative mind and her love of Rodin and the arts. When she learned that Emma was diligently working to obtain her Ph.D., she invited her to dinner several times a week just to get her out of the laboratory.

CHAPTER

Fifteen months' later - September 18, 1996

Emma was thrilled when senior faculty chose her to attend the yearly two-day Biotech Showcase Seminar at the South San Francisco Conference Center. The conferences covered a consortium of researchers seeking new treatments for diseases of the immune system. There were also several biopharmaceutical companies that were focused on acquiring, developing, and commercializing innovative anti-cancer agents in the United States. Emma's interest was with a biotechnology company engaged in the growth of human organ tissues for transplantation use.

When the morning session broke for lunch, she decided to eat at the buffet she'd noticed on her way to the conference room. The line had just begun to form, so she quickly stepped behind a tall gentleman. Within seconds, there were more than twenty people behind her.

Suddenly, when the gentleman in front of her spun around to glance at who was behind him, he frightened Emma. She gulped a quick inhale of breath and jumped back. Her mouth gaped open; she stared back at him in astonishment.

When he saw her reaction, he said, "Oh, I'm so sorry. I didn't mean to frighten you."

"Oh." She glanced down self-consciously. "You startled me for a moment."

Waves of warmth immediately ran through his body when he looked at her. She had to be the loveliest young woman he'd ever seen. She had large blue-violet eyes with thick lashes, her frothy shoulder-length curly brown hair framed her face, her lips were full, and she had a soft pink flush on her cheeks; she took his breath away.

"Again, I'm terribly sorry."

Emma was embarrassed. She had no idea what to say. She smiled and braced herself.

"Would you care to join me at a table?" he politely asked her.

Before answering, Emma hesitated, looked down and to the side to make certain that he had spoken to her. Then she raised her eyes to his and said, "No thanks, I'm waiting for someone." She lowered her eyes and then tilted her head and looked up and smiled. She couldn't tell if he was shocked or amused at what she had just said to him.

"You're not waiting for anyone," he blurted.

Surprised by his remark, Emma's lips poked out a little as she shrugged her shoulders and then asked, "And how could you possibly know that?"

"I can tell by your eyes."

"And exactly what are my eyes telling you?"

"Well, it's a commonly held belief that when someone is not telling you the truth, their eyes dilate."

Emma felt her face begin to flush and she suddenly had a case of the flutters, which she thought was because of the way he looked at her—as if she was the tastiest thing in the buffet line. She felt his gaze search her soul. While she felt uneasy, at the same time this handsome stranger intrigued her.

"Life's too short for drama. Come on sit with me. You're alone, I'm alone. I promise I won't bite you," he said with a chuckle.

She liked the way he laughed, nearly enough to consider his request to sit with him. Emma smirked as she ran her fingers through her hair while studying him silently. He was tall, athletic-looking, with a lion's mane of golden blonde hair, brown eyes, and a perfect complexion. He was strikingly handsome—an Adonis dressed in a navy blue sports jacket with gray slacks. His shirt was white and crisp, his tie, maroon with narrow diagonal navy stripes and his shoes were cordovan loafers. He was perfect... or perhaps not.

There was something not quite tame about this man. She could see it in his devilish eyes. He had the look of the bad boy that all women went crazy over. *This is just a strong case of physical attraction*, she told herself while acknowledging the fact that she had never felt like this before.

"Are you sure about that?" Emma said to him, smiling with satisfaction.

Looking somewhat amused by what she said, he responded, "What makes you think I would say something that wasn't true?"

Emma's eyes widened and then she laughed. Her eyes twinkled before she said, "It's a commonly held belief that if you want to spot a liar, watch their hands when they speak. Your hand went directly to your earlobe."

He liked the intelligence and determination in her violet-blue eyes. He liked her confidence. Actually, he liked the whole damn package. Wes was not in the habit of pursuing women who showed a lack of interest, or who sent out mixed signals, but when he met a woman who attracted him, he became relentless.

A flicker of a smile came into his eyes when he responded, "Well, now, we do have to have lunch together. There's no turning back at this point. I've got to find out who you are. You intrigue me."

Emma had no doubt that she probably did, although she was suspect that he was not as straightforward as his statement. *This guy is really good*, she thought. He knows how to treat a woman and make her feel special. She wondered if his technique was instinctive or possibly something he'd been practicing for years.

"Are you flirting with me?" Emma asked, smilingly.

"I don't know. Am I?" he replied with a crooked grin.

She glanced up at him, directly meeting his gaze. "I do believe you are."

"Wes," he said. "My name is Wes Blair, and today I'm attending the accounting seminar."

Emma nodded but did not say his name. He had a quiet kind of confidence, a trait she was particularly attracted to.

"What's your name?" he asked when she remained silent.

Emma started laughing and couldn't think of a response that seemed any better than inadequate, so she politely said, "I'm Emma Griffin, and I'm attending the Biotech Showcase Seminar."

"Now that we know each other, will you have lunch with me, Emma Griffin?" Wes asked.

"No way. I don't know you. I know nothing about you."

"That's exactly why I want to have lunch with you," he said patiently.

She hesitated and then turned to him with a smile and asked, "Why do you wish to have lunch with me?"

"So you can get to know me better and I can get to know you better."

Oh, this man was used to women falling for his charm. "Why me?"

For a long moment, he simply stared at her before saying, "Why you? You're probably the smartest gal in this buffet line, and I like talking to you. You're different than most girls; you're bright and exciting, and you're not exactly hard on the eyes."

With her gaze fixed on him, she knew that he was interested, but she was not an idiot—she felt an attraction toward him. She couldn't deny that and, after all, he was very handsome.

"Okay," she finally conceded. "I guess those are good enough reasons to have lunch together."

"Boy, you're one tough lady."

"Yes, and don't you forget it."

After working their way through the buffet line, Wes was able to find a table and he motioned for Emma to join him. They set their trays down and immediately went into a conversation which led them to share stories and laugh. It was a harmless lunch, and it didn't mean anything. He was very open about his life and shared the fact that he had a girlfriend, but it wasn't serious. He had lived in San Jose for five years and worked as an accounting analyst for a large accounting firm that attracted prestigious multinational clients. He was born in Spokane, Washington on April 1, 1966, which made him thirty years old. He graduated from Eastern Washington University with a bachelor of arts in business administration.

"Tell me about your family," Emma asked.

"Ah, my family. An unusual situation, I must say. I am the only child of Howard and Ida Blair, who sold their home in Spokane while I was in the Navy and decided to retire to the Fiji Islands. My parents and I have a mutual dislike for one another. My mother was a woman with absolutely no maternal instincts. She was a self-serving woman who considered her only child a burden. And my father... well, as hard as I tried, I could never live up to my father's standards. Needless to say, we never got along."

Emma's brows drew together in dismay. "I'm sorry to hear that."

Wes just shrugged his shoulders. "It happens in the best of families."

"So you haven't seen your parents, for how many years now?"

"Seven years," he replied, his voice tight. "I've been gone from their lives almost as long as I was in it."

Emma's nose wrinkled and her eyes softened with sympathy. "That's a long time."

After a few moments of silence, he said, "They never even tried to contact me," he replied with a deep hurt in his voice.

"Do you ever regret not seeing them?"

A faraway look had entered his eyes before he answered, "No, not at all."

In an attempt to shift the conversation in another direction, Wes blurted out, "So, tell me all about Emma Griffin."

Emma's eyes widened. "Oh. Let me see. Well, I was born in Los Angeles on March 9, 1970. I am an only child and grew up in Washington, D.C. I moved to Palo Alto a year and a half ago, right after graduating from George Washington University because I had a job offer in the research lab. I am a doctoral candidate and currently conducting my research under the tutelage of my research professor and if all goes as planned, I hope to attain my dream. My ultimate goal is to be a professor at Stanford."

"Wow. You certainly know how to keep yourself busy," Wes said. "Are you seeing anyone?"

Emma hesitated. She did not want to say that she had not dated anyone since coming to California, and certainly did not want him to know she had sociability issues, so she said, "I've been much too busy at work."

They planned to meet and have lunch again on the second day of their seminars.

Again, the next day, they had conversations about politics, the environment, movies, and the best places to dine. They were comfortable together. Emma felt Wes was very easy to talk with and she really enjoyed his company, but she figured he was in a hurry to get back to his girlfriend and she would never see him again.

To her surprise, on the following day, she received a dozen red roses at her office followed by a phone call from Wes that afternoon asking her to have dinner with him Friday evening. He explained to her that he had broken up with his girlfriend.

Wes was totally unfamiliar as a stranger would be yet Emma was completely at ease with him. He intrigued her. He was different; everything about him felt new and exciting. There was no doubt in her mind that he aroused a portion of her soul that had never been stirred before.

Emma cautiously held him at bay for a while but as their relationship grew stronger, she found herself falling blindly in love with Wes. He had a great sense of humor, she enjoyed being with him, and her friends thought he was handsome and a great catch. He had captivated her entirely.

She did, however, have moments of concern and doubt about her newfound love. How was it possible after such a short period of time that she felt like she'd known him for a lifetime? Everything was so easy—their first embrace, their first kiss, their first lovemaking—all so natural. Had God blessed her with true love? Surely fate brought them together.

They began to spend most of their weekends together, but, there were also many weekends when she would not hear from Wes at all. He would just say he had things to do. Then, he would reappear Monday evening as if nothing was out of the ordinary.

Although some of her mutual friends thought he was wonderful, a few thought he was dangerous. Some of them even warned her about him, but she never saw any danger in him. She couldn't see his faults. Wes just filled up the sky above her, and she couldn't see around him to see if he was good, bad, or stupid, or anything else for that matter. She felt that her life didn't begin until she met Wes.

Her lab associates told her that that's the way chemistry works. She just happened to find the combination of luck and chemistry: *the magic potion.*

She understood chemistry just fine, but she was also aware that volatile experiments could blow up in your face. She had all the answers to chemistry equations, but falling in love was an equation she knew nothing about. She never had any type of love interest in her life unless she counted Bobby, a timid boy in her sixth-grade class who had the most unforgettable gray eyes with a tinge of aqua.

Secretly she wondered if other couples felt the way she felt about Wes. Her love for him didn't seem run of the mill. It wasn't natural how he had come to mean everything to her. Perhaps the relationship was moving too fast. She didn't really know him very well.

Perhaps that was what he wanted—someone who would never really get to know the *real* Wes.

It was Sunday afternoon, fifteen minutes past twelve and Emma was in the kitchen making a sandwich, when she heard the doorbell ring.

She pulled open the door, and her Uncle Ross stood there smiling. "Surprise!"

He immediately saw disappointment in Emma's eyes, before she said, "What a wonderful surprise." Without any further words, they hugged.

"You look like you were expecting someone? Am I intruding?"

"No, not at all, come in. I'm so happy to see you. What brings you to the west coast, Uncle Ross?"

"I have an urgent meeting tomorrow morning in San Francisco and I just thought I'd swing by to spend some time with you and take you to dinner tonight."

"That sounds wonderful. Are you staying in the city overnight?"

"Yes, I have to fly back tomorrow evening. Are you sure, I'm not intruding on any plans you may have had? I don't want to interfere with your social life."

"No. No plans. I just thought it was Wes."

"Who is Wes?"

"He's a man I've been seeing for a few weeks," Emma said with a crooked grin.

"And you didn't tell me about him?" he said with disappointment in his voice.

"Am I expected to ask permission to date someone?"

"I believe you intended to hide this relationship from me. I worry about you, darlin'."

"No need to worry. I'm able to take care of myself. I know what I'm doing."

"I'd like to know what's going on, that's all. Where did the two of you meet?"

"We met at a two day conference in San Francisco a few weeks ago."

"Do the two of you have plans this evening? I don't want to barge in."

"You're not intruding, Uncle Ross. We have no plans. I was just making a light lunch. Would you like a sandwich?"

"Sure. Are you making your famous grilled cheese?"

Emma laughed. "Yes, as a matter of fact that's exactly what I'm making. Come on, make yourself comfortable, and we'll eat in the kitchen."

When they finished lunch, the doorbell buzzed. Emma jumped up and opened the door.

"Wes! How nice to see you," she said as she wiggled free of Wes's arms wrapped around her waist and cursed the easiness with which her cheeks flushed crimson over her pale complexion. "Come in and meet my Uncle Ross. He just surprised me with a visit."

Ross walked into the room just as Wes turned to leave.

"Come inside, Wes," Emma said.

Wes hadn't planned on meeting Emma's uncle and immediately felt he was not going to make a good first impression with unruly hair and unshaven face. He started to step inside, but stopped abruptly. "No, I don't want to intrude."

Ross walked up to Emma. "You must be Wes."

"Yes," he said as he stepped inside, studying this tall, distinguished looking man walking toward him.

"It's nice to meet you Wes." Ross said with his arm stretched out.

Wes shook hands, and said, "I've heard a lot about you, sir. I just dropped by to see if Emma wanted to have lunch."

"My uncle and I just had lunch but we're going out for dinner and perhaps you could join us?" she pleaded, as she turned to look at her uncle.

"By all means, join us for dinner," Ross demanded. "It'll give us a chance to get to know one another. I insist."

Emma watched Wes transform right in front of her eyes. The casual, friendly, demeanor of the Wes she knew immediately changed into a cold, defiant stranger who was suddenly panic-stricken. "I can't tonight. Perhaps another time," he sputtered.

"But Wes, my uncle doesn't get out here that often."

"I'm sorry, but I have other plans this evening. I'll call you later, Emma." He turned, walked out, and closed the door.

Ross turned to Emma and said, "It appears that your boyfriend doesn't care for me."

"Oh, he's sort of a loner," she said, making an excuse for his behavior, but deep down, she was disappointed in Wes' attitude, and the embarrassment caused her stomach to flutter.

"Does he do this often?" Ross asked.

"Do what often?"

"Act like a twelve year old."

CHAPTER

8

Emma had been dating Wes for four months when he surprised her and whisked her off to Napa Valley for the weekend.

"Where are we going?" Emma asked.

"It's a surprise," Wes responded.

"Can't you tell me now?"

"No. If I tell you now, it won't be a surprise."

"It's obvious that we're going to Napa Valley. All the vineyards and rolling hills. It's beautiful here, isn't it?"

"Yes, it is."

"Are we almost there?"

"Yes," Wes said, "We're almost there." He turned off the main highway, drove down a quiet private street, pulled his car right around the circular driveway, and stopped in front of the beautiful Yountville Inn— the ultimate escape for a romantic getaway.

"Oh, Wes, what a splendid surprise. This is beautiful."

"I thought you'd enjoy a little escape. You've been working horrendous hours. You needed a break."

"Oh, I did. I do." Emma wrapped her arms around Wes and gave him a hug and kiss.

The door attendant held open the large ornate door for them and once inside, they immediately took notice of the tranquil environment and the attention to detail. The décor was international marble in rich earth tones of sand and gold. The room was warm, scented with flowers and designed with some cozy corners for guests to lounge while they enjoy the wine tastings. Emma's sensitive nostrils also picked up the pervasive smell of greed.

Their spa suite had a steam shower for two and a luxurious double hydrotherapy tub, and Italian marble everywhere, the floors, the dual vanities, the shower.

"This is magnificent, Wes."

"I'm glad you like it. I made reservations for us to get a Quattro Mani massage later this evening after dinner."

"What's a Quattro Mani massage?"

"It's an Asian-inspired massage where two therapists work in unison for ninety minutes, and they're known to melt all tension and stress away."

"Oh, that sounds too good. They will absolutely melt me. Does that mean we'll be sleeping the rest of our time in Napa Valley?"

"Sleeping? I don't think so. Relaxing and enjoying each other. Yes."

Emma smiled lovingly and wrapped her arms around Wes' neck. "And what else have you planned?"

"Tonight, we have reservations at Bouchon's which is right up the street from us. This is a quaint little town and everything is within walking distance from here. But first, let's go and get something to eat. I'm famished. There's a restaurant up the street called, Grandma's Pancake House."

"That's perfect. I'm hungry too. Let's go."

They walked hand in hand up the street until they reached a small stone building with ivy growing all over the front of the building. Large oak and pine trees stood tall on both sides of the building. It looked like a grandma's house in the forest. As soon as Wes opened the door, they were greeted with aromas of coffee, cinnamon, and ham. A cheerful little woman with snow-white hair and small oval glasses perched on her little nose walked up to them. "Welcome to Grandma's. Table for two?"

"Yes," Wes said.

Dressed in a checkered pinafore with a little crisp white apron, she said, "Right this way." She seated them in a corner booth and placed two menus on the wooden table. A large pitcher of water was already set on the table with two glasses.

"Isn't this cozy," Emma said. "Looks like a grandma's house should look, with all the knickknacks on the walls."

"This is as quaint as you can get," Wes said with a laugh as he squeezed in next to Emma.

"I love it. Hand over the menu, and let's see what Grandma's cooking today."

After a few minutes, Emma announced, "I'm going to have the Swedish lingonberry thin pancakes. How about you, Wes? Have you decided?"

After a few moments, he said, "I've decided on the California omelet."

"This is just the most perfect day, isn't it?" Emma cried out. "It's so beautiful up here. I have never been to Napa before. When I went to the university, I never had time to go anywhere with all the tough classes I took my first year."

She reached over and gave Wes a kiss on the cheek. "Thank you, sweetie. This was an excellent idea and very thoughtful."

"I'm glad you're enjoying yourself. I thought you'd enjoy Napa. What's not to like, eh?"

Grandma returned with two coffees and a creamer in the shape of a cow. She placed the coffees in front of each of them and before she walked away, she said, "Your breakfasts should be ready in a few minutes."

"Umm, the coffee is delicious," Wes said. "If breakfast is as good as the coffee, we're in for a real treat."

"So what's on the agenda while we're here?" Emma asked.

"We've got reservations for the hot air balloon ride Saturday morning. They take off right from the road where we turned in, but there's only one catch—we have to be there at five-fifteen in the morning."

"Oh, that's no problem. I've never been on a hot air balloon ride before. This is going to be so much fun. We'll be able to see the whole valley. How exciting is that?" Emma exclaimed.

"I have never been up in a hot air balloon either," Wes admitted. "Napa Valley is one of the most beautiful places on earth, not only for growing wine grapes, but also for soaring in colorful hot air balloons. Once you're up in the air, it'll put the world below into perspective. The view will be astonishing when we're above it all."

Grandma appeared at the table with a basket of syrups dangling from one finger and carrying two hot plates, which she immediately set down in front of them. "Here you are. There are four different syrups in this basket," she said as she unhooked it from her finger. "If you need anything else, please let me know. I'll get more coffee for you right now."

"Oh, this really looks incredible," Emma said with wide eyes. "Grandma's come a long way with her passion for food. I've heard that all the best chefs are located in Napa Valley."

"That's what I've heard too," Wes replied. "A lot of European's came to Napa Valley to grow grapes. There's a strong influence of German, Italian, and Swiss winemakers in the valley. Most of them were chefs who came here to make wine. The combination turned out to be quite explosive."

Suddenly the talking stopped and the eating began, followed by lots of *Umms, Ohs,* and *Wows.* "Grandma can cook for me anytime," Wes announced.

Within twenty minutes, the plates were left clean, the coffee was gone and they were content. "The food was fabulous. Grandma's very creative," Emma said.

"Amen to that," Wes added.

"You look content now that you're fed," Emma said.

"Food has a tendency to do that to people," Wes responded as he stretched his body upward and patted his stomach.

"Let's try to walk off this breakfast. There's a marketplace up the street. Let's go browse that area," Wes suggested.

They strolled up Washington Street to the marketplace and walked around all the little shops. Emma bought a pair of shoes, and Wes found a tan cashmere jacket.

"Why don't we go back to the hotel and go for a swim and then a Jacuzzi?" Wes suggested.

"That sounds like a plan. What time is dinner?" Emma inquired.

"Dinner is at seven so that leaves us a couple of hours."

Wes took her hand as they turned and walked casually toward the hotel.

Suddenly, without any warning, Wes let go of her hand and gave Emma his jacket to hold. When Emma looked at him, she saw menace in his eyes. He was beyond angry; he was enraged. He rushed down a small alleyway and screamed at a young man who was urinating against the side of a building. "You moron! There are restrooms right down the street," he yelled out. Before the young man could turn around, Wes brutally shoved his face against the building. Dazed, the man fell to the ground, his mouth and nose bleeding.

"Get the hell out of here," Wes yelled as he gave him a swift kick in the side of his body.

Emma kept walking and never turned around. His unexpected anger dismayed her. If there was one thing about Wes that she did not like, it was his temper.

Wes caught up to her and grabbed the jacket from her hand. "I'm sorry about that, Em," he whispered while he held her hand and continued their walk as if nothing happened.

"It's all right, Wes. He shouldn't have done that. You didn't hurt him, did you?"

"No, but I scared him."

Once inside the room, Wes swept his arms under Emma's knees. Her breath caught as he lifted her off her feet, and held her in his arms. When his mouth met hers, she sank into the kiss with a soft murmur of pleasure. She kicked off her shoes as he carried her into the bedroom—they both fell backward onto the bed.

Wes raised his head; he put his hands on her face, and said, "I love you so much. Let's go to Tahoe and get married."

Emma's eyebrows shot up. "Get married? Now? Why now?"

"For the simple reason that I don't want to wait any longer."

"I had no idea we were waiting."

"I've wanted to marry you the first moment I laid eyes on you. I love you so very much," he said as he pulled her closer. "I can't imagine my life without you. Please say you'll marry me," he begged.

He reached under his pillow, pulled out a small pink velvet case, and handed it to Emma.

"For me?" she said as a smile broke out on her face. Slowly she pried open the elegant case. The hinges resisted slightly before it popped open. Emma's eyes went wide, completely overwhelmed by surprise. It was a huge pink diamond ring.

"Oh!" she screamed. Her eyes glistened with tears.

"We can take it back if you don't like it, and you can exchange it for something you like."

Emma wiped the tears away with the back of her hand. "It's so beautiful."

He took the ring from the box and without a word, she gave him her hand. He slipped the ring on her finger and said, "Will you marry me, Emma Griffin?"

She gazed lovingly into Wes' eyes and with no hesitation, she said, "Yes."

Wes gave a startled laugh and said, "You've made me the happiest man in the world."

With a guttural sound, he wrapped his arms around her and kissed her mouth lovingly, passionately. "Let's drive up to Tahoe tomorrow and get married," he murmured against her hair.

A deep sigh rippled through her as she reached up and touched his face. "Oh, "I'm going to become Mrs. Wes Blair."

"Yes, you are," he said as he clutched her in his arms."

"Oh, Wes, I'm so happy." Emma knew in her heart that she was going to marry the man of her dreams.

"You're the love of my life, Emma. You *are* my life."

"I'm yours, forever," Emma said in a loving whisper.

Those were the *exact* words Wes needed to hear.

CHAPTER

9

Emma Griffin allowed herself few certainties in life, but she was absolutely sure of one thing—she was deeply in love with Wes. He was her first love, her only love and she wanted to become Mrs. Wes Blair.

No big ceremony… just the two of them standing in front of a heavyset minister with unruly gray hair and a round jowly face. After a ten-minute civil ceremony, they were husband and wife. Emma was euphoric and very enchanted by the thought of Wes *forsaking all others so long as they both shall live… forever and ever… a promise till death do us part.*

They dined in Friday's Station on the top floor of Harrah's. It was a perfect romantic dinner with an incredible majestic view of Lake Tahoe. After dinner, Wes said, "Let' go down to the casino floor. I'd like to spend a little time at the blackjack table."

Emma had never been to a casino before so she said, "Oh, that'll be fun. I'll play the slot machines. This was not exactly the wedding night Emma dreamed of, but after she had hit a thousand dollar jackpot, she was all smiles and couldn't wait to tell Wes. She took her winnings and immediately went over to him at the blackjack table.

"Guess what?" she said as she put her arms around him.

"What?" he asked as he turned toward her.

"I just won a thousand dollars on a slot machine," she said with a huge smile.

"That's great, honey. Can I have five hundred dollars? I haven't won yet."

Hesitantly, Emma said, "Sure." Reluctantly, she reached into her purse and counted out five one hundred dollar bills, which he plucked from her hand before she uttered, "Here you are."

"Thanks, Em."

"When are we going to go up to our room?"

"In a little while. You go win some more money."

"No, I don't feel like playing anymore. I want to go up to the room."

"You're not going to start nagging me already, are you?"

Emma tugged on his jacket, "Come on, Wes."

"I'm not going up right now," he snapped with fierceness in his expression that she had never seen before. "You go up to the room."

When Emma turned away, heat rose in her cheeks as her whole body vibrated with outrage. Not wanting to make a scene, she squared her shoulders, marched straight to the bank of elevators, and jabbed the button. With her eyes glued to the digital display over the elevator doors, she tried to maintain her emotions.

Ding. Seconds later, one of the elevator doors opened. Once inside, tears filled her eyes. *What have I done? He would rather stay and gamble on our wedding night than come with me to our room? Since when did he gamble? He never mentioned that he played cards. Did I just make a mistake marrying this man?* "What did I get myself into," she whispered.

Ding, the elevator doors glided open. Slowly, she walked down the carpeted corridor toward the room. Squaring her shoulders, she inserted the key card in the slot and reached for the doorknob.

She opened the door and stepped across the threshold into a shadowy hall but hesitated before moving forward. The heavy door closed with a quick snap, making her jump.

A deep loneliness filled the darkened room. Here she was, alone… on her honeymoon, a night which should be the biggest night of her life. Just hours ago she said, *I do* in front of a judge, and already, she bitterly regretted that she ever uttered those words.

She plopped down on the sofa, staring out the window into the darkness of the night, her stomach queasy. She sat there motionless; the darkness seemed only seemed to make her fears rush forward. She felt numb, unaware of what to do now that the evening had taken an abrupt turn. *It had been ridiculous for us to get married… eloping like a couple of crazy teenagers. What was I thinking? What do I do now?* she thought as tears flooded her eyes and trickled down her cheeks. She sat for a long time surrounded by silence. *Perhaps things will seem different in the light of day.*

It was three o'clock in the morning before Wes staggered into their suite. He quietly crossed the room as his eyes adjusted to the darkness. Emma was asleep in the bed with the TV playing. He turned the TV off, took off all his clothes, and lay down on the bed gently so as not to disturb her.

When Emma woke in the morning, she saw Wes passed out on top of the bed covers. Furiously, she grabbed her clothes from the closet, went into the bathroom, and when she emerged, she was fully dressed and ready to leave.

As much as she hated scenes and melodramas, she felt this was going to be a confrontation worthy of a soap opera. She walked over to the side of the bed and vigorously shook Wes.

"What? What happened?" he groggily asked as he rubbed his eyes and quickly sat up on the edge of the bed.

With a temper that she seldom showed, Emma said emphatically, "Get dressed, we're leaving."

"What's the problem, honey?"

"Don't call me honey," Emma yelled in a frosty tone. "I don't have a problem, you do. I want to leave right now," she demanded.

"What do you mean you want to leave? Why are we leaving? This is our honeymoon."

"Yes, I thought it was our honeymoon, but it seems you would rather sit at a blackjack table all night than be here with me. Getting married on the spur of the moment was ridiculous."

"Honey, that's not true. Come here," he said as he grabbed her arm. "Sit down on the bed."

She sat on the bed, tears streaming down her cheeks.

"Honey, don't cry. It's our honeymoon. I'm sorry I didn't come up to the room earlier, but I was on a winning streak. You *don't* leave the table when you're winning."

She hesitated for several seconds before she asked, "How much did you win?"

"I won twenty-two thousand dollars after you gave me the five hundred."

"What?" she screamed out with a huge smile. "You won twenty-two thousand dollars?"

"Yeah. That's the reason I was so late in coming up to the room," he said, somewhat relieved.

"Oh, that's wonderful, Wes," Emma said. She put her arms around him and kissed him.

"Why don't you come back to bed and I'll show you what a real honeymoon is all about?"

Emma blushed. "I guess I was premature in getting angry with you. It's really not my nature to get angry. I don't know what came over me. I'm sorry, Wes. I really am."

"You're forgiven," Wes said as he grabbed her and threw her flat on the bed. She was giggling and squirming, but she soon settled down when he brushed his lips over hers and traced her mouth with the tip of his tongue.

"I love you so much," he said, biting her ear with exquisite care, sending shivers through her body. The sensuality in his voice did dangerous and bizarre things to Emma. When his mouth came down and covered hers, the world stopped—it was a sensually ravenous experience.

The only person not entirely overjoyed by the news of the sudden marriage was Emma's Uncle Ross. "Why the rush to get married, darlin'?" Ross asked as his stomach churned.

"Why should we wait?" she responded. "We want to be together, and there's really no reason to drag it out with a long engagement."

"Jesus, Emma." He closed his eyes. "You really haven't known Wes very long. I wish you paused long enough to think about what you were doing and that you talked with me earlier about getting married."

"We didn't plan it. It just happened. I'm in love with Wes and he's in love with me. I did think about it and the more I thought about it, the less crazy it seemed."

Ross cringed at her impulsive action. "I see… well, as upset as I am right now…"

"Uncle Ross! Why are you upset? This is not what I expected you to say," Emma shouted.

"I may as well tell you that I don't believe Wes is the right man for you. But what is done is done and there is no one who wishes you more joy in life than I do. If you're happy, then I'm happy for you."

"Oh, Uncle Ross, when you get to know Wes, you'll like him. Wes is a dream come true and I love him deeply."

"I can only hope the both of you will be blessed with a wonderful marriage."

"Thank you, Uncle Ross. Your blessing means a lot to me."

Ross put the phone down and held his hand firmly over it as if to lock the cyclone of bad news out. He may have told Emma he was happy for her, but he was extremely distressed by her impulsive decision. He always felt this nagged annoyance in his gut whenever he heard Wes's name mentioned.

Nine months later, Lucas was born on November 17, 1997, and ten months later, Adam was born September 12, 1998. Emma and Wes had the family they wanted, and Emma had reached her personal goal—she obtained her Ph.D. and was now a biochemistry professor at Stanford. Wes did well at work, and had earned several advancements in the company.

Life was good.

CHAPTER

10

Four years later – November 2001

Wes slammed the door of his office so hard the hanger holding his sports jacket fell off the back of the door and fell in a heap onto the floor. He looked around the room—it was the biggest office in the building. He had eight years of hard work and now he was being kicked out on his ass by his boss, with no stock options, no severance pay! "Fuck him!"

He yanked open his desk drawer only to see a coffee mug. He had no pictures of his family; nothing of a personal nature to take with him.

The door opened. It was the human resources manager. "I brought you a box for your personal things," she uttered.

"Don't waste your time," he said as he angrily slammed the drawer shut. "There's nothing I want from this company."

"Your medical and dental insurance for you and your family will be in effect for the next twelve months. Here's a copy of your final termination papers. I'll need your badge and the keys to the building."

Wes nervously bit his bottom lip. He unhooked the badge from his shirt pocket and threw it on his desk. He fished in his pocket for the keys and tossed them on the desk next to his badge.

"This isn't the only electronics company in this valley. I've had plenty of offers from other firms over the last six years," Wes shouted as he picked up his jacket and walked through the doorway. Everyone in the outer office turned and looked at him. *Damn, they know.*

Wes examined all their faces. How they ogled. He straightened his shoulders, stood tall and said, "If I've hurt you in any way, I'd like to take this opportunity to say from the bottom of my heart, I really don't give a damn."

With a firm salute, he walked to the elevator, pushed the button, and disappeared behind closed doors.

He hopped in his car, started the engine, and said, "Fuck you all."

"Clear out my office," he mumbled to himself. "What a joke, and they send someone in to make sure I don't take any of their valuable shit."

His next thoughts were of Emma and the boys. *I'll get another job. My 401K was good. But, what if things get worse? How long would that last with a wife and two small kids? Maybe a full year?*

CHAPTER

11

"I have some news," Wes said when he walked into the kitchen from the garage. "You are not going to believe what happened today. I should make you guess, but you'd never get it."

"Oh, did you get another promotion at work?" Emma smiled as she turned to look at Wes. Instantly her smile faded when she saw the look of death on his face. "What happened?" she asked as she strolled over to him. His body stiffened when she kissed his cheek.

"I lost my job. I got fired."

Emma's mouth gaped open. "How? What happened?"

"We had a financial meeting this afternoon and I called my boss an idiot and I was fired on the spot, right in the middle of the meeting."

"Oh, Wes. How awful. Why did you say that?"

"Hey, he doesn't know what's really going on in the company, and he comes off like he's actually involved when he's not. He *is* an idiot!"

"Maybe so, but you don't tell your boss that. What will you do now?"

"I've been offered jobs at other companies—I'll find another job."

With the sudden detour in his career, Wes became agitated after weeks of searching for another position. He realized he was in trouble with the loss of income, and he just couldn't make anything happen. Between his unsuccessful attempt to find a job and his inability to cope with his failure and the needs of a wife and two sons, he distanced himself from them and started drinking heavily and gambling at the Garden City Casino, rarely making it home before midnight.

Almost overnight, Wes became a stranger to his family. Emma questioned how a man could go from an attentive, loving father to a father who had lost all interest in his sons. She was heartbroken every time the boys asked, "*Where's Daddy?*"

For weeks, there had been no real union—they were nothing more than passengers on a train grouped together through circumstance. Inwardly, Emma suffered the silent trepidation of a wife faced with a failed marriage.

She immediately began to rethink all the aspects of her marriage that evidently had been running on autopilot for the past few years. She had been so busy doing, she never stepped back to see *how* she was doing, or how *they* were doing. As much as she wanted to find something that would trigger what and when something went wrong, she only found herself more frustrated as she grappled for answers.

In an attempt to understand her husband's behavior, Emma pored over dozens of books on abnormal psychology and dysfunctional conditions. It was a cold comfort for her to see herself headed into an abysmal spin that she had no idea how to explain. Certainly, there had to be something she could do to turn her marriage around. She was happy two months ago; she could be happy again. Her focus was to keep the family together. She must talk with Wes about marriage counseling.

The night was cold and windy. Emma could hear the branches brush against the house. The living room was dark except for the thin lines of moonlight that seeped through the blinds. Dressed in a zip-up pink robe, her hair tied up in a ponytail, she paced nervously in random circles around the living room just like she had done every night of the week for the past several weeks.

She heard the garage door lumber up on its tracks. Her heart was pounding fiercely. She closed her eyes and took several deep breaths in an attempt to appear resilient. Her eyes focused on the hallway.

The erratic shuffle of Wes' shoes produced a whispery sound coming toward her. Wes squinted at his watch when he saw her. "How come you're up?"

"I thought we could talk."

"That's what you thought? Well, you'd be wrong."

"Wes, we need to sit down and talk rationally if we're going to save our marriage."

"Talk, talk, talk. You always want to talk. Every goddamn day all you want to do is talk. Okay, what is it today?"

"I think we should go to marriage counseling so we can work on solving whatever it is that's tearing our marriage apart. We need to find out what the problem is."

"You're the problem," Wes snapped. "Doesn't take a marriage counselor to figure that out. Our marriage never worked. You think you're something special because you're a professor at Stanford. You're worthless, you and your higher-than-mighty attitude. You think you're better than me."

"That's not true. How can you say that?"

"Yes, it's true. All of it is true. I'm not going to any marriage counselor. You, my dear wife, are the one with the problem. You go spend your money talking to a stranger who'll listen to *your* problems."

Silence filled the room for several moments before Emma asked, "How did we lose it, Wes?"

"Lose what?" he growled.

"We were once in love," Emma whispered, her eyes filled with tears. "So this was all for nothing. We have nothing now? When the hell did this happen? I don't understand any of this."

"For a professor, you don't seem to understand anything. Well know this," Wes said firmly, "I'm through listening to any of *your* problems. I don't want to hear about any of this crap. Don't think for one minute that I'm gonna do anything you want me to do. It's not gonna happen, so stop telling me what to do. Just stop! No one tells Wes Blair what to do. No one!"

What happened to us? How did we get to this point? Emma asked herself as she sat on the edge of the bed that she shared with her husband of four years. *There was a time when we were compatible… we wanted to make each other happy and we would talk and laugh. She hadn't heard laughter come out of Wes in months. He's certainly not happy and could care less if she's happy. All he does now is complain about everything. She can't do anything to please him. When did everything start to change?*

Emma lay back on the bed and closed her eyes trying to remember the very beginning, before they were married. *Perhaps nothing had really changed. Yes, there were signs. She ignored the damn warning signs of trouble coming. Huh… this has actually been going on since the day we met. Does falling in love do this to a person? Make you deaf and blind?*

She always felt that there was something different about Wes. He had a disconcerting way of staring with an inscrutable expression on his face giving no indication of what he was thinking. He was an expert at concealing his thoughts and only let you know what he wanted you to know. He made you feel unsteady and took pleasure in the fact that you were not sure about something. He kept you off balance.

That isn't normal behavior. What was I thinking?

In the days that followed, Emma convinced herself that Wes' depression was just a temporary phase. They had fallen into a rut that a lot of married couples do, and when he finds another job, he'll be his old self again and their family will be back to normal.

Somehow, after a month of being unemployed, Wes managed to get a job offer from a mortgage company as the western regional manager. It turned out that Kate Lee, a woman he had met at the bar he frequented, was the operations manager at Capital Mortgage & Loan in San Jose and she was recruiting for this position.

Emma thought things would change once he found a job but his attitude toward her only worsened and created an atmosphere of even more tension between them with his constant mood changes and emotional outbursts. What she thought, no longer mattered. She was never right; he was never wrong. He badgered her over trivial things that eventually had her believe that there really was something wrong with *her*.

CHAPTER

12

Tonight will be different....

"I feel like I'm being strangled in this marriage," Emma mumbled to herself. *I can't take this anymore. Something has to change. I can't go on living like this. This is not healthy for me or for the boys.*

She cringed when she heard the garage door roll down and then slam shut with a final rumbling shudder. She moved some loose hairs out of her face. The room suddenly seemed to get smaller and airless as she waited.

She swallowed convulsively as he staggered toward her. She backed away, but he caught her. She felt his hand close around her neck in a grip that made her wince.

He smiled when he saw the look of terror in her wide, fearful eyes—exhilarated by the power he had. *He was the man in charge.*

What is he smiling at? Emma wondered. She had not seen him smile in weeks. "You seem happy this evening," she blurted out.

Wes immediately let go of her. "Why should I be happy? What happened?"

"Nothing happened. You walked in here smiling. I just wondered why you were smiling, that's all."

His shoulders started to shake with a suppressed laugh. "I just like looking at your face, that's all," he replied as he plopped down on the sofa.

After several moments of silence, Emma cleared her throat and said, "Wes."

He looked up at her.

"We need to talk."

"Oh, here you go, again. All you ever want to do is talk," he yelled. "Talk about what?"

"Talk about our life together, or I should say, lack of a life together," Emma cried. "This marriage is not working out. Surely you can see that."

"You can't be thinking about leaving me," he blurted out as he sat up. "Is that what you're thinking? You goddamned well know that I will never let you walk out on me. That ain't gonna happen. You're not going anywhere with my sons," he shouted.

"Don't yell at Mommy!"

"Lucas!" Emma said as she jumped up and ran to him. "Honey, are you okay?"

Lucas stared at the two of them. "I heard Daddy yelling at you."

"Oh, sweetie, we're just talking. Come on, let's go upstairs and I'll tuck you in. Everything is fine."

Five minutes later, Emma came back downstairs and sat on the sofa, her head in her hands. How ugly, she thought. The two of them filling their home with rage.

"Are you happy now? Your son heard us fighting!" Emma said.

Wes sat quietly for several minutes, seemingly disturbed that his son heard them quarrelling.

Emma stood up, took a deep breath, and said, "Why in the name of Christ do you want to live like this? I don't understand any of this. You are not a responsible father, you are never here, and when you are here, it's after midnight. You would rather spend all your time gambling at the casino than come home to your family."

Wes looked at her, totally offended by what she said. With no sign of emotion on his face, he stood and moved toward her.

Emma immediately backed away. However, not fast enough to avoid being slapped with a quick sharp blow to the right side of her face, snapping her head back. She yelled out in pain as she held both her trembling hands to her face and fell on the sofa. Her hand felt wet. She looked at it, all covered in blood. Dazed, she stared up at him—the hatred in his eyes, a face she hardly recognized at all. "You're like a stranger to me. So uncaring… so brutal."

Silence filled the room for several minutes. Emma got all tight-mouthed, and started plucking at her nails. With a trembling voice and tears streaming down her cheeks, she said, "I don't know who you are anymore. I don't understand any of this." Fiercely she wiped the damned humiliating tears away with the back of her hand. She vowed not to shed any more tears over him.

"Do you actually believe that I'd let you take my boys and walk outta here just like that?" he said, snapping his fingers in front of her face. "Is that what you think is really gonna happen?" he snarled, smothering the last word with laughter.

Emma stared at him, her spine stiffening as she gained control of herself. With her hands clasped in front of her, she said, "Wes, I want a divorce. I cannot… No, I *will not* live this way any longer. The boys and I deserve better."

Wes walked over to the sofa, grabbed Emma by the shoulders and stood her up. "There will never be any divorce, Emma," Wes said emphatically. "Never gonna happen."

"What do you want from me?" Emma pleaded. "We can't go on living this way. This isn't how two rational people who have been married for over four years behave. In case you haven't noticed, we have more than the normal bickering between married couples going on here."

"Will you listen to what I'm telling you?" he said raising his voice. "There…will…be… no…divorce. I can't make it any clearer than that. You will never stop me from seeing my boys, and you dare not try to leave California, or *else*.

"Or else what?" Emma demanded.

Wes grabbed her by the throat, paused for several seconds and stared directly into her eyes. "If you leave, I will find you and when I do my face will be the last thing you see just before I kill you," he said in a low gravelly snarl.

"You'll never get away with…"

"I won't get away with it?" he interrupted. "You know me better than that. If you think for one minute that I haven't planned this all out, then you'd be wrong."

If Emma knew nothing else about Wes, she did know he never made idle threats.

CHAPTER

13

Jolted awake like a jack-in-the-box, Emma gasped for breath. The dream... the frightening dream was so intense, so real and so terrifying. Possessed with panic, she stumbled out of bed into the dark, soundless room, to grab her robe and wrap it around her shivering body.

Her bare feet hit the cold hardwood floor when she entered the kitchen. The scrape of the stool was the only noise heard when she pulled it out from under the kitchen counter. She sat rigidly on the backless bar stool, holding the thick robe close to her body, overwhelmed by the blackness—the horror of her nightmare.

She was alone in a filthy hellhole prison cell. There were no sounds as if the rest of the world was nowhere. She did not belong here in this insufferable cell with gray cement walls and a small barred window infected with soot and spider webs.

The clang of metal on metal parted the stillness as she banged the rusty metal bars with a large spoon screaming out her innocence. "I'm not an evil person! It wasn't my fault! I didn't do it."

A battalion of guards dressed in black capes with hoods advanced through the shadows. They all wore goggles that shined light into the cell. They opened the door and grabbed her arms and beat her with their night sticks before they dragged her bloody body down to the shower room and turned the high pressure shower head on her. Blood trickled down her pale nude body and circled around and around before it flowed down the drain.

Motionless, she sat in the dark, trying to manipulate the dream knowing that real life problems were the instigators of dreams. To make sense of it—the prison cell—the beating. After several minutes, tears welled in her eyes as she drearily uttered, "My failed marriage. The blood circled around as it flowed down the drain; years of work gone down the drain."

Without warning, a shiver ran through her body. She felt as if her life suddenly ripped out of her. She tugged at her robe to bring it closer to her body as she walked over to the sofa and plopped down, feeling defeated.

She ran her fingers through her long dark brown hair and wiped the tears from her eyes with the back of her hand. She winced when her hand rubbed over the stitches. Wes had put the cut on her cheek, and the bruises on her neck.

Entangled in the web of deplorable regrets, her lips tightened when Wes' image-provoking words throbbed in her mind... *If you leave, I will find you and when I do my face will be the last thing you see just before I kill you.*

He had her trapped—if she stayed, she would live with pain and suffering. If she left, she would be free from all the pain and suffering. Of course there was the possibility he might find her. Then she would be dead.

She knew her life wasn't supposed to turn out like this—sitting alone in a darkened room, crying. She had never imagined herself as any sort of martyr—enduring loneliness and living every day in fear. She just assumed that things would just go on indefinitely in their imperfect unacceptable way because human nerves rapidly get accustomed to the most unimaginable conditions and circumstances. *Could it be that she's become a victim of human adaptability? Had the abuse eroded her sense of self-confidence and self-worth? Had she adapted to her misery? Perhaps it was easier to adapt than to change*, she thought.

She leaned her head back, closed her eyes, and uttered, "God help me. Has he done this to me? Have I allowed him to do this to me and my sons?"

CHAPTER

14

Christmas Party at Professor Stanton's home

"I've been looking for you!" a man's harsh voice rang out.

The violent disturbance abruptly filled the air with complete silence.

Emma turned. It was Wes! Thoughts immediately ran through her head. *Why is he embarrassing me in front of my co-workers?* To make light of the situation, she cried out, "I'm... oh, I guess I completely lost track of the time."

"I guess you did. I'll be waiting in the car."

Emma, completely embarrassed, walked toward Professor Stanton. "I am so sorry for the intrusion. I must go now. Thank you so much for a lovely party and my very best wishes for a Merry Christmas. Good night."

She ran into the bedroom, grabbed her coat and purse and quietly left the home. She heard the engine running as she walked down the path toward the car. "Damn him!" she cried out. "Who does he think he is?"

She jumped into the car. Wes, who never turned his head, sat stiffly and immediately pressed the accelerator, making the car jerk violently.

"How dare you embarrass me in front of the people I work with? What in the hell is wrong with you?" she yelled out.

"Nothing is wrong with me. You're the one with the problem."

"What problem might that be? You deliberately embarrassed me in front of the people I work with and now I'm the one with the problem?"

"Oh, I saw a problem all right. You were talking with all those men. I saw you! I saw the way those men looked at you."

"How they looked at me? What are you talking about?"

"A man looks at things differently than women do. I see things from a man's point of view."

"So a man looked at me. Don't make such a big deal out of nothing."

"Don't make a big deal out of nothing? One of them had his arm on your shoulder! I saw that too! *You* owe *me* an apology," Wes demanded.

"An apology! Are you insane? I am not apologizing to you. You are the one who should apologize. I did nothing wrong."

"I saw you in the company of several men. I was the one who was embarrassed," Wes flared.

"I've watched you with other women. You beam when a beautiful woman talks to you and don't you dare say you don't because I've seen it a hundred times."

"Don't you dare try to turn this around, Emma! I swear to God…"

"You have the nerve to bring God into this conversation? All of a sudden you're filled with the Holy Spirit?"

"So I'm not religious, but I have moral principles," Wes said.

"Don't be so sanctimonious around me. Let's stop this bickering right now. This conversation is going nowhere."

The ride home created a new meaning for the word silence.

As soon as they entered the house, Emma slipped her coat off and threw it on a chair. She turned to face Wes. His eyes were in a rage, and in a violent force, his open hand slapped her face. Smack!

Stunned by the attack, she screamed out as she went flying across the room falling hard against the front door. "What is wrong with you?"

"Don't play that innocent card with me."

"What are you talking about?" she yelled back as she held her hand to the stinging pain on her face, where she felt welts on her face.

"You just love to go to these parties with all those smart young people. You fit right in with them."

"Those are the people I work with every day. What is wrong with you, Wes?"

"There's nothing wrong with me. It's you who has a problem. You think you're so damn smart," he said as he rushed toward her, grabbed her by the hair, and punched her in the stomach.

Emma cried out, but there was no one there to hear her. The boys were at the neighbors on a sleepover. Not that she *ever* wanted them to see her like this.

Suddenly, there was a knock on the front door.

Wes looked through the peephole. It was Debbie, the neighbor who had the boys. He opened the door just as Emma turned and ran into the bedroom and slammed the door.

"Hi Debbie. Are the boys okay? Is there something wrong?" Wes asked in a caring manner.

Debbie stood there and glared past Wes. "Oh, no, nothing's wrong, I just had a thought I wanted to share with Emma. Is she okay?"

"She's not feeling well. We think it was something she ate at the party."

"Oh, if there's anything I can do, let me know."

"She'll be fine."

"Let Emma know I came by."

"I will."

"Oh, dear God. Debbie knows. She saw me run. She probably heard us fighting. What am I going to do now?" Emma cried out.

Emma was frantic. The shame, the cowardly shame she suddenly felt as if she were a criminal who got caught in the act. Angry tears began to form as they did every time her emotions got the best of her.

"What will I do now?" she whispered feeling defeated by guilt. She knew she couldn't keep this bottled up forever. But who could she possibly tell? Uncle Ross? Oh, he would kill Wes in an instant. Susan? Jimmy? They would not know what to do.

She decided that she would keep it to herself. She'll figure out a solution. That's what she does.

No sleep came. Every muscle, every nerve, was tense as she constructed what she would say to Debbie tomorrow morning when she picked up the boys.

Nervously, she knocked on the door.

When the door opened, Debbie said, "Emma? Are you feeling better?

"Yes. I'm fine."

"The boys are just finishing breakfast. Come on in."

Emma looked into Debbie's eyes. Eyes tell the story. She was putting on a front to pretend she did not see or hear anything last night.

"I only have a minute. I hope they behaved themselves?" Emma said as she stepped inside.

"Yes, they were great. We set up a tent in the playroom upstairs and they 'camped out.' They slept in sleeping bags and they loved it. How was the Christmas party?"

Nervously, Emma paused a moment before responding. "Debbie, I know you heard us arguing last night. Wes was upset because I lost track of time and he walked in looking for me. He was quite angry when he saw me talking to a few of my co-workers. It was my fault. People get angry all the time. Wes got irritable, and it was my fault for not watching the clock."

Debbie stood quietly for a few seconds before she said, "I heard something going on and I heard you slam the door. What happened to your face? It's all red."

"Yes, I know. Evidently, I was allergic to something I ate at the party. It's nothing."

CHAPTER

15

... *"Was I not right?" said the little mouse. "Little friends may prove great friends,"* Emma said, as she closed the book after she finished the bedtime story, *Lion and the Mouse*.

"I liked that story, Mommy," Lucas said as he yawned. "Just cause the Lion is bigger than the mouse, doesn't mean the mouse can't help him when he got in trouble."

"Yeah," Adam said. "You can have small friends. I'm smaller than Lucas but I could help him if he got in trouble."

"That's right, Adam," Emma said as she rumpled his blonde curly hair. "You're only three but you're strong and when you're four, you'll be big, like Lucas."

"Good night, Lucas. Good night, Adam. I love you guys."

"I love you, Mommy," Lucas said, rubbing his eyes.

"Me too, Mommy. I love you," Adam squealed.

She looked at them lovingly before she closed their bedroom door and went downstairs to finish the dinner dishes and do some laundry.

The phone rang just before she stepped into the kitchen. She grabbed the phone in the living room and sat on the sofa.

"Hello?"

"Hi, Emma," the familiar voice of her Uncle Ross uttered. "How are you and the boys doing?"

"Oh, how nice to hear your voice," Emma said as she smiled into the phone. "I just put the kids to bed. You're calling rather late this evening. Are you home?"

"Yes, I just got home and thought I'd give you a call. I've been thinking about you all day. What's going on out there on the west coast?"

"Nothing really new out here. The boys are doing well in school. I'm very proud of them."

"They take after their mother."

"Yes, they do. They really enjoy school."

"How are your classes going at the college?"

"My classes are going exceptionally well. I have some very creative students, who are wonderful for my brain as well as theirs. They keep me on my toes."

"And how is Wes doing?" he reluctantly asked, just to keep peace in the family.

"Oh, he's fine and really likes his new job at the mortgage company," Emma said as guilt flashed through her mind because she lied to her uncle.

"That's good. You sound different, sweetie. Is everything okay?"

"Yes, everything's fine." She had to quickly change the subject. He seemed to have an uncanny way of finding out the truth. "Have you decided where you and Ellie are going on vacation this summer?"

"Well, actually, we're thinking about coming to San Francisco in July and perhaps we'll drive up to Lake Tahoe for a few days. Just relax, take a cruise on the lake, do some gambling, and have a good time."

"Oh, that's wonderful. I can't wait to see you both. It's been a while since we all got together."

"Yes, it has been too long. I'm looking forward to seeing you and the boys. They've probably grown taller than you by now."

"Well, not quite," she giggled. "You do realize they're only three and four years old."

"Yeah, but they're gonna be big guys with long legs like their mother."

"I hope so. We can't have any runts in our family."

"I bumped into Hawk a couple of weeks ago. He said to say hello to you. He really misses you, you know."

"I know, Uncle Ross. I miss him too. Things will change, and I'll give him a call."

Ross knew that she never called Hawk because Wes had forbidden it. "He'd like that. You know, he started his own investigation business. I've used him on a couple of cases. He's become very well respected for his forensic talents, and it's keeping him extremely busy. He even hired a guy from NCIS to work in the lab. He's got a lab that will knock your socks off. It's got everything that NCIS had in their lab. He's pretty proud of his business. He's even got himself a boat now. I haven't seen it yet, but he talks about it."

"Oh, he's got girls all over him now if he's got a boat," Emma laughingly said.

"As a matter of fact, he doesn't have a girlfriend anymore. He told me his new mistress is his work. He spends all his time at work. Says it keeps him out of trouble. His boat is for getting away from everyone and relaxing every now and then. He's got it moored at one of the local Yacht Clubs, so it's easy for him to go there. A change of scenery is always good for the psyche."

"Oh, I agree. Say hello to Hawk next time you see him, and tell him I love him."

"I will. Well, I better let you go. I know how busy you are with school and the kids. You always have something to do. I just wanted to touch base with you. Love you, darlin'."

"I love you too, Uncle Ross. Give my love to Ellie."

Emma hesitated a moment before hanging up the phone. She hated to lie. She and her uncle made a pack when she was ten years old that they would tell each other the truth no matter how bad things were. Now, feeling like such a failure, she just couldn't bring herself to tell him how unhappy she was with Wes. She took a deep breath, got up from the sofa and turned to go into the kitchen.

She came to an abrupt halt—her breath caught in her throat. Wes was sitting on a chair at the kitchen table with a beer in his hand. "Oh, I didn't know you were home."

"I overheard your conversation with Ross. I also heard you say, *Say hello to Hawk next time you see him and tell him I love him.* So you're still in love with this Hawk guy? You miss giving him a blow job? I just bet he misses you."

"Why do you say things intentionally crude, insulting, and hurtful?"

"Oh, yeah, and I don't know what I just heard you say."

"You don't know what you're talking about. Why don't you just shut-up so I don't have to listen to your disgusting comments?"

Wes slammed his beer down on the table. "Don't tell me to shut-up and stop telling me what to do." He rose up from the chair and walked toward her with his arms flailing in the air. "You sound just like my parents, telling me what to do and when to do it." His face was contorted and built-up anger reddened his eyes. "Yes, sir. Yes, ma'am. "Kiss your ass? Jump how high? Always ready with commands. Just shut up!" he screamed. "I'm the one in control here, not you, and not my parents."

His words; the way he spoke, so cold left her gasping for breath. She didn't know where to turn or what to do. "Don't come near me," Emma warned.

"There you go again, telling me what to do. Will you just shut the fuck up for once?" He grabbed her arm and pulled her close to him. The veins in his forehead bulged, and she could feel the warmth of his foul breath just inches from her face.

Thwack. Emma's head snapped to one side when Wes delivered an open-handed slap to her head.

"Oh!" she moaned when a shaft of pain hurled unexpectedly, and her hand flew to her head. Blinking, she saw stars and the room blurred for several seconds as she wiggled herself away from him.

"Just leave me alone. I'm through with you, Wes. I'm not going to be quiet. I'm tired of giving you so much space you don't even see me anymore, even though I'm right here. You don't want to be with me? I'm not good enough for you? Well, read my lips. I don't want to put up with you any longer. Either you get out right now or I'll call the police. You are not going to slap me around. You got that?" Emma yelled, her eyes jittery with fear.

"Oh, aren't you the tough one." He grabbed her by the shoulders and began fiercely shaking her. "Yeow," he screamed when he felt a sharp rivet of pain shoot through his arm. Emma's teeth were buried in the soft tissue of his forearm. He grabbed her with his other arm and she bit him again. This time, her teeth went deeper.

"You bitch. You fucking biting bitch," he screamed out, his arm painful, dripping with blood. Enraged, he was quick to respond, hitting her again and again until she fell to the floor groaning in agony. Engulfed with fear, she didn't get up.

"Don't you ever tell me what to do again. If you do, you die. Understood?"

Terror shot through her veins. She knew if she got up, the situation would only escalate. She didn't utter a word. She lay still on the floor finding it impossible to figure out who Wes was anymore. He seemed to have some horrible character flaw that surfaced and she appeared to be his only target.

CHAPTER

16

Emma dropped the boys off at the Stanford Museum for a *Wizard of Oz* presentation that Susan had planned for pre-school children. The boys were always excited whenever Susan asked them to join the group. She and her husband, Jimmy, were godparents to both boys and they took them to various outings whenever possible.

She hurried home to prepare dinner for everyone, which left her two hours to bake an apple pie and put a chicken in the oven. When she pressed the remote to open the garage door, she saw Wes' car parked inside. "Hmm," she said softly. *He's never home during the day.*

She stepped inside the house and heard noise in the bedroom. When she went into the room, Wes stared at her for a second, and then pulled a suitcase from the closet and opened it on the bed.

"What are you doing?" Emma asked.

"I'm moving out."

Silence.

"Did you hear what I said," he yelled.

"Yes, I heard you," she said in a whisper. "Don't you want to talk about it?"

"I've got better things to do than listen to you talk, and talk, and talk. I'm sick of it all."

"Just like that—you walk away?" she said.

"Yes, my dear Emma," he said in a slow, gravelly voice, "just like that."

"So your new girlfriend wants you to move in with her?"

"What new girlfriend?"

"The one who wears that cheap disgusting perfume that you reek of all the time."

"You don't know anything."

"Where are you going?" Emma asked.

"Goddamn you, Emma, stop asking me questions? I am sick and tired of listening to you. Where I'm going is none of your business."

More silence as Emma struggled with the words that were reluctant to be said and equally hard to actually say them. She took a deep breath, closed her eyes for several seconds, squared her shoulders, and said, "You have the nerve to stand there and tell me it's none of my business? Well, I'm glad you're leaving. Good riddance to you. Get your stuff and get the hell away from me and the boys! I don't want you around to contaminate my sons."

Like a whip, he surged upward and grabbed her shoulders and shook her.

Her chest heaved in wild horror. The combative light in his eyes hardened beneath furrowed brows and sent chills throughout her body. A face she hardly recognized at all. *How does such a handsome face turn ugly so quickly? There's something fanatical in his eyes. Hell, he looks like he's on drugs.*

"Let go of me," she cried out.

"I'll let go of you when I teach you a lesson."

"What lesson would that be?" she shouted, just before he struck her across the mouth with the back of his hand. She felt her lip split and something wet fall to her chin. When she raised her hand to her mouth blood covered the tips of her fingers.

"You never really understood that I'm the boss. I'm the one who gives the orders. You do not ever tell me what to do. You do not ask me where I'm going. You just won't listen."

He walked toward her and grasped her arms with his thumbs pressed against the very bone and vigorously shook her while he yelled, "I am the boss. Not you!" He dropped one arm and twisted the other arm behind her back. "I want you dead, you bitch. Do you understand me now?"

Fear crawled up from the pit of her stomach. She had to do something. With one quick move, she stomped on his foot, turned, and brought her elbow up to the bridge of his nose. She heard a crack followed by a howl and then saw blood gushing from his nostrils down to his mouth.

With his hands cupped over his face, he stepped back a few feet as he tried to gain his footing. His foot pained him so badly, he almost lost his balance. Maddened by the excruciating pain, he leaped at her. She let out a howl as she flew halfway across the room before she hit the floor, landing on her back. She sat up and quickly scrambled to her knees. She tried to stand, but he lunged toward her again and fell down on top of her, his hands firmly wrapped around her throat. Emma screamed and kicked and hit him repeatedly, but her defensive strength weakened as she gasped for breath. Blood from his nose gushed all over her face as he continued to squeeze her by the throat.

The last thing she remembered were his eyes, filled with immense satisfaction.

Her body lay unconscious on the floor.

CHAPTER

17

Jimmy knocked on the door several times and waited patiently on the front step with Susan and the boys. Not a sound came from the house. He waited a few moments and then knocked again calling out, "Emma! We're back." No answer—not good.

Susan nervously fumbled inside her purse to find her key to the house. She quickly handed it to Jimmy and he opened the door slowly, calling "Emma, are you here?" When the door fully opened, he saw Emma trying to stand up. "Emma!" he yelled as he rushed inside the house.

She did not answer, her gaze barely focused, her face covered in blood.

"What the hell... happened?" Jimmy asked as he kneeled down beside her. "Put your arms around my neck, and I'll lay you down on the sofa."

"Okay. Don't hurt yourself."

"You're a lightweight." He gently lifted her up in his arms and carried her over to the sofa. Susan had already laid a blanket on the cushions. He sat her gently on the couch. "There, does that feel better?" he asked.

"Yes, much better. Thank you, Jimmy," she said with a sigh as she rested her head on the back of the sofa.

"Mommy?" Adam asked, looking up with worry in his tear-stained eyes. He began to cry, reaching his arms up to his mother. "What happened to you, Mommy? You got all hurted."

Emma quickly responded. "Come here, sweetheart." She gave him a hug and said, "Mommy fell, sweetie. Don't cry. I'm okay."

"Lucas, would you please go and get me a wet face cloth and a towel please?"

Lucas stood staring at his mother, his lips pressed together in an effort not to cry. Within seconds he let out a wrenching sob and with arms outstretched, he reached for his mother and fell into her arms burying his face against her.

"It's okay honey. Mommy's going to be fine. Please go and get the facecloth for me."

"Okay, Mommy." Lucas said with tears streaming down his cheeks.

Jimmy sat next to her on the sofa. "Sue, honey, please get my medical bag from the car."

"Okay, come on, Adam, I need someone to help me carry Doctor Jimmy's medical bag."

"I'm real strong," Adam said, turning to hurry out the front door while rubbing the tears from his face with the back of his little hand.

"Where did all this blood come from?"

"It's not mine."

"Oh, I see. You've got some welts on your face and neck."

"I just bet I do, but you should see the other guy. This time, I gave back as good as he gave."

"Here's the wet cloth and towel, Mommy."

"Thank you, Lucas." She wiped her face with the towel and placed the wet facecloth on her forehead and sighed. "Oh, the coolness feels so good and it's relieving the stinging pain."

"Here's your bag, honey," Susan said as Adam helped carry it over to Jimmy.

Both boys stood motionless when Jimmy opened his bag to get the stethoscope.

"Go along with Susan now. Doctor Jimmy is here to take care of your Mommy."

"Are you okay, Mommy?" Lucas asked.

"Yes, boys, I'm all right."

"Come on, boys, let's go and make something for dinner. Doctor Jimmy's going to help your mommy right now. Come on."

"Okay," Lucas said. "Come on Adam, let's help Susan."

Jimmy checked Emma thoroughly. No broken bones, just bruises and a few scratches. He decided it was time he had a serious talk with Emma. She needed to file charges against Wes. "You know, you just can't go on living like this, Emma. Wes will eventually kill you."

"Wes moved out. He went crazy when I told him good riddance and that I didn't want him around contaminating my sons. He has so much hate built up inside him," Emma said, shaking her head.

"Honey, will you make an ice pack for Emma's face, please?" Jimmy shouted.

"Sure thing."

"You know, Em, I think it's about time I have a heart to heart talk with you."

"Oh, here it comes. Another lecture. This is the reason I don't tell anyone about my personal life. They start to tell me what I should do and how I should live my life."

"I've never lectured you. Actually, that's not my style, but I'm going to make an exception in this case because I care about your welfare and Susan and I are godparents to both your sons. As much as we've always wanted children, we don't want to get them because your husband killed you."

With tears streaming down her face, she uttered, "I know, I know. I never wanted this kind of life. I just don't know why this is happening to me. My life is a mess and I don't know what to do about it. Wes erupts every time I say anything. I can't remember when I had contentment or happiness in my life. What do I do now, Jimmy?"

"Emma, you've got to come to terms with your marriage. It's just not working out like you expected. He's going to kill you... he wants you dead. You cannot go on living in fear every day of your life. You and the boys deserve better."

"I know the boys deserve better. I just wanted it to work so badly. I've tried everything and I just don't know what else I can do. He seemed so perfect at the beginning of our marriage. How could I have been so wrong about him?"

"You weren't the only one who thought he was perfect. We all bought into his phony persona," Jimmy pointed out.

"Here's the ice pack," Susan said.

"Thanks honey. Let's put it on this side. You'll have to hold it there, Em."

"Okay." She covered her face and whispered, "He was the love of my life. He lit up my sky."

"I know, Em, but you have to accept that it is what it is, and the sooner you move on, the happier your life will be. Think of your sons... you'll be sparing your boys a lot of grief."

"You're right, Jimmy. I must first think about my sons."

"Wes threatened to kill you and there isn't *anything* you can do when someone else is threatening your life. You have no control over the situation."

Emma was silent for a few moments before she said, "I actually do have control in a way, but I want to do this my way."

"What do you mean you have control? I don't see anyone protecting you."

"I do have access to protection, but I just don't want anyone to know about Wes' problem."

"Wes' problem? Are you kidding? Is that what you call it, a problem? Sweetie, it's far more dangerous than a problem. This so-called problem is *not* going away. You have to take action to stop him from beating you. Let me call my brother, Charlie, and have him prepare and file a domestic violence restraining order against Wes. Will you, at least, let me do that?"

Emma stared at Jimmy for a few seconds. "A restraining order," she said aloud. Those words, those unthinkable bold words shocked the core of her being before she uttered, "Yes, I think that would be a start. Okay, please call him. I'd really appreciate it, Jimmy. Wes will really be angry when he gets that restraining order."

"Okay, you stay put and rest here and keep that ice pack on your face, and I'll give him a call now."

Susan sat on the sofa next to Emma. "You're doing the right thing, Emma." If Wes comes near your home again, you call the police and they will arrest him for violating the restraining order. I think he has to stay at least one hundred twenty-five feet from you. He's not stupid. He'll stay away."

"Wes is going to be so angry," Emma murmured. "He doesn't want to go to jail over this, so perhaps he will stay away from now on. What are the boys doing?"

"They're breaking up lettuce for the salad and eating carrots. I'll go check on them."

More than ever, Emma now realized that her future with Wes was doomed. Her efforts to make the marriage work had failed. She was unable and unwilling to continue to live a life of fear and abuse.

"Okay, I talked with my brother and I need to take pictures of your bruises for the court," Jimmy said. "The person applying for a restraining order must show the danger of some imminent harm. They require proof of abuse. We have proof. Raise your head a little and turn to the left so I can get the bruises and marks in one picture."

Emma followed Jimmy's instructions, and he snapped two pictures with his cell phone camera and forwarded them to his brother.

"My brother said he'll have the papers ready tomorrow morning. You'll have to sign them before he submits them to the court on Monday. He'll take care of everything for you. He'll get the process server to serve Wes at work. That's the best place to serve papers because they are usually there during business hours."

"How long does it take?" Emma inquired.

"The court clerk will hand your forms to a judge who will rule on whether the restraining order should go into effect. The judge will make the determination within a day. Usually, the clerk will give you a specific time to come back on the next business day.

"The court will give you a designated time to appear, and if the judge signs the order you will receive five copies of a temporary restraining order which are valid for three weeks. It goes into effect as soon as the judge signs the order. I'd say it'd take a couple of days."

"What happens after three weeks?"

"They'll have a hearing on the permanent restraining order. It goes into effect when the judge signs that order."

"Thank you, Jimmy. I'm so sorry to put you through all this."

"You're taking care of business now, Emma. Things will get better. Oh, before I forget, my brother said all of Wes's belongings must be removed from the house. You will need to get new locks put on all the doors and a security system installed. Are you okay with doing that?

"Of course, that's no problem."

"My brother has a buddy who does that type of work. I'll call him and see if he can come over late tomorrow afternoon. Does that work for you?"

"Yes, that'll be fine."

"Susan and I will stay with you once Wes gets served just in case he decides to make another visit."

"Thank you both. I don't know what I'd do without you."

CHAPTER

18

Emma Gains Consciousness in Hospital

The transition from sleep to wakefulness felt strange to Emma. The world was coming in and out of focus and she wasn't sure where she was. Her first coherent thought was *I'm alive.* She knew she was alive by the pain that emanated from her whole body. She tried to move, but the pain was unbearable. *Why can't I move?*

She was lying down, on her back, her head slightly elevated. This was not her bed. She tried to identify the rhythmic beep noise and the smell of alcohol. She was not in her bedroom. *Where am I?*

Her whole head felt tight as if bounded. She reached her hand up to her head and felt a cloth that covered her entire head where her hair was. *Why is there something covering my head?* She let her hand fall down to her face only to find a rough cloth over her nose and her left eye. *What happened to me? Why are my head and face all covered up? Why does my head feel like it would fall off if I move it?*

Slowly, painfully, she opened her right eye and stared at the white ceiling and wall. She heard a noise. She slowly turned her head and caught a glimpse of a figure, but she let out a moan when pain radiated from her head and neck.

What's going on? Why does my jaw hurt and why do my lips feel swollen? She tried to talk, but no sound came out.

"Try to sleep," a woman's soft voice said, "You need rest." A cool, soft hand rested on her arm. Emma felt her touch and slowly turned her head toward the voice. She saw a woman with blonde hair, dressed in white standing on the side of her bed. "You're in a hospital, and I'm Jeanne, your nurse."

Why am I in a hospital? What's going on? Emma wondered.

"She's beginning to come to, but she doesn't know where she is yet or what happened to her," the nurse said.

"You've experienced quite a trauma, Mrs. Blair. Do you know why you're here? Do you remember what happened to you?" a man asked.

Who are these people? Where am I?

"She can't speak right now, detective. I'm going to have to ask you to leave, please," the nurse said firmly.

"Do you remember what happened to you, Mrs. Blair?" the man's deep voice asked again. She saw what looked like a tall man, with a lot of hair ask her that question. He walked closer to her, but he was still blurry.

"Don't try to speak," the nurse's voice uttered softly. "You've got multiple facial wounds, numerous body bruises, and a concussion. Lie still, please. Any movement will only cause pain. Right now you need to rest." The nurse wiped her mouth with a warm face cloth.

"I'm Detective Quinn from the Palo Alto Police Department," the deep voice said as he tried to keep his voice soft. "Your neighbor went to your home and found you unconscious on the floor."

My neighbor... *"Oh, my boys. My boys. Where are they?"* she said.

No response. Did they hear me? My lips moved, but maybe there was no sound. *I need to know how my boys are.* Emma's mind raced and she tried to raise her hands up, tried to say something. *I must speak,* she thought. She began to move around. The nurse rushed over to hold her arms still and asked, "Do you want to write something down on paper?"

Emma nodded slightly.

The nurse reached into her pocket and pulled out a small paper pad and a pen. She placed the pad on Emma's chest and put the pen in her right hand. *Where are my 2 sons?* she scribbled out on the paper. The nurse read the note and then handed the slip of paper to the detective.

"Your neighbor has offered to care for your boys until you're released from the hospital. The police are guarding the house just in case your husband comes back. Your husband has fled the scene, and we have an APB out for him. Do you remember what happened to you?"

Emma's head dropped slightly when the wracking pain in her body flooded her memory with a recollection of what happened to her. It was all coming back. *I know who did this to me.*

"Last night we called your next of kin, your uncle, Ross Griffin. He should be here sometime tomorrow," Detective Quinn said.

Oh no, Emma immediately panicked. *He'll go insane when he sees me. He knows nothing about Wes's abusive behavior. Oh, dear God, he will kill Wes. I know he will. All hell is going to break out.*

"I'm sorry, sir, but you'll have to come back tomorrow," the nurse said when she saw Emma's blood pressure and heart rate significantly increase on the monitor.

Emma moved her head forward, away from the pillow and scribbled another note... *I must see him when he gets here.*

"Yes, he'll be coming straight to the hospital," Detective Quinn responded.

Emma relaxed her head back on the pillow. How will she explain this?

He will never forgive me for not saying anything to him. I only wanted to spare him worry. It was my stubborn pride getting in the way again. I just couldn't admit that my marriage failed miserably. He is going to be extremely upset with me, she thought.

When he sees what Wes had done to me, he won't listen, he will only act. I will talk to him... somehow, I will convey to him that he is not to harm Wes in any way. Unfortunately, he's more stubborn than I am. Oh God, help us all!

CHAPTER

19

Uncle Ross arrives - 4:45 am

A powerfully built man dressed in a gray overcoat walked briskly through the glass lobby doors at Stanford Hospital. Once inside, he took long strides toward the bank of elevators and pushed the 'up' button. Immediately the doors to one of the elevators swished open. He quickly stepped inside and turned to punch the third-floor button. The doors slid close. After several moments of silence, the digital readout ticked off each of the floor numbers with a ding. Just before he reached the third floor, the elevator slowed down to a crawl before it stopped, and the doors slid open. He stepped out of the elevator and immediately detected the pungent odor of antiseptics. He headed down the dimly lit corridor observing the descending room numbers that would take him to Room 321.

He could hear repetitive beeps from the monitor equipment within the semicircular nurses' station. Quietly he passed the vacant nurse's station and proceeded to the end of the corridor that was filled with shadows. At the end of the hallway, Room 321. He opened the door slowly and entered the somewhat darkened room, lit by soft integrated lights from above the headwall. A curtain was half drawn around the bed. He pulled it gently to one side.

He gasped. "Oh, my god," he cried out in anguish, his hands covering his mouth, a reflex he had no control over. He tried to muffle the sounds of pain he felt for his Emma. "Oh, Emma," he said in a strangled voice. He grunted, and soon tears filled his eyes as he stared at the flaccid skin and grayish pallor of his niece's body under the crisp white hospital sheets. He made the sign of the cross and uttered a silent prayer for his niece.

Her head, nose, and left eye covered in wide white bandages—oxygen prongs in her nostrils—an IV drip in her left arm. He had seen countless grisly beating victims but never one of a loved family member.

"I can't believe this," he murmured as he wiped his tears with the back of his hand.

He sucked air deep into his lungs and turned to look out the window. He blew it out hard as if trying to force out the disturbing image of Emma lying in bed. "That motherfucking bastard," Ross muttered softly as he bit down on his lip. "Why didn't she tell me this was going on?"

His hands clenched into fists, his face taut and reddened with hateful emotion. *I will kill that sonofabitch husband with my own hands. He will pay for what he is done to my little girl. He will pay, and he will suffer greatly!* He paced the room, fists bunched up as he tried to control himself. He ran his hands through his hair in frustration.

Suddenly the door opened, and a tall, blonde nurse pushed a small cart into the room. She wore rubber-soled shoes and made no sound when she entered. "Oh," she uttered when she noticed the compelling figure standing at the window. "Are you Mrs. Blair's uncle?"

Lost in thought about the punishment he would inflict on Wes, Ross turned toward her when he heard her voice.

"Yes, I'm Ross Griffin," he said as he held out his hand.

She reached to return the handshake. "I'm Jeanne O'Brian, R.N.," she said as she stared up at this man who stood well over six and a half feet.

"Nice to meet you," Ross said. "She looks terrible, but how is she really doing?"

"Her vitals are normal now. Earlier, she came to and she had some recollection of what happened to her, but Dr. Gordon wants her to rest all night. She's confused and rest is what she needs right now. Perhaps she'll be able to talk tomorrow."

"I'd like to stay with her tonight if that's possible," he said.

"I'll have to ask Dr. Gordon, but I don't see any reason why you can't stay with her. You've come a long way. From Washington, D.C., isn't it?"

"Yes, I flew out right after Dr. Gordon called me," he answered.

"You were lucky to catch a flight so quickly."

"I came out on a private jet."

"Oh, I see," she said with amazement. "I'm going to check her IV right now and then I'll page Dr. Gordon. He's on duty, and I know he'll want to speak with you."

She pushed her cart to the foot of the bed, checked the IV drip, and scribbled down her blood pressure, heartbeat, and temperature readouts shown on the monitor next to her bed. "She's doing very well. I'll try to contact Dr. Gordon."

"Thank you very much."

"I'll be back shortly," she said as she opened the door to wheel her cart into the corridor.

Ross pulled one of the side chairs up next to the bed, removed his overcoat, and laid it on the back of the chair. He sat close to her, with his hand on her arm, to comfort her. Thoughts of Wes collided in his mind as his eyes scanned over the outline of her body lying so still.

"Oh, my sweet baby," he murmured. "Just look at what he's done to you…. that motherfucking pervert…" His words trailed off as he sobbed uncontrollably.

He stood up from his chair and went into the bathroom to splash cold water on his face. He wiped his face with a paper towel and took a deep breath before he returned to Emma's side.

Again, he held her hand as he tried desperately to soothe her. He stroked her forearm expecting her eyes to open, but they did not. He felt utterly helpless as he watched the rise and fall of her chest as she breathed evenly while the air hissed from the tube into her nostrils.

If only she told me, he thought as he bit down on his lip. *She knows I would have stopped him. That's what I do. I do damage control. I never liked him. Never! She had to fall for a loser like that? Oh, Emma, look what he's done to you…* his thoughts trailed off as anger consumed him all over again.

"Hello, I'm Dr. Gordon," a man announced as he entered the room.

Ross turned his head to find a tall, rather slim man dressed in hospital greens with a string tied cotton cap covering most of his brown hair.

"Hello, I'm Emma's uncle, Ross Griffin."

Dr. Gordon extended his arm to shake hands with Ross and said, "Yes, we spoke on the telephone. I'm terribly sorry about what happened to your niece."

"Not as sorry as he's going to be," Ross blurted out.

After getting an awkward glance from the doctor's keen blue eyes, the doctor replied, "You really need to have faith in the law, Mr. Griffin. Let the police take care of whoever did this to your niece."

"Oh, by no means have I given up my faith in the law, Dr. Gordon. On the contrary, its justice I'm looking for."

After an unusually long staring match between the two of them, Dr. Gordon spoke.

"Emma's actually doing very well considering what she's been through. None of her injuries appear to be life-threatening, and she should make a full recovery. She had a few moments of consciousness earlier this evening, but she was confused, so we'll keep her asleep and see how she's doing in the morning."

"That's good news. What's with all the head and eye bandages? Is her eye damaged?"

"She had a cut on her head along with several facial wounds, and the reason for the bandaging is to keep her from using that eye due to a cut on her eyelid. We called in a plastic surgeon to stitch it up to minimize scarring. She did suffer a concussion along with multiple body bruises, but fortunately, she had no fractures. Her vitals are good, and I want to keep her sleeping for another six hours."

"Thank you for taking care of her, Dr. Gordon. May I stay in her room tonight? I'd really like to be near her right now," Ross asked.

"By all means," he responded. "By the way, when I spoke to you earlier today, you said you lived in Washington, D.C., right?"

"Yes, why?"

"How did you get here so quickly?"

"I have access to a private jet, and I was cleared to land at Moffett Field."

"Oh," Dr. Gordon said with raised eyebrows and a quizzical look. "That's interesting." He smiled, gave a little smirk and a headshake, waved his arm and turned to leave the room.

After Dr. Gordon had left the room, he stopped at the nursing station. "Jeanne, who is this guy anyway? He comes out in a private jet? Do we know anything about him?"

"Well, it's her uncle is all I know and he sure is one hunk of a man. Wow. He looks like Tom Selleck. I don't really have to know anything else."

"Women!" he cried out. "I'll never understand them."

"What do you mean by that remark? If it was her aunt and she looked like Angelina Jolie, you'd be all goo-goo-eyed too. You're not kidding anyone with that shy look you have plastered on your face. You don't fool me for a second."

"Ha! After that remark, I'm going down to have some breakfast."

CHAPTER

20

Ross rested in the chair beside Emma's bed. He should have slept, but as much as he tried to clear his mind of what Wes did to Emma, sleep never came to him. The thought of Emma going through this terror in her life consumed him. *Why did she put herself through this? I brought her up to be independent and now look at her life. Perhaps I should have been more coddling and kept her in D.C. after she graduated. I should have kept her close to me. That bastard is going to get what he deserves. If he has any luck on his side at all, we will never meet again.*

He wished he could have talked to Emma last evening to judge her state of mind, to see how coherent she was. For a woman to be beaten by her husband had to be a ghastly experience.

He heard a groan. He turned to see Emma move restlessly on the bed. Her eyelashes fluttered when she became aware that someone was there.

"Don't move darlin'."

Slowly she opened her unbandaged eye in an attempt to focus in the direction of the voice. She smiled when she saw him but quickly grimaced in pain. Her jaw hurt when she smiled and her lips were so dry they cracked. She tried to lick her dry lips, but pain radiated from the top of her head to her jaw. She started to panic. *What's wrong with me? Why am I in so much pain? Why can't I move?* Her breathing became more labored and she started to move her arms.

"Don't try to move or talk, darlin'. I just buzzed for the nurse. Please try to relax."

"Do you know where you are?" Ross asked as he clutched her hand.

Emma's blank expression told him, *no.*

"You're at Stanford Hospital. You came here yesterday—late last night."

Emma's mind searched for yesterday. She was unable to recall any yesterdays.

Suddenly the door opened and Jeanne, the nurse, came in cheery and bright, saying, "Good morning, Mr. Griffin. Oh, it looks like our patient is awake. How are you, Emma?"

Emma just stared and gave her head a slight nod but wondered who she was.

"Dr. Gordon will be starting his rounds in the next few hours. He'll probably remove some of those head bandages so you don't look like a mummy."

When the nurse said, "Mummy," Emma started flailing her arms. *Her sons. Where are they?*

"Oh," Jeanne said, "she wants to write something down." She grabbed the pen and notepad from her pocket and placed the pen in Emma's hand and laid the paper in front of her. "She did this yesterday. She wrote us messages."

"She was able to write yesterday?" Ross asked.

"Yes, she wanted to know how her boys were."

Emma wrote: *Have you seen boys?*

Ross grabbed the notepad and smiled which left a pattern of smile lines that crinkled around his eyes. "No, not yet, darlin', but I will see them today." He placed the notepad in front of her again.

Don't tell them. Say I was in car accident. PLEASE.

Again, Ross read the note, but didn't say anything. He put the notepad back in front of her. She wrote: *PLEASE say U will.*

He looked at her lying on the bed, slightly shook his head back and forth, took a deep breath, and said, "Okay, Em, I will tell them you were in a car accident."

Relieved, her head fell back on the pillow with a moan and a sigh.

Ross' fingers curled over the rail, his knuckles turned white as he gripped the rail.

Moments later, Ross reached for Emma's hand and cradled it. He groped for the right words, but soon gave up. There was nothing he could say that would give her comfort. She squeezed his hand for a second, but quickly relaxed her hand. Her spirit was willing, but her body was weak. She drifted back to sleep.

"I'm glad to see that she was alert this morning. That's a good sign," the nurse said. "She'll get some rest now. We'll probably get her up to walk around later this afternoon."

"How long do you think she'll be in the hospital?" Ross inquired.

"Probably for another couple of days. Ask Dr. Gordon when he makes his rounds."

"Yes, of course. I will do just that."

She turned and left the room.

Ross walked over to the window, stood, and stared outside into nothingness. His thoughts on how he would take care of business. *Whatever it takes, I will find that bastard. He can count on that.*

CHAPTER

21

Emma gradually felt the strength slowly return to her body, but she was weeks away from being at her normal fitness level. Though she moved stiffly and rather slowly, she no longer felt debilitated now that she was able to walk around by herself.

"Are you ready to go home?" Ross asked when he entered the room pushing a wheelchair.

"I am, Uncle Ross. I am."

Nurse Jeanne held Emma's arm and assisted her into the wheelchair. She placed a plastic bag on Emma's lap and said, "These are your medications and your personal items."

"Thank you, Jeanne. Thank you for all you've done for me."

"That's what we're all here for," she said as she wrapped her arms around Emma. "You've been an excellent patient."

"Okay, let's roll," Jeanne said as she grabbed the wheelchair and wheeled Emma out to the corridor. Ross walked ahead of the wheelchair and stopped at the row of elevators. *Ding.* The doors opened and Ross stepped inside to hold the door open. Jeanne pushed the wheelchair inside and down they went when he hit the lobby button.

"I'm parked right outside the entrance," Ross said.

"Okay, here we are," the nurse said as she pushed the wheelchair toward the automatic doors. The doors slid open and the nurse rolled Emma outside.

Immediately Emma breathed in the cold air. "Oh, it feels so good to be outside."

Ross ran ahead of them to open the door to his car.

"Okay, are you ready, Em?"

"I am," Emma responded and handed Ross the plastic bag on her lap. "Here, put my meds in the back."

Ross put the bag on his seat before he lifted Emma up from the chair and into the car with one swift swoop. "Are you comfortable, Em?" he asked as he buckled her seat belt.

"Yes. I'm all right."

He closed the door, turned to Nurse Jeanne, and gave her a hug as he whispered in her ear. "I can't begin to express my appreciation for the excellent care you gave my Emma. Thank you so very much," he said as he slipped an envelope into her pocket.

"It was my pleasure, Mr. Griffin."

On the way home, Emma repeatedly leaned over to touch Ross' arm. She felt secure when he was beside her. "Thanks for being here for me, Uncle Ross."

As he eased his car into the driveway, he said, "That's what family is all about. Helping each other whenever needed."

He pulled up close to the front door. "Here we are."

Emma sighed. "It feels so good to be home."

Ross jumped out and quickly went around the car to open the door for Emma. Awkwardly, he put his arm around Emma, and lifted her out. He steadied her when her feet stepped on the pavement. "Are you good?"

"Yes. I'm fine."

Before they reached the front door, it suddenly swung open. "Oh, Emma, you're doing so well," Susan called out. Right behind her, Lucas and Adam were hopping up and down and screaming, "Mommy's home, Mommy's home." Emma smiled and bent over to give them each a hug. So you boys missed me a little, eh?"

"Oh yes, Mommy, we both missed you bad. Are you okay? You don't look okay," Lucas said. "Why is your face all hurt? Did the car accident do that to you?"

"Yes, honey, it did, but Mommy's fine now."

"I got hurted too. See my knee," Adam said, pointing his chubby little forefinger at the Band-Aid on his knee.

"Oh, how did you do that Adam?" Emma said.

"I fell trying to catch a butterfly. It doesn't hurt now."

"I heard that you've been taking care of Uncle Ross? Is that true?"

"Oh, yes, we play with Uncle Ross and he wrestles with us. He's strong," Lucas said.

"He picks both of us up by hisself," Adam squealed.

"He says we're gonna be big and strong Marines."

"Oh, Marines is it? He can tell you so many stories about the Marines."

"Okay, boys, let your mother inside so she can sit down in her chair," Uncle Ross said.

"Move, Adam, so Mommy can go inside," Lucas instructed.

"Okay, Mommy, go inside," Adam ordered.

"Something smells delicious in here," Emma said as she stepped inside the house.

"The boys wanted to have something special *for when Mommy comes home*," Susan said, "so I fixed your favorite dinner, roasted chicken, mashed potatoes, squash, and peas. I know it won't be as good as yours, but I gave it my best shot. And… we have apple pie and vanilla bean ice cream for dessert."

"Sounds wonderful, Susan. That's sweet of you to go through all this trouble," Emma said as she made herself comfortable in her reclining chair.

"No trouble. The only trouble we've had is you not being here."

"Is Jimmy able to get out of the office and come for lunch?"

"Yes, he said he'd be able to get away about twelve-thirty."

"It's so good to be home. I missed all of you." With that, the boys ran to give their mother more hugs and kisses.

"Oh, Mommy we missed you so much," Lucas said.

"Don't leave us again, Mommy," Adam added.

"I won't leave you again, boys."

"Who wants to play ball before we eat?" Ross asked.

"I do, I do," Lucas and Adam squealed.

"Go up and change your clothes and get your baseball gear," Uncle Ross said.

They both raced upstairs squealing, excited with happiness.

"Have they tired you out yet, Uncle Ross?"

"They're great guys. Yeah, they have a lot of energy. You have done a fantastic job with them, Emma. I know it's been tough for you this past year, but you're tough, eh?"

"Today, I don't know about tough, but I am very proud of the boys. Have they asked about their father at all?"

"Yes, they asked once, and I told them he was away on a business trip. They never asked again. You mentioned that he didn't have much to do with them lately, so it seems they've lost interest in him."

"It looks that way, doesn't it?"

"Yes, it does. Not to change the subject, but what are you going to do now? I did not want to bring this up while you were in the hospital, but we need to talk about having you move back to D.C. where I can keep you safe from that bastard. The next thing he'll try to do is kidnap the boys and then we'll have bigger problems trying to find them."

"I was half-way expecting a sermon from you," she said, looking up at her uncle.

Ross just grinned—a concerned grin.

"You wouldn't be wrong by giving me one. I surely deserve it," Emma said softly.

A silence fell between them for several seconds.

"To think he was my entire world. I can't believe it's over. It was my fate to marry Wes."

"He didn't deserve you and fate had nothing to do with it," Ross quickly interjected. "Fate is only a reflection of our weaknesses and faults."

Emma shrugged her shoulders. "I apologize for not telling you about Wes' abusive behavior, but I know how you've always felt about him and I thought I could handle it myself. I was totally unprepared for his actions. Love does not conquer all."

"No, it does not."

"This last attack brought an end to all the excuses I made for him—he was depressed because he lost his job; he had anger problems because his father abused him; his parents haven't spoken to him in over ten years. All those hardships he suffered. One would think that having a loving wife and two beautiful sons would alleviate past hardships, but it seemed to make everything worse. It was as if he didn't deserve to be happy.

"I couldn't divulge Wes' abusive behavior to anyone. I was so ashamed to think I couldn't save our marriage. I thought I was the one to blame. Of course, Wes told me I was to blame. Since I never failed at anything before, I had no idea what it felt like to fail. The concealment seemed to make the reality tolerable. I thought that if I really tried, I could reach Wes. Every relationship has its challenges but he wouldn't talk to me, and when he did say something, it was derogatory, mean, and hurtful. His constant put-downs chipped away at my heart and spirit. *I allowed him to do that to me.* I think I'm the one who needs psychiatric help.

Ross sat down next to Emma and put his arms around her. "Darlin', all of us make decisions that don't turn out like we expect them to. You've been very fortunate to make many of your decisions based on impulse rather than logical reasoning, but marriage is one of the major decisions one makes in life and it can't be made on impulse or gut-feeling. You didn't know Wes long enough to see his faults and really know about his behavior. That was sheer immaturity on your part."

Emma sat still, tears filling her eyes.

"I understand how frustrated you got when you were unable to talk rationally to Wes. You were torn between failing as a wife and the desire to stay and try to help him. You had no idea Wes was mentally unstable.

"You've always been stubborn, Emma, and you thought you were doing the right thing by staying. We all make mistakes and that's how we learn—from our mistakes."

"I certainly made a doozie of a mistake."

"Yes, and that stubbornness in you has caused you all this pain and grief. Now, let's only look at the bright side of things. It's over and you and the boys are safe. And to keep you all safe, have you thought about what your next move is?"

"Yes, I've given it a lot of thought while I was in the hospital and yes, I've decided to take the boys and leave California before Wes does kill me. I have to get the boys away from Wes. I really miss you," she said warmly.

"It's been wonderful having you here, and we all need to be close to one another."

"There's nothing that would make me happier than to have you and the boys close to me." When do you want to move back? The sooner, the better."

"I want to finish out the semester with my students. Exams are in another six weeks. We'll leave right after exams so that'll put us leaving on March 29."

"But that's over a month away."

"I know, Uncle Ross, I know. However, I also know how Wes thinks. He thinks I'm afraid to leave because I didn't file any charges against him. He figured that I'm so scared I'll just sit back, cancel the restraining order, and everything will go back to the way it was. Wes isn't going to want to go to prison for me."

Ross pondered that statement for a moment before responding. "In that case, let me at least, get someone to watch you and the boys for those weeks. I can have someone here tomorrow."

"I've seen some of those big brutes you have working for you. They would be much too conspicuous in this area. I don't need anyone watching over us."

"Emma, for God's sake, stop being so stubborn for once in your life and listen to me. Wes wants to kill you. Do you understand the mind of a killer? He *will* kill you. Believe me, when I say this…" he paused. "I have an idea. Why don't I get a woman to watch over you? Would that work out for you?"

Exasperated, she threw up her hands. "Okay, get a woman to look after us," Emma said as she glared stubbornly at him.

"Finally, I'm able to penetrate that head of yours. You need help, Emma. I can at least help you to stay safe. I have just the gal for you. You'll love her. She's one of my best. Her name is Stella, and the boys will be crazy about her."

"Stella. Is she Italian?"

"As a matter of fact, she is. Stella Stesito. She is a former FBI agent, and she's as tough as any man. I trained her."

"Why did she leave the FBI?"

"She got tired of the bureaucracy and when I took this job, she was my first recruit."

"What will we tell the boys?" Emma asked.

Ross thought for a second and then said, "She's about your age. We'll tell them that she's a friend of yours from college. How's that?"

"Okay? That should work."

"At last. Now I can get some much-needed sleep, and perhaps I'll stop getting more gray hairs from worrying about you and the boys."

"Since we're going to be leaving California, I think it would be wise to change our identities. I don't want Wes to find us. Are you able to get that done for us?"

"I can do that. What names do you want to use? Won't the boys get confused with new names?"

"They'll go along with it. They like role-playing. They've learned that in school. Actually, they've become pretty convincing young actors."

"Why don't you keep your first names and just change the last name to Ross?"

"Emma Ross, Lucas and Adam Ross, The Ross Family... that sounds pretty good. Okay, let's keep it simple. Ross it is."

"We'll need birth certificates, and I'll need a new driver's license for Washington, D.C. You can do all that?" How about baptismal papers, too?"

"No problem. Give me copies of all the documents you have, and I'll take care of the rest. Once I get back to D.C., I'll find a safe place for you to live. There's some new construction going on near the Capitol. I'll check into it."

"When are you planning to go back to D.C?" Emma asked.

"I think I'll leave tomorrow. There's a flight out from Moffett early tomorrow morning. I'll have Stella get out before I leave."

"Wow, you sure do move fast."

"Have to. That's how things get done," he said as he grabbed his cell phone and punched in Stella's speed dial number. He talked for a few moments and hung up. "It's all taken care of. She'll be here this evening."

Boom, bang, clunk, down the stairs, rolled a baseball bat. "We're ready to play ball," Lucas squealed.

Ross ran over to pick up the bat. "Why is Adam trying to carry all the baseball gear? Lucas, help Adam out. He shouldn't be carrying everything."

"He wanted to carry it all himself."

"Can't you see he can't do it himself? You're his big brother and you need to help him."

"He didn't want me to help him."

"Here, Adam, give Lucas the glove," Ross said. "All right, let's go."

CHAPTER

22

Ding-dong… Ding-dong, suddenly rang throughout the home. "Ah, she's right on time, as usual," Ross announced as he ran to open the front door.

Stella stood on the stoop, suitcase in hand. "I was kinda hoping you were already in bed," she said jokingly. "Hello, Ross," she said in a raspy voice. "I wanted to wake you up in the middle of the night."

"Like you never have done that before," Ross said with a huge grin. "Come in, Stella. Come in. Let me take your suitcase."

"It's been a while since I had a gig in California. Thanks for thinking of me."

"It's great to see you, Stella, and I really appreciate you coming out here on such short notice. Come and meet my niece, Emma. Emma, this is Stella. You two gals talk. I'm going to put your suitcase in the den, Stella," Ross said.

Stella approvingly nodded her head.

Without saying anything for several moments, they studied each other. Emma carefully examined Stella—an attractive woman with an athletic body. Her face unlined with smoothness to her skin that gave no hint of her age. Her posture was straight; her chin tilted upward which showed independence in mind. It would be a mistake to underestimate this woman. She wore black jeans, her reddish-brown shoulder length hair was just long enough to be sexy, but her large, deep-set brown eyes immediately reflected that she was also intelligent.

At the same time, Stella measured Emma: *She's Ross' niece all right—long legs and dark hair. She has beautiful eyes, but they're filled with fear. Her scars tell the whole story. I can help this woman.*

"Looks like we're going to become college buddies during the next month," Emma said as she reached out to shake hands with Stella.

"Yes, your uncle has filled me in on what happened to you. I'm glad to see that you're doing well physically. It will take time for your face to heal. I had some facial injuries a few years ago and it took about six weeks to heal completely."

"Yes, the doctor told me it would take that long."

"You have two young boys, I hear."

"Yes, Lucas is four and a half, and Adam is three and a half. They're sleeping right now. You'll meet them in the morning."

"I'm looking forward to it. I love kids."

"Do you have any children?" Emma asked.

"No, I never married. I've been carrying around a torch for your uncle for too many years. It's terrible to meet a wonderful man when you're young because he then becomes the standard that no other man can measure up to. Believe me, I've tried, but I've never found anyone who comes close to him," Stella said with a hearty laugh while glancing at Ross, who was now laughing loudly.

"Oh, that sounds like a great story that Uncle Ross hasn't yet shared with me."

"Yes. And it's a story your Uncle Ross is never going to ever share with you," Ross announced firmly when he entered the room.

"Secrets of the past, is it?" Emma inquired.

"Call it what you want, but you'll never get anything outta me," Ross said stubbornly.

Both he and Stella had their own joke going and they both laughed hysterically.

"Now you two are making it a story I definitely want to hear about. One of you will break."

"I don't think so, do you, Stella?" Ross declared.

"She'll never get anything outta of me," Stella confirmed.

"Come, sit down Stella. Tell me all about yourself," Emma asked.

"Can I get you something to eat or drink, perhaps? Are you hungry?"

"No, I had dinner before I left, thank you. I would like a cup of tea if it's not too much trouble."

"No trouble at all. Come with me into the kitchen. We'll talk," Emma said.

"This is a beautiful place you have here. I love California. It's been about seven years since I've been to California."

"Did you live here before?"

"No, I've never lived here for more than a couple of months. The weather can sure spoil a person, except for those earthquakes you have here. I don't like those at all."

"We've not had an earthquake of any significance since the Oakland quake in 1989. I wasn't living here then. We haven't had any kind of movement since I've been here."

"When did you move here?"

"I came to California in 1995."

"So, what is it you do here?" Stella inquired.

"I'm a professor at Stanford University. I teach biochemistry."

"That sounds fascinating. Where did you go to college? Or perhaps, I should say, where did *we* go to college since we are supposed to be old college buddies?"

Emma laughed. "We went to George Washington University and graduated in 1995."

"Oh, that's good to hear. I did attend GW for a couple of years after high school."

"What were you majoring in?"

"Boys." They both laughed loudly, immediately getting Ross' attention.

"Okay, what are you two giggling about?"

"Just talking about our college days at GW," Stella said.

"Well, it looks like the two of you are going to get along just fine."

"We're buddies, remember?" Emma said. "I like Stella. Wish I did meet her at GW. We would have had those guys eating out of our hands. We would have been known as the Boobie Twins." They hugged each other and posed. "See, we even look alike!" They laughed and giggled until Ross had to leave the kitchen mumbling, "What am I creating?"

Thirty minutes later, Ross found Stella and Emma in deep conversation. "Well, what do you think of each other?"

Both girls smiled and Emma said, "We'll get along just fine, Uncle Ross. We're best friends already. Stella is perfect. Thank you for thinking of her."

"Yes, we've been talking," Stella said, "and I think the best idea is for me to keep surveillance on the boys. After everything Emma has told me about Wes, he may just try to kidnap the boys and that's the one thing we *don't* want to happen. The outcome of that could be disastrous. I'll take them back and forth from school and to any activities they have. Emma is safe at the university because there are too many people around for him to bother her there. He doesn't know his way around the campus, so he's unlikely to go there. We've made a tentative schedule and we'll tweak it this weekend. Shouldn't have any problems. I've got my cellphone and gun in my purse and I'll be sure to keep it safely out of sight from the boys."

Emma shrugged while she gestured with her hands and said, "See, everything worked out just fine."

"When are you leaving, Ross?" Stella inquired.

"I'll be taking off at four in the morning. I have an important meeting at two o'clock tomorrow afternoon that I cannot miss. Before I forget, Emma, if you want me to take some luggage or boxes back with me, I'd be happy to do that for you. I can take anything back on the jet."

"You know, I do have a few items. I have them in a box in my closet. I'll tape the box up and leave it next to your suitcase. Thanks for doing that."

"No problem, sweetie. I'll store it at my home until you get there. I'll leave you two alone to talk the night away. I'm going to watch TV for a while before I get some shut eye."

"Would you like me to help you with that box?" Stella asked.

"Yes, let's go into my bedroom and I'll pull it down from the closet shelf. I think I'll repack it and put it all in a suitcase so it's easier for Uncle Ross to transport."

"This must be very hard for you to do, Emma. The emotional impact will be with you for years, I'm afraid."

"I realize that. Divorce is like a death—the burial of the love of my life. The burial of all our photographs together as a family with four people in them. The burial of all the dreams of growing old together that will never be."

"You're young, beautiful and smart," Stella said as she wrapped her arm around Emma. "You'll find the perfect partner one day."

"I don't believe in anyone being the perfect person. That's exactly who I thought Wes Blair was. A man filled with impulsiveness and excitement that I had never known before. He made me feel like a woman. I thought together we were the greatest thing since Gable and Lombard, but there are no princes and no castles, only reality. There are times I think I don't ever want to go through this again. I wouldn't be able to endure the pain and heartache all over again."

"They say that time heals all wounds," Stella said.

"I don't actually believe that. Time only allows scar tissue to form so the wound eventually goes unnoticed. However, the inner scars will always be there. I made an appointment with the psychiatrist at the university. I hope he will be able to help me with how I feel now and perhaps he can give me some insight as to how I'll feel after I leave."

"That's a move in the right direction, Emma. You're talking about it. That's healthy."

Emma opened the closet door and looked up at the shelf. Stella jumped in front of her and said, "I'll get that down. Is it this box?" she asked when she touched one of the boxes on the shelf.

"Yes, that's the one."

Stella grabbed the box and placed it on the bed. "Where's the suitcase you want to repack?"

"It's under the bed, right where you're standing."

Stella kneeled down on the floor and pulled out the suitcase. "Is this the one?"

"Yes. I'm not taking anything from this house back to D.C. I'll just be taking some personal belongings like pictures of the boys when they were younger, some jewelry, and toiletries. I'm never coming back here."

Emma reached into the box and picked out a music box that was once her mothers. "This belonged to my mother. It's one of the few treasures I have from her. My dad gave it to her when they got married."

"Oh, that is so beautiful. Look at all the pearls covering that egg-shaped music box. What does it play?"

"It plays *'Somewhere Over The Rainbow.'* She played it for me while she sang along with it. I play it for the boys. I need to find a box to put it in so it doesn't break. Let me look in my dresser drawer. I think there's a box in there."

"It'll be safer traveling with Ross. Luggage doesn't get thrown around on a private jet," Stella pointed out.

"You're right. Here's a box that's the right size." She opened the lid, and said, "What is this?"

"The box isn't yours?" Stella asked.

"No. I don't know what this is," she said as she dumped the contents onto the bed. Passports and credit cards spilled out. "What the…?"

Emma flipped through one of the passports. It had a photo of Wes' face, but with a different name—Charles Whitman. "That's Wes!" she shouted. "What is he doing with a fake passport?"

Stella flipped through the other passport. "Do you know a Sara Benoit?" she asked as she showed Emma the photo.

Emma stared at the photo, and her head started to spin. "No, I don't know who that is. What is going on?"

Stella grabbed up the credit cards. "The cards are in both those names. We've got to show these to Ross."

"Wait; there is a manila envelope on the bottom of the box." Emma unfastened the clasp and slid out the contents—her jaw fell slack. "More passports and credit cards?"

Stella quickly flipped through them. "Same photos with different names. Kate Bell, Wes Black. Same names on the cards too. We'll have to show these to Ross."

CHAPTER

23

As soon as all her students departed her classroom, Emma grabbed a small carton of milk from her office refrigerator to calm her nervous stomach. It was not going to be easy to talk to a psychiatrist about her failed marriage. Failure had never been a word in her vocabulary.

Professional psychiatric therapy would make it official—it would confirm the existence of a problem. She knew that if she talked about her mixed feelings, she would be more able to cope with them in the future. She needed to feel confident that there would be better times ahead... something more than a life trapped in memories of the past.

His office was on the other side of the campus and it would take her, at least, five minutes to get there. She had five minutes to think about what to say as she made a mad dash across the campus gulping down her milk.

She had never spoken professionally to a psychiatrist before. She was the *problem solver* who now felt the need to seek help. *I never had trouble talking with David before*, she thought. But then again, she never talked about her personal life.

Nervous but determined, she climbed the stairs of the building, still feeling jittery and even a bit scared, but she knocked on his door anyway.

"Hello, Emma, come in, please. You're right on time," he said after opening the door.

"I really appreciate you taking the time to talk with me on such short notice, David."

"Not a problem, Emma. Can I get you something to drink?"

"No thank you. I just gulped down a carton of milk on my way over here."

"Come, sit down and tell me what's bothering you, and how I can help you."

Without pride, she said, "As much as I hate to say this, I should have come by sooner to talk with you."

Behind the black-framed glasses, his sharp blue eyes saw the hurt and embarrassment on Emma's flushed face. "I'm sorry to hear you've been distressed, Emma. Why didn't you come to see me sooner?"

She took a deep breath, tipped up her chin and said, "Pride! Freaking pride. How's that for someone in desperate need of psychiatric help?"

"That's a splendid start. Honesty!" he said with a half-smile.

"I wish all this was a nightmare instead of the truth, David. I'm going to get right to the point. I'm married to an abusive husband who wants to kill me. Is that truthful enough?"

He hesitated for a moment, before he said, "I had no idea, Emma. You're such a brilliant, innovative scientist and so well respected here at Stanford. Exactly what's been happening?"

"My worst nightmare is what is happening."

"How long has this been going on?"

"Too long. The man of my dreams wants to kill me and for no apparent reason other than I want to leave him and take my two boys with me. He's not been a father to them for months now and he no longer shows any concern for them or me. I've repeatedly tried to talk to him to save our marriage. I told him we could go for counseling. He refused. He won't listen to a word I say to him. The boys and I are not safe here anymore."

"So are we talking about physical abuse or mental abuse, or both?"

"Both. It began with mental abuse, which actually started about a year ago. The physical abuse came months ago after he lost his job because he argued with the vice president of finance where he worked.

"After he got fired, he started going out and began drinking heavily and would stay out all night. He was able to get another job and I thought he would feel better about himself, but our marriage seemed to escalate into total deterioration."

Emma hesitated for several moments. "He almost killed me a month ago. He"—her voice broke—"he beat me so badly that he put me in the hospital for five days. He knocked me unconscious."

The doctor winced. "Oh, my heavens. I wasn't aware. Usually, I'm alerted by the Dean when this type of violence happens. Did you press charges? Was he arrested?"

"No. That's probably why you weren't notified. I didn't file charges at that time. I thought it best not to provoke him any further. I guess I wasn't in the right state of mind. I thought he'd repent and make amends, but that never happened. I told the university that I was in a car accident, so that's probably the reason you weren't notified."

"Why did you make excuses for what your husband did to you?"

"I made excuses because I wanted to keep the dream. To me, marriage is like an Orb, a magical circle that outsiders must never enter. Once someone enters, the circle never closes again and chaos is all that remains. I kept my painful secret hidden from the world so no one would know my shame. If anyone found out, it would take away my dignity and most definitely vaporize my soul."

Emma sadly lowered her head and softly said, "All I ever wanted when I married was to be a good wife and mother for my family. I just wanted to be happy." Big tears begin to flow down her cheeks.

He handed her a tissue box, which she placed on the desk in front of her after she pulled a tissue out to wipe her tears.

"There are times I feel an uncanny frenzy of emotions; one minute I'm bewildered and the next minute I'm intensely terrified. I go from exhaustion to explosive in a second. There are moments when I thought I was losing my mind."

"So you've been going through this all alone and you've not talked to anyone?"

"Actually, I have talked to several social workers for abused women. I'm so stubborn. It took sheer determination to keep my feelings hidden all this time. It has taken me too long to admit that my marriage is over."

Dr. Jamison leaned over his desk, his hand on her arm. "Why did you stay with this man for so long?"

Because I kept hoping I would wake up beside the man I'd fallen in love with. Then, a miraculous thing happened. Suddenly I was able to understand that I was not only wasting my life, but I was doing more harm to my boys by pretending we were a family."

"You've been through a horrible ordeal, Emma, but now you know what it is you have to do. We are all individuals that work through our problems differently. What may work for one person, may not work for another. Each individual has their own way of doing things."

"Yes, but it's taken me so long to work this out in my head."

"But you did it. You decided to take control. You figured out that Wes is the only obstacle in your path to finding happiness. Now you are moving on. That takes a strong woman, Emma."

"Strong is not the word I would use. Stubborn is what I am."

"There's nothing wrong with being stubborn when you know where you're headed."

"It's been one hell of a ride, let me tell you. They'll be no more crying over him or putting up with his abuse. All I want is to live a happy life with my boys. I am unhooking myself from this marriage. I don't ever want to see him again. I want him out of my life."

"That's good, Emma. You're facing it head on, and you're putting out energy to remove the obstacle radically."

"I know I should have come to see you sooner, David, but I just have a hard time accepting the failure. I have failed as a wife."

"Now, Emma, you mustn't blame yourself for Wes' actions toward you and the boys. There were choices to make and he made those decisions all on his own. Abusive men have deep-rooted issues, and he's chosen to take them out on those closest to him—his family. There's nothing you can do about that. You've tried seeking help and he refuses to acknowledge that he's doing anything wrong; he's in denial."

"There was a part of me that kept holding on, hoping something would change. I have since put those thoughts out of my mind. I can't live my life, hoping that another person will change. What a fool I was," she murmured.

"You wanted a home with two parents in it. You were just trying to save the marriage, but in cases like this, unless both parties are willing to seek help together, it does not usually work out because abusers don't really think they're doing anything wrong. You have to look deeper. Wes is filled with fear. He doesn't think much of himself, that's why he has always had to be the dominant one. You were too anxious to please... to keep the family together."

"But, I'm running away from my problem. I've never done that before."

"You're not running from your failed marriage, you're running from an abusive husband who wants to kill you. You have two boys to think about. You, Emma, are facing it head on, and that's good. You've endured a lot of stress and a lot of physical pain and you need to remove it quickly from your life. Long term stress has a way of changing the chemistry of the brain which can make the person depressed or outraged."

"Oh, I've been both angry and depressed, but I'm also a fighter. I'm moving on."

"Where will you go?" David asked.

"I'm moving back to Washington, D.C. where my Uncle Ross lives."

"Is your Uncle Ross your father's brother?"

"Yes. He was my dad's only brother and my only living relative."

"Is he aware of how Wes has been treating you?"

"Yes, he's aware of what Wes is like, and he's furious with me for not letting him take care of Wes... if you know what I mean," Emma said, giving him a sideways glance with her eyes."

"You mean he wants to kill him?"

"Yes, he wants to kill him! My uncle is in the killing business. He recruits mercenaries over in Iraq and Afghanistan and all over Europe and the Middle East. He's vice president of Global Security and does business all over the world. He could easily take him out. All I would have to do is say the word."

"I had no idea. I better stay on the good side of you," he chuckled softly.

"Well, his profession isn't anything I tell my friends about. He raised me since I was ten years old, he's like my father, and we're very close. I miss him not being here, but we talk several times a week. I never had many friends, and I don't require a lot of people in my life. My Uncle Ross is my best friend, and we always confided in one another. This is the first time I did not confide in him because he would have had Wes killed. I know it."

"Your uncle would be a little difficult to explain to your friends. What do you tell your friends when they ask what he does for a living?"

"My uncle is a former Marine and war hero and has worked for NCIS for many years. He's highly respected so I tell them he's in the security business, which he is. They just don't know the extent of the business. Most people don't even know Global Security exists in the world."

"That is a fact. So why have you not acted on your situation sooner than this?"

"As I told you earlier, stubborn pride stopped me. And also the fact that I had many moments of sentimentality which were followed by moments I wished Wes was dead. Not that he'd ever been born, but that he'd get hit by a car or get himself killed in some violent way."

"Your emotions seem to be going in a zigzag direction, from totally terrorized to sentimental moods. This is not something that is bad. You will reach a point in time where there will be more *everything is okay* patches and fewer frightening ones. However, the mind cannot handle emotions like terror for a sustained period of time and you've been frightened for quite a while now. Considering everything you've told me, the fact that you're leaving the situation and ending the relationship is the healthiest resolution and moving back to Washington, D.C., where you evidently have someone to protect you, is a smart move. Soon your comfort zone will return, and you'll once again be able to lead a normal life. When you leave the area where the terror is, your fear will gradually fade, and your life will resume to a normal rhythm. Soon, all this will be just a memory.

"I don't want to remember him. I don't want to ever see him again. This man is deadly."

"So you honestly believe your husband will kill you and that he's not just saying that to prevent you from leaving?"

"Oh, this isn't paranoia. I have the scars to prove it. He will come after me. Fortunately, he does not know where my uncle lives. He thinks he lives in Chicago, but he moved to D.C. over a year ago. I never told Wes."

"So he'll find you in D.C. Then what?"

"Uncle Ross has found a secure building for us to move into. If he says it's secure, believe me, it's secure."

"How will you live and support yourself and your boys?"

"Fortunately, money isn't one of my problems. I have a vast financial portfolio that is entrusted to my Uncle Ross that Wes knows nothing about. My parents were killed when I was ten years old and my father had a lucrative electronics business in Torrance, California. Being an only child, I inherited all of their estate and business holdings. My Uncle Ross takes care of my money for me. I've never touched any of it except for my college education."

"How were your parents killed?"

"They were on that American Airlines DC-10 that crashed in Chicago on May 25, 1979. They were heading back to Los Angeles. Do you remember that accident?"

"Yes, I do remember. That was a terrible accident. A dear friend of my family's, Larry Silva, was killed in that crash."

"It changed my life, just as my failed marriage is about to change my life once more."

"Why did you keep the fact that you had an inheritance a secret from your husband?"

"Perhaps I instinctively kept back my only valuable secret. As much as I loved Wes at the time, he enjoyed gambling and playing the horses and was very loose with money. There was really no reason to tell him because we both held good positions at work with excellent salaries, and we didn't really need the money."

"In retrospect, that was a smart thing for you to do."

"Uncle Ross suggested it to me, and I simply went along with it."

"So being an only child, you went to live with your Uncle Ross after your parents were killed?"

"Yes, he took care of me. We have a great relationship and he was so much like my father, he became my dad very easily."

"So it was a good time for you?"

"Oh, yes. I've been pretty happy most of my life until a year ago. For some time now, I've been in a terrible state of uncertainty. I felt unwanted and alone. I've never felt so miserable living a life without much to look forward to. Now that I am finally out of denial, I realize that I am the only person that can change my life. My biggest fear right now is telling Wes that we're leaving. It's not the telling him that I'm afraid of, it's the backlash of telling him."

"Don't tell him. Just make your plans and leave. Your husband has some deep rooted issues and I'm afraid, from what you've said, that he will try to harm you or kill you, so clearly it would be in your best interest to be silent about any of your plans."

Emma nodded, but she *was* going to have a final meeting with Wes in public where he would never show his true self to protect his precious image. "We're planning to fly out of San Francisco the day after exams. My Uncle Ross will have our tickets at the airport. He's also able to get us new identities. I should receive them here at the university in a day or two."

"I can imagine he could do that easily with his connections. That's a smart move. So are you ready to walk in someone else's shoes?" he asked.

"What do you mean?"

"If you're going to take on a new name and become someone else you will need to know how to walk in someone else's shoes, right?"

"I hadn't thought about that."

"Well, think about someone you know. You have to shed Emma Blair and assume this new person. The person you will become. You've got to walk in this person's shoes and get into their skin and become them. Assessments are based on how one looks, how one talks, how one dresses, and what hairstyles they wear. You may even decide to change your hair color. When you're out in public, you've got to change the way you would ordinarily look and become someone else. It could be fun for you if you make it fun. Be someone else. Practice with your closest friends. Shop for clothes you would never ordinarily wear. I would stay away from any flashy or sexual looking clothes because you do not want attention drawn to yourself. You're a beautiful woman and you'll attract people's attention. Downplay your looks. Wear floppy hats and sunglasses, perhaps even get a pair of clear glasses to wear all the time.

"The important part is the fact that you have to shed Emma Blair and assume the identity of this new person. Make it a game and have fun with it. Do you have friends in D.C. who are able to go along with you on this?"

"Oh, yes, I do. This will give me something else to think about and plan for. I will make it fun. I need all new clothes anyway because we're just taking a few things with us. I'm beginning to feel a *happy* type of excitement about this now."

"Good. Give it some thought and you'll do just fine. You only have to do this when you're out in public."

"Yes, you're right. Well, thank you for all the valuable information and ideas."

"No problem."

"Who knows what's hidden in my psyche? Perhaps I have talent in play acting!"

"One never knows," he said laughingly. "Will you be filing for divorce before you leave?"

"I was thinking about that."

"Do you have a divorce lawyer?"

"No, I don't."

"I have a friend who's a divorce lawyer and he's right here in Palo Alto. If you'd like me to give him a call, I'd be more than happy to call him right now."

"Oh, that would be wonderful. Thanks, David."

He immediately picked up the phone and made a call to Mr. Walter Strauss. He explained the necessary urgency to him. "He can see you at four-thirty today. Does that work for you?"

"Yes," she said with certainty. She took a deep breath.

Things are now moving in the right direction.
Finally.

CHAPTER

24

Emma stepped outside, closed the door and fumbled in her purse for the keys to lock the deadbolt. She turned and walked over to her car and threw her purse on the front seat through the opened window. Her whole body trembled when she opened the door and slipped inside.

She sat for a few moments just staring at the steering wheel. She waited a long time for this day. She must remain strong. Today will be an enormous step for her. She will meet with Wes one last time to let him know of *her* decisions. He made his decision to leave and she was now making her decision to divorce him and move on with her life. She will not tell him when or where she is going—only that she is leaving.

She called him last evening and asked him to meet her at The Caffee, one of the restaurants they once frequented together in downtown Palo Alto. She did not want to be alone with him. She knew all too well what Wes was capable of when he was angry, and she was confident he would become inflamed once he found out she was leaving the area.

She also knew Wes would never do anything threatening to her with an audience looking on. He would be very sure to protect his image at all costs. *His image…* it meant everything to him. He always had the need to impress the public. If only he cared enough to impress *her* after they got married.

Emma knew they'd be an abundance of shoppers in the downtown area of Palo Alto because the Farmer's Market sold fresh fruits, vegetables, a variety of cheeses, pastries, and freshly made kettle corn. She was once one of those shoppers who pushed her sons in their stroller when they were young. She would never stroll through this farmer's market again.

Wes changed all that.

After taking several deep breaths, she slipped the key in the ignition, gripped her hands firmly around the steering wheel, and backed out of the driveway.

Only a short drive from her home, Emma soon found a tree-shaded parking spot around the corner from the restaurant. She faced the car so she could make a quick getaway and purposely left it unlocked. Slinging her purse over her shoulder, she got out of the car, walked to the parking meter, and inserted two quarters. She wouldn't need much time.

When she turned the corner to walk down University Avenue, she inhaled the sweet aroma of coffee and bakery products. The pleasant aromas made her stomach growl. She was much too nervous this morning to eat anything.

The closer she got to The Caffee the more tension she felt. She spotted Wes as she neared the restaurant. One could hardly miss his tall frame and his thick wavy blond hair with his big brown eyes—quite a handsome man— she had to admit. Not the kind of face one would expect to see on such an evil monster of a man.

He was impeccably dressed in a black silk shirt and beige slacks, and he looked quite calm and relaxed sitting at one of the outside patio tables having coffee and talking with two young women sitting at the next table who were laughing at whatever he had just said to them.

Ah, yes, she thought. *I too was once attracted to him.*

Indeed, there was not the slightest indication in his appearance that hinted at <u>the</u> cruelty that lay within. He was a manipulative sociopath. He was so good looking and so charming and so damned smart, he got away with it. He could be incredibly charismatic when he wanted to be, but under the charismatic, charming façade was a simmering rage that could erupt in a second. Then again, there was the other side of Wes. You never knew what he was thinking. He always tried to find your inner weaknesses, so he could weaken your mind to make you feel insecure. *Had Wes always been this way? What happened to make him turn into such a hateful, wicked man?*

She was amazed at how detached she now felt about him. Actually, she was more than detached, she was utterly repulsed by him. *Yes*, she thought, *the boys and I desperately need to get as far away from this man as we can.*

Having no intentions of sitting at a table with him, she stopped abruptly several feet away from the table and stared at him without any trace of warmth.

Wes stood up and walked toward her. "Come and sit down, Emma," he said politely, waving his arm to come closer.

She didn't respond—the words stuck in her throat. *I must do this, I must,* she told herself.

"No, Wes, I didn't come here to sit and have coffee with you. The time for loving welcomes has long past. I'm here to let you know of my intentions. I'm leaving the area."

"You can't do that," Wes hissed venomously.

"Oh, no? Watch me."

"Why are you leaving the area? Where are you going? You can't take the boys away from me."

"What exactly will you do, Wes? Beat me to a pulp again? You're pathetic. While I take full responsibility for allowing you to beat me because I was once afraid of you, my boys deserve better. In my eyes, you are insane and I will not let the boys anywhere near you ever again. I probably saw the real you early on in our marriage, but I did not act on it. I believed we could work it out, but you shut me out and now I'm shutting you out. I'm leaving."

"You can't leave," he said as anger spilled into his voice. "I won't allow it."

"You won't allow it? Are you kidding me? The judge already restricted you from any visitation rights with the boys. Do you not listen to anyone?"

"They're my sons, and I have a right to see them whenever I want."

"Tell it to the judge," she responded angrily.

Wes' jaw tightened and his eyes narrowed to slits as blood roared in his ears. "I don't give a damn what some judge says."

"You've changed, Wes. You're not..." she said, as she lowered her head... "the person I thought you were. You have become a nightmare for the boys and me, and I can't and won't cope with it any longer. You've made your choices, and now I'm making mine. It's really quite that simple."

"Emma..." He moved toward her with his arm outstretched, but didn't touch her. "Emma, can't we sit down and talk about this?"

Her chin went up in defiance. All the anger she had packed away suddenly came pouring out—the volcano in her head erupted. "Oh. Now you want to talk. You have the nerve to stand there and tell me you want to talk. How dare you! Who in the hell do you think you are? You're nothing more than a psychopathic nut case who only wanted to control me and psychologically destroy me." She leaned her head forward and said, "Well you didn't do it! Your plan didn't work you sick sonofabitch."

As she backed away from him she said, "I don't want to ever hear your name or see you or talk to you."

Their eyes met for a moment. She could see his emotions flood his body with rage. His eyes became savage looking; his complexion white, like all the blood in his body had withdrawn from his being. With his fists clenched tightly beside his body he just stood there alone as if frozen, protecting his *precious image*.

"Hey," he yelled. "Don't walk away from me." He no sooner said that, when he became aware that a small group had turned around and was looking at him. He forced a smile, then turned and sat down.

Her heart pounded; she stepped back to get further away. *Is he going to come after me?* she wondered for a second. Not likely. He would wait until she disappeared from his audience who were now watching his every move. She knew he would not cause a scene in public. *It's all about his image.*

She stared at him as she took another step backward—then another, until he was no longer in her sight. A sense of exhilarated relief flooded through her, but at the same time, she also felt fear as she spun around and ran to her car, opened the door and flung herself into the front seat and locked the door as if that would keep out her fear. She jammed the key into the ignition, started the engine, turned her head around, looked at the road, punched the accelerator and tore down the street, leaving only exhaust fumes. In seconds, she was gone. Delirious with joy, she did not know whether to laugh or cry.

Her eyes watched in the rearview mirror to see if he was following her. As the distance between her and Wes increased, she felt a profound relief while driving directly to her classroom at Stanford to finish her termination paperwork.

It was a sad day for her. Leaving what she loved. She would never walk through the campus again or visit the Rodin Garden, or see her students again. Wes had taken away the life she loved, and the only thing she has now is the heart for escape.

CHAPTER

25

Thursday - March 28, 2002

It was close to seven o'clock on a misty evening when Major Hawk Shaw pushed opened the door to Finn MacCool's, a popular restaurant and watering hole in downtown Washington, D.C. The long mahogany bar was surrounded by locals who were jabbering policies and politics.

The pub, alive and happy, was dominated by government workers, lawyers, Marines, teachers and students from the nearby college who lived within walking distance. Strangers didn't frequent Finn's very often, but those that did happen to wander in rarely stayed very long. For the regulars, it felt like a meeting of the minds refuge—intelligent conversation, good food, and friends. People sat at round tables and drank beers as they munched on bowls of pretzels and popcorn and yelled or cheered for their team on the wide-screened television.

He signaled J.C., the bartender with a wave. J.C. quickly raised his hand, flexed his wrist and pointed to a meeting room in the back of the tavern.

Hawk glanced around the crowded room and waved at a few friends and winked at the waitresses. Across the room was the glowing neon Rockola jukebox belting out Bill Haley's, *Rock Around The Clock*.

Hawk was a natural musician born with music in his soul. When he felt the beat of the drums, the rhythmic twanging of the guitar, his feet and voice became one with the music. *"We're gonna rock around the clock tonight; we're gonna rock, rock, rock, 'till broad daylight; we're gonna rock, gonna rock around the clock tonight...* he belted out as the crowd cheered for more. He spun the waitress around twice before he waved and bowed as he made his way to the back of the tavern.

When Hawk turned the corner, he could hear a murmur of conversation from behind the closed door of the meeting room. He paused for a moment when his cell phone jingled. He glanced down at the ID: 'Emma.'

It was Emma! His Emma? He wondered why she would be calling him. He hadn't heard her voice in over five years. He only kept her on his phone just in case she ever needed him. Once she hooked up with Wes, they never talked; Wes would not hear of it. However, every year he would get a birthday card from her and at Christmas, a card with pictures of the boys.

"Emma, my dearest, what a pleasant surprise."

"Hi, Hawk. I hope I'm not interrupting anything."

"Emma, you could never interrupt me or bother me. What's going on?"

"I'm leaving California tomorrow morning to move back to D.C. The boys and I will be living in D.C. now."

"You're always full of surprises, Emma. What's causing you to move back east?"

"Oh, Hawk, my life has turned into a huge mess. My marriage is a complete failure. I've made a horrible mistake marrying Wes; a horrible, horrible mistake. He's changed. He's no longer the man I married. He wants to kill me so he can take my boys away from me."

After a long pause, he said, "Emma... when did all this come about? I thought all these years you were happy."

"Well, for the first three years, everything was fine, but Wes changed this past year. He wants to kill me, Hawk. He really does."

"Oh, he's probably just saying that, Emma. Men say stupid things when they're angry."

"I wish I could say that was the case, but it's not. He *is* going to kill me. I know it. I've been living with an abusive husband for months now, and I can't take it anymore."

Another pause… a really long pause, while the *abusive husband's* statement had a chance to sink in. *This bastard has struck my Emma?*

"Whoa… wait a second. Are you saying that bastard actually hit you?"

"Yes, that's exactly what I'm saying. He's sent me to the hospital a few times. I just can't live like this any longer. I've talked to the police, a social worker, and a psychiatrist. I've tried reasoning with him, I've suggested counseling, but he won't go. He doesn't want our marriage to work. I feel like I'm losing my mind, Hawk."

More silence on the phone. If she had told him Wes turned into a vampire at midnight every night, it would have been easier to believe. Hawk could feel his pulse pounding in his ears; instinctively his hands clenched tightly turning his knuckles white as he held the phone. Did he hear correctly what Emma had just told him? His mind could not accept what he had just heard.

"Emma, listen to me. You're not losing your mind. All the tension you have been living with is causing you to not think logically."

"It's more than that, Hawk. I don't know who I am anymore. I have unpredictable mood swings, I can't eat or sleep. And, truth be told, my blood feels like it's intoxicated with carbon dioxide, and I'm spiraling toward insanity. My life could not be more abnormal than it is right now."

"I want to come out there, Emma. I'll take care of that weasel for you. Just say the word. I can be out on the next flight tonight. I will make the source of your problem be eliminated," he said in an angry matter of fact tone.

Emma was silent for a few moments as she thought about what Hawk had just said. He actually could do this. Like Houdini, she knew in her heart he could make Wes disappear. She would never have to look over her shoulder or be frightened, or ever have any fear of losing her children. But, one could never ask any questions about Hawk's methods because you really didn't want to know.

"Emma, please listen. I can make it all just go away. Just say the word."

"No, Hawk. As tempting as your offer is, it won't be necessary. Uncle Ross is picking us up at the airport tomorrow. We get in around four-thirty.

"Well, that's the best news I've heard in seven years."

"I knew you'd be happy to hear that I'm coming back."

"I'm elated. What great news. Wes won't be bothering you while you're here with Ross and me watching over you."

"Have you talked with my Uncle Ross lately?"

"As a matter of fact, he called and wants to get together tomorrow morning."

"He probably wants to let you know I'm coming back home."

"I wish you had called me sooner, my sweet. I know how to handle those bastards who beat up women. He wouldn't be walking or talking by the time I finished with him and he for sure in hell wouldn't be able to strike anyone ever again."

"I'm quite aware of that, Hawk, and that's precisely why I *didn't* call you."

Hawk quickly changed the subject. "Well, you're coming back home. That's the important factor. Where are you going to be living? I want to come by and see you and the boys."

"I don't know the address yet. Uncle Ross found an apartment in one of the new high-rises, not too far from the Capitol, but I don't have the details yet. I'm not keeping this phone, so I'll call you when I get settled, okay? I just wanted to let you know I'm moving back home. I never thought I'd be making this call."

"I'm glad you called. It's wonderful to hear your voice, and I'm certainly looking forward to seeing all of you. If anything happens before you get on that plane, you be sure and call me. Keep the phone until you board the plane and then take out the SIMM card and throw the phone in the trash just before you board, okay?"

"That's a good idea. I'll do just that. Thanks, Hawk, and I can't wait to see you. Love you."

"Love you too, Emma, my sweet. Looking forward to seeing you. Bye now."

Emma's call caught Hawk completely off guard. He stood there for a few moments. His thoughts went directly to Emma's husband. *He actually struck her?* Once more, he felt his blood boil throughout his body. *That weasel, Wes Blair is going to pay for what he's done to my Emma,* he thought with suppressed rage. *I can only hope he comes to D.C. to look for her.*

Gradually, fond memories conjured up in his mind when he began to think about all the roles Emma had filled in his life. She was the sister he never had, his best friend, his mentor, his study partner, but never his lover even though he fell in love with her the first moment he laid eyes on her twelve years ago at GW. Their classes were almost identical and they had a wonderful friendship for four years.

When he clipped his phone on his belt, his mouth curled into a smile at the thought of her being close to him once again. He took a deep breath before he pushed open the door to the meeting room.

CHAPTER

26

Hawk had glanced at his watch after he left the meeting room. *Twenty past twelve. It would be twenty past nine on the west coast and Emma might be sleeping by now,* he thought to himself. *That's if she were able to sleep with death threats from her husband. Emma sounded terrified. She's never been one to be easily frightened—she was tough,* he remembered.

Her call had unsettled him to a point where he probably would not get much sleep tonight. He felt handicapped by not being close to her so he could watch over her and protect her. *Why didn't she call me?* he wondered. *I would have gone out there and flew back with them to make sure nothing happened.* Now he would have to wait until they arrived in D.C.

He waved his arm to J.C. and sat on the last stool at the bar. Within seconds, he had his Jack Daniels in front of him.

On a personal level, her call had undoubtedly disturbed him. This was a level he wasn't quite sure he knew how to handle. He never expected just by hearing her voice again that it would stir up emotions he once had for her. But it was obvious he still loved her more than he cared to admit. She was in his blood. He never stopped thinking about her after she moved to California.

He remembered how excited she was when she called to tell him she was getting married. The moment she uttered those words, his heart stopped beating; it felt like a knife went through his chest. She rambled on about how she found the perfect partner, the man of her dreams, her soul mate. He forced himself to lie to her and told her how happy he was for her.

He never thought much of her choice for a husband. He didn't like Wes. Though he never met Wes, he *knew his type*. He was always jealous and possessive about Emma. Wes actually forbid Emma to have any contact with him, which slowly isolated her from her family and friends. *A true narcissist.*

Hawk always felt that somehow this day would come. His beautiful Emma—so loving, so intelligent, so independent, so caring—she's coming back home. Our talks, our laughs, our thoughts about everything in the universe will be enjoyed again. She's special in so many ways.

Though elated that she would now be living in D.C., he had mixed emotions: elation that seemed overpowered by fear. He wasn't confident he could handle this type of turbulence in his so-called 'private life.' He did not want to be roused from the existence he created for himself. He had worked too hard to guard his personal life against any and all intrusions. He'd been through relationships—women played too many games and he was done with all of them.

He suddenly feared that his mental strength would crash once the two of them were together again. God only knows what will happen to his physical side of this predicament.

His life, as he now knows it, will be over. That he was certain of.

CHAPTER

27

Hawk pulled up the collar of his jacket and shivered as the damp wind bit at his face—typical March weather when he walked down the street to Matteo's for a meeting with Ross.

When he opened the door to the crowded restaurant, the regular thirty or so customers were having their morning infusions of caffeine. As he wriggled out of his jacket he spotted Ross waving his arm in the air and quickly maneuvered himself through the tables to where Ross sat with a cup of coffee in his hand.

"I hope you've not been waiting long?" Hawk said as he held out his hand.

Ross stood up and gave him a firm handshake. "No, not at all, I came early to get a table. This place can get crowded. How are you, Hawk?"

"Oh, I've been quite busy, which is good. Unfortunately, the crime business always seems to be booming. I'm doing great."

Before Hawk had a chance to sit down, Matteo already had his Espresso Sambuca on the table in front of him. "Thanks, Matt."

Matteo gave him a two finger salute before he turned and walked back to the counter.

How have you been, Ross?"

"I gotta tell ya," Ross said with excitement in his eyes. "I'm thrilled that Em's moving back home with her sons. That's why I wanted to meet with you before she gets into town. You do know she's coming in later today, right? She said she called you."

"Yes, she called me last night."

"Before she gets here, we need to have a serious conversation to discuss my Emma."

Hawk's left eyebrow arched. "Oh, now there's an interesting topic of conversation. She evidently doesn't know you're here to talk about her, right?"

"No, she'd kill me if she even thought I was talking about her. You know how she is about anyone meddling in her life."

"Oh, yes, I do remember how private she is."

"Whether she likes it or not, I just feel she needs someone solid in her life. That's where you come in."

"Me? What are you trying to get at?"

"We've got to look at this realistically," Ross said in a serious tone. "Emma was in love with you once. You do realize that, don't you? What exactly happened with the two of you?"

Hawk gave a casual shrug of his shoulders. Of course, he knew she had been in love with him, just as he had been in love with her. In all his years he's never really been in love. He had a lot of girlfriends and several serious relationships, but somehow they never worked out. After all these years he still has never found a woman like Emma. She *is* special.

"We made a decision to just be friends rather than lovers. Because we were so young and because love came so easy for us, we thought it best not to get romantic. Actually, it may have been more of what I wanted than what Emma wanted. I was a young guy, and I figured I still had oats to sow."

"So you both decided this?" Ross asked as he took a gulp of his coffee all the while staring into Hawk's eyes.

"Yes, we both gave it a lot of thought. You know how Emma has to analyze and dissect everything to death treating it like she was dissecting a dogfish shark. After all the facts had been presented, the final analysis was, we'd just be friends. As young as we were, we were smart enough to value our friendship.

"We came along at an awkward time in our life. I was just out of the Marines, which made me all I could be and I was going to give my life all that I had to give. Meeting Emma was the best thing that ever happened to me. I can honestly say she pretty well grounded me, and in reality, I needed to be grounded. If it weren't for her, I probably wouldn't be doing what I'm doing today."

"Yes," Ross said. "My dear Emma was also the best thing that happened in my life. It would be difficult for me to begin to imagine my life without her. I know what you mean about her ability to 'ground' someone. She certainly had me wrapped around her little finger."

Hawk smiled, knowing exactly what Ross meant. "She was the sister I never had. The only way I could describe Emma was that she was a beautiful, brainy, brilliantly funny woman with an impermeable shell protecting her from heartache and pain. When I found out that her parents were killed in that Chicago air crash when she was ten years old, it pretty well explained everything about her. My Emma was not going to have further heartache and pain in her life. At that time in our relationship, Emma only wanted a friendship. We were always best buddies."

"You were the rock she needed at that stage in her life," Ross said. "You were her mentor. She had boundless ambition and enthusiasm with absolutely no focus. You were able to focus her."

Hawk shook his head in agreement. "How were we to know at the time that it might have been the real thing? Emma and I continued to be best friends, studying together, enjoying life together and then one day Becky turned up during the spring semester. I became totally dazzled when she flashed her megaton sex appeal at me. She was a bronzed bombshell with sexy, seductive eyes and dressed in the tiniest outfit that was barer than there. She might as well have worn a neon sign saying, 'Wanna have sex with me?' She was totally hot and irresistible—temptation packed for easy access. She was a real firecracker, and she wanted me and I was there for the taking. That semester had a lot of intense heat."

Ross grinned and just shook his head, understanding.

"Being young," Hawk acknowledged, "we do stupid things that seem right at the moment, but looking back, I always felt, given more time, that Emma and I would hook up eventually. But right after graduation, Emma flew off to California and I became a Special Agent at NCIS. It wasn't too long after that she wrote and informed me that she was in love with a guy named Wes Blair and that she was going to marry *the man of her dreams*. I was utterly devastated. Heartbroken doesn't begin to describe how I felt. She wanted me to meet him. I couldn't bring myself to fly out there. I didn't even want to know him."

"Wes was definitely not the man for her, and I knew it from the get-go," Ross said. "He's got a cue stick up his ass."

"I always thought you approved of Wes," Hawk responded.

"The hell I did. I tried, for her sake, to get along with the jerk. I guess Wes waited and saw his chance and grabbed her up. Their marriage was a real quickie. He took her to Nevada and got married on the spot. He didn't want anyone else around."

"Wow. I had no idea. All these years I was under the impression that you liked him."

"Not even close. There was something about the guy that was colder than ice, but for Emma's sake, I kept my feelings hidden in the dark part of my heart all these years. I never warmed up to that asshole. Now look at the predicament she's in. The man of her dreams, my ass. She deserves something better than that piece of crap. She needs someone who's real. He's a phony, and I spotted it as soon as I met him and he knew it. He stayed away from me. But, she was in love. Can't tell a woman anything when they think they're in love."

"I hear you," Hawk said, shaking his head.

"My niece never needed any assistance when it came to finding men. Believe me; I've watched a parade of them come through over the years. She's dated a doctor, a couple of young lawyers, a professor, even a judge, and she ends up with this creep, Wes. She could have anyone she wanted and believe me, they all wanted her."

"Yeah, who wouldn't want her?" Hawk murmured in a low voice.

"Damn right. I'm not saying this because she's my niece, but she's an amazing girl. Wes was always putting her down. After a while, she started believing that this mess was all her fault. Bullshit! He's a psycho nut case.

"She needs to find her equal. She's got a brilliant mind. You know what I mean? Someone who can keep up with her both mentally and physically. If she ever asks me for advice, that's exactly what I'd tell her."

"That would be great advice," Hawk said. "She does have a lot of energy and she's got an IQ off the charts. I think that's why we hit it off when we first met."

"And now I have some advice for you, Mr. High IQ. I'm not going to wait until you ask me. Take it or leave it."

"Okay, Ross, sock it to me. What advice do you have for me?"

"You need to make up for lost time, young man."

"Lost time for what?"

"You know—do I have to spell it out for you? I'm an old man and spent a lot of years making costly mistakes that I've now learned how to avoid. I'm going to give you my expert advice for free."

"Okay, fire away," Hawk said laughingly. "I can always use advice from my elders."

"Oh, you're real funny. There's a gift waiting for you to open."

"There is? What gift would that be?"

"The truth lies in who you are and how you feel about Emma. Life only gives you one true love, Hawk—only one. Sure, there are certain things that catch your eye, but you must never lose sight of the one who captures your heart. When you find that true love, and you throw it back because it didn't 'sizzle' enough, then you will spend the rest of your life regretting and searching for that one gift from God. You've been bouncing around this earth like a football and the gift from God has been right in front of you all along."

Was Ross giving him a directive to try to win Emma back? Hawk thought. As much as Hawk wanted to ask, the words caught in his throat. "What are you trying to say?" Hawk asked, looking directly into Ross' eyes.

"Are you blind? Ah, forget it. What the hell business do I have venting my spleen to you of all people? You're smart in the IQ department, but your love life is the pits. Let's just change the subject. "Do you still do work for the Pentagon?"

Hawk changed the subject matter as quickly as Ross did, saying, "Yes, they contract me five or six times a year."

"You like working for them?"

"Yes, as a matter of fact, I do. In the beginning, when it was my first-ever visit to the Pentagon, I didn't know what to do nor how to do it. I was as nervous as a kid on his first day of kindergarten. I was so uptight and kept wondering if I was dressed properly in my lightweight beige suit or whether I should have donned my khaki chief's uniform.

"I had the map of the building memorized so I wouldn't be roaming around like an idiot, so I was able to find my way around. When I entered the office I was going to, a petty officer said, "Yes?"

"Major Hawk Shaw," I responded. "I have an appointment with Admiral Swayze."

"Please take a seat, sir," the petty officer instructed.

"The waiting room was pretty crowded, so I figured I'd be there a long time, but in a few seconds a voice called, 'Mr. Shaw?' I raised my hand and stood up and walked to the door the petty officer had opened for me. After it had closed, a red do-not-disturb light kept blinking inside and outside the room to let people know not to enter that door.

"As soon as I went into the room, Admiral Swayze asked me to have a seat at the table. I couldn't help feel uneasy in the presence of a flag officer and to make matters worse, another door opened up and three more men entered the room. One was dressed in civilian clothes, the other was a Rear Admiral, wearing all the "I was there" ribbons and the other man was an Aviator Captain with a medal of honor. Talk about being intimidated. Wow.

"The civilian walked over to me and said that he's heard a lot about me. All I could say was, 'Thank you, sir.' I didn't know what else to say. What had he heard about me and who has he been talking to? Yes, that was a day to remember. I'll never forget it."

"What type of work do they call you for?" Ross inquired.

"You know my background, so I do psych evals on vets coming back from combat, and on occasion, they call me in as a weapons expert for court trials. And last month they called me in to evaluate a murder/rape case for the Army. That was a tough one. I spent over a month investigating that one. There was no evidence, but one hell of a motive, but I finally dug deep and got the evidence needed to convict that sonofabitch."

"You're a good man, Hawk. Men like you are one in a million. Are you sure you don't want to come and work for me? I could sure use someone with your extensive knowledge and talents."

"I'm honored," Hawk responded with an entirely humble look. "I have the greatest respect for you, sir… always have had. Emma was so fortunate to have you as a role model. She's very proud of you, you know."

"Yeah, I'm pretty proud of her too. I raised her to be independent, and she certainly exceeded my expectations. Leaving Wes as she did, in a cloud of smoke, I'm sure Emma left the smell of sulfur well up Wes' nose. He's going to hunt her down. I just know it. That sonofabitch is the kind of guy who's never had a logical thought in his entire life. He came out of the womb as a psychological nut case, always doing what he damn well wanted to when he wanted to. He's a real selfish bastard. This attitude of his is what's going to take him down. Did you know he was dishonorably discharged from the Navy?"

"You're kidding? No, I didn't know that. What the hell did he do?"

"You're gonna love this… willfully disobeying the lawful order of a superior commissioned officer, assault consummated by a battery on a commissioned officer, and assault with a dangerous weapon on a commissioned officer. He got the full *Duck Dinner*. His sentence was two hundred days in the brig and a dishonorable discharge."

"Did Emma know about this when she married him?" Hawk inquired.

"Hell no, she didn't know anything about it. Of course, he's not going to boast about it. His parents were disgusted with him so they put him through college in the state of Washington after he got out of the brig and they moved to the Fiji Islands and retired, far away from Wes."

"Did he graduate from college?"

"Actually, he did graduate with a bachelor's degree in accounting."

"So he's an accountant?"

"Yeah, I guess so. He's working at some mortgage company. You know, Hawk, this whole damn problem she's having started with you."

"How's that?" Hawk asked, his brow furrowed.

"This whole problem started with you wanting sizzle over true love. If you had married Emma, we wouldn't be having this conversation about her husband wanting to kill her."

Hawk laughed at that remark. "You're right about that."

"Emma would surely kill me if she knew I was over here talking to you like this," Ross said.

"I'm sure she would be angry at both of us for discussing how she should live her life," Hawk replied.

"You know, I'm going to tell you something you are never to repeat to anyone," Ross said, looking straight into Hawk's eyes.

"Okay, it'll be our secret. What?"

"I wanted to take Wes out if you know what I mean. Would have been a simple task to do and no one would have ever known. But, he is the father of two great boys and it was for them that I didn't go after that sonofabitch. When Emma was in the hospital, she made me promise not to touch him."

"Yeah, I offered to go after him when Emma called me last night. Every time I think of him striking her, my blood boils. I would've killed the bastard. She wouldn't hear of it. She wanted to handle it herself."

"I know," Ross said, throwing his arms in the air. "She figures he'll just fade away out of her life, but you and I both know that ain't never gonna happen. He's going to search her down. I can feel it," Ross snarled.

"Well, I hope he tries. Does Wes have any idea what you do for a living?" Hawk inquired.

"No, he thinks I'm some kind of old security guard. Ha! Ha! Ha!"

"Now that's hysterical," Hawk said, laughing out loud.

"Does he know what you do for a living?" Ross asked Hawk.

"No, he doesn't have a clue, poor bastard. Yeah, let him come here to try and get *our Emma.*"

"Ha, ha, ha, ha," they laughed loudly, clinked their coffee mugs, drank up, and never noticed the heads of people at other tables turning toward the raucous laughter.

CHAPTER

28

Emma slept fitfully throughout the night anticipating the long journey ahead of her. Awake for an hour she watched the red numerals on the digital clock turn over, waiting for the night to end and for the sun to slide in, to call it morning. Finally, flickers of sunlight radiated through the trees, and the first ray of dawn pushed against the window.

She gently pulled back the bed covering and sat on the edge of the bed for a moment trying *not* to think about how her life had come to this point. The nightmarish life she'd been living for the past year would soon be behind her and for that, she was thankful.

In less than a week's time, and with the help of her associates at Stanford University, Emma was able to resign her position at the college, clear her desk, get her divorce started, and saw Wes for the last time. She closed all the bank accounts, cancelled the credit cards, and also arranged to have Wes served the divorce papers at work after she arrived in D.C. All completed without his knowledge.

Once Uncle Ross sent the new identification papers for her and the boys, she began to feel anxious about having to relocate and start all over again. At the age of thirty-two, she was ill-prepared for the single parent life. She was frightened of what the future had in store for her and her two sons. But she knew her panic would disappear as soon as they were all on the plane headed east.

She quickly showered and dried herself off and dressed in her gray slacks with a pink silk sweatshirt that felt so luxurious against her skin. She tousled her long curly dark brown hair with her hands, applied pink lipstick to her lips, and smoothed gray eyeshadow above her violet-blue eyes, which, for some strange reason, only seemed to reflect her saddened mood.

She slipped her gray wedge shoes on her feet, which made her several inches taller than her actual five-foot-nine-inch height. Suddenly, she heard her stomach growl. She had been so nervous last night that she had scarcely eaten anything at all. *We'll all have breakfast on the airplane,* she thought.

She had been very careful with what she packed to take with them. She had her overnight bag, a small suitcase, and her purse. There was one large suitcase for the boys. She would shop for everyone when she reached their destination.

"Come on boys, it's time to get up now. We've got to get moving."

"Okay, Mommy," Adam said as he popped out of bed and ran to the bathroom.

"Don't forget to brush your teeth."

"Okay, I will," he responded.

Lucas just laid there for a minute before he got up from bed. "I'm going to get dressed while Adam is in the bathroom."

"Good idea. Be sure to brush your teeth."

"Okay, Mommy. I can't wait to see Uncle Ross."

"Yes, he's very happy that we're going to see him. Hurry now, we have a plane to catch."

"Okay, Mommy. I'll move Adam along."

"I'm sure you will. And no fighting." Adam walked away shaking his head back and forth.

Emma hastily carried the luggage into the living room where Susan and Jimmy were sitting on the sofa watching the news on the TV. When they heard that Stella left California late last night, they offered to stay with them for the night just in case Wes showed up. If Wes did drive by and saw their car in the driveway, he would never come into the house.

"Hi, you two. I just can't thank you enough for staying with us," Emma said while setting the luggage down. "I just know Wes would have come to the house last night if your car wasn't in the driveway. Thanks again for being here for us. I'm going to miss the both of you," Emma said as she started to cry just thinking about leaving her best friends.

"It was our pleasure, really," Susan said as she turned the TV off and walked toward Emma to give her hug. "I'm glad we were able to help you out. We're going to miss all of you. Jimmy and I were just talking about coming out to visit you at Christmastime, if that's all right with you."

"Oh, I would absolutely love that. Did you hear that, boys? Jimmy and Susan are coming to see us at Christmas."

"Yeah!" Both boys screamed and ran to give them hugs.

"Christmas it is," Emma said with a big smile as she wiped her tears with her hand.

"Are those suitcases ready to go?" Jimmy asked.

"Yes, the taxi should be here any minute now."

"I'll put them in the foyer for you."

"Thanks, Jimmy."

Emma glanced at her watch and said, "Let me help you with your shoes, Adam."

"We're going up in the air, Mommy," Adam cried out.

"Yes, we are, sweetie. There," she said tying the lace on the last shoe. "Let's go and see if the taxi is here to pick us up."

They both ran to the front door, jabbering to each other.

"The cab is here," Jimmy shouted.

"Okay, we're all ready," Emma said as she grabbed her purse and scurried the boys outside.

She armed the security system, stepped outside, and closed the door. The only thing she now had the heart for was escape—freedom to get her life back and to give her boys a life filled with love and caring. "On with the next chapter," she muttered to herself.

The green and white taxi had backed up to the doorway, and the driver had the trunk open to load the luggage. The taxi driver greeted them, picked up the luggage, and placed them in the trunk.

"Is that everything?" the driver inquired.

"Yes," Jimmy said, closing the trunk.

Emma hustled the boys over to Jimmy and Susan for a goodbye hug before she ushered them into the rear seat of the taxi and buckled them in safely. She turned to Susan and Jimmy and gave them a hug and thanked them again for staying with her.

Emma went to the other side of the taxi where the driver was standing with the door opened. She waved to Jimmy and Susan as they drove away. When she got inside, she turned and saw that the boys were smiling and eager to go. They were off.

Or were they? When the taxi pulled out the driveway, Emma gazed down the street only to see Wes' SUV parked half way down the street. He was just sitting there, watching.

"Oh, my God, no!" she said out loud as she put her hands to her face.

"What's the matter, Mommy?" Lucas asked. "Did you forget something?"

"No, sweetie. Driver, please drive so that the white SUV across the street doesn't follow us. Can you do that?"

"Yes, ma'am, I can do that."

Emma panicked. *Could he have seen the suitcases being loaded into the taxi? From where he was parked, the garage would have obstructed his view of the front door. Good, he hadn't seen the suitcases.* She relaxed.

She made it a point to leave her car in the driveway all week with the hood up so he would assume the car wasn't running. He would think nothing about a taxi picking them up.

CHAPTER

29

From the air, Washington, D.C. seemed to exude a somewhat mystical charm. She missed this city. As the jet touched down onto Reagan National Airport, she felt an inner excitement laced with underlying fear—a fear sharper than the fear of being found by Wes. She feared that her uncle would see that she was not the same woman she once was. She had been under unremitting stress for months, and her nerves were shot. She hoped that her nervousness was not apparent to her Uncle Ross. If he did notice... *if he did notice? Who is she kidding?* He notices everything. Perhaps he would blame it on jet lag.

She gathered the jackets and helped the boys pack their backpacks. The jet had taxied for a few minutes before it came to a complete stop. When the *unbuckle seat belt* light blinked, the sound of confusion and panic from the passengers were heard as they scurried about to find their belongings. The boys unbuckled their seat belts and Emma handed them their jackets. She slipped on her jacket and maneuvered the backpacks on both boys.

First Class passengers were the first to exit the plane as were parents with children. She held both their hands firmly as they walked up the ramp into the terminal. The plane was only a few minutes late, but Ross Griffin's face looked worried and troubled when he fastened his gaze on his niece's face as she walked with both boys clutching each of her hands. Emma was surprised to see her uncle waiting right outside the passenger door. *He must have used his credentials to get through the gates.*

He stared at her; her violet blue eyes caught him and she instantly flashed him a smile. There was bleakness in his face that hadn't been there before. She knew it was because of her; he hadn't been able to keep her safe.

Ross wrapped his arms around Emma. Suddenly, like magic, the fatigue of the long flight and the tension of the past months melted from her body leaving her feeling instant relief and the heavy hand of loneliness that plagued her seemed to leave her body. She felt a sudden sense of safety, not because of her family ties, but returning to the familiarity of a place that she was acquainted with—where nothing had ever gone wrong for her.

"How are you, my princess?" he said, hugging her tightly.

"I'm fine now. It's wonderful to be home again," she said, leaving Ross grinning from ear to ear.

"Look at you, Adam," Ross said as he slid his both arms around him to pick him up. Adam's chubby little fingers gripped his forearm. "I have something special for the two of you. Lucas, reach in my coat pocket and see what I have for both of you."

Lucas reached deep into his pocket and his little fingers pulled out two FBI badges strung on purple cords. "Wow, look at this Adam."

Ross reached for one of them and put it around Adam's neck. Lucas slipped the purple cord over his head. They both gleamed.

"Uncle Ross always gets us the coolest things," Lucas said. "Thank you, Uncle Ross."

"Oh, boy. Now we're investors, Lucas," Adam said.

"Not investors. Investigators," Lucas corrected him.

"Yeah, I want to be one of them," Adam responded.

"I picked up a luggage cart," Uncle Ross said. "Here you go, Adam, you ride up here. Lucas, you sit right here. Let's put the backpacks in this little side basket. There, now you both hang on tight, and don't move around or you'll fall off."

"Oh, boy," Adam squealed. This is fun. Don't fall off Lucas!"

"I won't. I'm holding on tight."

Emma held onto the cart while her uncle pushed it, and they all strolled toward a sign that read baggage pickup followed by an arrow pointing straight ahead.

"It's wonderful seeing you again. You have no idea how happy I am right now. It's been so hectic lately with the end of the semester and getting ready to leave."

"You made it here safely. That's the important thing. Did you have any problems?"

"No, actually, we didn't have any problems. The boys couldn't wait until they saw you. You've really captured their hearts."

"That's what uncles are for, eh?"

"You've always been my savior," Emma said, giving him a peck on the cheek.

"You're the daughter I never had and when you came to live with me, I didn't know anything about raising kids, let alone a ten-year-old girl. After the first day we spent together, I was so proud to be there for you—you immediately stole my heart. You're the best thing that's ever happened to me, Emma."

Emma lovingly leaned her head on his shoulder. "You were so much like my father. You'd sit with me on the sofa for hours just holding me while we watched television. That meant so much to me after feeling so alone."

"I will never leave you alone, princess. Never."

"I know that."

"I've found a lovely home for you to live in, and it's fully furnished. You can do your own thing with decorating."

"It's furnished? Who furnished it?"

"It was one of the model homes and I really liked the floor plan, so I thought, why not? Now you don't have to shop for furniture. I'm pretty sure you'll love it. It's really quite nice."

"I love it already. A model home. Wow, that's pretty impressive."

"I knew you'd like that part. The main reason for getting this particular home was the fact that it has full security because of the many foreign diplomats who live there. You're on the fifth floor and the view is spectacular. The boys will love it up there, don't you think?"

"Wow, did you hear that boys? We're going to be living in a big tall building."

"Oh boy! I'll fly my plane out the window," Adam squealed in excitement.

"Well, I don't think that's a good idea," Ross said. "What if the plane hits someone on the street? Then what?"

"Oh. I don't want that," Adam responded.

"I'm going to stay with you for a couple of weeks if you don't mind. I want to make sure you settle in okay and no one bothers you. I'm taking a couple of weeks off to be with you and check out the security guys that work there. Is that okay with you?"

"Of course, it's okay. We have a lot of catching up to do. So tell me about the place? How many bedrooms and how many baths?"

"It's not too large and not too small. It's about twenty-seven hundred square feet and has four bedrooms, four and a half baths and, of course, a large kitchen and dining area and living room, and a den you can use for your office."

"I'm so excited. It sounds perfect for us."

"The fourth bedroom and bath are like a guest suite and is separate from the rest of the house. I thought I'd stay there. You'll like it. They have a pool, Jacuzzi, steam baths and a spa and fitness center on the first floor and loads of other amenities. Schools for the boys are close by, and they have a pickup and drop off for the kids. They will love driving in a limo now, won't they?"

"It'll be a total change for all of us. I'm so glad you advised me not to ever tell anyone that I had money. Thanks to you I never told Wes. That's one of the smartest things I did while I was married to him. I also never told him that you transferred here from Chicago last year. He'll never find us living in such luxury in D.C. If he knew I had that money, he'd want half of it, or probably all of it."

"Well, you had it long before you met him, so there's no way he could get any of it, and I'm the trustee so everything is in my name, not yours."

"Oh, that's right!"

"Did you close out all your joint accounts?"

"Yes, I closed all the bank accounts, checking accounts, and credit cards."

Ross nodded his head in approval. "Good. Now let's get the luggage. Take a right at the next corner."

"There it is. The second one down on the right," Emma said. We didn't take many things with us. We can go shopping for some new clothes and toys tomorrow. I only have two suitcases and my overnighter."

"Mommy, I have to go to the bathroom," Adam cried out.

"I'll take the boys to the bathroom while you find your luggage, okay?" Ross said.

"Good. Lucas, you go with Uncle Ross and Adam while I look for our luggage, okay?"

"Okay, Mommy," Lucas replied.

People were crowded around the baggage carousel waiting to claim their belongings. The conveyor system was just beginning to operate so Emma pushed the luggage cart near the carousel. By the time it went around a few times, she had spotted her two suitcases and the overnighter as they brushed through the weather flaps and went around the track to where she was standing. She grabbed them up quickly as they passed by bumping them over the rim onto the floor.

Ross and the boys were standing right behind her. Ross grabbed the luggage with little effort and placed them on the cart. "Okay, the car is close by once we get out of this building. Follow me."

Ross clicked the remote to his car and the boys' eyes lit up. "Wow, you got a Hummer? We never rode in a Hummer. Wow, Uncle Ross, this is super."

"You can see they love cars and how excited they get when they see one they haven't yet ridden in."

"I see that. Okay, is everyone ready?" Ross asked.

"Yes," the boys squealed.

"We're only about twenty minutes from the apartment and since traffic is heavy tonight, why don't we stop at this great pizza place. It's right on the way home."

CHAPTER

30

As they approached the downtown area of Washington, D.C. Emma took notice of the traffic on the wide streets and the steady stream of tourists and pedestrians on the sidewalks. Oh, how she remembered the heavy traffic, the snarled intersections, and the perpetual construction.

The car slowed down, and with the press of Ross' finger to the remote, massive iron gates slid open to an underground parking area. He drove into the space right beside a bank of four elevators and parked the car. "This is your parking spot. This one and the one next to it."

"Why is there a car parked in that spot," Emma said.

"Because that car is yours, Emma."

"Mine? You got me a car? A Lincoln Navigator?" she screamed.

"Yes, and from the sound of your voice, I guess you kinda like it."

"I love it. Oh, this is too much. You are so full of surprises," she said, smiling ecstatically.

"It's great to see you smile again, sweetie."

With smile lines creasing her face, she turned to him and said, "You are priceless."

"It's your coming back home present. You've made me so happy moving back home."

"I know. It really feels good to be home, Uncle Ross."

"Look, Adam, we got a new car," Lucas said.

"I like the Hummer," Adam said.

"Yeah, but that's Uncle Ross' car. This one is ours."

"Okay. I like it."

Ross unloaded the luggage from the back of the Hummer while Emma helped the boys unbuckle themselves from their seat belts and lift them out.

"Wow, look at that, Adam," Lucas said as he pointed to a long limousine parked along the wall.

"That's big," Adam replied.

"Okay, I think we've got everything," Uncle Ross said. "Lucas, go and punch the elevator button.

"Okay, Uncle Ross." They both ran over to the elevators and Lucas quickly pushed the big yellow button.

Almost immediately, the doors to the second elevator swished open. The boys stepped in first, followed by Emma and Ross. "Okay, Adam, you punch the button this time. Hit the number five button," Uncle Ross instructed.

"I know my numbers," Adam said, punching the number five button with his little fist. The doors quietly closed and a whirling sound was heard and the sensation of movement was faintly felt. The boys watched the rhythmic tones of the digital readout tick off the floor numbers while they both counted, "two, three, four, five," and the elevator slowed to a gentle halt. Soon the doors swished open to reveal a large gray marble-walled foyer with gray and red streaked carpeting.

"Take a left and we're two doors down on the right," Ross said.

One by one they all emerged, walking to the left down the corridor. Ross quickly put the suitcases down and flipped through his keys before finding the right one.

He put the key in the lock, gently pushed the door open and softly said, "Voilè!"

Completely unaware of what to expect, Emma stepped inside. Her mouth opened wide, her eyes were astonished. Clearly the apartment had been entirely designed to perfection.

"Uncle Ross, this is beautiful. I love it."

"Can we go see our bedrooms?" Lucas asked.

"Yes, go see them," Emma responded, feeling like this was a dream.

"Pinch me. I can't believe this is actually happening."

"Come and see the view," Ross said, pointing toward the patio.

They walked over the plush muted toned carpeting through the living room which had a low and inviting sofa upholstered in a bold color of indigo and rust. Overlooking the living room horizontal blinds hung at the large expanse of glass leading to a large multi-colored terrazzo-tiled patio. Beyond was a spectacular panoramic view of the Capitol.

"Oh, my. What a breathtaking view. I am *so* impressed." Tears filled up Emma's eyes. She was overwhelmed as she turned to her Uncle Ross and gave him a hug and kiss on the cheek. "You are too much. I just don't know what to say. I believe for once in your life you've left me speechless."

"Well, it's nothing to cry over, darlin'."

"These are tears of joy and happiness. I'm home and I feel safe from the outside world."

"I'm glad you like it. What do you think boys?" Ross asked as they came running and squealing hysterically, from the bedrooms.

"Mommy. Mommy. We've got our own bedrooms and it's so cool," Lucas said. "I got a jet plane for a bed. How did you know I like planes, Uncle Ross?"

"I just took a wild guess," Ross said, smiling.

"I'm gonna sleep in a boat," Adam said. "This is the best bed I ever got, and I go to sleep in my own room. Thank you, Uncle Ross." Adam said.

"I'm glad you like them, boys. I wish I had a bedroom like those when I was young," Ross said.

"You didn't have a room like ours?" Lucas asked.

"No, I had a room with a bunk bed it in. Your grandfather slept on the top bunk because he was older, and I slept on the bottom bunk. I always wanted to sleep up on the top bunk, but never got to do that. When we got older, we got our own separate bedrooms. The bunk beds came apart and made two single beds for each of our rooms."

"You can sleep in my bed if you want," Lucas said.

Ross and Emma had laughed before Ross managed to respond, "It's your bed, Lucas."

"Mommy, come see our bedrooms," Lucas said, pulling his mother's arm.

"Okay, let's go see the bedrooms."

CHAPTER

31

Hawk Shaw looked up from his desk and glanced out his office window. It had begun to rain. He checked his watch. Seven-thirty—time to pack it in and lock up. His six foot four frame stood up to stretch his arms above his head and run his hands through his dark curly hair. His beige designer linen shirt was partially unbuttoned revealing a heavy gold chain around his neck adorned with a large gold hawk's head.

He moved with the grace of a trained boxer as he walked toward his forensics lab with keys in hand to lock the door and set the lab's security alarm. He grabbed his beige jacket from the coat stand, locked his desk and file cabinet, and headed out the door—but not before he set the office security alarm. Security was high on his list of importance. It always had been, was, and still is.

Hawk worked hard to get where he was. As a former Marine, NCIS Agent, forensics and gun expert, and martial arts expert with a law degree, he was at liberty to choose whatever cases he wanted to work on.

Up until the time he was thirty, Hawk believed it was possible to protect the vulnerable from the grasp of institutional control. He'd tried in vain to do just that, but too often he went away, wondering whether the case was a win or a loss. There were too many questions left unanswered whenever the scoundrels got off due to legal technicality screw-ups. It became difficult to tell the victories from the defeats.

He loved the plight. He loved the fight. But once the adrenaline-high seeped away, all that remained was exhaustion and self-doubt. He felt that perhaps he could've done better.

He gave it all up and went into private forensic investigations. His clients, represented by large law firms, didn't have the manpower to research the cases as thoroughly as they should have been, so they employ Hawk to investigate all the angles to prove their client innocent—to do whatever it takes. Now with all the facts on the table, it felt like he actually had come out victorious in his efforts.

It was a steady rain when Hawk reached the street. He pulled up the collar of his jacket and made a quick dash down the street to Finn's. He pushed open the door and shook the rain from his head before taking off his jacket. Whenever he entered Finn's, he stopped for a moment to salute the memory wall at the entrance of the pub. The cedar- planked wall was covered with hundreds of plaques of Marines who were killed in the line of duty.

He waved at J.B., the barman as he worked his way down the long mahogany bar to his regular stool at the end. He hung his jacket on the back of the stool and then turned and looked around as he nodded his head to some familiar faces and waved to a few of the men that surrounded the pool table.

By the time he put his jacket on the back of the bar stool, J.B. had already placed his drink down in front of him. Almost nightly, you could find Hawk in the stool, his glass of Jack Daniels on the bar as he listened to Fifties music that emanated from the old Rockola.

Hawk stared at the glass in front of him but did not pick it up. His mind drifted toward thoughts of Emma. That's all he could think of since she called him last night.

He couldn't seem to shake her from his mind. He picked up his drink and gulped it down. He clutched the empty glass as he sat for a few minutes. The barman asked if he'd like another. "No, I've got to be going. Thanks, J.B." He placed the money under his glass, grabbed his jacket from the back of his bar stool and headed for the door, waving a friendly farewell to the barman.

Although the rain had eased somewhat by the time Hawk left Finn's at half past eight, lightning flickered way off in the distance, followed by a rumble of thunder. Hawk hunched his shoulders and dashed across the street to his apartment building, taking the stairs two at a time. He reached into his pocket for the key to unlock the entrance door. The door slammed closed with a thud as he scraped his damp shoes on the floor mat. He again looked through his keys to open his mailbox. He scooped up three letter-sized envelopes before he scrambled up the stairs to his third-floor apartment. He rarely took the elevator.

He slipped the key into the door lock and opened the door. Once inside, he dropped the mail on the table in the small foyer, kicked the door closed, and in a reflex gesture pushed his heel down on the floor bolt.

It was a modern apartment with a living room overlooking a covered large patio, two bedrooms, two bathrooms and a den, kitchen, and guest powder room. He'd been living here for three years and up until now, he thought of it as a comfortable haven. Now it's his think-tank space where no one can interfere with his life—a quiet solitude to purge his mind of undesirable elements.

He emptied his pockets, tossed his wallet and some coins on the table before he slipped off his jacket and hung it in the hall closet. He had glanced through the mail before he dumped it into the trash basket under the table.

He unbuttoned his shirt as he walked through the darkened living room toward his recliner chair that faced the patio. Easing himself into the chair, he stretched his long legs out in front of him. He was dead beat. He stared out beyond the window. The night sky was stained the color of lead and sounds from the street were hushed.

He caught a glimpse of the red light that blinked from his telephone resting on the end table beside his chair. He reached over and pressed the 'play' button.

Rubbing the back of his neck, he listened to the message. "Hi Hawk, this is Emma. I just wanted to let you know we arrived safely. Would you like to meet on Monday? I can come over to your office. I'd like very much to see you. I'll try calling you again later this evening." He pressed the 'end' button.

An intense uneasiness swept over him. This was an odd sensation for him... hearing Emma's voice... he felt overwhelmed just thinking how she could change the life he now seemingly enjoyed. He felt overpowered; that's what was most unsettling. Those fluctuating emotions were not part of who he really was. But at the same time, just the thought of Emma's return weakened every damn emotion in his being.

There was a time when all he ever dreamt about was to have her close to him again. But now, after all these years, he's concerned that once he sees her, his life will change. Fear is what he felt. Fear that Emma's return will jolt his seemingly enjoyable personal life.

Suddenly, Ross' words echoed in his mind. He had smacked the lonely, sad truth that was his life squarely on the head. What was even worse is that these words came from a man he fundamentally admired which made their bite abysmally painful. In reality, he had no personal life. Work was his mistress now. He has no room for romance in his life. Relationships? Ugh. He tried relationships, but none of them worked out for him. He had no time for needy women who only liked to play games. He had no time for their games.

However, the siren call came and Emma now needed his help.

It had been a long tiring day for him and with the rhythmic sound of rainwater drumming on the patio, sleep came to him quickly.

There's no telling how long the ringtone on his phone played *Taps* before it snapped him awake from a deep sleep. He sat up on the edge of his recliner and blinked several times to sure himself that he wasn't still asleep. His neck burned from being bent in the wrong position. Groggily, he reached out and punched the speaker button and said in a hoarse voice, "Hawk" as he rubbed his eyes and looked at his watch. It was almost half past ten.

"Hi, Hawk? It's Emma," a soft voice said.

"Emma, my love. You made the trip safely, I see," he stated in a gruff voice. His throat was parched, and his voice sounded rusty.

"Am I calling at a bad time?"

"No, not at all. How are you?" Hawk asked as he picked up the receiver and reclined his chair. He squeezed his eyes shut in an attempt to gain some sort of awakeness while he ran his hand through his hair.

"I'm just fine and glad to be back in D.C. My sons are enjoying it here. Uncle Ross found a beautiful apartment for us to live in with a view of the Capitol. The boys love *living up in the sky*," she said laughingly.

"Well, it's certainly wonderful to hear your voice, Em. I did get your earlier message and Monday works. I'm looking forward to seeing you."

"Wonderful. Uncle Ross will be taking the boys over to his place Sunday to meet Ellie and they'll be on a sleepover for a few days, so Monday's perfect. I'll come down to your office. Uncle Ross tells me you have quite a setup there with an elaborate forensics lab of your own. I'm totally impressed."

"Oh, you'll really be impressed when you see it. Hopefully, I'll be able to convince you to work with me in the lab. You are unemployed, aren't you?"

"Yes, of course, I am. I just got here today."

"Your arrival time means nothing. I can remember when you were offered a job in California before you graduated. Remember that?"

"Yes," she said with a sigh. "I remember."

"I just want to snatch you up before you get any other offers. I really can't think of a more qualified person other than myself to run my lab. Would you be interested in working with me?"

"Wow, that's quite an offer, Hawk. Let's talk about it when I see you on Monday, okay?"

"Okay, only if you promise me that you won't accept any job offers between now and Monday."

Emma laughed. "Okay, I promise."

"Sounds great, Emma. So it's one o'clock at my office. Do you know where it is?"

"Oh, yes, Uncle Ross told me. So, I'll see you Monday. I hope I didn't disturb you tonight."

"Not at all. See you on Monday. Good night, Em."

"Good night, Hawk. I can't wait to see you. Bye."

Hawk pushed himself up from the chair and scrambled to the kitchen for a glass of water to help clear his parched throat.

She can't wait to see me. Wow

CHAPTER

32

"I smelled the coffee wafting through the house," Emma announced when she entered the kitchen. "It smells delicious."

"Well, good morning, Miss Sunshine. You're up earlier than I thought you would be with the time difference. How was your first night in your new home?" Uncle Ross asked.

Emma smiled. "At first, I didn't know where I was, but it didn't take me long to realize I was in my new home. I love it here. It's beautiful and has a very comfortable feel to it. You have done an excellent job, Uncle Ross."

"I'm glad you like it. The boys are still sleeping. They were so tired from the trip. They'll probably sleep for another hour or two."

"What would you like for breakfast?" Emma asked.

"Well, I bought a little of everything. We have cereal, eggs, bacon, orange juice, grapefruit, and lots of different kinds of bread because I didn't know what the boys liked. We have bagels, blueberry muffins, English muffins, whole wheat bread, and white bread. We have pancake mix too, and maple syrup."

"Right now, coffee and a blueberry muffin sound good to me. What do you want?"

"I'll have the same. Thanks, Emma."

"I'll just heat up these muffins in the toaster oven," she said as she popped them into the oven. "This kitchen has everything in it. Did it come like this or did you buy all the extras?"

"No, strangely enough, it came with everything. They pretty much put everything in the homes because most of the buyers are from foreign countries and they likely wouldn't have all these things with them."

"That's true."

"What's on the agenda today, Em?"

"I thought we'd do some shopping. We all need some clothes and the way the boys are growing, it seems I have to shop all the time for them. They'll also need some new toys. Do you want to come with us?"

"Of course, I want to go with you. I wouldn't dream of missing it. I'll carry the packages," Ross said with a big smile. "So we'll take the boys out on a shopping spree. I talked with Ellie this morning and she's looking forward to having the boys over for a sleepover tomorrow. She's off work for three days."

"The kids will love it. That'll be perfect because I'm going over to Hawk's office Monday afternoon."

Ding, ding, ding. "Ah, the muffins are ready. Here you go. Hot muffins," Emma said as she slipped them onto a plate.

They sat at the counter and sipped their coffee in silence for several minutes.

Emma was in deep thought—wondering how long it would take Wes to call the police after he was served the divorce papers at work and he went to the house and found it empty. He would drop everything at work to run over to the house and probably go to the university too.

"Uncle Ross, how long do you think it'll take for Wes to find us?"

"Emma, I don't want you worrying about Wes finding you. You've done everything I've asked you to do and with your new identities, he won't find you. For one thing, he doesn't know you have any money, so he's not going to be checking out these owner apartments. You're not to worry about him finding you. You let me keep tabs on where he is. You do know I can keep tabs on him, right?"

"Yes, I do know that you can keep tabs on anyone. It's a huge relief just knowing that."

"Then you don't need to worry your pretty little head about Wes. Let me take care of him. So you called Hawk last night?"

"Yes, we talked a little while. He's already offered me a job working in his forensics lab."

"Didn't take you long to find a job now, did it?" Ross said with a hearty laugh. "That's my girl, never wasting a minute of her time. He's got quite a business going. Does he know you changed your name?"

"No, I haven't told him yet. He just knows we're all out here and that I'm divorcing Wes. I filled him in on Wes' behavior the night before we left for D.C."

"Oh, I bet he just loved hearing about that."

"You know Hawk. He's just like you… ready to fly out to California to take care of Wes. But I convinced him that it's better this way and no one will get hurt."

Ross smiled. "Yes, we are alike. We take care of business."

In an attempt to change the subject, Emma asked, "Did you happen to get a list of the schools in the area? I want to sign the boys up for school, but I think I'll wait until next week to do that so they'll have some time to adjust to all the changes."

"As a matter of fact," Ross responded, "I did get that information for you. I have the list in my room."

Suddenly, a gentle bickering between the boys wafted through the house. Emma immediately looked for movement in the hallway.

"I do believe the boys are awake," Ross said

CHAPTER

33

San Jose, CA - April 1, 2002

"Wes Blair, there's a gentleman to see you in the lobby," the receptionist announced over the conference room's intercom system.

Wes glanced down at his watch. "Ah, nine-forty-five. It must be Mr. Walsh. Excuse me, gentlemen. I'll be right back."

He took the last gulp of his coffee before he pitched his cup in the trash bin and rushed down the corridor to the reception area. He straightened his tie, buttoned his jacket, and ran his hands through his hair to meet who he hoped would be his new client.

"Hello, I'm Wes Blair," he said with a warm smile while extending his arm to shake hands.

"I'm here to serve you papers from the court, Mr. Blair," the gentlemen announced as he smoothly handed him an envelope in his extended arm.

"Papers? What papers? What the...?"

"Please sign right here, sir, to show that I did, in fact, hand this envelope to you."

Wes looked around the lobby to see who observed him being served papers. He saw the receptionist and another older woman on the far side of the lobby. As it happened, both women stared at him when the process server handed him the envelope. *Were they staring because I'm good looking or because I was getting served papers from the court?*

He gave them both a dirty look as he grasped the pen and erratically scratched out his signature. Veins bulged on his forehead and his face became flushed with rage.

"What the hell?" he said as he spun around to walk back down the long corridor to his office while he just stared at the envelope as if it was an endangered species. *This can't be. This has got to be a joke. That's what this is! This is a joke! Those guys are playing a joke on me. It's my birthday and they're playing a prank on me. That's what this is all about.*

Wes walked directly to the conference room with a big smile on his face. Slumping back in his chair, he threw the envelope on the table and announced, "I get it, you guys. You're a bunch of dumbshits to think I'm gonna fall for this prank."

The V.P. of finance looked up at him and asked, "What are you talking about? What prank?"

"This envelope. The process server. The divorce papers. You really had me going there for a while. You guys got me good."

"I don't have any idea what you're talking about, Wes."

He glanced around the room and no one smiled. They were all serious and had no idea what he had been talking about. It wasn't a joke; humiliation found him like a flash of lightning.

"You know, it seems I've made a horrible mistake. I'm sorry. I apologize to all of you. I've made a terrible assumption. Please excuse me. I have something I need to do right now."

He grabbed the envelope and walked out of the meeting, his fists clenched, his face beet red, veins in his neck pulsed with tension. He hurriedly slipped into his office and locked the door. Once inside, he slapped the envelope down on his desk. Instantly, his mind filled with craziness. He put his hands on his head, pulling at his hair, shaking his head from side to side. He flailed his arms in the air yelling, "That bitch, that fucking bitch. I can't believe she did this to me."

He ripped open the envelope grabbing each and every sheet before he threw it in the air. Between clenched teeth, he uttered, "She made me humiliate myself in front of the people I work with. She's not going to get away with this. How dare she think she can divorce me? She's not gonna take my boys from me. Never going to happen. NOT! NEVER!"

Pacing in circles, he had to think and plot his next move. What to do, how to do it. His mind, like a giant jigsaw puzzle, sorted all the pieces before they stumbled into place to form *his plan*; carefully formulated to *not* fail. I must *kill that bitch*.

CHAPTER

34

Major Hawk Shaw glanced up from his desk when he heard the office door open. There she was—*His Emma,* standing right in front of him with a big smile.

He sat quietly for a moment to think about the last time he had seen her. His prodigious memory bank quickly scanned back to all the wonderful college years they spent together. He hadn't laid eyes on her since the summer they graduated and that was almost seven years ago June 1995.

He never once took his eyes off her. He noted every detail about her. Her posture showed competence; her cheekbones showed strength; the soft curve of her mouth as she smiled—her full lips showed sex and the curve of her body showed... *God, she's just as beautiful as ever. Why did I ever let her go?* It had been a case of bad timing. Now she's alone, frightened, and her life's been torn apart. *She needs me*, he thought, *and now I've got to be here for her.*

Patience has always been one of his strong suits. It has to be in his line of work. Having Emma close to him again is his dream come true. *He will not let her go again.*

She looked straight into his eyes with a stare that seemed to penetrate his mind as if she could read his thoughts. Though he knew she couldn't read his mind, for a brief moment, he felt violated.

"So you finally made it back to D.C.," he announced.

"Yes, I did. I wasn't sure you'd recognize me since it's been seven years. I thought you would have forgotten all about me," she said as she turned to close the door. She just stood there, a little nervous, but couldn't explain why. Perhaps her mind was a lot more battered than she thought, a kind of invisible damage that left her unsure of herself. She hoped Hawk wouldn't notice her uneasiness.

"You thought I'd actually forgotten about you? You should know me better than that. I still have a remarkable memory bank."

"Well," she said with her hands out placating, "since you say you remember me and you say you've missed me, why am I standing here all alone?"

"Where are my manners? Let me formally welcome you back, Miss Emma," Hawk said, as he jumped up from his chair and walked toward Emma with outstretched arms singing his rendition of *Hello Dolly... "Hello, Emma... Well hello, Emma... It's so nice to have you back where you belong..."*

Emma started laughing as he approached her. "I see you're still singing..."

Hawk gazed down at her, thinking, *why did I ever let her go? How could I have been so stupid?* He slipped his arms around her waist and kissed her lips hard and long—he didn't want to ever leave her touch. She was still wearing that lavender scent he remembered all too well.

They parted somewhat but continued to look into each other's eyes while holding their bodies close. "Oh, my," Emma gasped, feeling weak in his arms. He felt so good in her arms, the kind of good that tingled her body from head to toe. "I guess actions actually do speak louder than words. You *really did* miss me," Emma said as she tried to compose herself. "I had no idea you missed me *that* much, Major Hawk Shaw."

"I've missed you since you left for California seven years ago. How could I not miss you? Look at you. You haven't changed one bit… but, why mess with perfection. You look absolutely fantastic."

"You're looking pretty incredible yourself. I see you're keeping in shape."

"I try to huff out five miles a day, just so I can convince myself that I'm not getting any older."

"It's working. You look the same as you did seven years ago."

Hawk loosened the hold he had on her and Emma straightened her posture as they separated. Her smile faded, and the nerves she'd been trying to hide showed in the line of her mouth. She drew in a deep breath and said, "Seven years ago… so much has happened since then, Hawk." She looked at his earnest face and intense eyes and she could feel his deep concern.

"So, I've heard. Come, sit down or are you hungry? I can order in or we can go somewhere. It'll be like old times. Let's go to our old *thinking tank* restaurant. Remember, *The Diner*? It'll be just like the old days. We have so much to catch up on," Hawk said, "and we can talk until the wee hours of the morning. Or we can go to my place. It's right across the street."

"Oh, I think The Diner is the safest idea," Emma said with a chuckle.

"All right, I get your point. You aren't going to let me sweep you off your feet and into my bed," he replied as he exhaled heavily, feeling defeated.

"Hawk, I came here for your help. The last thing I'm looking for is a relationship with you or anyone else."

"I'm kidding with you, Emma. Don't you remember what a big kidder I am?"

"I'm sorry. My life has been so without kidding, that it's going to take some time for me to get back to the woman I used to be."

"Oh, Em, I'm so sorry. Please forgive me. No more kidding around," he said as he gave her a warm shoulder hug and kissed her forehead. "I'm so glad you're here. I'll always be here for you, Em."

What has that bastard done to my Emma? Hawk thought as he tried to control his emotions. Just thinking about that louse of a husband striking *his* Emma made his blood boil.

"The Diner sounds perfect. I'm not very hungry right now, but I'm sure if we stay long enough, I'll get hungry. It feels like old times already," she said as she touched his hand. "It's really great seeing you again, Hawk. I missed you, too." She laid her head on his shoulder, and he put his arm around her and held her close for a few moments.

"I'll make the reservations right now," he said as he rounded the desk to grab the phone.

"Has The Diner upgraded to reservations now?"

"No, but I'll have Sam save the booth at the end for us," he said as he picked up the phone, dialed, cradled the receiver on his shoulder, turned off his computer and locked his desk.

Emma stood there watching Hawk as he spoke on the phone. He had the shoulders and biceps of a prizefighter but his overall appearance hadn't seemed to change, although he seemed a bit taller than she had remembered. He kept himself in prime physical shape because he was alpha and his body was the tool he used to keep the wild animals away. She noticed the military training was still there in the way he moved, the way he took charge. Hawk Shaw was a wild man, a Marine, but, always, always a gentleman first.

It was difficult to think that he wasn't really what she wanted twelve years ago. *Who wouldn't want Hawk Shaw?* He was very personable, highly intelligent with an extraordinary memory, and he had a terrific sense of humor and he could sing a ballad like no one else she knew. She had to be crazy not to want him back then. *What was wrong with me?* she asked herself.

He was still as handsome as ever—piercing blue eyes, neatly trimmed dark curly hair and those darling dimples when he smiled. It was that smile of his that belied the tough exterior and he used it for his own benefit. He would smile at everything, be it a betrayal or a casual romance. You never knew what he was thinking at the time. How could you? He grinned when he was irked and when he was outraged, the grin widened.

She looked at him and conjured up wonderful memories that gave her a warm feeling of real friendship. She felt safe near him.

CHAPTER

35

The aroma of coffee, toast, and hamburgers greeted them when they stepped into the crowded diner. The large dining area hummed with activity and noise when plates and silverware clattered.

A young hostess with hair as straight as a horse's tail immediately approached them. "Hi, Hawk," she said with a drawl and a smile that clearly stated she wanted to please him in any way. "I saved the last booth at the end for you, just like you asked me to."

"That's my girl. Thanks, Debbie. You're the best," he said as he slipped her a folded ten-dollar bill.

"Right this way," she instructed them. Hawk slid his arm around Emma's waist as he pivoted her toward the aisle to the last booth.

"Melissa will be right down to take your order," Debbie said as she stopped abruptly and placed two menus on the table. She then gestured with her arm for Emma to slip onto the red vinyl booth bench as she eyed her every move.

"Thanks, Debbie," Hawk said as he slid into the booth across from Emma—their knees touching. Hawk carried most of his height in his long legs.

"Some things never change. I can't believe this place still looks the same since the first time we were here some eleven years ago," Emma says. "It's amazing."

"Don't change what works. That way it just keeps working for you."

"Little Debbie really likes you although I don't think she likes me very much."

"Why do you say that?"

"She kept giving me strange looks. But when she looks at you, oh boy, she likes what she sees. So what do you think about that?"

Hawk laughed out loud and said "A young lady with excellent eyesight."

Emma's face was covered with shock followed by laughter. She never expected that response from Hawk.

"She's just a kid. I've never come in here with a woman before. You just threw her off-guard and I suspect her smile was in anticipation of my generous tip."

"So why don't you come here with other women?"

"I don't know. I just never have. You're the only woman I've ever taken here."

"So I guess it's safe to say that this is what one would call, 'our place?' she said with a laugh.

"Yeah, I guess so, eh?" he said as he grinned at her outrageously, making his dimples deepen.

"Our little hide-a-way. We've had some good times here, haven't we, Hawk?"

"We would debate for hours, going over class discussions. We were going to solve all the crimes in the world, remember?"

"Oh, I remember very well."

They sat silently for a few moments. "This is nice, eh?" Emma asked.

"Just like old times," Hawk responded uneasily. This was difficult for him, sitting across from the woman he once shared his every thought with and now he's acting as if he'd just met her a few seconds ago.

Emma stared at Hawk as she remembered how much they meant to each other in the past. He was the brother she never had. He always watched out for her. It felt good to be next to her protector. He was just what she needed right now: comfort, safety, and a sense of security.

"So, tell me about your sons," Hawk asked with interest.

"They're the sunshine in my life," Emma said as her face immediately lit up. "Lucas is four and a half and wears Batman pajamas all the time. He's the rough and tumble guy who's eager to please and quick to laugh. Adam is three and a half and has a love for race cars of all things. The faster, the better. Actually, they both like cars. He's a thoughtful, lovable little guy, but doesn't allow anyone to push him around. They're both great little guys."

"You have your hands full with two young boys to care for. Do they go to preschool?"

"Yes, they attended preschool in Palo Alto and have already learned to read and write.

"So it's pretty obvious they take after their mother," Hawk said.

Emma chuckled before she said, "They can't wait to meet you."

"You told them about me?"

"Of course, I told them about you."

"I can't wait to meet them."

"So, tell me Hawk, what have you been up to for the past seven years?" Emma asked as she settled back into the seat with a smile. "But first, I'd like you to tell me why you're still single?"

The flippant answer that came automatically to his lips froze the second he glanced at her sincere expression. He remembered that she had a way of listening with total attention as if he were the most important person on earth. She *was* really interested in his answer.

"Well, let's see, where do I start? I lived with a girl for a few months after college."

This was something he'd never told her before. "What happened?" Emma asked as her violet-blue eyes shimmered with wonder.

"She never seemed to get over her first true love. The guy left her standing at the altar. Evidently he was cheating on her and fell in love with a woman almost twice his age. She just could never make peace with it."

"I'm sorry."

Hawk shrugged his shoulders. "I was young," he admitted. "I just made a poor choice." In reality, I guess I didn't really care about her anyway. It only took me a few days to get over her."

Emma smiled back at him connecting with him the way she used to. They would have entire conversations without a spoken word. It was their innate understanding of how the other felt.

"So, what about after her? With your good looks, surely you had other girlfriends drooling all over you," Emma said.

"Oh, yeah. I'm a real ladies' man."

"As I recall, you were quite the stud in college."

"Well, that was then and this is now."

"Oh, so you've grown up, have you?"

"I guess one could say that."

"Okay, back to your love life events."

Hawk gave Emma one of his left eyebrow raises and then went on. "Later, there was only one other serious relationship. Her name was Alexis Santa Maria."

"What a beautiful name. She wasn't in love with someone else too, was she?" Emma asked inquisitively.

Hawk smiled one of those fabulous smiles and shook his head. "No, not exactly *with* someone, but *something*. The law was her first love."

"Ah, so she was a lawyer?" Emma asked.

"A defense attorney."

"Oh," Emma said as she leaned her elbows on the table and moved closer. "So what happened to her?"

"My grandfather died."

"Oh," Emma said, her hands covering her mouth. "I didn't know. I'm so sorry to hear that. You spent your younger years with him," Emma said as she slid her hand over to his arm resting on the table. "It must have been a terrible time for you."

"Yes, actually it was. I felt lonelier than anyone can imagine. He was the most astounding individual who lived his life with passion and commitment. He was quite a role model for me. He had his own self-styled path in life and there was nothing that got in his way. I think of him every day, and I try to live up to his standards."

Emma grabbed both his hands and held them tightly. "Your grandfather would be so proud of you. He loved you so much. He never stopped talking about you. You'd think he was the only one that had a grandson."

Hawk smiled as he held back tears. The gentle touch of her hand on his conveyed so much more than words could ever have said. Hawk immediately knew that she understood how he felt. He was amazed at the expressiveness of her eyes. How they had positively glowed with empathy for him.

Suddenly a tall, older woman appeared at their table. "Hello, my name is Melissa. May I get you both something to drink?"

"Emma?" Hawk asked as he released their hands.

"I'll have iced tea, please," Emma said.

"I'll have iced coffee. Thank you."

"I'll be right back with your drinks," Melissa replied as she swiveled around and walked over to another table.

"So, go on with your story about Ms. Santa Maria," Emma said eagerly.

"Ah, yes, Ms. Santa Maria. Well, rather than accompany me to the funeral, she chose to bail one of her wealthy clients out of jail. Her actions pretty well made the decision for me. I decided right at that moment that I didn't want to be around her anymore. There was no way our relationship was ever going to work. She became a high-priced defense attorney trying to keep the high-level drug guys out of prison and here I was attempting to put them away in the slammer. There were definitely some career conflicts in our relationship."

"So, where did you two meet?"

"Oh. I guess you don't know this. I went back to college for my law degree."

"Wow," Emma said with a surprised look. "No, I did not know. That's wonderful, Hawk. I'm so proud of you."

She gave him a smile that was all teeth, crossed her arms, and leaned back against the booth. "Just who are you, Major Hawk Shaw? When I knew you way back when you were an intellect with genius intelligence, a scientist, and a lover boy, and now you've added lawyer to your list of achievements. I must say, I'm impressed."

Emma's eyes squinted some as she stared at him for several moments. "You've changed somehow. I haven't quite put my finger on it yet, but I will. Yes... you've changed."

"The truth be known... yes, I have changed—but, for the better. My new life has transformed me into another person. Perhaps it will transform me into the person I was always meant to be... an advocate for the innocent prisoners in prison, the poor who are not treated equally, and for all the less fortunate men and women who just need assistance to survive in this crazy world.

"My former life was all about wine, women, and song... money, greed, and possessions. I was somebody that everyone looked up to. Now, I'm just a nobody, like my clients. I'm pretty sure everyone thinks I've lost my mind, but actually, I think being a saint-type will actually enrich my life in an entirely different way," he said with a broad grin.

"Oh, a saint you are now," Emma said with a questioning look on her face followed by a laugh. "Well, I'm impressed if that means anything to you."

"Of course, it means *everything* to me. Will you still be my best friend when I'm poor and don't have any place to live?" Hawk asked, trying hard to keep a straight face.

She laughed. "Oh, Hawk, you've got plenty of money. Don't attempt to kid a kidder. I think your life will be utterly changed mentally, but change is good, so I'm finding out. Don't underestimate change and challenge in your life. We'll be experiencing challenges together now, won't we?"

Her voice was genuine. Oh, how he missed her. "I may just have to ask you to marry me, Emma."

"Oh, I don't think you're quite up to that much of a challenge in your life. A divorced woman with two small children? You'd most definitely be a pauper soon and how would we survive? How will we send the boys to college?"

Hawk changed his serious look to a smile. "I'm still madly in love with you," he said in almost a whisper.

"I love you too, Hawk," Emma said, covering his hands with hers. "I can't be anything to anyone right now. I've changed."

"Life has a habit of making changes in everyone," Hawk said. "Whenever you're ready, I'll be right here."

"Loving someone and being in love are two different things, aren't they?

"I don't know. Are they different?" Hawk asked.

After a long silence, Emma said, "We were inseparable in college. Do you remember that, Hawk?"

"Yes, I remember it quite well."

"We were young, Hawk. You'll always be very special to me, but to be perfectly honest with you, I don't want a relationship. My marriage turned out to be such a complete failure, I doubt whether I would ever again want the companionship of a man. Men change after they get married, and I'm afraid it will happen again. Many women professors I worked with at Stanford talked about that same problem. It seems that it made no difference if they married another professor or married an electrician; the husbands always appeared to change. I can't ever allow that to happen in my life again."

"You'll find the right person. Someone, who'll protect you and take care of you."

With her self-esteem at an all-time low and her emotions in a confused state, she said, "That won't be an easy task. I now have baggage, resentments, and insecurities thanks to marrying the wrong man. I will never permit a man to alter my life, no matter how golden his skin is or how muscled his body is, or how smooth he can talk. Never again!"

She stopped talking. A knot of grief had lodged in her throat. She wondered how much time it would take before she would no longer think about Wes. She shivered at the vivid memory of Wes' violence as it flashed in her mind. Her cheeks suddenly became tear-stained.

"Oh, Emma," Hawk said, as he quickly got up from his seat and moved in next to her. He wrapped his arms around her and wiped her tears with a napkin. "What did he do to you?"

"Oh, Hawk, she said. "It was awful."

"Emma, what," he repeated slowly, "did he do to you?"

"He made me face the truth."

"Such as?"

"That I was a pitifully boring wife to live with and boring as all hell in the bedroom."

"He convinced you that everything was your fault?"

Emma sobbed and then said, "Yes, everything *was* my fault."

"Oh, Emma," Hawk said as he looked into her teary eyes. "You should never cry. It doesn't become you."

Emma started laughing as she wiped her tears away with her hand. "Doesn't become me? Oh, Hawk, you're so silly with your words. You always seem to find a way to make me laugh."

Hawk, suddenly relieved, said, "We won't delve into your past anymore. Deal?"

"It's a deal. My past is my past—my *before* life. I want to live in my *now* life."

Hawk moved back to his seat across from Emma keeping his emotions under control. His thoughts were sprinting in his mind... all he could think about was getting his hands on the man who hurt *his* Emma.

After several moments of silence, Emma said, shifting the conversation, "Go on with your story about Ms. Santa Maria. You met her in one of your law classes?"

"Oh. Yes, that's where I met Alexis. She was in one of my evening classes. She was smart, very ambitious, and eager to follow in her family's footsteps."

"So her father was a lawyer?"

"Oh, yes. He runs a very successful law firm that specializes pretty much in corporate law and criminal law. His father also was a lawyer, so it pretty much ran in the family."

Melissa appeared at the table with the drinks as she managed to smile a little more brightly at Hawk than she did Emma. "Thank you," Hawk said.

"Have you decided what you want to eat?" she asked as she stood there with pen and pad in hand.

Hawk spoke up and said, "To start with, would you bring us some of those fantastic onion rings with tartar sauce, please?"

"Certainly, thank you," she said as she quickly spun around to return to the kitchen.

"Ah, yes, I haven't had onion rings like they make here since I left D.C.," Emma said with delight.

"You haven't had a lot of things since you left D.C.," Hawk replied with a big laugh.

"So you say. Get on with your story. Was that the end of Ms. Santa Maria?"

"Pretty much. After I left NCIS and began my own investigation business, I really haven't had time for women."

"My, you have changed. I can remember when you *only* had time for women."

Hawk ousted a loud laugh. "Yeah, those were the days, weren't they?"

"Why did you leave NCIS? I thought you were happy there?"

"I didn't care for the director. His only reason for getting up in the morning was to jerk us around. He trampled on far too many people's feelings and the worst of it was he really seemed to enjoy it. It was better that I left when I did."

They lingered over their drinks and after a long pause, Hawk asked, "So, have you noticed a lot of changes in D.C?"

"Oh, yes. Physical changes so far. I haven't been here long enough to find out if the city is still the same."

"Oh, it's pretty much the same. We still have a lot of crime going on."

"That must keep you pretty busy."

"Oh, yes indeedy. I'm swamped. About two months ago I hired Theo Pappas to work in my lab. The workload just became too much and I couldn't keep up with it."

"How's he working out?"

"He's damn good. He's thorough and doesn't make mistakes. He thrives on pride."

"Not a bad trait to have."

"Now that you're here, how about coming to work with me?" Hawk blurted out. He had no idea how he was going to ask her and this was his opening.

"You're looking for another employee? Can your budget afford that?"

"Oh, I have this *huge* budget that you wouldn't believe," he said with a broad smile.

"So when did you come into all this wealth?"

"My grandfather made it possible. He was the financial fertilizer that made this all happen when he left me his fortune. That's the primary reason I quit NCIS and formed my new company. I've never been happier," *he lied.* He wasn't actually that happy but with Emma sitting in front of him with those eyes attached to him, he now felt entirely happy so it wasn't a total lie.

"I'm glad for you Hawk," Emma said as she grabbed both his hands again. "Being here with you now makes me nostalgic for the good old days. It's like going back in time when we were silly, immature, and happy."

"So does that mean a *yes?*' You've got that look in your eye."

Emma thought for a while before responding. "While there's nothing I'd rather do than work beside you and be able to focus on something that interests me deeply; my life is changing, and I'm going to have to change with it. So before I make any commitments, my mind needs to clean out all the pain and suffering I've been through this past year so I'll be able to focus on my career. I need time, Hawk. Let's just take this a day at a time. I've only been here a few days," Emma said with a chuckle. "Give me a few weeks to get the boys settled, and we'll talk about it. Okay?"

His expression quickly softened. He reached over and squeezed her hand. "You take all the time you need, my sweet."

Hawk could see that beneath the laughter and her gentle smiles there was a lingering sadness about her. "What is it, Emma?"

She sat there quietly for a few moments. "Now that I'm back, I regret ever having left.

CHAPTER

36

Wes hurried through traffic to meet Kate for their six-thirty reservation for dinner at Tao Tao's. He was ten minutes late when his cell phone rang. He grabbed the phone like it was a winning lottery ticket and immediately said, "I'm two minutes away."

"Okay, just wanted to let you know I'm in the booth in the back room. See you in a few minutes."

"Okay," he said as he hung up.

There were no parking spaces available, so he stopped at the valet. He ran inside and maneuvered through the crowd toward the back room. He was anxious to tell Kate the latest news.

"Hi. Sorry, I'm late. I have news… bad news," he said as he slid into the booth opposite her.

"What kind of bad news?"

"Emma is suing me for a divorce," Wes blurted out.

"How did you find that out?"

"Well, for starters, I got the divorce papers served at work today."

"When did all this happen?

"When you were away at your off-site meeting. Let me tell you the story in chronological order, just to make it clear. This morning, at nine-forty-five, that bitch had the papers served on me at work. Can you believe that? Right at work?"

Kate shook her head. "Oh, and on your birthday?" she said as she put her hand to her mouth.

"Yeah, how about that? Wes said as he raised both arms up in frustration. "She's going to pay big time for doing that to me."

Kate sat silently and reached across the table and put her hand on his arm.

"I'm in a meeting trying to close a massive half-million dollar job and the receptionist called me and said someone was in the reception area for me. I thought it was Mr. Walsh, who called and said he was running late, so I excused myself from the meeting and headed to the reception area. I've never met this guy before, so I walked up to the only man in the lobby and introduced myself, and when I put my arm out to shake hands, he handed me an envelope. He was a damn process server. I opened up the envelope and it's my divorce papers! I look around and I think it's a joke. I think it's one of the guys at work playing a prank."

"Oh no, you didn't," Kate's mouth fell open.

"Wait, it gets worse. I go back to the meeting and drop the envelope into the center of the table and I tell them I wasn't born yesterday and I wasn't about to fall for something like this. All the while I'm thinking it's a joke on my birthday. They all look at me and the serious looks on their faces immediately tell me they have no idea what I'm talking about. It's no joke. Everyone at the meeting is looking at me like, 'you poor sonofabitch.'"

"Oh no, Wes," Kate cringed.

"I apologized and excused myself from the meeting. I immediately went to my office and called Emma on her cell, but she didn't answer. I decided to call the university, but it turned out she's wasn't there so I went to the house. The house is quiet but her car is still in the driveway with the hood up... it's not been running for a while. As soon as I went into the house an alarm went off. That bitch put in an alarm system. I took a quick run through the house before the police arrived, and no one was there.

"How do you know she left? Was there anything in the house? Furniture, clothes?"

"Oh, yeah, everything was still in the house, but I could tell no one had been there since I saw them leave in that taxi on Saturday morning. I just figured she was going somewhere for the day and took a taxi because her car wasn't running. She must have been on her way to the airport with the boys. Goddamn her."

"How do you know no one had been there?"

"The house was all dark and chilly. The furnace was turned down to fifty-five degrees. The plants were drooping. The kitchen lights were still on. She's gone. She's as good as dead. She may have left California, but I will hunt her down. I'm gonna find her if it's the last thing I do, and I *will* kill her the next time I see her."

Kate reached out and put her hands over Wes' hands to hold them until he settled down.

"There's more," he said as his expression hardened. "I checked all my bank balances and she took all the money out of our joint accounts. She closed out all the credit cards. I'm now broke and without any credit cards. I just never thought she would have the guts to leave!" he shouted as fury rose inside him like an Avenal vapor. "I told her I'd kill her if she ever left. She ran home to her Uncle Ross in Chicago. If she thinks that old man is going to protect her, she's deadly mistaken. She's made a very, very wrong move."

"Don't worry, Wes. We'll be all right. I met with the Russians after my off-site meeting and learned that they are about ready to close up shop here to end this portion of their plan. They told me that together we would have a little over six million dollars. We don't have to work anymore. If we keep a low profile, we'll be on our way toward retirement before you know it. We'll find her and the boys. In another few weeks, we'll be leaving California and we'll be on our way to being wealthy."

"I must get my boys back," he said, unable to calm down. "I will find them and I will find her. I have a strategy all planned. After we get the boys, we'll leave this country and retire in South America. With enough money and connections, there are hundreds of places to live."

Wes smoldered like a hot coal. His mind began to form disconnected images with tormented thoughts of his father who beat him and all his childhood fighting experiences that had become embedded in his personality when he was just a young boy. His breathing quickened as the half-formed images kept coming faster and faster in his mind.

"Wes, are you all right?" Kate asked, as she grabbed his hand and held it tightly.

He took a deep breath, noticed that she had already ordered his Crown Royal on the rocks and quickly gulped it down. The tension slowly left his body.

After a few quiet minutes, he murmured, "I'm all right. I'm okay now."

"It's your birthday, Wes. Just relax and have another drink," Kate said.

"She's really pissed me off big-time, and I'm gonna make her pay. I now have only one mission in life, and I will wait for the perfect moment. I will strike back no matter what it takes and when I do, the ground beneath my dear wife will tremble when I find her. My face will be the last thing she sees just before I kill her. One shot to her pretty little head."

CHAPTER

37

Emma gave her cappuccino a stir after she dropped a sugar cube into the mug. She stirred it gently, as she walked toward the patio terrace. It was a dark, gloomy day, totally in conflict with how she felt today. She was feeling warm, loved, and happy because her first thoughts when she woke this morning were of Hawk and their time together yesterday.

She walked over to her recliner and set the cappuccino on the end table. The boys, busy coloring a large poster board, dropped their crayons and ran toward her. She raised her arms over her head and imitated a silent scream and they both smothered her with hugs and kisses.

The sudden ring of the telephone startled her. She reached over to the end table and picked it up. "Hello?"

"Miss Ross, this is Allen at the security desk in the lobby. You have a Federal Express package that just arrived. Would you like me to bring it up to you?"

Emma thought for a moment, wondering who had her new address? "Oh, yes," she said as she remembered her lawyer in California had the divorce papers for her to sign. "That would be wonderful. Thank you, Allen."

"Was that Allen from downstairs?" Lucas asked as he let go of her leg.

"Yes, he's going to be bringing up a package for me."

Several minutes later, the doorbell rang. Adam and Lucas ran for the door.

"Slow down before you fall!" Emma shouted.

"Hi, Allen," Adam said.

"Hello, Adam, Lucas. How you boys doin' today?"

"I'm okay. You have a package for my Mommy?" Adam asked.

"Yes, I do."

Emma, who was standing right behind both boys, said, "Good morning, Allen."

"Miss Ross," Allen said with a nod of his head. "Here's your package." He handed her the orange and blue FedEx envelope that had traveled many miles and showed the wear.

"Thank you very much, Allen."

"You're welcome. You boys be good now. Bye."

"Bye," Emma said as she closed the door. She carried the envelope to her recliner while the boys went off to play in front of the fireplace with their train set.

She gazed around her luxurious home. Nothing was here from her married life—nothing. This is what she wanted; a clean break and a new start in life. She was a different person a week earlier—scared, alone, and depressed. She will never be that person again.

She tapped her fingers against the blue and orange FedEx logo with one hand and took a sip of coffee with her other hand as she relaxed in her chair. She hesitated to open the envelope. She closed her eyes for a few moments as she recalled the words, 'till death do us part.' *What a crock*, she thought. If that statement were true, she'd be dead at thirty-two. But she's alive and intends to stay that way.

They'll be no more threats, no more beatings, and no more arguments. No more tears and certainly no more heartache. The day he threatened to kill her and take her boys was the day any love she had for him vanished. It ended right there. It was like the turn of a faucet and it was over. *No one* will ever threaten her again.

The divorce papers will make it all go away. It will change her life. She will now legally be Emma Griffin, a single divorcee with two children. *My signature on these papers will finalize and bring an end to this hellish nightmare of a marriage.*

She grabbed the envelope and with a twisted, torsional strain in an attempt to try to pry the flap loose on the non-tearable, tamper proof, Tyvek envelope, she got totally frustrated. She reached into the end table drawer, grabbed the scissors and cut the damn envelope open. She must do this now. Sign it, mail it back, and be done with it.

"It's over," she mumbled to herself and smiled.

CHAPTER

38

Friday, April 5 - Auditors at Kate & Wes' Office

At precisely 5:20 p.m., a series of sharp piercing successive taps on the outside of the glass door echoed throughout the bank.

The young, beefy security guard in uniform quickly turned his head toward the door and observed an older, gray-haired man waving his arm at him. The man was wearing a business suit and carried a large black briefcase. As the guard approached the door, the man held up an identification badge that he pressed against the glass door. The guard carefully inspected it before he unlocked the door to let the gentlemen inside.

Once inside, the man quickly announced, "My name is Neil Bronson, and I'm from the audit department at headquarters and we're here tonight to conduct an internal audit."

"I only see you. How many auditors are with you?" the guard asked.

"They'll be seven…" Suddenly proliferation occurred and a regiment streamed into the bank like floodwaters.

"Please, all of you, wait right here," the guard announced. Have your credentials out so I can check them. You all have to sign your name in the log book, the time you arrived, and your employee number. Thank you."

The security guard immediately phoned Kate. "Miss Lee, there's a Mr. Neil Bronson with seven other people in the lobby who are from headquarters audit department."

Her eyes widened in surprise. "I'll be right out. Thank you," she said in a calm voice. She hung up, sucked in her breath, and dialed Wes' office.

"Hi, what's up?" Wes asked.

"We're getting audited. A group from corporate just arrived. I just wanted you to know."

"Thanks. Talk with you later."

"Mr. Bronson?" a voice spoke out loudly. "I'm Kate Lee, the operations manager. How may I help you?" she asked as she moved toward the group of men.

"We're here to do an internal audit, Ms. Lee."

"Will this be a full-dress audit?" Kate inquired.

"Yes, it will," Neil Bronson responded.

Kate smiled politely as she concealed her surprise at this intrusion and said, "Come this way, Mr. Bronson. You can set up in the conference room. We're here to assist you, so whatever assistance you may need, please let the staff know and they'll be more than happy to help you. I'll notify the employees that they will be working late tonight."

"Thank you," he replied as she gestured with her arm toward the conference room. He walked into the conference room and plunked his briefcase onto the table with a loud thud. He removed his jacket and hung it on the back of the chair and immediately rolled up his shirt sleeves. He swiveled his briefcase around and reached for the two brass catches, snapping them open simultaneously. With a rustle of papers, his fingers quickly found the file folder he was searching for. He removed it and laid it on the table in front of him. He was now ready.

Kate walked over to the staff members that were now all huddled together curious to know if they were being audited. "There will be a full-dress audit this evening and I'm going to ask your indulgence and also ask that you remain at your desks until you're given permission to leave. I know this is inconvenient for some of you with families, but all I can offer you at this time is pizza, soft drinks, and cookies. Sue, will you please take care of that?"

"Consider it done, Kate."

A low rumble of uneasiness between the staff as some members groaned and voiced their dissatisfaction. "They have to do this on a Friday night of all nights. Damn them. I have reservations at a concert. Are they going to reimburse me for those tickets? No!"… "Don't these auditors have a life?"

"No. Haven't you heard they're not human?"

Kate walked into Wes' office and closed the door. His head was down, resting in his hands. "Looks like we're through here, Kate," he said as he raised his head up.

"Everything is going to be okay, Wes. Once the Russian's hear about this audit, they'll disappear. We'll disappear too. Let's wait and see what they uncover. Right now, they don't have anything, and they're not telling me if they have already found something wrong. Have they been in your office yet?"

"No, no one has come here yet, but the night is young. I'll go out and talk to the folks here and have pizza with them. I don't want to look nervous at this point."

"Good, I'll join you a little later."

All the ledgers were soon taken over and scrutinized in the conference room where several auditors seated themselves around the oblong table spreading paperwork that covered the table.

After the pizza, the staff accepted their surprise arrival and soon all the tellers were asked to leave after the vault reserve cash balanced and their cash had balanced.

By nine o'clock a notable amount of work had been accomplished and the staff began to thin out. The bank manager and his secretary were kept busy as they searched for information and answered questions for the auditors. It was past ten o'clock when Neil Branson walked into Kate's office.

"How is the audit going," Kate asked.

"We're making progress, but unfortunately it isn't going well for the branch. We've located a deal more than anyone expected."

"What did you find?" Kate asked calmly, even though she was deeply worried.

"There were a significant number of large transactions that were unethical and should have never been allowed. We also found some illegal transactions which must be reported to the FBI."

"The FBI?" Kate exclaimed as she tried to hide the anxiety attack she felt coming on.

"Yes, ma'am. The FBI is now involved due to the discrepancies we've found. Please don't leak this information to anyone else, Ms. Lee. You didn't hear it from me and this conversation never took place."

CHAPTER

39

April 6, 7:00pm

Hawk guided the Jaguar right to the front door of the 1789 Restaurant. A valet attendant, dressed in a red vest, immediately ran up to his car to open the door for Hawk. "Good evening, sir," the young man said, handing him a ticket stub.

"Don't get a scratch on it," Hawk said when he stepped out.

"No, sir," the young man immediately replied, his eyes large with wonder and excitement. "Don't see many XK8's around here," he sputtered. "That's a beautiful Jag."

"You're right, and I'm planning on keeping it that way. I'm counting on you to take good care of it," Hawk said as he handed him a Jackson.

"Absolutely, sir."

Hawk opened the oversized walnut door that led into the restaurant. The foyer inside the entrance door offered marble floors, masterpiece art, and cozy love seats. To the right of the entrance was a bar with intimate tables dimly lit with candles occupied by several couples deep in conversation. A schmaltzy lounge tune filled the air.

Hawk walked up to the attractive hostess who stood behind a podium style desk. "Reservations for Shaw at seven o'clock. I'll be waiting for my lady friend at the bar."

"Very well, Mr. Shaw. Your table is ready when your guest arrives."

"Thanks," he said as he turned and walked over toward the bar and settled on a stool close to the entrance. He ordered a Jack Daniels while waiting for Emma.

Uncle Ross had picked up Emma and the boys because he and Ellie planned to keep them overnight after he dropped Emma off at the restaurant to meet up with Hawk.

Punctual as usual, Emma breezed through the door looking spectacular. Her hair fell softly to her shoulders and the diamond studs in her ears glittered when she walked. Wearing a lilac-colored sheath with a scooped neckline and a lilac cashmere wrap trimmed with small crystals gently thrown around her shoulders indicated that she had an instinctive flair for selecting eye-catching clothes. She immediately noticed Hawk when he waved his arm.

A flicker of a smile came into his eyes as he walked toward her. He didn't speak it out loud, but he thought, *Wow!*

"You look very handsome, Mr. Shaw."

Startled by the compliment, he smiled and said, "Ah, yes. It's amazing what a suit will do for a man."

She shook her head. "No, the amazing thing is what you do for that suit. You could be a male model."

With a roar of laughter, he spouted, "I really don't think so. Now you on the other hand," he said as he stepped back and gazed deliberately down to her strappy lavender high heels and slowly moved his eyes up her body as he climbed back to her eyes, "are the one who looks good enough to eat."

Emma had blushed before she responded, "In your dreams, Mr. Shaw." She leaned into his body and with a fleeting touch of her lips on his cheek, she whispered with a shy smile, "In your dreams."

Hawk chuckled softly but said nothing. How could he? She always left him tongue-tied whenever she greeted him. *I've got to spend more time at the Dojo—she's going to kill me if my heart keeps beating this fast,* he thought. *She's wearing that lavender scent that drives a man wild.*

Emma barely had enough time to absorb her surroundings before the maître d' hurried over to greet them. "Mr. Shaw, your table is ready if you'd care to be seated. Shall I take your wrap, Miss?"

"Certainly," Emma said.

Hawk threw the maître d' a quick wink and stepped in front of him as if to say, *"I'll take it from here.* His arms slipped around Emma's shoulders with a smooth sideways motion. He let his fingers linger to free her hair from the wrap before he gently slipped it off. Emma looked over her shoulder—her face teasingly close to his. She smiled as they held a brief gaze.

The wrap was whisked away, and they were led into a private dining room already prepared for a cozy table for two. There were gorgeous flowers in a vase surrounded by amber candles that shimmered on the table while soft music drifted through the air. Silk-shaded brass oil lamps provided a perfect atmosphere.

"I hope this is suitable for your evening?" the maître d' asked.

"It's perfect," Hawk responded.

"Madam," the maître d' gestured with his arm as he pulled her chair out. When Emma sat down, he picked up the napkin that rested on the table and shook it gently to unfold before he placed it on her lap.

"May I," the maître d' asked, as he gestured toward a large silver bucket filled with ice to create a cold, if humble, nest for a bottle of Cristal.

"Yes, please," Hawk answered.

He put a crisp white towel over his arm before he peeled the gold foil off the top of the bottle to free the wire cage. He carefully loosened the cage while he placed his thumb on the cork so there would be no surprises. With the cage off, he put the towel over the cork with one hand and held the base of the bottle with the other hand as he turned the bottle gently to ease the cork off with a soft '*whoof*' rather than a loud pop.

Emma heard the excited fizz of air and watched the wine rise in the neck of the bottle. "I love that sound," she said.

The maître d' smiled with satisfaction. He folded the towel and then wrapped it around the neck of the bottle and poured the bubbly into two very tall champagne glasses. "For you, madam," he said with a smile, handing her the glass.

"Sir," he said quietly as he placed the glass next to Hawk's hand.

"Ah," Hawk said after taking a sip. "It's wonderful."

The maître d' bowed his head coyly and smiled as if pretending that he was personally responsible for the wonderfulness of the champagne.

"If you wish for anything, you have only to ask. Please, enjoy." He slipped out to leave them alone—as alone as one could be with a waiter stationed discreetly just outside the room.

"When you do something, Hawk," Emma said after a moment, "You really do it."

"You know I don't like to do things halfway. He lifted his glass; she lifted her glass. The crystal stems chimed when they clinked them together. "To all our moments: the past, present, and those in our future."

"That's beautiful, Hawk." She sipped approvingly. She took another sip while she stared over the rim at Hawk. "Okay, I'm impressed." She looked around the room, so private, so romantic—the flowers, the candles on the table and the soft music. "This is all very romantic, Hawk."

He reached for her hand and said, "I just wanted to be alone with you. Don't spoil the evening. It's just dinner with an old friend."

"*Just* dinner? In a private room like this?"

"Just one evening. It doesn't mean anything, Emma. Can't you just relax?"

Emma lowered her head in thought for a few moments. *He's gone through a lot of trouble to plan this evening. The last thing I want to do is upset him by complaining about spending one evening at a beautiful restaurant with a handsome gentleman. Most girls would consider this a dream date.*

With a hint of apology in her voice, she looked up at Hawk and said, "You're absolutely right, Hawk. We're *just* friends, and we're both right here so let's just relax and enjoy the moment." She picked up her glass, clinked his glass, and sipped. She allowed herself to get all worked up about what might happen next. She'll just enjoy Hawk's company and go with the flow. She must learn to relax and enjoy the moments in front of her.

Music suddenly filled the air, and immediately Hawk leaned across the table and sang softly the opening lines of *'Just to be with you'… "Just to be with you…There is nothing I wouldn't do, just to be with you."*

Emma smiled, then put her hand on top of his and said, "I was hoping you'd sing."

"I meant every word of it," Hawk said before he kissed her hand. *I am secretly romancing you,* he wanted to tell her, but he could never get the words out. That had never been part of their past relationship, and this was not the time to talk about it.

Hawk gave a friendly nod to the white-jacketed waiter standing by the door and the young man quickly handed them menus.

"So, what would you suggest for dinner?" Emma asked.

"I know how you love crab cakes and they make *the best*. There's one other item we have to have and that's their glazed donuts with tangelo ice cream. You're gonna think you died and went to heaven."

"You still like desserts, I see."

"Oh, this is more than a dessert. It's an aphrodisiac."

Emma laughed, almost choking on her champagne. "All right, I'll take your word for it. That's exactly what I'll have. Crab cakes and glazed donuts. Sounds pretty good to me. What are you going to have?"

"I'm going to have the chicken with chestnut polenta. I haven't tried that yet."

"So you come here often?"

"I try to when I have a free night."

"You're a workaholic, Hawk Shaw."

"Oh, no… well, maybe… some weeks I am. "But not this week? At least not tonight."

Emma stared at Hawk as he sipped his champagne. *What a remarkable man, my friend, Hawk. I have really missed him.* "You really are comfortable with yourself, aren't you, Hawk?"

"That's a strange play on words. Comfortable with myself? I guess one could say I like what I do. There are times that I'm not sure if I love my job or I'm addicted to it. Actually, I do like it most of the time. I'm going to really enjoy it with you by my side. Are you ready to start work on Monday?"

"Yes, as a matter of fact I am anxious to start. The boys are registered in school, and I need something to occupy my mind."

"That's great, Emma."

"This evening is perfect, Hawk. I do need to relax and enjoy life again. I need time to figure out my life."

"You take all the time you need."

"We're different people now, Hawk. These past few months have really changed me."

"Our challenges in life continue to change us, but basically, we're the same people."

"I can't say I'm the same person I was five years ago. When you lose yourself in another human being and he becomes the world to you, you actually open your heart to grief. Being in love is a huge risk, and yet people willingly long for it. Why is that?"

"If I could once feel the way you felt about Wes, I would take the risk."

"Really? You? The confirmed bachelor? The man who was allergic to wedding rings."

"I've wanted to get married and have children. I just never found the right girl."

"Ah, the key phrase… *finding the right girl.* I thought I found the right man."

"Perhaps you married too soon. You only knew him for a few months. You can't really get to know anyone in that short period of time."

"You could be right. I don't think I ever really knew Wes. I have had a really difficult time trying to understand how he could be so two-faced. He turned into a real Jekyll and Hyde."

Hawk raised an eyebrow and said, "Anyone is capable of being two-faced."

"You're not."

"I can be if the situation calls for it."

"Then, you too have changed, Hawk."

"No. Actually, I've grown up."

"I don't believe that. You are telling me you're all grown up now?" Emma said as she laughed in his face.

"So that makes you laugh. I love to hear you laugh. You used to laugh all the time, remember?"

"Yes, I remember. So, tell me about the job I'll be doing…"

They talked and talked for hours and reminisced about all the things they did in the past. He went over in detail what type of work she would be doing in the lab. Hawk explained everything precisely. He was the best at what he did.

Dinner came and went and dessert was most definitely a sexual pleasure.

"Dinner was extraordinary. Thank you so much for asking me to join you. I'd almost forgotten how much I enjoy talking with you. You're a good man, Major Hawk Shaw… a really fine gentleman. Your grandfather would certainly be most proud of you."

Hawk suddenly felt awkward and didn't know exactly how to respond. He didn't take compliments easily. "Compliments are for politicians; they need the constant pumping up."

"Why do you get embarrassed when someone compliments you? I wasn't trying to make you feel awkward, Hawk. I'm just…"

"It's a beautiful evening," he interrupted. Why don't we stroll around the area before we drive back?"

"Is that your way of saying I ate too much and I need to walk it off?"

"Not at all. I just want to spend time alone with you."

Her wrap reappeared and Hawk gently placed it around her shoulders and he held her for a moment, giving her a kiss on her forehead. She took his arm, and he steered through the people who crowded the entryway.

Arm in arm they walked through the Georgetown streets passing noisy nightclubs and bars. "Do you hear that music?" Hawk asked Emma.

"Yes, it's coming from farther up the street. What do you think it is?"

"I see a large group of people gathered up there. It looks like we've encountered some type of music festival. Let's go find out what's going on."

As they neared the gathering, music filled the air as a group of musicians belted out rock and roll tunes and the crowd enjoyed every beat while they danced.

"They're pretty good," Emma said. No sooner did she say that, Hawk grabbed her and spun her around a few times. Surprise came over her face and before she knew it she was dancing to the rendition of Elton John's, *'I Don't Wannna Go On With You Like That'*.

Soon after, they were swaying to, *'When I Fall in Love.'* "I always liked dancing with you," Emma said. "I never told you that did I?"

"No… no, you never did." *'When I give my heart, it will be completely,'* Hawk sang in her ear. "You and I moved to a lot of music when we were young. See Emma, we're the same people, just seven years later and still having fun."

Suddenly, he managed to dip her once, spin her around and dip her again. He showed her some of his Travolta moves, and did some dance steps he called, 'How to Dodge the Bullets.' She laughed hysterically and watched him with that cocky half-smile on his face.

"I've missed you, Hawk. The more I'm around you, the more I realize how much I adore you."

Without saying a word, Hawk pulled her close and they continued to dance the night away.

It was past midnight and the air was cool when they walked back to the restaurant arm in arm.

"Tonight, I feel like I've met you for the first time. It's odd," Emma said.

"What's odd about it?"

"Remembering you. I've known you for so long, yet I feel as if I've just learned who you really are. It's like seeing you how others see you. You're still handsome, intelligent, and funny, but you've grown into one hell of a man!"

"You're making me blush," Hawk said.

"Don't I feel like a stranger to you? Don't I seem like a different version than you remembered?"

"Yes, in a very subtle way. What I regret is that I was not around to watch you blossom into such a beautiful woman."

"Truth be known, I feel like another person. Some person I've never met."

"You're the same person, Emma. You just need time to get your life back to some form of normalcy."

CHAPTER

40

Traffic was almost non-existent, which made the drive home relaxing at this late time of night. The muted wail of a distant siren filtered into the car and the streetlights and traffic lights intermittently broke the darkness. Hawk slowed as he pulled up to the entrance curb in front of Emma's apartment building.

When he turned and glanced at Emma, he noticed she had a smile on her face. "What are you thinking about?"

"I was just thinking about the day we first met. Do you remember?" Emma asked.

"Of course, I remember. You were sitting in the audience at Bojo's, the nightclub all the students rallied to every Friday and Saturday night."

"Yes, you're right," she said and started laughing. "You were sitting at the piano, playing *Bad, Bad, Leroy Brown.* You had a pretty little redhead sitting on one side and a tall blonde on the other side and you were singing, *'The baddest man in the whole damned town...'*

When you finished singing, you made a quick detour toward the men's room. The band began playing a Latin set and you came out of the men's room doing a little cha-cha-cha step. You were singing softly... *'Its cherry pink and apple blossom white when your true lover comes your way'...* that's when you stopped right in front of me. I told you how much I enjoyed listening to you and then I asked you where you learned to play the piano like that."

"Yes, and then I asked you, "Where did you ever get those beautiful violet eyes?" You blushed when I asked you that. You were quite shy."

"Yes, I was. It's a wonder I spoke to you at all."

"Then I grabbed your hands and said, 'They're playing our song.'"

Emma laughed. "Yes, that's right. I don't even remember going on the dance floor."

"You were too beautiful to be alone on a Friday night so I just curved my arm around your waist, and we plowed our way to the dance floor."

"Those were good times, weren't they, Hawk?"

"Yes, they were the best. We had some great times."

"We were a great team," Emma muttered.

"That we were," Hawk responded.

Jumping out of the car to open the door for Emma, he held out his hand and when she took it, he pulled her close and buried his face in her hair. She wrapped her arms around his neck and gave him a gentle kiss. He felt wonderful.

"This has been an extraordinary evening, Hawk. One I will never forget."

"Thanks for keeping me company. If you're up to it in the morning, I'd like to take you out on my boat."

"Yes, Uncle Ross mentioned that you had a boat," Emma said with surprise.

"I do. Why do you look surprised?"

"I don't know. Probably because you're so busy working all the time, I don't know when you could possibly have time for a boat."

"I make time for relaxing. Call me when you wake up, okay?"

"I will do that. Thank you for an enjoyable evening, Hawk. Goodnight."

"Goodnight," he said as he kissed her hand.

He watched her walk away. He observed every detail about her—everything from the curve of her hips and the sway of her walk made him think of other things. He knew he wanted her, but he also knew he had to be patient or he'd lose her.

"Good evening, Miss Ross," the doorman greeted her with a tip of his cap.

"Good evening, Paul." He nodded as he opened the door. "Thank you," Emma said as she turned and waved at Hawk.

Once inside, she crossed the dimmed lobby with its antiques and relics and went directly to the bank of elevators and stepped inside. She poked the button and dreamily leaned against the wall.

She closed and bolted the door to her apartment. She felt dreamy. It had been a very long time since she had so much fun. She stripped off her clothes, jumped in the shower and stood under the hot spray while reliving the moments when she was dancing with Hawk. *He is so entertaining and he took my mind off all the bad things happening in my life. I couldn't have done that by myself. He certainly is a special man, and I'm lucky to have him in my life.*

Clean and a little dizzy from the wine, she toweled off, wrapped up in her robe and blew her hair dry. She turned down the bed, fluffed up the pillows, and hopped in bed. Unable to get her mind off Hawk she closed her eyes only to have images of Hawk appear in her mind. "No," she said out loud, sitting up in bed. "No, no, no! This is wrong."

Moments later, she fell back onto the pillow wondering if it was okay to have these feelings. We were just having a good time. It was nothing more than that, just like Hawk said, *It's just dinner with an old friend.*

CHAPTER

41

The telephone rang. Hawk glanced at his watch, grabbed the phone and saw Emma's name on the ID. "Good morning, Miss Emma. How are you this morning?"

"Hi, Hawk. I'm fine. I talked with the boys earlier this morning and they are having a blast spending time with Ellie and Ross. It's so good to see them happy and to finally have some family connections. They have really taken a liking to Ellie. She's spoiling them."

"Kids need spoiling once in a while. Ross enjoys children. I guess because he never had any of his own."

"How can you say that? He had me!"

"That's right. But boys are different. They'll challenge him."

With a loud laugh, Emma said, "Oh, I think I've already challenged him. Are we on for the boat ride today?"

"I checked the weather and it's really not a good day for going out. It's going to rain today, and the water will be very choppy. But why don't you come over anyway?"

"Okay. I have a few things I have to do to get the boys ready for school tomorrow, so why don't I pick up something to eat and I'll be over about one o'clock. Does that work for you?

"That works out fine."

"Where exactly is this boat of yours?"

"Actually, the dock is not far from where you live. It's at the Capitol Yacht Club."

"Oh, I know where that is. What's your dock number?"

"It's thirty-three and you can't miss it. It's right on the water."

"Oh, very funny. I'll see you at one o'clock."

"Looking forward to it. See you then." Click.

Hawk listened to the rumble of thunder and went to the port side deck to watch for Emma. Outside, he saw no lightning flashes, but the air itself seemed charged. Raindrops began to patter a few hesitant taps on the deck. Suddenly lightning cracked open the sky and clashes of thunder roared. The cool air rippled his blue nautical shirt.

With another hard crack, the sky broke releasing gushes of rain. He saw a car pull up at the end of the dock. Moments later he saw Emma dash from her car carrying a red sack. She made a run down the paved path toward the boat dock. With his head bent down Hawk ran up to her, grabbed the sack and wrapped his arms around her as they hopped up on the boat. In seconds, they were inside.

"Wow. I never thought I'd have to swim to get to your boat," Emma yelled.

Hawk laughed while he held her when she stepped on the gangway to get on the deck.

"Whew, what a storm," she said, kicking her shoes off.

Hawk chuckled when he saw her all wet and bedraggled. "Come on, I'll get us some towels."

"I think I'm beyond towels," she said as she pushed her wet hair off her face and as unobtrusively as possible, she plucked her tank top away from her breasts. "Maybe I should just stand outside and take a shower."

"You don't want a cold shower. Follow me. You're going to love this shower."

"Do you have something for me to wear? My clothes are soaked and splattered with mud."

"No problem." Let's go down below," he said as he descended the stairs. He went to the galley and placed the sack on the counter. "Come with me. The bathroom's right down this hall."

"I thought you said you had a boat? This isn't a boat. This is a house on the water. Wow, this is absolutely beautiful, Hawk. I had no idea it was so huge. I've never been on a yacht before. What kind of a yacht is this?"

"It's an Azimut, seventy footer."

"Oh, my God. That's huge."

"Yeah, it's a pretty large vessel."

"How can you afford this?" Emma laughed.

"Oh, now that's a really long story. I didn't actually pay for it."

"Another payment from one of your clients, it sounds like."

"Yeah, I guess you could say that."

"Wow, look at the size of this bathroom. Double sinks and all this beautiful woodwork. What kind of wood is this?

"The interior is all American Cherry woodwork and the cockpit and all the exterior woodwork are teak."

"I bet you've had a lot of company since you acquired this baby."

"Not really. I come here on the weekends to get away from everyone. I've only had it for about six months. There's a stack of towels over there on the shelf, and I'll fetch you a robe."

"Thanks, Hawk. I really appreciate it."

Hawk went into the master cabin and grabbed a blue ultra-terry robe for Emma. "Here, this ought to wrap you up pretty well."

"Ewe, this is so soft. Thank you. Boy, you've got it all here, Hawk. I don't think I'd ever leave this yacht."

"It is pretty nice, huh? Maybe we could take it out when the weather is nicer, and we'll take the boys with us. They'll love it."

"Oh, wouldn't they just have a blast," Emma exclaimed.

"Take your time, and I'll get the beers on ice," Hawk said as he closed the bathroom door.

A moment later, he heard the shower running, and he could hear Emma singing. *She never could hold a note,* he thought with a grimace. While she had many gifts, her voice was not one of them.

He set large white plates and silverware on the dining room table, dimmed the lights and put on some easy listening Dean Martin music all the while thinking, *this is a great start. She's already nude, and soon she'll be wearing my bathrobe. Not bad,* he thought as he released a deep breath with a look of satisfaction on his face.

Naw, its only dinner, he thought again. *It's just one evening under the same roof with the love of my life. But, I can't make a move. It's too soon. I've got to play it cool. I'm not going to lose her again.*

He heard the shower turn off. In a few minutes, he heard her footsteps coming up the stairs and suddenly she was standing there with her hair bundled up in a white towel and the blue robe skimming her knees. She smelled warm and soapy and intensely sexy. *Down boy, you don't want to lose her,* he thought.

"You don't mind eating with a Barefoot Contessa, do you?" she asked. "My shoes were soaked."

Hawk laughed. "Tell you what, I'll go barefoot too. We'll pretend we're at the beach. A beach without any sand."

"Why no sand?"

"I hate sand on my feet," he said as he slipped out of his deck shoes and went to the refrigerator. "Are you ready for a cold beer? Or, if you prefer, I make a mean hot buttered rum."

"That hot buttered rum sounds perfect," Emma said as she curled up on the massive leather sofa. This yacht is just too comfortable, Hawk... oh, you've got a piano on the boat?"

"Can't live without my Steinway."

"Who ever heard of a baby grand piano on a boat? That is too funny. Doesn't it move around when you're on the water?"

"No, it's sealed to the floor. It won't move."

"You've got it all. This is just too unbelievable. It's like a fairyland."

He quickly stirred up her rum drink, heated it in the microwave and before long, *ding, ding, ding.* He removed it from the micro, shook a can of whipped cream several times and squirted it over the top of the drink, "Ah, perfect," he said. He grabbed his bottle of beer from the refrigerator and handed Emma her hot buttered rum drink.

She held it in her hands. "Oh, this smells delicious. Thank you, Hawk."

Hawk sat down on the other end of the sofa, tilted his head back and took a big gulp of beer before saying, "You're very welcome."

"UMM, that's so good," Emma said after taking a sip of her drink. "Where did you learn to make this?"

"Actually, my Mom used to make them. A real New England drink to keep you warm during those blizzards."

"How is your Mom doing?"

"She's just fine and keeps busy with her Bridge buddies. She's traveling a lot now."

"Does she come down to see you?"

"Yes, as a matter of fact, she's planning to come down in May."

"It'll be great to see her. She's always fun and interesting to talk with and she's the best cook. Speaking of food, I'm suddenly hungry," Emma said as she removed the towel from her head.

He watched her damp hair fall into ringlets, all the while thinking about her being here with him—naked under that blue robe. She looked so relaxed in her bare feet. He observed her closely when she got up and walked into the galley to open the red insulated sack she had brought with her. He liked the way she walked, slowly and carelessly.

"So what are we having for dinner?" Hawk asked. "That sack was pretty heavy."

"It's a surprise. Come and see." He walked over to the counter and reached into the sack and grabbed two hot foil-wrapped packets and a carton of butter. He reached in again and grabbed a large plastic container that was very hot to the touch, so he carefully peeked in the container which revealed two steamy, whole red lobsters. "Holy cow," he yelled out. "I've never had whole lobsters before. What kind of power tools do we need to open these puppies up? A chain-saw or a sledgehammer, maybe?"

"Tell me you're kidding? You really don't know how to crack a lobster open?

"I'm sure I can figure it out. There's probably nothing to it."

Emma reached into the sack and pulled out two red shaped lobster claw nutcrackers. "Here you go. They say it's all in the technique."

"A nutcracker? Now you're making me very nervous. These are for the lobster, right?"

"Oh, God. You guys always think women are ready to crack open your family jewels."

"I'll have you know that *us* guys never know what women have on their minds."

Emma started giggling. "Wait. We need to prepare ourselves for this feast."

"What is it we need to do? Start praying that they don't come alive and eat us all up?"

She reached into the side pocket of the sack and pulled out two gigantic white plastic bibs with a red lobster printed on them.

"You have got to be kidding."

"No," she said as she circled around behind him and quickly slipped the bib around his shoulders and over his chest and tied it neatly in a bow behind his neck.

He felt her warm body next to his and he could smell the faint fragrance of the shampoo when her hair brushed his face. *Oh, maybe I better start drinking more if we're going to keep being friends without benefits.*

"Here, let me put your bib on," Hawk said as he reached around her, lifted her damp ringlets up, and tied the bib around her neck while he did his damnedest not to think about her being naked under the robe.

"Now we both look stupid," Hawk said as he lifted his bottle of beer and took a gulp.

"Okay, ready, set, go!" Emma yelled out. They both grabbed a lobster and burst out laughing when they dropped them on their plates. "I don't like their eyes looking at me," Emma squealed.

Hawk dropped the foiled baked potatoes and ears of corn on each dish. They unwrapped the foil and oodled the carton of melted butter all over them.

The rain pounded on the deck as they cracked shells to pop out chunks of lobster meat from the claws. They ate with butter dripping from their fingers and laughed hysterically when they tried to open bottles of beer. This was their own private picnic; both barefoot with buttery faces, slickery fingers, and non-existent table manners.

"Is this fun or what?" Emma asked. "Eating without silverware is a trip." I've got a confession. I've never eaten lobster this way before."

"I thought not, the way you squirmed when you picked up the lobster."

"So it was that obvious?" Emma said as she reached for her napkin to wipe her buttery mouth.

"I have to admit, this is a lot more fun than eating with a fork."

"Have you ever eaten lobster with your bare hands before?" Emma asked.

"No. I haven't. Believe it or not, this is the first time I've encountered one that wasn't already cracked open." He reached for a napkin to wipe the butter off his mouth and fingers before he grabbed the bottle of beer with his hands. He took a big gulp before setting it down on the table.

"So, now we've both done something together for the first time. I should add for the first time as adults," Emma said with a big smile.

"It's the first of many, I'm sure," Hawk said as he raised his beer bottle to clink her bottle.

"Right now, I'm surprising myself."

"How is that?"

"First, I had the delicious buttered rum drink, and after that, I had two bottles of beer. Let me tell you, I'm already feeling it. Is this your scheme to get me drunk so you can take advantage of me?"

With a wolfish grin, he said, "That scenario does have distinct possibilities which I'd definitely like to pursue, but not tonight."

"You know what? It feels so good to just relax and have fun with my best buddy."

"I've never seen you like this. You would never even take a sip of alcohol when we were in college."

"Yeah, I know, but I'm all grown up now."

"Yes, you are, Emma. Yes. You certainly are."

CHAPTER

FBI Uncovers Fraud

San Jose Mercury News
Tuesday, April 9,
2002

LOAN FRAUD SCHEME UNCOVERED IN SAN JOSE

San Jose, CA. - The FBI uncovered a $200 million dollar mortgage and loan fraud scheme in San Jose, California. An eight-count indictment charge also involved defendants, Aleksa Lakevich, Alex Igor, and Mariska Lubikin, who are known members of the Russian Organized Crime family. They have been charged with conspiracy to commit bank fraud and wire fraud in connection with the procurement of specific mortgage and home equity loans. The fraud also involved paying individuals who fit a certain financial profile to act as phony purchasers, or "straw buyers" of the target properties.

Twenty-two individuals were charged with fraud by participating in an illegal scheme to defraud banks and financial institutions. Court appearances are scheduled for April 15, 2002.

The charges arise from an investigation by a joint task force of the FBI, the San Jose Police Department, and the Immigrations and Customs Enforcement Agency (ICE). Chief of Police, David X. Miranda and Mayor Atticus Adams of San Jose praised the efforts of these departments.

# # #

CHAPTER

43

Monday, April 15, 2002, 8:15 am
San Jose Courthouse

"You're in a shitload of trouble, Wes. You could be facing some serious prison time," his lawyer said.

"I can't do prison," Wes responded.

"You should have thought about that when you absconded with tens of thousands of dollars of people's savings and hard-earned money.

Wes directed a dirty look toward him and then said, "I've got to go to the bathroom."

"Come right back here when you're through," the lawyer instructed.

He walked down the corridor toward the restroom. The door swished open, and a man exited. Inside the door, his nose was assaulted by an intense scent of pine. He walked over and stood in front of the sink. In the length-long mirror than hung over the row of empty basins, he stared at himself. "I can't do this," he said to himself. "I've got to get out of here."

Distraught, he splashed cold water on his face and neck with both hands, practically submerging his head in the basin. He raised his head, reached for a paper towel, and dried his face. He balled up the paper towel and flipped it in the trash can. He glanced at himself in the mirror and ran his hands through his hair. Standing right behind him he saw the face of a middle-aged man wearing glasses and carrying a hat and overcoat. The man looked steaming mad—face red, mouth tightened, fists clenched.

In a flash, before Wes could turn around, the man threw his overcoat and hat in the air and lunged at Wes, knocking him to the ground.

In a rage, the man yelled out, "You stole my life. I have no home, no marriage, no money, and no place to live." He punched Wes several times in the face before Wes grabbed the man's arm with brutal force and twisted it behind him.

"Yeow," the man screamed out in pain.

"Shut the fuck up!" Wes yelled out. He stood up and kicked the man on the back of his head several times causing his glasses to hang cockeyed on his head. He moaned a few times and then passed out.

Wes grabbed the glasses, picked up the man's hat and overcoat and quickly put them on. Once dressed, he walked out of the bathroom, rushed down the stairs and walked out the courthouse doors.

With a million dollar bail on him and ten minutes before his trial, Wes disappeared.

The U.S. Marshals were immediately alerted and the search for Wes Blair had begun. Unaware that Wes and Kate were connected in any way other than at work, the first stop they made was to the address listed on his employee paperwork. They went to the home he once lived in with his family. No one was there. They called Stanford University looking for his wife. She no longer worked there. They questioned the neighbors but no one knew where they were. They were told that they had not seen anyone at the house for several weeks. They were now left with no leads.

Wes drove two blocks away from Kate's condo and abandoned his car. He walked down the back alleyway to her home where she waited for him. Wes and Kate had planned everything in strict order for their getaway. They had new cell phones, new ID's, and new passports packed in their backpacks. They would be dressed like a couple of college students, backpacks and all.

With a growing disquiet, Wes moved from room to room as he peeked through the window blinds and curtains for someone on the street who may have looked suspicious. He was fully aware that if the heat were out there, he would never be able to spot them because they knew how to blend in and make themselves invisible. He knew he had every reason to feel paranoid.

He suddenly saw a Jeep slow down half a block away. The red brake lights lit up as it pulled over to the curb. He waited for someone to emerge, but no one did. Perhaps they're listening to the radio or calling on their cell phone. Feeling jittery, he walked in circles as he tried to formulate some explanation for them to pull up to the curb and not get out of the car.

Again, he returned to the window lifting the slat in the window blind to watch. Several minutes later, he noticed the Jeep's brake lights come on. He watched as it pulled away from the curb. He observed the car as it continued down to the end of the street and vanished around the corner.

Traffic flowed as usual with no suspicious-looking vehicles parked at the curb. No pedestrians stood around with a newspaper in their hands, and there were no utility trucks or utility men on the street. Wes struggled with a twitchy paranoia—he may not have seen anyone, but he knew they were out there somewhere. Sure as Little Red Riding Hood met the big bad wolf, he knew he was under surveillance. He let the blinds go and nervously bit at his lip. His mind was working overtime planning his every move. He had plans A, B, and C embedded in his brain. He must be prepared for every anomaly. He paced in circles, going over every move, over and over again.

Again, he parted the blinds with his fingers and watched from the living room window for several minutes. No one looked out of the ordinary. Their carefully prepared plan was in place. He went into the bedroom to let Kate know that they had to leave and leave very soon before whoever was out there, decided to come through the front door. Their new car was parked a block away, and the suitcases were already loaded in the trunk. They would put on their disguises and leave separately by the back alley. If they walked slowly and didn't draw any attention to themselves, they would have a quick, clean getaway.

Kate was already dressed, and she quickly put on her dark brown long curly wig and sunglasses. Dressed in skinny jeans with a black shirt, white socks, and tennis shoes she looked like a typical student when she left through the rear door and walked down the back alley toward the car. Wes kept a watch on her until she was out of sight.

His cell phone rang. His heart jumped. He let the slat in the window blind drop back into place and answered the phone. "Hello?"

"It's just me. Everything is clear. I didn't see anything or anyone that looked suspicious. No one was watching me. I'm in the car waiting for you."

"Okay, I'm going to leave now." He closed the phone and hooked it on his belt before he hurried across the room to put on his brown hairpiece. He put a navy blue baseball cap over his now brown hair and donned his sunglasses. He was dressed in jeans, tennis shoes, and a light black jacket with a gray backpack filled with enough money to last them until they located the boys and left the states.

The bulk of their money was wired to the Cook Islands Trust, which was known to offer the strongest asset protection. When a court demands payment, the trust company is not obligated to comply with the court order. The thirty-plus-year-old trust company keeps all your assets out of harm's way, so to speak. A properly structured Cook Islands trust can protect client's assets from any legal challenge.

Adrenaline rushing, heart beating rapidly, as the high caffeine 5150 Juice shot throughout his body, he quietly closed the door and headed down the alley toward Kate. He had to be calm, though he was a nervous wreck, and he had to walk like a student, not in any hurry to get anywhere. Placing his hands in the pockets of his jacket, he walked slowly down the alley looking like an average kid with seemingly no purpose in mind.

He jumped when he heard a gravel noise, like someone close behind him. In his peripheral vision, he saw a cyclist dressed in goofy tight royal blue shorts and shirt with a white helmet whip past him, causing him to jump out of the way. "Watch where you're going," he yelled out. The cyclist raised his arm and gave him the finger. He saw no one else in the alley as he continued to walk toward the car.

Kate sat patiently on the passenger side of the beige Honda sedan. Wes slid his backpack off and handed it to Kate as he slipped inside on the driver's side. Kate had already placed the keys in the ignition and Wes immediately started the engine, gently stepped on the accelerator and pulled into traffic headed east to Las Vegas.

"We're done here, Kate. We've got all the means to disappear and never be found—fake ID's, offshore bank accounts, and new passports, new car, new life, new everything. We're on our way to freedom." He leaned toward her to wrap his arm around her shoulders and gave her a hug. "Our plan is now in operation."

"Anyone see you?" Kate asked.

"Only some guy on a bike who almost broadsided me."

CHAPTER

44

The alarm buzzed at six-thirty. Emma turned the buzzer off, flung back the covers, walked to the bathroom, used the toilet and jumped in the shower while she sang with her usual off-note fashion. She felt ecstatic and totally excited though she didn't know if she was more excited for her boys who were about to start school or her visit to Hawk's office to decide if she wanted to work with him.

She dried her hair, put on a pair of dress jeans, a white blouse, and a tan leather vest. She even wore cowboy boots. Her psychiatrist had told her to dress differently to fit the new person that she's become, and that's exactly what she was doing. She is no longer Emma Blair. Hello, Emma Ross.

She had to get the boys ready by seven-thirty. Uncle Ross made sure they bathed last night so they just needed to get dressed in the clothes she laid out for them. Ross insisted that he take them to school on their first day, even though the chauffeur service drove all the children who lived in the apartment building to school. He watched over the boys like the concerned father in him.

They met their teacher and several students last week when she enrolled them. The teacher welcomed them into her classroom and introduced them to the other children. They were very excited about going to school.

As soon as she opened her bedroom door, the smell of brewing coffee permeated the air. She followed the scent toward the kitchen. "You've already started breakfast?" she said as she entered the kitchen. The boys were chomping on pancakes and eggs.

"Good morning, boys," she said as she rumpled both their heads and gave them a kiss."

"We beat you, Mommy," Adam said.

"Yes, you certainly did. Did you both sleep well last night?"

"Yes, Mommy," Lucas said.

"Are you excited about school?"

"We're going to meet new friends and they can come over and play with us," Lucas said.

"That would be nice. The school you're going to is the same type of school you went to in California. Both of you should fit right in."

"They're both excited, Em," Uncle Ross said. "I didn't think they'd ever fall asleep last night. What time did you get in?"

"Oh, it was about eleven o'clock. The rain just wouldn't let up. It looks pretty nice this morning. I love the air after it rains."

"It's going to be a nice sunny day today," Ross said.

"What did you boys do at Ellie's home? You couldn't go outside to play because of the rain."

"Oh, we had so much fun. We played games, watched movies, ate hot dogs and French fries and Ellie made us a carrot cake. It was so good," Lucas said. "She has a dog, Mommy. Her name is Violet."

"What kind of dog is it?" Emma asked.

"I don't know. She's cute and small," Lucas answered.

"She took a nap with me," Adam said.

"Can we get a dog, Mommy?" Lucas asked.

"Oh, I have to think about that. What will the dog do all day long all alone?"

"We'll get two dogs. One for Adam, and one for me and then they won't be alone."

Emma's eyebrows shot up. "Two dogs? We'll wait a while and talk about it later, okay?" Emma said as she glanced in Ross' direction. "I see you laughing under your breath."

She rounded the kitchen counter and grabbed a cup of coffee. Ross just sat there and ate his eggs and chuckled "It's only just beginning, darlin'."

"Yes, I know it's only just beginning."

"Not to change the subject, what did you and Hawk do yesterday? You couldn't take the boat out because of the weather."

"We had the best time eating whole lobsters in the shell. Neither of us had ever had lobster that way. It was pretty messy."

"Did you play any games?" Ross asked while he cast his eyes down at his plate. She quickly noticed the mischief at the corner of her uncle's mouth as he tried to keep a straight face.

"No, we didn't play *any* games, but thanks so much for asking."

"Just wondering. That's all."

"Have you seen Hawk's boat yet?" Emma inquired.

"No, I haven't. What's it like?"

"It's not exactly a boat. It's a seventy-foot yacht, is what it is."

"Are you kidding me? Seventy feet! Wow, how does he manage that financially?"

"I asked him the same question. All he told me was that he didn't actually pay for it."

Ross laughed out loudly. "That guy has a way of accumulating things that no one else can afford to even think about. You gotta love his style."

"That's all you have to say about it?"

"What do you want me to say? He's the only person I know who can acquire expensive items and never have to pay a cent for them. The guy is a genius."

After she had thought about it for several moments, she said, "Yes, I guess you could say that."

"What time are you leaving for work?" Ross asked.

"We're starting at eight. I'm going to walk over to the boy's school during lunch and check on the two of them. It's not far from Hawk's office."

"You think Hawk is gonna give you a lunch break? Ha ha ha ha ha."

"Oh, you're real funny this morning, aren't you?"

"I'd say you were the funny one. You're the one making me laugh."

"So you don't think he'll give me a lunch break?"

"I guess you don't know the *businessman* side of Hawk. He's not known to be very lenient."

"Lenient? Is that what you call it? I call it against the law to not give someone a break."

"Oh, boy, you two are going to have a lot of fun at work today! Ha!"

Emma gave him a scowled look.

"Come on boys, it's time to get your jackets on. Don't want to be late on your first day of school," Ross said.

"Come on, Adam, let's get our jackets," Lucas said.

"Okay, I'm coming."

"Here, let me help you, sweetie," Emma said as she held out the sleeves for Adam to slip in his arms. I'm going to come over to the school and see you after your lunchtime. I'll watch you on the playground, okay?"

"We'll look for you Mommy," Lucas said as he gave his mother a kiss and a hug.

"Come and kiss Mommy goodbye, Adam." She hoisted him up in her arms and kissed the top of his head and then kissed both his cheeks before she set him back down on the floor.

"I love you, Mommy," Adam said.

"I love you too, Adam. Have fun in school."

"Bye, Mommy," they both squealed as they walked out the door.

"I'll see you this evening, sweetie," Uncle Ross said. "That's if Hawk gives you the evening off." Ha!"

Emma laughed now as she closed the door, shaking her head. The phone rang.

She ran to the kitchen to answer it. "Hello?"

"Hi, Emma. Would you like me to come by and pick you up? I'm going right past your apartment."

"Sure, that'll be fine, Hawk. When will you be here?"

"In about ten minutes. Are you ready?"

"Yes, I'm ready. I'll meet you downstairs at the entrance."

"Okay. See you in ten."

She ran to her bedroom to put a little makeup on her face, grabbed her purse and went to the kitchen to put the breakfast plates in the dishwasher. She wiped the counter down and swept the floor where the boys sat. She could always tell where they had been by the crumbs they left behind.

Emma waited at the entrance for a few minutes before Hawk pulled up to the curb. She was feeling euphoric and at the same time, she felt uneasy. With her self-esteem at an all-time low and her emotions in a confused state, she wondered if her emotions would prevent her from staying focused on any work that Hawk wanted her to do. She would soon find out.

Her life had changed and she had to change with it. She's now free to follow her talent and begin to focus on something that interested her deeply. She would be using her studies on criminal intelligence to put murderers behind bars by way of profiling and forensic evidence.

Hawk pulled up to the curb in his black Jag XK8 and Jack, the doorman, immediately ran to open the car door for Emma.

"Thank you, Paul."

"My pleasure, Ms.Ross."

"Hi, Hawk."

"Good morning, Ms. Emma. How are you this morning?"

"Just fine. I'm just so excited that the boys are starting school. Uncle Ross insisted on taking them on their first day."

"He's very good with your boys, and they like him."

"Yes, they certainly do. It's good that they have a family now," Emma said with a sad tone.

"What's the matter, Em? You sound sad."

"Everything is moving forward so fast and there are times my mind gets stuck in the past. How do I erase the past and get on with my life?"

"Emma, my dearest, it will take time," Hawk said as he took her hand in his. "When you feel the unnerving breath of the past surrounding you, stop for a second to reflect and you'll begin to realize that the memories of the past, are just that, the past. They don't matter anymore. Your future is here and now. Every morning when you wake up, a new future is in front of you. You owe it to yourself and to your boys to get on with your life."

Emma squeezed Hawk's hand, turned to him and said, "You are so good for me. I want you to know that your friendship and advice is sincerely appreciated. In my state of mind, I need you to put me straight." Emma leaned toward Hawk and kissed him on the cheek.

They drove quietly for a few moments, before Emma said, "The boys are not too far from your office, and I was hoping to walk down to see them after their lunch break. I enjoy watching them play in the school-yard."

"I'll walk down with you. We'll stop for lunch after we see them. What time is their playtime?"

"They have lunch at eleven forty-five and then they play until twelve forty-five."

"Good. Perhaps Theo will come with along with us."

"He's your assistant, right?"

"Yes, you'll meet him this morning. I told him all about you and he's very anxious to meet you."

"So, tell me about Theo."

"You'll love him. He's thirty-two years old, very Greek, not married and he's a computer nerd, a health nut, and he's got an IQ off the charts, just like you. You two will get along great."

"Who did you snatch him away from?"

"NCIS. He worked there for seven years, got a lot of experience and then he wanted a change. I was able to help him make that change happen."

"You sure have a way with people, Hawk. You're a good person."

"Here we are," he said as he zipped his car into the underground parking area. "Let's go see what Theo is up to." He ran around the other side of the car to open the door for Emma.

It was a quick ride up to the fourth floor in the elevator and once they exited, they stood in front of the office door.

Unexpectedly, Theo opened the door before Hawk. "Good morning, Majordomo." His eyes went immediately to Emma. "Ah, this is the beautiful and intelligent Emma. Come in, come in, we need to talk."

His voice was deep and the tone pleasant when he greeted her. He wasn't tall, but he didn't need height to add to the impression he made with his gregarious personality and charm. He was dressed in a one-button black lambskin leather blazer with army green cargo pants and Gore-Tex boots. He looked freshly scrubbed and shaved and definitely possessed the basic essentials to make a good first impression. He held out his arm and she wrapped her arm around his as he led her into the office. When he let go of her arm, he held her hand, raised it to his lips and kissed it.

"Aren't you the charming one? I didn't think they made men like you anymore," she said as she gave Hawk a sideways glance.

Their eyes connected, but only for a millisecond before he slipped his tan jacket on the back of his chair and said, "Oh, I guess I forgot to tell you. Theo's a real charmer—a real ladies' man."

"Hawk never mentioned how good-looking you were," she said to Theo.

"Did he forget to tell you that?"

"Yes, he did. It's nice to meet you, Theo."

"Did he mention to you that I was a bit shorter than him?"

"No, he didn't mention anything about your height."

"Just so you're aware, we have a constant feud between us. Being tall, dark, and handsome is such an unearned physical advantage; it's no more than a mere payoff from an accident of birth."

Emma laughed. "Being tall has nothing to do with character, Theo. You're very charming and very handsome."

"Thank you, Miss Emma. I can see we're going to become wonderful friends. You and I are the same height, no?"

"I'm five-foot-nine inches tall in my bare feet. How tall are you, Theo?"

"I'm five-foot-nine inches tall. Perfect!" Theo proudly stated.

"Come into our laboratory, it's the epitome of technical perfection. We're going to do some magical wizardry in this lab, you and I. Wonderful things will happen here."

"Oh, I see you have one of the scribbling quotes from college over the door to the lab," Emma said as she looked at the sign.

"Yes, I do," Hawk interjected. I always liked that quote: *Every Contact Leaves a Trace* by Edmond Locard. That pretty well depicts what we do around here."

"Come, let's explore," Theo insisted. He pulled Emma into the lab.

CHAPTER

45

Partners in Crime

Wes continuously checked the speedometer, making sure it wasn't even one mile over the speed limit. As anxious as they were to get far away, they couldn't risk being stopped. For most of the drive in California, they stuck to side roads, taking wide detours to avoid the major highways where Kate expected the police to be looking for them, if in fact they were looking for them. They stopped only once at an out of the way gas station to fill up with gas, grab some chips, a couple of sodas, use the bathroom, and immediately left the area.

Every now and then, his gaze would shift from the road ahead to the rearview mirror. He was convinced that every car on the Interstate was a police cruiser, and any minute now he was sure he'd see the sudden flicker of red and blue lights start up on the roof of a distant vehicle.

After the first few hours on the road, the steady, grinding tension was making Wes an irritable bundle of nerves, in spite of the fact that their escape from California had gone almost without a hitch. Kate gave him a pain killer to try to relax him so he would stop panicking every time he saw a police cruiser.

His throat was parched, and he had finished the last of the sodas they bought at the rest stop more than an hour ago. He didn't dare make another stop. Not yet. Not until he had crossed the border to Nevada. Even then, it might not be safe. In fact, he knew in his mind that he might never be safe again.

Kate listened intensely to various talk radio stations on AM but, at least so far, she hadn't heard anything about authorities on the lookout for a woman or a man who had skipped bail and were wanted by the FBI.

Once out of California, the driving on the flat, straight road was easy and mindless, so Wes allowed himself some thinking time. As the road continued to unroll in front of him, he settled back in his seat wondering if he was going to have to face the rest of his life like this; always looking over his shoulder and up ahead.

With Kate's insistence that they not stop in Las Vegas, Wes drove until they found themselves twenty-two miles east of Las Vegas at the quaint Boulder Dam Hotel in the historic district of clean, green Boulder City, as the huge sign indicated.

Kate pulled her sunglasses down on her nose and squinted from beneath the brim of her hat as she gazed at the outline of this magnificent hotel in the middle of what once was a desert. It seemed hardly feasible that someone could successfully turn this desert into an elegance of yesteryear. It was somewhat of an oasis in the desert.

Wes pulled up to the curb in front of the hotel and the doorman opened the car door for Kate. Wes got out of the car, stretched, and surveyed the area. The doorman immediately walked toward the hotel and held open the large, ornately designed door for them.

Steps sounded on the marble floor, and a moment later, a woman had crossed the foyer to greet them. "Would you care for a glass of freshly made lemonade?" she asked.

"Yes, that would be wonderful," Kate replied.

She immediately filled two large crystal glasses and handed each of them a drink. "Thank you. Your hotel is certainly a refuge from the hustle and bustle of Las Vegas."

"Yes, many people enjoy being away from all the glitter of Las Vegas."

"We'd like a room for the night," Wes said impatiently after he gulped down his drink.

"Certainly. Come right this way, and I'll be happy to assist you." She quickly moved behind the marble counter. "Would you care for a suite? We currently have one available."

"Kate?" Wes asked as he turned to look at her.

"Yes, by all means. A suite would be perfect. Thank you," Kate responded before taking a sip of lemonade.

"Do you have a restaurant?" Wes asked.

"Yes, we have a wonderful on-site restaurant, Mariano's. You'll enjoy his creations."

They checked in with their new ID's and paid cash for the evening. Wes went outside, followed by the bellboy with the luggage cart. He unlocked the trunk and the bellboy retrieved their luggage and arranged it neatly on the cart.

"Right this way, sir," the bellboy instructed.

They followed him down the corridor to their suite. When the door swung open, they both stood, wide-eyed, with a look of astonishment on their faces. One would never have thought that an old historic hotel would have such extravagant rooms.

A marble foyer, an enormous living area with hardwood floors and an Oriental rug. The décor was all beige and white and a dining table overlooked an enclosed patio. The bedroom had a king-size sleigh bed upholstered in white damask with custom duck down bedding. The adjoining bathroom had a beautiful marble garden tub.

"Here you go," Wes said as he handed the bellboy a Jackson and then asked, "Would you please make reservations for two in your restaurant for dinner at six o'clock?"

"Certainly, sir. I'll be happy to take care of that for you. Thank you, sir." He turned quickly to exit the room.

"This is the kind of life we'll be living from now on," Wes said, as he embraced Kate.

"This is a beautiful suite," Kate said as she gave Wes a quick kiss. "It's kind of shocking to find such an elegant room in this old town. How does it feel to leave California for good?"

"It feels fantastic. Let's change clothes and get ready for dinner. I'm starving. We've got thirty minutes to get ready. I'm going to jump in the shower," Wes said.

"Okay, I'll unpack our clothes for tonight and tomorrow. What time are we going to leave in the morning?"

"Let's take our time. We need to slow down and enjoy ourselves. We'll leave after we have our breakfast," Wes said as he headed for the shower.

"Sounds good to me."

CHAPTER

46

Kate was awakened by the shrill ringing of a telephone. She fought to stay asleep, but the ringing wouldn't stop. She squinted at the luminous numbers on the bedside clock. Five-twenty-three... in the morning. "Who—?"

She sat up groggily and groped for the phone. "H'lo?" Her voice a hoarse mumble.

"Rob Parker?"

"I beg your pardon? Who is this?" Silence on the phone. Suddenly, panic brought her wide awake. She held the dead phone to her ear for several seconds before she hung up. She reached behind to rouse Wes, but his side of the bed was empty. She switched on the lamp. He hadn't even been to bed. If the early telephone call weren't enough to wake her up, then Wes' unexplained absence certainly was. She threw off the covers, got out of bed and reached for her robe. She searched the living room—Wes wasn't there.

She heard the door open and seconds later he emerged from the hallway and strolled into the darkened living room carrying his shoes. Kate flipped on the lights. Rage flashed through her. "Where in the hell have you been all night?" She could already tell by his bloodshot eyes and his rumpled hair that he'd been up all night.

Her biting tone stopped him dead in his tracks. He arched an eyebrow in silent disapproval of the third degree she was about to lash at him. "I decided to go out gambling."

"And exactly *where* did you go gambling?"

"I went to Las Vegas."

"You did what? Are you a complete idiot? Did I not tell you that going to Las Vegas would be a bad idea? We're on the run, for crissake. Both the cops and the FBI are after us. Do you not understand that? Do you *want* to go to prison?"

"No one spotted me. They probably haven't even disseminated the information about us yet. We only ran yesterday. It'll take weeks for the FBI to get postings sent around the country."

"You're going to screw this whole thing up. I can feel it now," she shouted. "Our carefully thought out plan is going down the tubes, thanks to you."

"Nothing's going to go wrong. We're leaving today anyway."

"It can't be soon enough," Kate mumbled. "I just got woken by a phone call. It was a wrong number. How can a hotel operator connect to the wrong room? No one knows we're here, so there should be no phone calls. From now on, everywhere we stay, we will be disconnecting the damn phone."

Blah, Blah, Blah. Why can't I please anyone? Wes wondered. *No matter what I do, it's always wrong. I just can't do anything right for women. They all think they're so damn smart.*

He tried to please his parents so they would be proud of him. Even when he excelled, they weren't proud of him. His father would make scathing remarks cutting him down. Once when he was twelve, he made the mistake of raising his hand to his father. Before he could blink, he was sprawled out on the floor with his father standing over him—his mother watching. God, how he hated them both.

Kate is beginning to get on my nerves with all this worrying. She never even asked me if I won any money.

CHAPTER

47

"I don't want to alarm you, Emma," Ross said.

"What happened?" a wide-eyed Emma asked.

"I just heard that both Wes and his girlfriend, Kate Lee, are now fugitives from the law.

"What? No, I don't believe it."

"Well, believe it. They're both wanted in California for unlawful flight to avoid prosecution. They were due in front of a judge yesterday and they decided to make a run for it. A federal arrest warrant for failure to appear was issued for each of them and now the FBI is also on the hunt for them."

"What did they do to have the FBI looking for them?" Emma asked.

"Well, my dear, it seems that they were involved with the Russian Mob, of all people, and were caught in a massive two hundred million dollar loan fraud business. A company called Capital Mortgage and Loan in San Jose. Isn't that where Wes worked?"

"Oh, my God," she said, horrified. "So that's what they were up to, with those fake passports and credit cards. They're planning on leaving the country."

"It gets better. Seems Wes was at the courthouse with his lawyer waiting for a preliminary hearing when he decided to go to the bathroom. One of the men he played his mortgage fraud game on followed him in there and attacked him. Wes ended up beating the crap out of the guy and left him lying on the floor unconscious. Wes grabbed the guy's jacket, hat and glasses, put them on and disappeared down the courtroom steps with a million dollar bail on his head. He managed to skip out of the courtroom fifteen minutes before his trial. They searched everywhere but never found him. He's gone. That's why the FBI is after him now."

"So where are they now?"

"Their whereabouts are currently unknown, but I'm sure they'll be caught within a few days. There are only a small percentage of fugitives who succeed in hiding simply because, like humans, they'll make mistakes and there's always someone who will pick up on those mistakes. However, those who do not get caught, well... let's just say they're either very lucky, smart, or just really good at hiding and escaping from the law. I don't know much about his girlfriend, but I know Wes doesn't fall into any of those categories. With his wild temperament, he *will* make a mistake."

"I hope he's not coming to look for the boys or me," Emma said with a worried look on her face.

"With that much money, and the Russian's after their asses, they've probably already left the country. And, don't forget, they have the FBI after them too. I hope it's the Russians who find them. Ha!"

"I hope you're right," Emma said softly. "But, he wants the boys and he usually gets what he wants."

"Now, Emma, don't start thinking those thoughts. If he does come to D.C. to look for you, he won't find you. You've changed your name and there's no reason for him to come here looking for you," he assured her. "Your divorce will be final in another couple of months, and that will be that."

"I only hope that's true. I freak out whenever I hear his name."

"Okay, worst case, he knows you're here. There is no way he's going to get into this building. One of the reasons I picked this apartment for you and the boys to live in is because it has such high security. There are a lot of high-ranking government officials living here and they all demand tight security. He still doesn't know that you have money, so why would he even come here looking for you?"

"I guess you're right," she said softly. "If you could have seen his face when he told me he was going to kill me, you would change your mind. He never makes idle threats. That I know for a fact. He wants the boys and one way or another he always manages to get what he wants."

"Well, if you really think he's coming here, I can get a private detective to watch over you and the boys. Would you like that? I don't want you all worried and tied up in knots."

"Let's wait a while and see what the authorities find out. If you hear that he's in the area, yes, I would feel better if someone were here with us, especially when we go out somewhere."

"You'll be okay at the office with Hawk around. He won't let anyone near you. Let him know Wes may be in the area and show him a picture of him. He ain't named Hawk for nothing."

"I'll let him know."

"From now on I'll be getting all the updates on Wes' whereabouts so when anything turns up, I'll be the first to know about it. I've got a picture of him, so I'll also put out a local BOLO to my guys and see what turns up from that. I'll give the head of security for the building a copy of his picture and alert them that he may try and get into the building. They'll be on the lookout too. He'll get

caught if he comes near this building. The security guys
are all former Marines and are top notch."

CHAPTER

48

Unaware of where Ross lived, Wes did remember that he spent time at Mercy Hospital on Michigan Avenue, visiting his many Marine friends. With any luck, he might find out where he worked from someone who worked in the hospital.

They parked the car and walked through the revolving doors. A woman who sat behind a circular reception desk asked, "May I help you?"

"Ah, yes. Where is the cafeteria?" Wes asked.

"Just follow the red line on the floor," she said, "and you'll run right into it."

"Thank you," Kate said with a smile.

As they walked down the corridor, Wes heard someone behind them. With a reflex now ingrained into his behavior, he turned to look— it was two nurses with rubber-soled shoes that squeaked on the glossy vinyl floor.

The aroma of coffee, bacon, and toast mingled in the air as they came to the end of the red line. Wes wasted no time and immediately scanned the cafeteria to determine what would be the most advantageous place to sit down.

There were about forty tables scattered throughout the cafeteria. Several groups of nurses were huddled at three of the tables, and several other people sat alone at separate tables. A few doctors were in deep conversation at one of the tables by the window.

A long counter with about fifteen red leather bar stools lined the far wall. Two people were sitting at the counter and three women dressed in pink candy-striped aprons were behind the counter.

The hostess approached them and asked, "Are there just two of you?"

"Yes, and I think we'll sit at the counter if that's all right," Wes asked. He thought his chances of striking up a conversation with one of the volunteer waitresses would give him the information he was looking for.

"That'll be fine, just take any seat at the counter."

They walked over to the long gold-flecked gray counter and slid onto the red vinyl stools at the end, which had already been set with silverware, napkins, and a menu. They both casually glanced at the plastic covered breakfast menu for a few moments.

The waitress, a tall, dark-haired woman, probably in her sixties, with a big smile, had just served coffee to the couple four seats down from Kate. She walked over to them and cheerfully, said, "Good Morning, My name is Betty. Can you believe spring is here already?"

It immediately gave Wes the opening he wanted and he turned on the charm. "This is my favorite time of year. We're from Arizona so it's a bit colder here in Chicago."

"Well, how about some nice hot coffee to warm you up?"

"Sure, we'll each have coffee, thank you," Wes said.

She immediately reached under the counter and placed a coffee mug in front of each of them and turned to grab the coffee pot from the warmer and poured the coffee. "Here's some cream," she said as she reached under the counter and placed a small bowl of various creamers between them.

"Have you decided what you want or do you need more time?" she asked as she pulled out a small notepad from her pocket."

"Oh, I think we've decided. Kate, what would you like?"

"I'll have the French toast, please."

"Okay, I'll bring jam and syrup for you. And, for you, sir?"

"I'll have bacon and scrambled eggs with hash browns and wheat toast," Wes said.

"Okay, I'll be back shortly with your orders."

Wanting to strike up a conversation with the waitress, Wes asked before she turned to place the orders, "What are all those pins on your apron?"

"Oh, these," she said with a huge smile and proudly touched them with her hand. "These are pins for every year that I've been a volunteer at the hospital. I will be getting my eleven-year pin at the end of this month."

Acting totally impressed, Wes responded, "So you've been here for eleven years!"

"That's a pretty long time," Kate added.

"I'd be lost if I didn't come to the hospital three or four times a week. I only work the breakfast crowd, so I'm only here about three hours a day. My husband passed away twelve years ago, and my three kids are married and don't live in this area anymore so I keep myself busy being around people here in the hospital. Otherwise, what would I do?"

"Yes, it's good to keep busy. I guess it must be pretty fulfilling," Kate said as she rearranged her napkin to form a neat square. "You must get to meet a lot of interesting people."

"I should say so," Betty replied. "Are you visiting a patient here at the hospital or are you waiting for someone?"

"No, we're actually trying to find a friend of ours. He used to come to this hospital to visit his veteran friends," Wes said as he pulled out a picture of Ross from his suit pocket.

"Oh, that's Mr. Griffin," she exclaimed. Mr. Ross Griffin. He used to come in here all the time. I sure do miss having him around. Is that the man you're looking for?"

"Oh, so you recognize this man?" Wes asked as he pointed his finger at the picture.

"Oh, I should say so. He came in every morning at seven sharp for breakfast and sat right here at the counter."

"Does he still come here?" Kate inquired.

"No, No. He doesn't work in Chicago anymore. He moved to Washington, D.C. about a year ago. He got himself a job at some big security company. He's some bigwig there, some vice president or something like that. Sure do miss seeing him around here. He always came to see his friends and a couple times a year, he would bring in some celebrity to visit with the children. Oh, Mr. Griffin was something special. Just about everyone here in this hospital knows Mr. Ross Griffin."

And with that said, she pivoted away from the counter and slipped down the aisle to place their order.

"Looks like my wife didn't tell me what her uncle was up to. Her and her damn secrets; I always wondered how many secrets she was keeping from me. She once told me that hearts were created as safes for keeping secrets and intelligence was the lock. She never seemed to totally open up to anyone. I guess that's why she didn't have a lot of friends. You could feel there was a lot more to her than what she let you believe."

"She never told you her uncle moved to D.C.?" Kate asked.

"No, she rarely ever said anything to me about her uncle. It's as if his life was a secret. She was always trying to protect him. I never understood it. So he's some big shot now at a security company."

"Did you ever meet her uncle?"

"Yeah, he came out every now and then. He's just some old guy. Actually, he gave me the creeps. I never liked him, and he didn't like me. Guess you could say we both had a mutual dislike for one another."

"What kind of a secret would it be to know that he moved? That's pretty strange."

"I've been telling you all along she was strange. They're both strange. Let them keep their secrets. Now that we know he's some big shot in D.C., he won't be too hard to find, will he? He's probably with some hire-a-cop security company. Those so-called security guards are like cheap home alarms—useless. They're all just a bunch of old croakers depriving a village somewhere of an idiot. Not too bright in the head department and uneducated."

Now that he had the info he needed and in a hurry to get back on the road, Wes' gesture to the waitress changed from a polite beckon to one of mimicking writing the check so they could get out of there.

CHAPTER

49

Emma grabbed a spoon to taste the spaghetti sauce that simmered in a large pot on the front burner. "Ah, perfect," she said as she gave it a stir and gently dropped in the meatballs she had baked in the oven earlier. Satisfied, she put the cover on the pot and lowered the burner down to a simmer. She filled a large stockpot full of water and put it on the burner after she added salt and olive oil to it.

She made herself a cup of hot tea and carried it to the end table next to her recliner. She was quick to notice the gray clouds that filled the sky as she sat in her recliner. "It's looking mighty gloomy out there," she announced.

"Mommy, look at the picture I just colored. The sun is shining in my picture."

"That's very nice, Adam," she replied. "What are you coloring over there, Lucas?"

"I'm coloring a herd of horses. They sure are big. I'm coloring them all in different colors, and I'm going to name them all."

"What will you name them?" Adam asked.

"I don't know. I have to wait till they're all colored," Lucas replied.

Two minutes later, the doorbell rang. "I'll get it," Lucas said, as he quickly ran for the door. Emma jumped up to follow right behind Lucas. "Mommy, there's a big man…"

"Hi, Hawk, come on in," Emma said with a smile. "Come in and meet the boys. Lucas, this is my friend Hawk that I was telling you about."

"I thought a hawk was a bird," Lucas said as he looked up at Hawk.

"Well, a hawk is a bird, a huge bird. My parents named me after the bird," Hawk said.

"I don't know anyone with that name," Adam said sheepishly.

"Yeah, there's not too many of us around," Hawk responded. "How old are you, Lucas?"

"I'm almost four and a half. My birthday is November seventeenth. I'm going to be five," he said with five fingers held up, "and after that I start my age on my other hand."

"Hey, I'm Adam," a high-pitched squeaky voice said as he pushed Lucas aside.

"Adam doesn't want to be left out of any conversation," Emma laughed.

"Wow, you're a pretty big boy. How old are you, Adam? You look like your four and a half too."

"No. I'm only three and a half. My birthday is September twelfth and that's when I'll be four."

"It's certainly nice to meet you guys."

"Nice to meet you too, Hawk," Lucas said as he turned to run back to his coloring.

"You're tall," Adam said as he stared at him.

"Yes, I am. Come here. I'll show you how it feels to be as tall as I am." Hawk picked him up and put him over his shoulders. "There, do you like it up there?"

"This is fun. You can see everything from up here. Just like a real hawk."

Emma and Hawk laughed as Adam dropped gently down to the floor in Hawk's arms.

"Let me see from up there too," Lucas squealed as he ran toward Hawk.

"Okay, here you go," Hawk said, lifting him high on his shoulders in a piggyback fashion.

"I want to be tall," Lucas cried out. Hawk got down on all fours to let Lucas climb off.

"He's real strong, Mommy," Lucas said as he ran off to join Adam in his coloring.

"Yes, he's strong, sweetie."

"You've got some great looking kids, Emma. I imagine they keep you pretty busy."

"Yes, they do. They're a lot of fun."

"This is a great looking apartment, Em," Hawk said as he scanned the area. "Very nice indeed."

"I love it here. It was a model home so it came completely furnished. How nice is that?"

"It suits you perfectly," Hawk replied as he stared at Emma. She was wearing an apron, of all things. This is a role he had never visualized her playing—an ordinary housewife. This was not *his* Emma.

His Emma? He took a deep breath as the ramifications of that thought exploded in his head. Since when had he been thinking of her as *his*? Since... realistically? *Forever*, he suddenly realized. He's wanted her for years. He's loved her for years. Denying it would be impossible. He couldn't take the risk of losing her again by telling her or he'd be out the door before the sentence left his lips.

"What?" You're looking at me like you've never seen me before."

"Well, to be perfectly honest, I have never seen *this* Emma before. A housewife wearing an apron? I never visualized you in this role."

They both stood speechless until Hawk finally sputtered, "I've got a lot of catching up to do, don't I?"

"I guess you do. I do housework, make lunches for the boys, and cook. It's what I am now, a mom, and I enjoy being a mom every day."

"Motherhood most definitely agrees with you," Hawk replied. "You're beautiful. I just never pictured you in this role. You've become a woman. I only know the brilliant, fun-loving spirit of the old Emma when you were a young girl. This is more exciting than I could ever have imagined—the new Emma with her family. I couldn't ask for anything more unique."

"Now that I have introduced the new Emma to you, may I offer you some Prosecco?"

"What's Prosecco?" Hawk inquired with a big grin.

"It's a Brut Sparkling Wine. I like it better than Champagne."

"That sounds good. I'll try it. Whatever you're cooking smells terrific," Hawk said as he followed Emma into the kitchen.

"I'm making spaghetti and meatballs. Uncle Ross and Ellie are coming over and they should be here any moment. Have you met Ellie yet?"

"No, I haven't. Ross talks about her all the time," Hawk responded.

Ding Dong, Ding Dong. "No sooner said, and there they are," Emma said when she heard the doorbell ring.

Lucas already opened the door. "It's Uncle Ross and Ellie," he squealed.

"Hi, big fella," Ross said as he reached down to pick Lucas up in his arms. "How are you doing, big boy?"

"I'm good. We're having pesgetti and meatballs for dinner."

"Oh, boy, that's my favorite," Ross said.

"Hi, Ellie," Lucas said as he reached over to kiss her before Ross lowered him down to the floor.

"Hi, Lucas. Where's that brother of yours?"

"He's coming. He's not as fast as me."

"I can see that. There he is. Hi, sweetie."

"Hi, Ellie. I missed you," Adam said.

"I missed you too," Ellie said as he gave her a big hug.

"Where's your mom?" Ross inquired.

"She's in the kitchen with Hawk," Lucas replied.

"There you are. Hi, Ellie. Hi, Uncle Ross. Come in. Let me take your coats," Emma said with Hawk right behind her.

"Hi, Ross," Hawk said as he extended his arm to shake hands.

"Good to see you, Hawk. I'd like you to meet the love of my life, Ellie West, MD."

"I've heard a lot about you, and it's nice that Ross's finally letting you meet other guys," Hawk said. "I can see why he's been hiding you. You're beautiful."

"Yes, all the guys tell me that," Ellie said as she flipped her long red hair with her hand. "It's nice to finally meet you too, Hawk. And I just have to return the compliment. You're not bad on the eyes either. Ross never told me you were tall, dark, and handsome. You're a lucky gal there, Emma. I work at Walter Reed Medical Center and all I see all day long are grumpy old men with a lot of gas."

They all laughed hysterically. Even the boys were snickering.

"That's my Ellie. Always telling it like it is. She can work anywhere she wants to, but she's a real American and wants to do everything she can for the men who served in the armed forces for our country."

Emma came into the living room with two glasses of Prosecco for Ross and Ellie. "Yes, Hawk too is all-American and *such* a Marine," she said proudly.

"Why do you say that?" Hawk asked.

"You stop to talk to every serviceman you see and you salute them all. You always stand tall, dress impeccably, never a hair out of place. You remember everything. How do you live with yourself? The only bad habits I see are that you crack your knuckles, you drink coffee all day long and you smile when you're mad."

"Is that bad?"

Emma laughs. "No, of course not. I'm not criticizing you. We all have habits."

"What are yours?" Hawk inquired.

"You should know," Emma replied.

"Let me see if I *remember*?" Hawk said, as he emphasized the word 'remember' and put his index finger to his temple. "You can eat a tub of ice cream at one sitting. You steeple your fingers when you're concentrating. You like to read over someone's shoulder. You can read upside down and backward. You keep a messy desk," he said as he glided closer to her. And… you're a bit of a nosey bug—you have to know everything."

Emma smiled, wrapped her arms around his neck, and kissed him gently on the lips.

"What just happened here?" Hawk asked.

"I just wanted to make sure you know how much I adore you," she said with a smile. "Now you know. Oh, there's also the fact that I've already had two glasses of Prosecco."

"With that," Hawk glanced at Emma, "I'd like to make a toast if I may?"

"Of course, go right ahead," Emma said.

"Tonight we are in the company of friends and family. Some new friends," he said as he nodded at Ellie, "and some old friends," he looked at Emma and Ross. "You can shut me up anytime you feel like it. I'm like a nuclear reactor—you push the button and I go off, so feel free to tell me when to stop."

"Fair enough," Ellie said. "I just pushed the button."

"The button's been pushed and I'm feeling very nostalgic this evening. My first surprise of the evening was finding Emma in an apron! Wow! I've never seen her in this role. My second surprise was seeing her two boys. They are the size of eight-year-olds. I think they're going to be taller than me!"

"I do believe you're going to be right about that," Ross said.

"And, with much regret," Hawk said, hanging his head down, "I'm sorry to say that I feel left out. Yes," he said, raising his head, "I missed seeing Emma grow into a beautiful woman and mother. I only know her as a scholar and a real go getter. She is definitely getting better with age. Look at her."

They all looked at Emma.

"You're making me blush, Hawk."

"Yes, I'm making you blush. It only makes you more beautiful. And now, I'm introduced to Miss Ellie. This room is going to explode from all this beauty. I've heard nothing but great things about you, and I'm sure to treasure your friendship as much as I treasure Ross'.

"This evening has been overwhelming for me, and I haven't even tasted Emma's spaghetti and meatballs yet. Maybe that's what will take the air out of my balloon."

Ha, ha, ha, ha, ha. "Cheers!"

"Very amusing, Mr. Shaw. Very amusing," Emma said, punching him in the arm.

"Well, now it's my turn," Ross said. "Let's just take a moment to talk about Mr. Major Hawk Shaw, if we may. I'm sorry you missed out watching Emma become a woman and mother, but that's your fault. If you played your cards right from the beginning, you would not have been left out of the picture. You would have been in the picture."

Emma glared at her uncle and then looked over at Hawk. "What is this all about? Where are you going with this?"

"You two were meant for each other is where I'm going with this. I've kept my mouth shut long enough and I can't or won't do it any longer. But, that's for the two of you to decide and work out."

"Uncle Ross?" Emma squealed.

"Hawk is one of the most intelligent, honest, hard-working men I've ever met. He has the unique ability to talk and negotiate better than anyone I know. But... and that's a huge *but*, he has a double-edged sword technique. I call him the Double Equalizer. Now if he can't talk his way into any discussion that goes dead, you don't want to see the other half of the equalizer. He will get you when you least expect it, and he will get whatever he wants to get from you.

"Now we get to my Ellie. Isn't she the greatest? I just love her to death. And, don't get any ideas, Hawk. She's mine."

"Oh, I wouldn't think of it. That's great news, Ross. So, are the wedding bells going to be ringing anytime soon?" Hawk inquired.

Ellie and Ross glanced at one another and then burst out in laughter.

"No," Ellie declared. "They'll be no bells ringing. We don't want to spoil what we have, so we'll remain status quo."

"I'll drink to that," Ross said.

CHAPTER

50

"What a great evening this was," Hawk declared. "I can't remember enjoying myself as much as I have this evening. It must have been the company."

"My Uncle Ross was certainly outspoken this evening," Emma said.

"Oh, he's just looking out for you."

"Sounds like he's ready to have me marry you."

"Oh, don't get angry with him. He only wants what's best for you."

"I suppose you're the best for me?"

Hawk smiled, shrugged his shoulders and then laughed. "I *am* the best for you, and you know it."

"Now, Hawk, you know I'm not about to jump into any relationship. If I'm scrupulously honest with my feelings, I'm pretty much convinced that I can't handle the physical closeness of a relationship right now. The last thing I want to do is to hurt you in any way. I don't want any regrets—regrets can't be undone."

"I agree."

"I've taken the first step by moving here. I'm going to have to take a step at a time. The last five months have been the worst months of my life. I need to get my feet on the ground again. I'm still living in fear of Wes finding me. I still have nightmares when I relive what I went through and the details are still sharply defined in my mind. I feel emotionally paralyzed, and I seemed to have built a protective wall around my heart. I've got to have time to get over this episode, or chapter, if you may, in my life."

"I agree wholeheartedly with you. You need time, Emma."

"I've always loved you, but after I had met Wes, I believed the love I had for you was a brotherly love. Like unrelated siblings."

"At that particular time, it probably was brotherly love," Hawk said. "We never took the time to romance one another because we were best friends, but now we're different people."

"I'm just not ready to lose myself in another relationship. If it went bad, then I would be opening my heart to more grief. Really, Hawk, I don't think I can handle any more grief."

"I would kill myself first before I would cause you a moment of grief."

She smiled, never dropping her gaze from his. "You're very special to me, Hawk, and you always will be."

He stepped closer and wrapped his arms around her waist. She gasped. This was not supposed to happen. This was her best friend, not her lover. She felt the thudding of her heart when he drew her close to his body. His body excited her—he felt absolutely amazing. It had been a long time since she'd been this close to a man.

"This is so wrong," Emma said in a whisper, trying to push away from Hawk unsuccessfully. "I'm not ready to jump into any…"

He pressed his finger to her lips. "Must you analyze everything to death? Save it for the lab."

She went still. Absolutely still. She tilted her head up and when she saw the gleam in his eyes—she melted in his arms. She knew she didn't have a chance.

He covered her lips with his mouth and they surrendered to one another in a way they never had before.

With her arms locked around his neck, she kissed him back, never wanting to let him go. She hadn't felt passion like this in such a long time, she'd forgotten how good a kiss could make her feel. Oh, how she missed the sensation of having a man's arms around her—of being loved.

His mouth lifted away from hers, just barely. Torn by conflicting emotions, she whispered, "I need more time…"

He kissed her again, long and hard. Emma just let herself be held and loved. The feel of his body amazed her. *We were so close for so many years without having any of this. I must have been totally blind.*

When his mouth left hers, he pressed his lips to her throat, her shoulder…. the scent of her only made him want her more. "You're not alone in this you know," he whispered in her ear.

Emma felt his lips brush her ear as he spoke.

"I will always be by your side. You mean more to me than anything in my life, and I can promise you one thing, no one will ever hurt you again."

His words, calm and soothing, seeped into her battered heart. Until this moment, she felt happier now than she ever believed possible a few short months ago.

For years she had leaned on his shoulder—he had been her only friend she could utterly rely on. She may have been too blind to see the real man when she was younger, but now she knew that he was something more… something astoundingly more.

CHAPTER

51

Wes & Kate in D.C.

"What was that address number?" Wes asked Kate when he stopped for a red light.

"Five Twenty North Capitol Street, Northwest is what the brochure says."

"We're getting close," he said as he peered out from under the brim of a White Sox cap he picked up in Chicago. When the light turned green, a huge truck pulled out in front of him and blocked his way. Wes honked impatiently and leaned out the window and yelled, "Get outta the way."

The truck driver yelled back, "*You* get outta the way, you asshole."

Kate grabbed Wes' arm when she saw his jaw tighten, and his anxiety turn to anger. "Just stay in the car. You've got to calm down. We can't afford to make a scene here."

Wes groaned and quickly shrugged Kate's arm away. "Jerk-off driver stopping traffic in both directions."

Suddenly, the shrill of a police whistle was heard in the back of them. Quick as lightening, they both panicked. Kate's face went white, her eyes anticipated the worst...

Wes' heart rate increased, perspiration covered his forehead.

Kate quickly turned around and Wes glanced out the rearview mirror. They watched as a cop yelled at a pedestrian who had not crossed the street at a crosswalk. They both gave a big sigh and moan of relief to know there was no sign of present danger.

Traffic had now become a snarl of cars. It had taken several minutes before traffic cleared and Wes could finally move. He made a sharp right turn and headed down Capitol Street. "Here we go, five oh two... it's on the other side of the street."

"I see the sign, Phoenix Park Hotel. See it?" Kate asked.

"Yeah, I see it now." He made a left turn into the entrance and pulled his car alongside the curb before he hit the brakes. "I'm glad we're out of that traffic mess."

"They certainly seem to drive differently on the east coast."

"I'll stay in the car," Wes said. Why don't you go in alone and see if they have any rooms."

"Okay. I'll be right back. If they do, I'll find out where to park the car."

The doorman opened the large glass door for her, and she stepped into the massive lobby and noticed a clerk standing behind the counter. She made her way to the desk and stood at the counter for a moment before the clerk noticed her.

"Good afternoon. Welcome to the Phoenix Park Hotel. How may I help you?"

"We just arrived in D.C. and we need a place to stay for three nights. Would you have anything available?"

The clerk gave a slight frown, possibly because she preferred someone with reservations. "Let me take a look. She viewed the computer for a few moments before she responded, "Ah. Yes, we have a suite on the seventh floor for six hundred fifty dollars a night plus taxes, of course."

"That's perfect. I'd like to book that room, please," Kate responded politely.

The clerk's eyebrows went up for a moment before she said, "I'll get the paperwork. It's vacant so you may have it now. Check-in is usually at three o'clock. How many nights will you be spending with us?"

"Three nights. That's if it's available."

"Yes, it's available," the clerk said.

"Thank you so much. Do you accept American Express?"

"Certainly we do. If you'll be so kind as to fill out this sheet, I'll get you registered in no time."

Kate quickly filled out the necessary information— none of it authentic. She wrote down a fake Arizona address and phone number. Wes had taken license plates off an Arizona car, so no one would suspect anything. "Where is the parking located?"

"If you just drive around the entrance and take a right, there's a parking entrance there and here is your parking card to allow you to enter." Kate took the card and put it in her pocket.

"Do you need help with your luggage?"

"No, we're fine, thank you."

"Okay, everything seems to be in order, Ms. Dell. Your room number is 704. If there's anything we can do to help, just call us. Thank you so much for staying at the Phoenix."

"Thank you... Helen," she said when she noticed her name printed on a nameplate that rested on the countertop.

The room was unusually dull with window scenery that looked out at a brick building wall. "We'll stay here a few nights and then look for something else," Kate muttered. "This is a boring place. I thought we'd have some kind of view from the seventh floor. It's blah."

"We'll get a feel of the city while we're here. The location is central to everything," Wes said as he lifted his suitcase onto the luggage rack. "Let's unpack a few things and we'll go and get something to eat."

"Okay. Would you like to eat at the hotel or do you want to take a walk and see what's around this area?" Kate asked.

"Let's take a walk. We've been doing nothing but driving."

"You're right. I'll be ready in ten minutes."

They walked down the street until they came to a quaint French restaurant, Le Petite Bistro. They were ushered to a little private booth with high-backed leather seats.

"I know Emma is here," Wes said.

"And exactly how would you know that?"

"I just know. Our plan is about to begin. She'll be before me very soon. All I want is to get my boys back and the sooner we get them, the sooner we leave for South America. I can't wait until we get there. I'm so sick of the U.S."

"We'll find them, Wes. Let's take in a movie tonight."

"Okay, let's scout the area. I picked up a few maps from the hotel lobby," he said as he opened a city map of D.C. He grabbed a pen from his jacket and drew a large circle around a random neighborhood area southwest of the shopping mall. "It looks like there's a large movie theater near the shopping mall. Let's walk down. It should only be a few blocks."

CHAPTER

52

Wes' long legs covered a block in minutes with his giant strides and Kate was in a near jog to keep up with him. "How much farther is the hotel?" Kate asked. "It's ten o'clock at night and we should have taken a cab."

"Just a half block or so. We're almost there."

Suddenly, Wes turned the corner into a long, dark alley with no lights but one solitary street lamp at the other end that cast a muddled stream of light that did little to suppress the shadows.

With an edge of panic in her voice, after she stepped over broken glass and God only knows what else, Kate asked, "Can't we use the sidewalks? It's pretty dark here."

"This is a shortcut, and it's quicker. The hotel is right down the end of the alley," Wes snapped.

An intolerable stench of rotting food and urine almost gagged Kate... *this is a shortcut?*

Halfway down the alley, two figures stepped out of the shadows. One of the figures had a baseball bat in his hand. Kate's heart skipped a beat. "Let's go back to the street," she begged.

Wes stopped walking and pushed Kate behind him, a tactical retreat. "Stay behind me," he whispered, as his peripheral vision took in both sides of the alleyway, looking at all the shadows and doorways.

There was a scuffling noise behind them. Kate nervously glanced over her shoulder and gasped in horror. "There are two more men in back of us, Wes! They've sealed us off," she cried out. "I told you we should have walked on the street!"

Wes turned, saw the two men, and pushed Kate against the wall next to a Dumpster. "Don't worry," he said calmly as adrenaline flooded his body. "Whatever happens, don't move."

The men closed in from both ends of the alley. The man with the baseball bat was now just ten feet away from them. With a smile on his bearded face, he said, "Give me your wallet, rings, and watches."

Wes didn't move. His adrenaline roared through his veins, his pulse quickened—he was ready for all of them.

"Just give them what they want and they'll let us go," Kate pleaded.

"Don't be so eager to give them anything," Wes said. "It'll only fuel their expectations and by then who knows what else they'll want."

"You want my wallet?" Wes asked, holding it up in front of him. "Come and get it."

After the smile had left his bearded face, his expression changed. Anger contorted his face as he groaned and swung the bat several times. "Give us the woman," he demanded.

"Go fuck yourself," Wes yelled back.

A short, bulky man with a tough jaw and squinty eyes pulled a knife out from under his jacket and stepped closer while the other men fanned out to surround them.

"So, you want to dig up the hatchet, do you?" Wes said. He made a quick step movement forward and swung his body around. They all quickly jumped back.

A slender man with a full mustache moved toward Wes swinging his knife back and forth... *swish*... *swish*. Wes studied the man's every move. The man had taken another threatening step closer before he lunged headlong toward Wes. With lightning speed, Wes kicked the man in the head, swooped him off his feet and hurled him to the pavement with a heavy thud. The man shrieked in pain, holding his head. Wes kicked him a second time, full in the face, sending him sprawling on the pavement, unconscious.

"One down, three to go," Wes yelled out in excitement.

The man with the baseball bat burst forward and swung wildly. Missed him. He swung again. Fused with anger, Wes grabbed his arm, snapped it backward and left the man on the ground howling in a drawn out scream of pain.

Kate heard the snap and realized Wes had broken the man's arm.

With his leg, Wes rolled the man over onto his back. Surprisingly, the man seized Wes by the leg. Wes fell to the ground, but was able to quickly get to his knees and with a mighty fist to the man's head, he knocked him unconscious.

"Two down, two to go," Wes announced as he stood up.

With a grim look of resolve, the other two men lunged at Wes; Wes pulled his Sig .380 ACP pistol from his jacket and like a cannonball two gunshots exploded.

Instantly, everything went silent. Kate muffled a scream with both hands. "What are you doing?" she screamed out. "You just killed two men! What's wrong with you?"

Without saying a word, he turned and fired a shot at each of the wounded men lying on the ground. "Leave no witnesses," he said. "They wanted war, they got it. Let's get out of here," he said while he searched for the shell casings. "Someone probably heard the shots."

Kate stood still. In those seconds of stillness, her heart stopped. *He just killed four people. A fight turned into a slaughter.* Her throat closed, she clutched at her chest and gasped for air.

Wes whirled her around, grabbed her arm and made a mad dash down the darkened alley toward the street.

Twenty-two year old, Jenny Dumas felt moisture in the air when a gentle wind blew her hair back as she walked briskly down the dark street, listening to soft music from her earphones. Dressed in a black jacket and jeans and a backpack worn high on her back, she was deep in concentration, thinking about her final exams. Finally, she will graduate. It felt like she'd been in school for a hundred years. She endeavored to take all the required classes that would allow her a career path to work for the FBI as an Intelligence Analyst. Earlier this month she submitted her resume at the career fair and was granted an interview. She was excited that she actually landed an interview, but at the same time she was a bit overwhelmed. Everything was happening at once.

Her concentration was suddenly broken. She heard rapid footsteps coming toward her. Terror erased every thought in her mind as she froze and just stood there. By the time she looked up, she had been violently knocked out of the way by a man and a woman. She staggered backward, her arms flailing and her feet scrambling on the pavement, trying to support herself. Just as she caught her balance, she found herself staring right at the man's panic-stricken face.

With a hysterical instinct for life, Jenny turned and ran down the street looking for someone—anyone. Surely, there were other people around. She kept looking back over her shoulder. *"Where did they go,"* she wondered. She didn't see anyone. The street was deserted.

"Go get the car," Wes said to Kate. "Take a right at the end of the alley. The hotel is there. Meet me back here."

Kate scurried away like a mouse in the dark.

Wes stood there a few moments. By the time he took a few deep breaths and straightened out his jacket, he had planned his next move. The girl saw his face. He had to get rid of her.

Trembling inside, Jenny's heart pounded feverishly. She's just two blocks from home. Out of the corner of her eye, she noticed a flickering light. It was a young boy on a bicycle on the other side of the street. She fled down the street without a backward glance, but within seconds, she could see a shadow on the pavement, getting larger and larger. Overwhelmed with fear, she reached in the pocket of her jacket for the pepper spray she kept chained to her house keys. The elongated shadow moved closer and closer to her. With the pepper spray canister clenched in her fist, she stopped abruptly, whirled around and in a split second she processed the sight of her pursuer—the same man! She pressed the button on the canister aimed right at her assailant's face.

He let out a howl—a screech of hurt and shock—a sound she had never heard a human make.

Wes just stood for a few seconds, disoriented and blinded before he fell to his knees and shrieked another cry of pain. He began to rub his eyes and then began to wheeze, completely overwhelmed by a sense of suffocation. He gasped and moaned and cried out—the burn was pure torture.

"Oh, my God," Jenny said as she staggered backward and watched in horror—the man was kneeling down on the pavement crying in pain, his hands clapped over his face. She screamed as she ran down the street and prayed someone would hear her yells.

Headlights suddenly illuminated the night when a car rocked over ruts making the headlights jump as it rumbled down the street. For an instant, Jenny was relieved… maybe not. She heard acceleration. She could see that the driver was a blonde woman. The car headed straight toward her… gaining speed… the car drove right into her!

Terrified, Jenny immediately leaped away, but in seconds, she felt her body lift off the ground. Her backpack strap had locked onto the side view mirror and she was being dragged by the speeding car; dragged some two hundred feet down the road before the strap snapped and she tumbled across the unforgiving asphalt. She moaned as her body came to a stop. Her arms and feet felt shredded and stung badly.

Rooted to the spot with horror, she lay there as if paralyzed, barely able to breathe. *Why would anyone want to kill me?* she wondered.

She watched the car's tail-lights as it drove down the road. Brake lights came on. The car stopped, picked up the groaning assailant and tires screeched as the car quickly turned and shot down the alley disappearing into the darkness.

The smell of car exhaust swept up her nose, threatening to choke her. She must get off the street. Pain shot through her when she tried to pull herself to her feet. When she looked at her feet, there were no shoes, only raw skin and blood. Her shoes must have fallen off while she was being dragged by the car. She crawled to the curb and grabbed hold of a lamp post to pull herself up. Blood trickled down her face as she hugged the lamp post. Her head throbbed and her heart pounded feverishly. She was frightened and knew that somehow, she had to get away. They may come back after her.

Suddenly, she heard sirens coming from several directions. She saw headlights flash and briefly flood the street with light. It was a black Hummer, and it pulled up in front of her. A man rolled down the window and asked, "Are you okay?"

Fighting to be understood through her shuddering sobs, she said, "No... I... I need help. I've been attacked. A man with a gun chased me... he could still be here."

The man jumped out of the Hummer and kneeled beside her. "I'll get you to a doctor that can help you. My name is Ross Griffin and I work with the police." He quickly slipped a black wallet from the back pocket of his pants and displayed his ID badge.

"Oh, thank you so much. My name is Jenny Dumas. I can't walk very well."

"Okay," he said as he slipped his wallet inside his jacket. "Put your arms around my neck so I can carry you. I'll get you to a doctor."

She did as he instructed.

"Ready?"

"Yes," she said, weakly.

"Here we go," he said as he lifted her body up and ran over to his car. He opened the door with one hand and reached in to push a button to recline the seat. His strong arms lifted her gently onto the seat and she laid her head back.

"I'll get some blankets from the back."

He grabbed the blankets from the rear of the car and placed them gently over her body.

"Are you all right?"

"Yes. This feels good. Thank you, sir." He quickly snapped the seat belt over her body and ran to the other side to position himself in the driver's seat. He gripped his hands firmly around the steering wheel and pulled into traffic toward Georgetown to Ellie's home. Several light-pulsing cruisers' sirens blew past him.

Within ten minutes, he pulled up in front of Ellie's home and quickly turned off his lights. He reached under the dashboard and removed the fuse that controlled the interior lights before he jumped out and ran around to open the passenger door. No one must see them.

He undid the seat belt and felt her body shiver despite the warmth in the car. She was asleep. He nudged her gently. "Can you hear me?"

She moaned and turned toward him. "Are we at the doctors?"

"Yes. Are you able to sit up?"

"I think so."

"Let me raise the seat." He pushed the button and the back of the seat slowly came up. "I'll help you down. Sit for a moment."

"Okay," she said, taking a deep breath. "I don't feel very well."

"It'll only be another minute and I'll have you inside the house. Grab me around the neck and I'll carry you."

The pain was almost unbearable when she put her arms around his neck. He managed to hold her and carry her up to the front door. At this lonely hour, there were no movements on the street.

He pressed the doorbell several times.

CHAPTER

53

Usually, there are no reverberating chimes of the doorbell ringing at eleven-fifteen in the evening. At first, Ellie thought she had dreamt it. When she finally opened her eyes, she heard the doorbell chime over and over, seemingly more urgent this time. *Jesus, mercy. Who in the world could that be at this hour?*

As soon as she put on her bathrobe, she hurried downstairs, feet still bare. The bell stopped ringing as she descended the stairs. Cautiously, she approached the front door and peeked out the side window. It was Ross, holding a young girl. She flipped the light switch and unlocked the door. When she opened the door, a deep, raspy voice said, "Turn that light out!"

She quickly flipped the switch off. "What happened, Ross? Are you all right? Is she all right?" Ellie asked with urgency in her voice. "She looks horrible."

"I'm fine, but the girl isn't," he said as he gently carried Jenny into the house and closed the door with his foot. "This girl needs help and I'm not able to help her, at least not right now. I've got to go. I have other problems to take care of right now. I need you to look at her."

"Okay, let's take her downstairs, please."

Within a few seconds, Ross had her downstairs and placed her on a soft chair.

"What happened to her, Ross? What's going on? She's shivering."

"She's damn lucky to be alive, Ellie" You've got to call in sick. I need your help. I need you to take care of this girl. Her name is Jenny," Ross said, speaking in a low confidential level as if it were a secret no one should hear even though there was no one else around to hear him.

"Someone is after this girl. They attacked her, and tried to run her over, but she got away. Please take care of her. She really needs someone right now."

"Has she been shot or raped?"

"No. She was attacked and dragged down the street on the side of a car."

Ellie put her arms around Jenny and said, "Hi, Jenny. I'm a doctor, and I'm going to take care of you."

"Thanks, Ellie," Ross said. "I'll call you in a few hours." He turned, went up the stairs, opened the door and quickly headed toward his car, disappearing into the darkness.

Ellie had a slender, almost delicate build; a combination that gave the illusion of frailty. On the contrary, working out in the gym every day and putting in double shifts at the hospital, she always managed to have fuel cells left over. The woman was tireless and always ready to pitch in and help others when in need.

Jenny looked at Ellie and said, "Why am I trembling?

"This happens because your body responds to traumatic experiences and releases a flood of adrenaline and cortisol in your system. Your blood pressure gets elevated and your heart rate accelerates. This is caused from being frightened. A person can shake, feel nauseated, and have muscle soreness. They're all symptoms one can expect to experience."

"I'm so tired and I hurt all over."

"There's a bedroom and bathroom for you. Come, let's go get washed up so we can see what needs to be taken care of."

Ellie's home was designed with three split-levels, with only five stairs between levels. She held Jenny's body as they slowly stepped toward the bathroom. "Let's start here so you can take a shower," she said, pushing the door open for her.

When Jenny started to undress to take a shower, Ellie was horrified at the extensive bruises on the young girl's body. Her arms, knees, and feet were bleeding and black and blue bruises darkened her skin in odd places. "Oh, someone did a real number on you, didn't they?"

"Yes," Jenny said as she held her stomach with one hand and put her other hand to her mouth. "I think I'm going to be sick."

"Here," Ellie said as she lifted the toilet lid. She held Jenny as she bent over and emptied whatever she had in her stomach into the pink porcelain bowl. Before Ellie reached over to turn on the shower, she dropped two thick towels over the tiles to help soothe Jenny's feet. She grabbed a face cloth and ran it under cold water. "Here, hold this face cloth on your face. It'll make you feel better."

"I'm so sorry," Jenny said as she flushed the toilet.

"There's nothing to feel sorry about. Do you feel better now?"

"Oh, yes. A lot better. Thank you," Jenny replied.

"Okay, do you feel strong enough to take a shower and shampoo your hair? There are handicap bars in the shower that you can hold on to."

"Yes. I feel so much better now. I'll be okay."

"I'll fetch you some clothes to wear while you shower."

"Thank you."

"I'll make you some warm milk with graham crackers. Your stomach should be able to handle that."

"All right, I'll be through in a few minutes."

"Don't rush, honey, take your time."

Jenny stepped into the shower under the warm spray. How good it felt. She was safe. The man that brought her here saved her life. "Oh, God, thank you," she murmured.

Ellie rummaged through her clothes and found a pink sweat suit that would fit Jenny. She placed it just outside the bathroom and said, "I'm leaving some clothes just outside the door."

"Okay. Thank you."

Ellie ran up the stairs and walked into the kitchen, her thoughts were about Ross and the trust he occasionally demanded of her. *This was not the first time he's done this and it probably won't be the last. It's probably good for me to see what dreadful things go on in the world,* she thought. It's been quite a few years since she's worked in an emergency room; she really didn't like it.

Her job now as chief of cardiac and thoracic surgery at Walter Reed Army Hospital was less stressful in a different way. She was chosen as the warmest and caring individual with a great willingness to be a team builder in every aspect of her career. Cardiothoracic surgery was her specialty and she felt quite comfortable with her well-trained staff. Ellie worked very hard to get this position. She was a Duke University School of Medicine graduate and also did her residency and senior residency at Duke before heading to Walter Reed.

Luckily I'm not on call this week, she thought. There were no surgeries scheduled till Tuesday morning.

She grabbed the box of graham crackers from the cabinet while she warmed a cup of milk in the microwave for one minute. She put the crackers on a dish and poured the warm milk in a coffee cup. She put them both on a tray and hustled down to the bedroom to see how Jenny was doing.

"How are you doing Jenny?" Ellie asked when she saw that the clothes had been picked up.

Jenny opened the door and stepped out. "I feel much better."

"Good. Let's take a look at you and see if you need any stitches," Ellie said. "Well, your head wound doesn't look as bad as I thought it would. Heads tend to bleed a lot. It seems to have stopped bleeding, so I'm going to put some ointment on it so it doesn't get infected, okay?"

"Okay," Jenny said. "I feel a lot better now after the shower."

"I just bet you do. You were pretty beaten up, young lady."

"Yeah, I know. My left wrist hurts a bit."

"Ah, let me see. Yes, it's starting to show bruising. You probably sprained it. It's not broken," Ellie said as she moved the wrist in several positions. "I'll wrap it for you."

"I'm also going to give you an antibiotic shot to prevent any infections, okay?"

"Okay."

"Your feet look pretty badly scraped. Were you dragged?"

"Yes. I was dragged down the street when my backpack caught on the car's side mirror," Jenny explained. "My feet feel like they're on fire."

"Well, they need to be cleaned up. Sit down here, and I'll get something to clean them. After I get them clean, I'm going to apply some ointment on the both of them and wrap them in a gauge bandage. It'll make them feel a whole lot better and by tomorrow, you should be much improved."

"Thank you so much for doing this," Jenny said.

"That's what doctors are for, to make you feel better. I'm happy to do it for you. Tell me about yourself, Jenny. Are you on any type of medications?"

"No, I don't take any meds. I'm not a smoker, I don't drink alcohol, and I don't do drugs."

"I'm glad to hear that, Jenny."

Ellie quickly injected the antibiotic shot and proceeded to clean all the debris from her feet with an antibacterial wash. Jenny jumped from the stinging a few times, but they were soon clean. Ellie grabbed the ointment and gauze from the medicine cabinet and worked quickly as she applied the ointment and wrapped her feet in gauze. She finished in a few minutes and put socks over the gauze. She wrapped a stretch bandage around her hand and wrist and sealed it with a clasp.

"Now I would like you to drink this warm milk and have some crackers with it. It'll settle your stomach. Okay?"

"All right," Jenny said. "I think I need to go to bed after. I'm so tired."

"Yes, sleep will be good for you. Here, let me undo the bed for you. She pulled down the covers and said, "Sit here and have your warm milk. When you're finished, turn off the light and get some rest and I'll be here when you wake up. If you need me, just call. I'll come in and check on you too."

"Thanks so much, Ellie."

"My pleasure." Ellie left the room, leaving the door half way open and went into the kitchen. She glanced at her watch. It was twelve-thirty. She made herself a pot of tea, grabbed a couple of graham crackers and went into the living room to watch some TV for a while, just in case Jenny called for her.

CHAPTER

54

"What the hell happened back there?" Kate yelled. "I never intended for anyone to be killed. Now we're wanted for four murders!"

"That fuckin' bitch had pepper spray."

"What? Oh, God, no! Are you all right?" Kate asked.

"No, I'm not all right. I can't see a fuckin' thing and I'm in agony. I'll kill that little bitch."

Damn him with his revenge, Kate thought. *He's going to screw this whole thing up—I can feel it! Why can't he see the big picture? Grasp the future, you idiot!*

"You're not going back after her. Just forget about her. Right now we need to get some milk and some Dawn detergent."

"Is that what takes this stuff off?" Wes asked.

"Yes. The milk will cool it off and the detergent will take off the capsicum oils."

"What the hell is capsicum?" Wes asked.

"Capsicum oil is from the pepper, and it creates heat and minor nerve irritation. The pain can last anywhere from thirty minutes to several hours. Let me see your face," Kate said.

Wes released his hands from his face so Kate could inspect the damage.

"You'll be fine," she said, trying to calm him down.

"How do you know about all this?" Wes asked.

"A friend of mine got sprayed. I'll drive to the grocery store up the end of this street and get what we need."

"Hurry up. I'm burning up."

"Okay. Lay your head back and relax."

"That's fuckin' easy for you to say."

He laid his head back, wondering what went wrong. The bitter realization that his plan had gone wrong was when he tasted viscid alkaline bile in his mouth blended with hatred for Emma.

"I know, Wes. But try to relax a bit," she said as she pulled up to the front of the store. "I'll be right back," she said as she hurried into the store.

Kate pulled the door open and walked to the back of the store where the refrigerated products were located and pulled out a half gallon of milk. She looked for the aisle that displayed detergents and grabbed a large bottle of Dawn and an empty spray bottle. At this hour, no one was in line at the checkout, so she was quick to return back to the car.

"Here we go," she said while she jumped back in the car. "We'll be at the apartment in a few minutes. How are you doing?"

"Hanging in there."

"Good."

"Our whole plan is backfiring on us," Wes mumbled.

"Not necessarily. What we need to do next is get rid of this car," Kate said. "The girl saw the car and may even know the license number now."

"Yeah, we'll get another car in the morning."

"You rubbed your eyes, and by doing that you spread it farther and made it worse. Rubbing only causes it to penetrate deeper into your skin."

"So how are we going to get this off my face? What's the Dawn for?"

"We'll start by spraying milk on your face. The milk should help take the burn away."

"I'm going to fill the bathroom basin with cold water and Dawn and you can dip your face into the mixture for fifteen or twenty seconds to dissolve the oil. We'll have to do this seven or eight times so the Dawn cuts the oil. After that, we'll put straight Dawn on your face to dissolve whatever is left. We don't want to rub your face. Some of the oil will have already been absorbed by your skin so we won't be able to get it all off."

An hour later, everything inside him quivered. The walls seemed to close in on him as he walked aimlessly through the apartment, stripping off his clothes and leaving them scattered on the floor. He was too nervous to lie down, but pain had settled between his shoulder blades, so he popped four aspirins and lay down on the bed.

Stretched out on his back, he stared at the ceiling in an attempt to calm down, but he could feel his heart pound. His mind, engulfed with a cloud of depression as he tried to force his thoughts to something else, but the depths of reflection from the night's event left him in panic mode. *He desperately needed a plan. He had no idea what to do now.*

After being horizontal for almost an hour, he rolled over to the edge of the bed to sit up but suddenly felt weak. With both hands curled over the edge of the mattress, he drew himself up to his feet, but he fell back down on the bed. Surprised at his weakened condition, he sat quietly for a few moments trying to figure out why he was so weak. The pain in his back gradually disappeared and he seemed calm now, so the aspirins worked. He decided to lie down again and try to get some sleep.

CHAPTER

55

It took several rings of the phone to reach her sleeping brain before she actually heard it ring. She fumbled for the phone. "Hello?" she said in a groggy, hoarse voice.

"Hi Ellie, it's Ross."

"What time is it?"

"It's almost six. How is Jenny doing? Is she all right?" Ross asked.

"Bruises on her body, abrasions on her feet and a sprained wrist. Otherwise, yes," Ellie said. "She's sleeping right now. She took a shower and I gave her a shot of antibiotics, taped her wrist up and wrapped her feet up. What in the hell happened to her? She told me a car hit her and dragged her down the street. Who is after this girl?"

"That we don't know yet. Is she awake?"

"No. I gave her a sedative and she's sleeping."

"This girl may have been a witness to a shooting last night. I'm about to find out more from the police. Call me if she says anything else. Okay?"

"Alright, I'll call you."

"Ellie, I want you to listen very carefully to what I'm about to tell you. This is crucial."

"Alright, I'm listening."

"First, don't tell anyone that Jenny is at your home. No one, Okay?"

"Okay, Ross. I won't tell anyone."

"Someone wants her dead, and until I find out what's going on, she needs to be protected. That's why I brought her to your place. I just couldn't leave her behind. Ellie, I'm really sorry I got you involved in this."

"Ross, it's okay. I can handle it, really."

"Okay, Ellie. Just be careful and don't let her out of your sight. Call me if she says anything else. Love you Ellie."

"Love you too Ross. I'll see you later. And don't worry about Jenny. She'll be fine and I will stay with her all day."

"No wonder I fell in love with you. You're terrific and always there when I need you most."

"You're welcome, Ross."

"Do you still have that .45 revolver I gave you a couple of years ago?"

"Yes, I do. Why? Am I going to finally have to use it? Ellie said laughingly.

"This is not funny. Yes, you may have to use it. Make sure you have it where you can get to it, just in case."

"Okay, I'll get it and put it in the end table drawer."

"Good. Thanks again, Ellie." The line clicked. He was gone.

She sat there for several minutes grateful that Ross was in her life. She's been involved with him for almost ten years and he still endangers his life to protect a stranger.

A remarkable man, my Ross.

CHAPTER

56

Hawk had just finished an early morning Espresso Sambuca at Matteo's Restaurant around the corner from his office and was in the middle of a delightful conversation with the owner when his cell phone vibrated. He glanced at the caller ID—Chief of Police Jack Morris.

"Yes, chief. What can I do for you?" Hawk inquired.

"Good morning, Hawk. I hope you're close by."

Going more by the urgency of the chief's tone than by his actual words, Hawk replied, "Yes. I'm having coffee at Matteo's. What happened?"

"There's been a shooting—four men fatally shot. The bodies were just discovered in an alley near Thomas Circle. We have four homicides on our hands. We received a formal request from the police commissioner this morning asking that you work on this investigation. It happens that one of the victims was the son of the commissioner's sister, Julie Segura. His name is Manuel Segura and he was twenty-three years old."

"What time did it happen?"

"Don't know for sure. The ME is on the scene now. Should know pretty soon."

"I'm on my way. Meet you there."

He cut the connection, turned and waved goodbye to Matteo, "See you later. Gotta go."

Hawk immediately dialed Theo on his way out the door of the restaurant.

"Pappas here."

"Theo, I need both you and Emma to meet me at Thomas Circle. There's been a shooting in an alley that left four men dead. Chief Morris received a call from the police commissioner and they're asking us to help out with the evidence analysis. Grab your gear and meet me there."

After a long pause, he took a deep breath and said, "You got it, boss," and hung up.

In an instant, memories he had placed deep in his mind, tumbled out. The call had taken him off guard, causing a shiver to run through him. He knew he had to hold himself together. He cleared his throat. "Emma, we need to meet up with Hawk at Thomas Circle. Grab the cases. We've got to leave now. Four men were found shot in an alley."

"Okay. You drive," Emma answered. "I'll grab the gear."

Theo ran to his office to snag his jacket from the back of his chair, grab his car keys, and the scratched aluminum case that held the photography equipment. Emma secured the lab and then the office before they exited down the stairs to the parking garage. He popped open the trunk and they placed the cases inside.

"How long will it take us to get there from here?" Emma inquired as she opened the door, quickly slid in and buckled her seat-belt.

"We should be there in a few minutes," he said as he slipped his sunglasses on. He backed up, swung around, and glanced in both directions before he jammed on the gas pedal and peeled out onto the street, causing the car to fishtail. Traffic was moderate and Theo kept the car just a little over the speed limit while he watched the activity in his rear-view mirror.

After several minutes, he hung a hard right, tires squealing, and turned toward the west side of 14th Street, which was alive with flashing blue and white cruiser lights. An ambulance and a fire truck had parked ahead of the lines of police cars and sirens sounded in the distance. Crime scene tape stretched across the area manned by a barricade of police officers.

Theo lowered his car window. "We're part of the strike crime force," he said while flashing his ID card.

"Yes, sir," the police officer said while examining his credentials. He pointed to a row of patrol cars, and said, "Park your car right over there, sir."

Theo nosed the car between a small herd of black-and-whites parked against the far wall.

"Did Hawk explain what happened?" Emma asked.

"He said four young men were shot and killed," Theo responded, his voice cracked as he spoke.

"Oh, how tragic."

When they stepped out of the car, Theo removed his black wraparound sunglasses when the transition from sunlight to shade hit his eyes. "I'll take these, you grab the other two cases," Theo said to Emma. Emma grabbed the two cases and they headed down the street toward the alley.

Immediately approached by a television news team reporting live from the street, a tall, red-haired woman dressed in a tailored black pantsuit recognized Theo and quickly ran toward him, her cameraman right behind her with the video camera perched on his shoulders as he zoomed in. Harsh lights instantly glared at them.

"Who is she?" Emma inquired.

"That's Faith Barnett. She's a reporter for the local TV channel."

"Isn't Hawk the one that gives interviews?"

Theo smiled. "Interviewing Hawk is about as likely as cozying up to a venomous snake."

Emma laughed, shaking her head in agreement.

"Mr. Pappas. Are you part of the crime strike force here to gather evidence?" she asked as she shoved the microphone an inch from his face.

"Yes, we are."

"What's the latest information?" she asked.

"Sorry ma'am. We just arrived, and we've not had time for any evaluations."

Suddenly, what sounded like gunfire filled the air. People in the area screamed and ran for cover. Raw adrenaline shot through Theo's veins. He instantly dropped the cases he was carrying to wrap his arms around Emma and drop her to the ground. Without any hesitation, he grabbed his gun, fully prepared for the unexpected.

Seconds later, when the screams stopped, he said, "Oh, I guess it's just a car backfiring." He stood up and put his gun back in the holster. "Are you okay, Emma?" he asked as he bent down to help her stand up.

Emma looked up at him and shot him a sharp glance. "Yes, I'm all right. You seem extremely high strung today," Emma said softly as she brushed gravel off her clothes. She noticed an unusual rigidity in her co-worker. It was as if he was about to be attacked at any moment.

"I hope I didn't hurt you. You can't be quick enough when you're in the middle of a crime scene. The person standing next to you could be the killer. There will be times when you have no time to think, only act. After a while, it becomes all reflex."

"Reflex, eh? You certainly have very fast reflexes, Theo."

"Yeah, I do," he murmured while still holding Emma's arm.

"What happened here?" Hawk asked as he approached them.

"Oh, some car backfired and it scared a few people," Theo reported.

"Follow me. We've got a lot of work to do," Hawk said as he turned and made a path through the crowd.

Emma's legs, resisting any attempt to turn around, followed closely behind Hawk and Theo as they walked under the barricade once Hawk whispered something to the officer who then held the tape up.

It was a filthy, narrow alley about a hundred yards long, lined with four Dumpsters, two on each side. There was a definite foul, sour smell of what seemed more or less permanent for an alley. Emma glanced down the alley, momentarily contemplating an escape.

"Are you okay?" Hawk asked as he turned to Emma and suddenly realized that his long legs moved too quickly. He waited a moment until Emma caught up with them. "Come on," he said, gripping her arm so she would not trail behind. "Let me have that case."

Emma gladly handed it to him. She wanted to hear all the details he was about to tell both of them.

"This is going to be a tough case. The media will be all over this. No one is to talk to the media. Got that?"

"Yes," Emma and Theo acknowledged at the same time.

"From all indications, each man was killed by a single gunshot. Two men, shot in the chest, and two men shot while lying on the ground. It doesn't seem that any gunshots were heard by anyone, so the killer may have used a silencer."

"Were they killed here in the alley?" Emma asked.

"Looks that way. There's smeared blood and the drag marks from shoes, so it looks like there was a struggle of some sort," Hawk said as he pointed to the marks on the ground leading to the victim's body.

"Who found the bodies?" Theo asked.

"A kitchen worker just stepped out for a smoke and saw the victims—they were already dead."

"Was any murder weapon found?" Theo asked.

"No. No weapon was found at the scene. However, there was some type of a scuffle at the end of the alley down on the street. There are blood splatters, and it seems like pepper spray was used. There was a young boy, Bobby Blake, on a bike who said he saw a girl get struck by a car. He ran home. He was scared because he wasn't supposed to be out that late at night. He said the car was a light colored Honda sedan and there was a woman driving. She hit the girl and then went and picked up the guy kneeling in the street, crying in pain. Detectives are also questioning other passersby who may have seen or heard something. Perhaps someone noticed the license plates."

The crime scene area had been cordoned off with yellow *Crime Scene-No Trespassing* tape. Police were scattered around the scene talking amongst themselves. Cameras flashed and a video of the bodies and the drag marks on the pavement were recorded. Evidence markers were set down, sketches were being drawn, and notes were being taken by various personnel.

Emma mouthed the words, *Oh my God,* but didn't say them out loud as she looked down into the lifeless faces of the four young men. She endeavored to not think of them as humans because the essence of the person was gone and all that remained was evidence at a crime scene—something that needed to be quickly processed and catalogued.

Hawk looked at Emma, and asked, "Are you all right?"

Emma nodded and mumbled, "I'm okay," she said, knowing that nothing in life prepares you for the day when four young men's lives are ended by an act of wanton cruelty. She soon felt her eyes fill with tears thinking of the loss their parents will feel. These men were alive yesterday and now they're going to wrap their bodies in clean white sheets and zip up the body bags.

She stared at the yellow chalk outlines around each of their bodies.

Theo's heart started hammering in his chest when his eyes gazed at the four young victims on the ground, five yards away. Memories of a prior lifetime suddenly flashed through his mind. He immediately closed his eyes for several seconds. It didn't help. Everything was the same when he opened them again. He closed his eyes a second time, telling himself: *relax, take a deep breath and get control of yourself. This is a disturbing sight for everyone.*

He opened his toolbox and extracted a top-of-the-line digital camera with resolution so sharp it could handle blowups up to one thousand percent. With a fifty-picture magazine, he would not have to reload. He turned to Emma as she was putting plastic booties over her shoes and said, "Scan the area for any trace evidence such as footprints, hair, fibers. I'll be taking photos."

"Sure thing," she responded while snapping latex gloves on her hands before collecting trace evidence.

She jumped right on it with her pen and evidence bags clamped on her clipboard and began to fill out a forensic entomology data form. "Do we have any names yet?" she asked Hawk.

"Just one. The commissioner's nephew, Manuel Segura, age twenty-three," Hawk replied.

"Was this a gang killing?" Emma asked Hawk.

"No, I don't believe so. The four men were not known to the police."

Emma filled in the information and quickly check-marked *pavement, alley, entire clothing, burgundy pants, black shirt, black tennis shoes.*

She swatted horseflies and other buzzing things that swarmed over the first body when she knelt on the cracked and broken concrete to examine the body.

Immediately, she felt like she was going to vomit—like she could throw up what had happened. She closed her eyes for a moment, knowing that this would stay with her for the rest of her life. She had taken a deep breath before she began her collection of trace evidence.

Hawk stood back and watched Emma as she collected several fibers from the victim's face and bagged them. When she searched the victim's extremities, she noticed that the right hand was clenched. She could see something inside the closed fist. "Hawk, come take a look at this."

Hawk bent down close to the body and said, "That looks like hair, doesn't it? Perhaps during the scuffle, he grabbed the assailant's hair. Let's not open the hand. Take a picture of his hand and I'll get tweezers and pull a strand out."

She quickly snapped a picture of the closed fist. Hawk held the tweezers and gently pulled out a strand of wavy blonde hair about four inches long. Emma bagged it, marked it and dropped it inside the scene kit.

Theo was filming the crime scene. Addressing the recording, he said, "Police on scene and perimeter established and taped off." He held his camera high to give it the same perspective he had. He videoed everything from every angle—everything he looked at or touched. He wanted no defense attorney to ever have the opportunity to say that the evidence was mishandled.

After he did the initial video taping, he immediately began taking pictures of what many may have thought were strange angles, but he knew what he needed to study when he returned to his lab. Theo was an expert in interpreting blood splatter patterns. Reading bloodstain patterns helps to figure out the positions of victim and attacker. The final location of a splatter can indicate the blood's velocity, what type of weapon was used, and even how many people may have been involved. The shape of the bloodstain can illustrate the direction in which it was traveling and the angle at which it struck.

Theo said, "I'll go out to the street and check for blood."

"When you get to the street," Hawk said, "be sure to get photos of everyone standing around. The killer may not have left the area yet, or perhaps came back to the scene."

"I'll stay here and process the other bodies, Theo," Emma said.

"After they go to the morgue, we'll get their clothing and see if we can get some fingerprints from the clothes."

"How do you get fingerprints off fabric?" Emma inquired.

"The fabric is put into a vacuum chamber and coated with either evaporated gold or zinc, which binds to the gold where there are no fingerprint marks. The impressions indicate where a finger of the hand had touched the fabric. It's pretty impressive."

"I'll say," Emma said with a surprisingly intense look.

"When both of you are finished here," Hawk said as he approached them, "let's meet up at the office. I want to go over a few things with both of you."

"We should be finished in the next couple of hours, Hawk," Theo responded.

"Good. Meet up with you at the office.

CHAPTER

57

Jenny's eyes opened. "Where am I?" she cried out in a hoarse, barely understandable voice.

Ellie laid the paper back down on the end table when she heard Jenny. "You're in my home, Jenny. How are you feeling?" she asked as she quickly walked over to the bed.

Jenny drew in a deep breath and tried to keep her voice from trembling. "I'm cold."

"I'll turn up the electric blanket. That should warm you in a few moments. How do you feel otherwise?"

After several moments, she answered, "Terrible." Her eyes closed, and she put her hand to her head. "My head hurts…"

"That's normal," Ellie said as she touched her forehead. "No fever, which is good." She felt for a pulse. Strong, regular, but a touch fast. Her skin was damp with perspiration. "Let me wipe your face," she said as she gently placed the cloth on her forehead. "It'll make you feel better."

"How did I get here?"

"A friend of mine brought you here. I'm a doctor, and I'm going to take care of you. You gave us quite a scare."

"How long have I been here?"

"Oh, about nine hours or so," Ellie said as she glanced at her watch. "Here, drink a little water. Your throat must be dry."

Jenny took several sips of water. "Yes, that feels good."

"Do you remember what happened to you?" Ellie asked.

"I do now."

"Do you want to talk about it?"

"It was terrible. I don't know why someone would want to do this to me. I was just walking home from work and suddenly two people running from an alley pushed me. The man told the woman to go and get the car and she left the area. I started running, looking for someone— anyone. I saw a flash of light across the street. It was a bicycle light, so I headed in that direction and then this dark shadow crept up behind me as if it were trying to catch up to me. When the footsteps sounded really close, I turned. The man had a gun pointed at me so I sprayed his face with the pepper spray canister that my dad got for me. The man fell down to the ground crying out in pain and made this ghastly sound that I have never heard a human make.

"I just don't understand why he wanted to hurt me. I didn't know this man. I just turned and ran down the street. All of a sudden, a car sped right at me and tried to run me over. A blonde-haired woman was driving. I dodged myself out of the way of the car, but my backpack caught on the side mirror and the car dragged me for about ten seconds before the strap broke. Next thing I remember, I was laying on the street. I saw the taillights of the car stop where the man was moaning and she picked him up. Then another car came by and stopped to help me. It was a man who said he would take care of me. He put me in his car and I guess he drove here to your home. I had no idea who this man was. Is this your friend?"

"Yes, he's my friend. That is what he does, he helps people in trouble. I am so glad he found you and brought you here. You will be safe now. No one will come after you here."

"You're a doctor?" Jenny asked.

"Yes, I work at Walter Reed Hospital. I'm a cardiology surgeon."

"Is your friend coming back?"

"Yes, he called to see how you were and he's coming back later this evening."

"What kind of work does he do?"

"He's a man that does a lot of good things for people and is always helping someone. He's in law enforcement."

"Hi, Ross? I have news," Ellie said on the phone.

"Has Jenny talked to you?"

"Yes, she certainly has. You need to come over and get her story. She saw the man who tried to kill her. She said she can identify him."

"Okay, I'll be over in about twenty minutes. Is she awake now?"

"Yes, she doesn't feel good, but she's awake."

"I'm on my way."

CHAPTER

58

"How is Jenny doing?" Ross asked as soon an Ellie opened the front door for him.

"She's doing pretty well considering what happened to her. She's an intelligent girl and has an interview for a position in the FBI. Come on, she's in the bedroom down stairs."

"Hello, Jenny, do you remember me?" Ross asked.

"Yes, Ross Griffin. I remember you saved my life."

"It was fortunate that I was there at that particular time to help you."

"Thank you so much," Jenny murmured softly.

"Can you tell me what happened to you?"

"Yes," Jenny said as she tried to sit up.

"No. Stay where you are. I can hear you just fine. I'm going to record what you say, okay?"

"Okay," Jenny said, laying her head back down on the pillow.

"She needs to get some rest, Ross. If she thinks of anything else, I'll call you," Ellie said.

"That's some story. Earlier this morning, I heard there was a shooting in an alley just about the time Jenny was walking home. I'm going to contact the chief and ask what went on. I do believe that Jenny was somehow involved. I'll call you later," Ross said as he gave Ellie a kiss and vanished out the front door.

CHAPTER

59

Wes was nervous. He did not like feeling nervous. He was a man who liked to feel that he was in control. However, now there was a glitch. He screwed up.

Stepping out of the shower, he said, "Let's get out of here and get something to eat. I'm starving."

"Okay, I'm ready. So you feel better, I see. Your face is still slightly red. Is the pain gone?"

"Yeah, it's gone. Now I look like I have a damn sunburn."

"It'll fade soon. After we have breakfast, we'll look for another car," Kate said. "Are we just going to leave this car somewhere or are we going to trade it in?"

"We can't trade that car in," he snapped. "That girl knows what I look like and saw the car you were driving."

"So what are we going to do with the car?" Kate asked.

"We'll head out toward the ocean after breakfast and bury it."

"I don't think that's a good idea. Why don't we find a wrecking yard? They'll get rid of it."

"No, that won't work. That'll only draw suspicion—wrecking a new car."

"It'll work just fine," she said through clenched jaws.

"Listen to me!" Wes said, jerking her arm back.

"Let go of me!" Kate yelled as she twisted away from his grasp.

"Will you just listen to me? I've got a plan."

Kate darted an evil look at him. "Don't you ever put your hands on me again. I am not your wife."

"I'm sorry, Kate. Really, I am, but I do have a plan," he said calmly, once his anger left him.

She started to tell him what he could do with his plan and then stopped herself. He wanted to do this his way. She could read it on his face. As much as she liked to have everything under her thumb, with some reluctance, she said, while rubbing her arm, "Okay, I'm listening."

"This is how we'll handle this problem," Wes said in a hushed tone. "We'll ride up the coast and sink it in the water. There are miles and miles of marshlands. It will sink to the bottom in no time and it'll be weeks before they find it, and by then we'll be in South America."

"And exactly how do you propose to drive it into the water," Kate protested.

"That won't be a problem. I can do it."

She gazed at him with a questionable look on her face. While she and Wes shared a number of common traits, she liked to have everything under her control. She was the *real* logical planner—Wes' plans were sudden, without much thought behind them—just like this plan of his. She knew when Wes landed on her doorstep four months ago that she'd been handed the one tool she needed to carry her plan off. What she didn't know at the time was that he was only focused on revenge. He only wanted his wife dead and wanted his two bratty kids back. Just what she didn't want... kids. *Well, maybe he will kill himself,* she thought. Go for it!

She shrugged her shoulders and said sarcastically, "So what's next on your master plan?"

"First, we need to remove all our things from the car. Second, we will go to the used car dealer right up the street and since we're not taking it with us when we fly off, there's no sense spending a lot of money for another car. Let's get everything out of the car."

"Okay, I'll just grab these sacks to put all the stuff in," Kate said.

Wes grabbed the keys and they left the apartment. The elevator doors opened just as they approached and a woman dressed in dark clothing stepped out without making eye contact. She quickly turned and walked down the corridor. Kate entered first with Wes right behind her. Kate hit the button to go down to the garage. The elevator dinged once, and the doors opened into a cavern of automobiles and the smell of stale oil and exhaust. Wes hit the remote button and the car lit up. He popped the trunk and grabbed an empty bag from Kate.

Kate went to the back seat of the car and put Wes' jacket, a package of cookies, and several maps into the bag.

"Okay, I think we've got everything," Wes said. "Oh, let's take the plates off. We'll use them on the car we buy here."

"Good idea," Kate said. "There's a screwdriver on this knife," she said, grabbing it out of her purse.

"This will only take me a second… wait," we can't drive without plates," Wes said. " I'll take them off just before I drive it into the ocean"

"Okay, let's go up and put this stuff in the apartment," Kate said.

When the elevator door opened, the same woman dressed in dark clothing hurriedly emerged from the elevator. Again, not making eye contact, she turned away from Wes and Kate and walked in the opposite direction.

"That's strange," Wes said. She got off on the seventh floor and now she's in the garage.

"She probably just forgot something in her apartment," Kate said.

"Yeah, you're probably right," Wes agreed. "Let me just drop these bags inside the apartment door. Here, give me the bag and hold the elevator door. I'll be right back."

"Okay."

Within seconds, Wes returned and the elevator went down. "That woman better not be in the elevator when we get off," Wes said. When the doors slid open, he looked in both directions. "Good, she's not here."

"Let's not get paranoid again," Kate warned.

"No, I'm not paranoid. Just careful of anyone who is around us and who may be looking our way. There's nothing wrong with being careful."

"Yes, you're right, Wes."

"Let's walk down and leave the car here. I've got money on me. We'll check it out and see if we spot something we like."

"All right, let's go this way," Kate said as she walked toward an exit.

"Charlie's Auto Sales. That's the place, and it looks like they're opened. Someone will pop out as soon as they see us on the lot."

"Let's get something that's not too flashy. There are some older cars over there," Kate said as she pointed to a row of cars.

Wes turned his head, and that was when he saw the black Honda. A four-door sedan parked along the boundary lines of the car lot. "That's the one we'll get."

"What year do you think it is?"

"It looks like a '99 Civic. Let's take it for a spin. Oh, here comes our sales guy. "Good morning, sir."

"How are you folks doing this morning? Need a car?" the salesman asked.

"Yes, we're looking at that black Civic. Can we take it for a drive?"

"Certainly, let me grab the keys and we'll take it out."

"What year is it?" Wes asked.

"It's a 1999 Civic."

"Yeah, I thought so."

"I'll be right back. By the way, my name is Charlie Gilbert."

"I'm Wes Black and this is Kate Dell."

"Nice to meet both of you. I'll just be a moment."

The test drive went well and they purchased the Civic with no problems. Cash always sold fast without any hassles.

"There's a restaurant up the street on the left. See that sign, 'Breakfast Served all Day,' Kate said as she pointed her finger across the street.

"Okay, let me swing the car around and we'll grab that parking spot near the entrance." Within seconds, he pulled into the spot and turned off the engine.

"After breakfast, we'll drive back to the apartment and pick up the other car. You can follow me up the coast," Wes said.

CHAPTER

60

The TV blared in the diner and people were glued to the screen, shocked by the latest broadcast about the murdered men found in an alley. It was a high-profile case and it was on every local channel.

Wes and Kate stood quietly as they watched the coverage. "Where do those people get their stories? They saw nothing," Wes whispered.

Kate leaned into Wes and said, "People need to get their 'one minute of fame' in front of a microphone. They'll make up any story just to be interviewed and the newscasters are right there spinning the news their way."

"There was no one in the area except that one girl who got away. They evidently didn't get any info from her."

"Not yet, they haven't," Kate said without any outward display of emotion, her gaze fixed on the television.

"If I weren't blinded, I'd have gone after her and killed her. Damn it! I left a witness!"

"Don't even think about her. We'll find Emma, and we'll be gone in a few days. Let's go and sit down at the counter."

"Yes, find Emma. Focus," Wes muttered as he scooted on a stool at the counter.

"Good morning," a pretty young woman with an Irish accent greeted them. "May I get you both something to drink?"

"Yes, we'll both have coffee," Kate said.

"So, you're from Ireland, are you?" Wes asked after he noticed the bright colored badge pinned on her apron that said, '*Deirdre—Ireland.*'

"Yes, sir," she said proudly with an Irish accent, as she poured the coffee.

"How long have you been in America?"

"I've been here a little over two years now."

"Do you like America?" Kate asked.

"Yes, very much so. I do miss my family and friends, though."

"And what brought you to America?" Wes asked.

"I married a United States Marine over in Ireland and when his tour was up, we moved here to Washington, D.C."

"And what does your husband do here?" Kate asked.

"He works for the government. He's an FBI agent."

"That sounds kind of interesting," Wes said calmly, even though his stomach suddenly felt tied in knots.

"He likes it and that's what's important," Deirdre said. "Have you decided what you'd like to have or do you need a little more time?"

Glancing at the menu Kate said, "We're ready now. I'm going to have French toast."

"Yes, and I think I'll have a spinach and Swiss cheese omelet with rye toast."

"Thank you. I'll put that order in right now," Deirdre said as she turned and went into the kitchen.

"Did you hear that? Her husband is an FBI agent and here we are sitting right here under her nose."

"Just sit still and don't draw attention to yourself," Kate said firmly. "We don't need to draw any attention from anyone."

Wes just loved Kate's naiveté. It seemed to amuse him.

"Kate, Kate, Kate. There's one thing you've got to remember, the police are incompetent fools. They have no clues, and they won't get any either. There's no connection with anyone. They cannot put the pieces together because they have nothing to go on. And from what we've seen and heard, the so-called witnesses who do come forward are complete idiots."

"Well, we need to concentrate on our search for Emma and the boys. We have no idea where they are yet. We need to find out where they live or if they're even here in D.C. Just because her uncle lives here, doesn't mean she moved back here."

"Oh, she's here. Trust me on that one."

"You don't know that for certain."

"Where else would she go? She has many friends here and she had a very good male friend named Hawk. She spent all her time with him during college."

"Did she have a romance with this Hawk guy?"

"No, they were just friends, both majoring in forensics and they studied together. Emma had quite a few male friends that she's not had romances with. She likes hanging with men."

"When was the last time she saw this Hawk guy? Is that his real name or is it a nickname?"

"You're gonna love this... his real name is Major Hawk Shaw. How's that for a name?"

"Huh. I think it sounds rather distinguished."

"I guess his parents wanted him to be in the military."

"Here you go," Deirdre announced. She placed the French toast in front of Kate and the spinach and Swiss cheese omelet in front of Wes. "If there's anything else I can get for you, please let me know."

"Oh, this looks great. Thanks, Deirdre," Kate said.

Moments later, Wes said, "Kate, I know Emma's here."

"Until we see her, we don't know that. Was this Major Hawk in the service?" Kate asked.

"Yes, as a matter of fact, he was. He was in the Marines."

"Did he make Major? Then he'd be Major Major Hawk Shaw," Kate said as she chuckled at how it sounded.

"No, I don't think he was a Major."

"Major Major Hawk Shaw. A comedian would have fun with a name like that. Have you ever met this guy?"

"No, never did. Emma never saw him or talked to him after we got married."

"So, just like that, she never emails him or calls him?"

"Nope. She stopped that once we got married. Emma is a one man woman. She would not think it was right to talk with him. She is so old-fashioned that way. Doesn't mean she hasn't called him since I left. I'm sure she has since he was her best friend."

"Top off your coffee?" With a hand on one hip, Deirdre was already filling Wes' mug with coffee.

"Thanks," Wes responded.

FBI Agent Michael O'Malley rushed over to his desk when he heard the telephone ring. "Agent O'Malley."

"Hi, honey, sorry to bother you at work, but you know those pictures you showed me a few nights ago? Those recent financial fraud perpetrators from California?"

"Yes."

"Well, right now I do believe that a man and a woman sitting at the counter are the same ones in the photos. I just served them breakfast. What should I do? I'm pretty certain they are the ones from California."

"You have a good eye, honey. Can you take a picture of them and email it to me?"

"Sure. They're sitting at the counter so I'll go into the kitchen and shoot it from the order station. They won't see me there."

"Have the chef take the picture."

"Yes, that's a good idea. I'll have Frank take it."

"Do you still have video cameras in the restaurant?"

"Yes, I'll write down the time so you can check it later."

"Okay, be careful, Deirdre. I'll wait for your email."

"All right. Bye, sweetie."

"Hey, Frank."

"Yeah?"

"Would you take a few pictures of that couple sitting at the counter for me?"

"Sure, honey. Give me the camera."

Click… Click…. Click.

"Are we about finished here?" Kate asked.

"Sure, we can get moving," Wes said as he wolfed down a large piece of toast in one voracious bite, followed by the last gulp of coffee.

CHAPTER

61

"You seem quiet, Theo," Emma said on the drive back to the office to meet up with Hawk. "Are you all right?"

"I'm fine," he said, managing a smile, but there was nothing in his voice or attitude that convinced her that he was fine.

"You are not fine, Theo. What is it?"

The horrible memory tumbled back in his mind. Once again hurt and anguish crept into his body. He had managed to push these memories into a locked vault deep within his brain all these years and now, it's all come back to haunt him once more no matter how much time had passed.

Emma waited eagerly as she watched Theo's uneasiness tighten his throat to the point that he had to squeeze out his words.

"I once had a wife," Theo said with discernible emotion as his hands tightened on the steering wheel. "Her name was Bella. She was the most incredible individual. We loved each other beyond imagination. She was seven months pregnant with our son when she was killed just walking down the street." His words became choked and tears streamed down his face.

"Oh," she gasped, reached out and took hold of his hand. "I'm so sorry. I didn't know," Emma said in a muffled voice. Suddenly everything became clear. Theo's reaction when he heard that the case they were about to work on involved young men who were gunned down. Certainly, when he saw the bodies it brought back memories of how his wife was killed.

She put her arm around his shoulders and murmured, "I'm so sorry."

He took a deep breath. "We were only in our mid-twenties with our whole lives ahead of us. She was in the residency program at Georgetown University studying to be a doctor. She lived for several hours after the shooting, and I told her the baby was fine and that I named him Jonah like she wanted. The truth is the baby didn't live; he never took a breath. She died right after she asked me to take care of our baby boy. It was a horrible time for me. I was holding her hand, trying to say good-bye, not wanting her to die. It was the worst day of my life when she slipped away. I lost the love of my life—she was the only woman I ever wanted to be with.

"The heartache and inconsolable grief were more than I could handle. I thought I would lose my mind. I felt so helpless; there was nothing I could do to put her death into perspective. My mind was unable to process her death. I felt like my heart was pulled out of my chest, and that I died with her. Oh, how I wanted to die.

"I withdrew from everyone and went through unbearable loneliness. The sorrow of losing them is still unendurable. There were times when I lost the will to live and wanted to kill myself. I became a physical invalid and had barely the strength to crawl out of bed, never mind kill myself. I had no purpose, no future. My life and happiness ended that very day.

"With terrible feelings of depression and anger, all I wanted to do was kill whoever caused my wife's death, fully aware that it would not solve my inner misery. I still miss her every day. Pain and heartache have been my companions for many years."

"Emma grabbed his hand. "I'm so sorry, Theo. So, very sorry. It must have been a very painful time for you. I can't find the words to console you, but I want you to know that I'm your friend and I'll be here for you if you ever need to talk about it."

"Thank you, Emma. You're truly a woman of compassion, and that means a great deal to me," he said as he raised her hand and kissed it, tears rolling down his cheeks.

"Does Hawk know about your wife?"

"Yes. If it weren't for Hawk, I would not be sitting here with you at this moment. He saved my sanity and my life. He's a very special man, Emma—a very special man indeed."

Emma sat silently in thought for several moments. *Hawk is special. He devotes his life to helping others. He is so unassuming; actually, for a man of his considerable talents, he is very modest. This is who Hawk really is. I'm very fortunate to have him in my life. I'll have to tell him that.*

Theo took a deep breath. He couldn't get lost in the memory now. He had to stay in the moment. "Well, back to work," he blurted out as he wiped his tears with a tissue.

"We've got to hustle back to the lab and evaluate the evidence. Hawk is counting on us."

CHAPTER

62

When Theo made the turn into the underground parking space, he was surprised to see that the first parking place, reserved for the boss, was vacant. "Looks like Hawk got caught up in something."

"I'm sure he'll be along any second now," Emma replied.

"You're right. Let's grab the gear and get up to the lab," he said as he popped the trunk.

Emma removed the scene kits and one of the cases and walked over to the elevator to push the button. Theo, carrying the other cases, was right behind her when they entered the elevator. The doors were closing slowly just as they heard car wheels squeal. Theo caught a glimpse of Hawk's car headed toward his parking space. Like lightning, his hand slipped in between the doors.

Emma just stared at him. "Good god, you've got quick reflexes, Theo."

Theo smiled as Hawk walked into the elevator. "You just made it, Majordomo."

"That gal reporter grabbed me. I thought you were the one she liked, Theo?"

"Oh," Theo said with a smile. "She grabbed me just when we first arrived on the scene, but when a car backfired, she suddenly disappeared with the rest of her crew."

When the elevator came to an abrupt stop, Hawk grabbed the case from Emma. "I want the three of us to meet in the conference room to go over the initial reports that Captain Morris handed me. I was able to take a quick look at them, and I have a strange feeling about this case. We're not dealing with a serial killer as the media proclaims. We're dealing with, I believe, a mass murderer."

"So it looks like we're going to be here for a while," Emma said.

"Yes, Em. Probably till early evening," Hawk said while slipping the key in the lock to open the office door. "You have to make arrangements for the boys?"

"Yes, no problem. I'll call and let Mrs. Healy know I'll be late."

"I ordered Chinese, and it should be here shortly."

Theo went to the lab with the scene kits, while Emma made her call to Mrs. Healy to watch the boys and give them the dinner she had prepared for them earlier this morning.

Within minutes, they both returned and sat at the conference table. Hawk had erased everything on the huge whiteboard. With a wide-tip black felt pen, he divided the board into four columns. The marker squeaked as he wrote, #1, #2, #3, #4, at the top of each column.

"Have all the victims been identified?" Hawk asked.

"Yes, they have," Theo said.

"Before we begin, I should let you know that the commissioner personally asked us to investigate this case because one of the victims was his nephew—his sister's son, Manuel Segura who was only twenty-three years old."

Emma looked at Theo in surprise.

"What are the names of the other victims, Theo?"

"The other three men were Jose Arroyo, twenty-four years old, a truck driver, five-seven, one-fifty, black hair. Next is Esteban Navarro, twenty-one years old, a restaurant worker, five-ten, one-sixty, black hair. The next victim was Cesar Ortega, twenty-three years old, a cashier at a grocery store, five-five, one-forty, black hair. The nephew was a college student, five-eight, one-seventy, brown hair.

Beneath the names, Hawk filled in the information—Name, age, occupation, approximate height, weight and hair color.

Hawk began to pace the floor. "Before we start working on what little evidence we have at this point," Hawk said, "I think this would be an excellent opportunity to go over the rules."

"What rules would that be?" Emma asked.

"Hawk's Rules," Theo responded with a grin.

"Oh. What kind of rules do you have, Hawk?"

"Rules on how to deal with anyone outside this office.

Rule #1: They'll be no talking to reporters. I'll talk with them when the time is right.

Rule #2: Do not reveal any evidence… it could turn out to be possible trial evidence.

Rule #3: Do not divulge any information about any case you may be working on to anyone. And by anyone, I mean *anyone*.

Rule #4: Got something to say? Got something that's bothering you? That's what the three of us are here for—open channels only among the three of us.

Rule #5: Whatever you do, do not talk to reporters.

Any questions about the rules?"

Silence.

Hawk's cell phone broke the silence when it buzzed and twirled on the table.

"Hello, chief."

"I have some additional information for you, Hawk. Information that should help you with the case. I'm sending one of my men down with a recording you need to listen to. Seems there was a young girl injured in this fiasco. She was just walking home from work and was attacked, but she managed to hit the guy in the face with pepper spray. Listen to the recording and perhaps one of your people can interview her tomorrow when she's feeling better. Ross Griffin was the person who found the girl injured in the street. She's staying with his girlfriend, Ellie West, who is a doctor."

"Really? Well, this is really going to help us. Thanks, chief. I'll get back to you after we've heard the recording."

"Yes, please do," the chief said. "Bye."

"Well, that was interesting," Hawk said as he placed his phone on the table. "Looks like we may have a break in the case. There was a girl involved and she's staying with Ellie," Hawk said looking at Emma.

"Ellie!" How in the world is she involved?" an astonished Emma asked.

"Seems your Uncle Ross picked Jenny up from the street after she was hit by a car and brought her to Ellie's."

"Oh, my. That's my Uncle Ross," was all Emma could say.

"The chief is sending over the recording that Ross made of Jenny's story. Should be here any moment."

"That's good news," Theo responded.

"Yes. It is. Okay, let's go over what we know right now. Since we have no viable evidence at this point, let's see what we are able to come up with. First, let's describe the killer's MO. Many homicide detectives confuse the killer's signature with his MO. The MO tells us something about *how* he did the killing, whereas the signature gives insight into *why* he did it."

Emma nodded her head to indicate she understood.

"Okay, let's see what we have for an MO. We'll start with location. What do we know?" Hawk asked," writing *Location* on the board in the fifth column.

"The attack was in an alleyway," Emma responded.

"The murders were committed sometime between 11p.m. and midnight," Theo said.

Hawk added a sixth column, *Time.*

"They were all shot once," Emma said.

"Yes," Hawk said as he walked over to Theo, stood him up, and said, "The killer walked up—bang—and shot two of the men in the chest." Hawk mimicked the shooting motion against Theo's chest and he fell to the floor.

"Or perhaps, the men walked up to the assailant and the assailant shot them both?" Emma said.

"Yes. That's very possible," Theo said as he jumped up from the floor.

Hawk paced from the whiteboard to the table and back again. "Okay, what else do we have?"

"He's left-handed," Theo said.

"How do we know he's left-handed?" Emma asked.

"By the angle the bullets hit the victims," Theo responded.

"Correct," Hawk said while writing *left-handed* under the seventh column, *Killer.* "So we now concentrate on left-handers."

Hawk sat down and stared at the whiteboard, his expression grim. He had trouble sitting still. He ran his fingers through his hair. The room went quiet.

"How did our killer pick *those* men? Did he pick them at random?" Hawk's expression was grim.

"Or perhaps by chance?" Emma said.

"This killer doesn't do anything by chance. He's too organized," Hawk said. "He picked up all the shell casings. He didn't want to leave anything behind."

"All four of the men lived in the same neighborhood," Emma said. "We have a restaurant worker, a college student, a grocery store clerk, and a truck driver. The one thing they seem to have in common is that they were all Latino's and they appeared to be friends," Emma said.

Hawk filled in *Latino* and *Friends*.

"They did try to defend themselves," Theo added. "There were defensive wounds on two of the men. Jose Arroyo had a broken arm, and Cesar Ortega was kicked in the head."

"So does this mean that they were killed because they were in the wrong place at the wrong time? That would make it a *chance* killing," Emma said.

"No. As I said a moment ago, he doesn't take chances."

"There're different variations of chance meetings," Emma said. "Suppose the killer was walking through the alleyway and these men challenged him. Or, the killer saw the men walking in the alley and thought they were a threat, and he shot them."

"I like that theory," Theo said. "Let's say the killer thought the men were a threat. There *was* a baseball bat found at the scene."

"And a knife," Emma announced.

"Okay, so here's one scenario—the four men walked up to the killer with a baseball bat and a knife. The killer fights with two of the men and throws them to the ground. Why didn't he just leave with two men down?" Hawk asked.

"This may have just started as an alley mugging," Theo said. "What happens is the men will come in from both ends of the alley, in an ambush style. The victims can't get away, they feel trapped. Perhaps they wanted his money and jewelry. These guys can be brutal as hell when they want something," Theo said as his voice cracked.

"Good job. Let's go with that scenario and we'll fill in the blanks after the two of you do your lab research," Hawk said. "Next, we need to describe the assailant.

"But we don't know what he looked like," Emma said.

"Profiler's maintain a list of descriptors that describe the *types of people* who commit these crimes. They're usually between the ages of thirty and forty years old, and they are almost always male. They don't usually cross racial lines. By that I mean, a white offender will kill a white, a black offender will kill a black."

"None of the victims were robbed," Emma said.

Hawk chalked in under *Killer*, no robbery.

"Profilers also break offenders down into organized and disorganized offenders. Organized offenders are likely to have some type of military background and are educated. Disorganized offenders are too unstable to hold a job for any length of time or be in the military for that matter. Is this assailant organized or disorganized?" Hawk asked.

"I believe him to be organized. Everything is neat and tidy. He leaves no trace of evidence behind," Emma said with some certainty.

"I have to agree with Emma," Theo said.

Hawk wrote down *Organized*. "He doesn't know his victims. This man is in control of his actions. There's a reason he's killing these people. He's *not* doing it for the pleasure of it. He's *not* hearing God command him to kill and he's *not* been ordered by any voices that he alone can hear. He's driven, but not in the sense that he's out of control. As a matter of fact, he is very much in control, in the conventional meaning of the word. He is aware of everything he is doing and knows exactly what the penalties are. I personally believe him to be quite intelligent."

A loud knock on the door interrupted them. "I'll get it," Emma said as she jumped up and walked into the lobby. She reached into her purse and took out a ten dollar bill before she opened the door. Kim, the delivery boy from the Chinese Restaurant stood with four large bags. "Hi, Kim. Thank you so much." She handed him his tip and she grabbed the bags.

"Thank you, Miss Emma."

"We've got plenty of food here," she said as she placed the bags on the center of the table.

"Okay, let's take a break while our food is hot." Hawk said.

Emma opened all the containers and placed them in a row. Theo grabbed the plates and silverware from the cabinet and handed them to everyone.

"I'm starving. Smells delicious," Hawk said.

"You know what the secret to good food is, don't you?" Emma asked.

"What's that," Theo inquired.

"Hunger!" Emma said, followed by laughter from the guys.

There was another knock on the door.

CHAPTER

63

"Okay, Theo, now that the chief's delivered us the girl's recording let's get rolling. This is a real break for us," Hawk said as he dragged a chair from the conference table, straddled it backward, and folded his arms over the back of it while Theo loaded the tape.

They sat quietly, listening to every word the girl had said. Every now and then, Emma's eyes and mouth would open in amazement—it was like uncovering a surprise packet.

"This is perfect," Hawk announced loudly. "We now have a real witness. She sprayed the son of a bitch with pepper spray. I love it! While she may not have witnessed the shootings in the alley, she came in direct contact with the assailant and his apparent accomplice. This helps us immensely."

Emma and Theo were all smiles. "This is now getting interesting," Emma said.

"Sure is," Theo said. "Who was the young boy Jenny said she saw on a bicycle?"

"What would a young boy be doing riding his bicycle that late at night?" Emma asked.

Hawk looked at Emma. "He probably wasn't supposed to be out that late so he may not come forward."

Emma, with a pained look on her face, said, "Yeah, you're right."

"Okay, let's get started. First, I want you," Hawk said, looking at Theo, "to call Jenny Dumas and set up a time to visit her and let her know you're coming to talk with her tomorrow morning. We'll work on the information she just gave us and when you see her tomorrow, perhaps she may remember more."

"Okay," Theo responded as he picked up the information sheet the Chief put inside the envelope with the recording.

"Let's get started on the whiteboard and get all the information we've just learned about inserted. Now we're getting somewhere," Hawk said enthusiastically.

The legs of Hawk's chair made an irritating screech on the tiled floor when he suddenly got up and filled in the sixth column with *Jenny Dumas*. He wrote: *pepper-sprayed killer.*

"I took notes from the recording," Emma said. "The attacker was Caucasian, about six feet tall, blond hair. The driver was also Caucasian and blonde. Perhaps they were brother and sister?"

No one answered Emma.

"The assailant told the woman to go and get the car and she left the scene," Theo said.

"He most definitely had a female accomplice," Hawk said. "The car stopped where the killer was crying in pain from the pepper spray, and she picked him up."

Hawk's cell phone vibrated again. "Hello, Hawk Shaw."

"This is Detective Jacobson, and I'm calling about the case you're working on for the commissioner. We've got a young boy who witnessed the girl who was hit by the car. His name is Bobby Blake. We have a report of what he told the officer who interviewed him, and I thought perhaps you'd like to see it. If you give me your fax number, I'll be happy to fax it over to you."

"That would be wonderful, Detective Jacobson. Thank you," he said, before he gave him his fax number.

"Looks like we're getting more than a few breaks in the case," Hawk said as he wrote in a seventh column: *Bobby Blake*. "It's very unusual that *two* people who don't know each other have information about the same case. *Very unusual,* indeed."

CHAPTER

64

They drove north for well over an hour before they reached any accessible waterways. They passed a few shallow duck ponds, but drove farther until they found a more suitable waterhole to drown the car.

"I see a quarry ledge area over on the right-hand side of the road just below that slope," Wes told Kate on his cell phone. "The water should be pretty deep there. Let's pull over on the shoulder."

"Okay, I'll follow you," Kate replied.

Wes eased the car over to the shoulder and stepped out, leaving the engine running. He wanted to make sure the water would be deep enough and that he would be able to jump to safety before he ditched the car. He paced the quarry's edge, not getting too close to the brim of the cliff. He had no intention of sliding down the stones and cracking his head open.

"Ah, yes. This is the perfect spot." With his size and strength, he figured the jump would be easy.

He walked back over to Kate, who remained in her car. "This looks like as good a spot as any. It's about a twenty-foot drop, and there's no one around. I'll go back down the road, and then speed the car up and jump out just before it goes over."

"You're going to kill yourself!" Kate yelled.

"No, I'll be okay. You wait right here," Wes demanded. "Here, hold my sunglasses."

She held his sunglasses in her hand, silently thinking, *nothing seems to be going right for him; perhaps he will kill himself. If he goes over with the car, I'll just hop on the next plane to South America. I'm safer alone than I am with him. His screw-ups are beginning to mount and he's fast becoming a liability. I need to get rid of this man before we both get caught and we spend the rest of our lives behind bars.*

He turned around and headed back toward the car. He was excited, euphoric, as adrenaline rushed through his veins like a narcotic. He jumped in the car and rode down the pavement several hundred feet before he made a U-turn. He stepped on the gas pedal to get the car up to about 40 mph, opened the door, and launched himself into the air, higher than he needed to. With his arms held over his head, he landed heavily. The impact knocked the breath out of him when he fell to the ground, just a split second before the car flew in the air and landed in the water.

Within a few seconds, he scrambled to his feet, waved to Kate to let her know he was not hurt, and then ran over to the ledge to see the results of his effort. "Ahh," he muttered, "it worked." The car was already half covered with water. He turned around to walk back to the car and gave Kate a big grin accompanied by a thumbs-up hand gesture.

"Damn," she murmured to herself while forcing a wave back at him. "Now he's a stunt driver."

"See, that wasn't bad, eh?" Wes said with a big childish grin. "That was kinda fun, actually," Wes said as he brushed himself off.

"Get in, Evel Knievel, and let's get out of here."

"It'll be buried in ten minutes. We're outta here."

CHAPTER

65

The Examiner, Washington, D.C.

Tuesday, April 23, 2002

Four Unidentified Bodies Found in Central D. C.

Shortly after 7 a.m. on Monday, April 22, 2002, a kitchen worker at a local restaurant spotted the bodies of four men lying in the alley beside a Dumpster. He immediately went over to one of the bodies, saw that he was dead, and called 911. Within minutes, police arrived at the scene. Moments later, a homicide detective came and quickly roped off the area while waiting for the crime-scene technicians to arrive.

The medical examiner concluded that the bodies were all young men. Two men were shot in the chest and the other two men were shot in the back while lying on the ground. All victims were in their early twenties. Time of the deaths was approximately between 11 p.m. and midnight Sunday evening. Identification is pending; no identification was found on or near the bodies.

Police spent the next few hours canvassing the area for clues. No one recalled seeing or hearing anything unusual that evening.

# # #

CHAPTER

66

After public outcry had demanded that something be done to insure the public's safety, Chief of Police Morris called an Information Homicide Department conference to determine and develop a city-wide effort to apprehend the killer. Those present at the meeting were members of various police divisions: patrol officers, homicide detectives, undercover officers, crime analysts and division investigation personnel. The FBI also sent a dozen special agents to the meeting.

Working twelve-hour shifts, the Homicide squad plus dozens of policemen from other departments were canvassing the area, following up every phone-in and every lead. Police came at the problem from several angles—more patrols in the area, confront all persons suspected of any involvement in criminal activity around the targeted area, retrieve information about open and past investigations of suspects in the area, and talk to their informants on the streets.

With no definite leads, investigators reviewed the FBI's ViCAP database of unsolved crimes for possible clues or connections to determine if there were other similar cases.

Knowing that the killer possessed the power to select victims who were walking down the street intensified personal mortality. As long as the killer remained uncaught he was free to kill again. Preoccupation with the murderer seemed to dominate all conversations—who was he, when would he kill again? An atmosphere of suspicion and mistrust emerged among the public because no one could be trusted, including the police, their neighbors and even those people who were once their friends. With the deaths of four young men, the buildup of fear grew exponentially among the public and the sheer magnitude of the case prompted the FBI to breach protocol and consult with experts.

"I'm glad you were able to assist in this case, Hawk," Police Commissioner Snyder said. Hawk reached out his arm to shake hands with him. A solid, square man with no neck and powerful shoulders. His face was as gray as his hair.

"I'm sorry for your loss, and my condolences to your sister. I'm here to assist in any way I can, commissioner. Same as always."

"This is a very sensitive case, Hawk. These young men were cut down in the prime of their lives, and the public wants answers."

"I will do my best, sir."

"I know you will, Hawk. I insisted on calling you because of your past experience with these types of murderers—lunatic psychotics." The commissioner paused a moment, then stared into Hawk's eyes, and said, "I'm going to send this killer straight to Hell."

"We'll catch him, commissioner."

When Chief Morris stepped up to the microphone, the buzz of conversation in the room immediately ceased. "I would like to take this opportunity to introduce you to a young man with extraordinary talents in both police science and psychiatric criminology. His talents have delivered criminals to justice that the police could not touch. His intense interests in the erratic acts of human nature have led to success in many of our cases. Commissioner Snyder has asked that he assist us with this particular case and he will now brief all of you on his findings. Major Hawk Shaw."

Hawk walked to the front of the audience and glanced around the room. All eyes were on him. He cleared his throat, and said, "Thank you. And thank you all for attending this briefing."

"I know what a lot of you are asking yourself right now. What is this guy doing here? I also know you're asking what can he find out that we can't find out for ourselves? I will hopefully be able to answer those questions for you today.

"I work, think, and investigate a little differently than most of you were taught to investigate a homicide. So what I would like to do is explain to all of you how I investigate a crime.

"My team and I view the scene of the crime as if it were a piece of art. Why? You might ask. Because there's an absence of motion... it's a still life. Our task is to collect the facts and evidence and reassemble the scene so that it comes alive. By the time my team has completed their analysis, we will have recreated what happened, when it happened, and how it happened. The only question we won't be able to answer immediately is *who* is responsible for these horrific crimes.

"My task today is to provide this talented group assembled here today with some insight into the mind of this particular killer." Hawk paced the floor in silence for a few moments. There wasn't a cough or whisper among the audience.

"Facts!" Hawk shouted as he paced the floor. "We collect facts and evidence to draw some type of conclusion but then it becomes nothing more than a bunch of theories, right?"

Hawk looked at the audience nodding their heads.

"Wrong!" Hawk shouts while he watches the response from his audience: shock in their eyes followed by loud murmurs and shoes shuffling on the floor.

"In order to solve these types of cases we need to listen to *all* the theories, *all* the reasons, and probabilities emanating from both the public and the media. Once we plow through all these conjectures, we will add the facts to the physical evidence left at the scene, thus allowing us to establish a firm ground so we can get a grip on this case."

Hawk was silent for a few seconds, as he again, carefully looked at his audience. "There are rumors out there that this was the work of a serial killer. What makes a serial killer? I don't think anyone knows for sure, but there are numerous factors that can influence such behavior and there are various theories of why a person becomes a serial killer. Serial killers all have excuses for their behavior—their upbringing, voices in their head, pornography made him do it, prison life turned him into a monster, an accident made them hypersexual, or they may even turn the blame around and say the victims deserved to die.

"But, how do we know that the man who killed these four young men isn't a serial killer? According to the Department of Justice, a mass murderer is defined when a single event at one location involves four or more people. So no, this is not the work of a serial killer. Serial killers kill in a series of events, and by that I mean there could be days or weeks between murders.

"Those who kill three to four people during a single event are what we call a 'mass murderer.' There is also a difference in the way a community reacts to a serial killer versus a mass murderer. Society tends to get briefly shocked by a mass murderer and they soon return to normal. Whereas a serial killer instills a lingering horror with lasting interest.

"Today, we'll just talk about this particular mass murderer along with some statistical information intermingled with the killer's psychological profile. Hopefully, it will be useful to all of you.

"Statistically speaking, the average mass murderer is a white male, usually in his forties or fifties, single or divorced and may have been physically or emotionally abused by his parents.

"We're looking for a killer who has a thirst for power and revenge. He seeks revenge because it is the typical response to a narcissistic personality and he will lash out in an effort to avoid what is within. He is clever, focused and angry and most definitely wants revenge.

"The killer is a probable combat veteran who has killing skills. He's trained to kill quickly and effectively. He may have been a Navy Seal, or possibly had some martial arts training. He keeps physically fit, and he's probably in his late thirties.

"Killing four young men in an alley and then running away from the scene with a woman tells me he's killing for the sake of it though there's a motivation making him disgruntled because he believes a certain someone or something is responsible for his problems in life. Something is pushing him."

"So you believe he had a partner?" an officer in the front row asked.

"Yes, he most definitely had an accomplice. The partner was the one driving the car that struck down the young woman. According to her, the driver was a woman with blonde hair. She drove the car directly at her, and then went and picked up the man crying in pain from the pepper spray."

The audience stirs; mumbles are heard.

"He's not one to leave any evidence or witnesses, so the fact that a young woman was able to escape after she pepper-sprayed his face, will undoubtedly cause him to try and find her."

An FBI agent raises his hand and asks, "So you really believe that he's going to try to find her and kill her?"

"He may, because she knows what he looks like. He's probably envisioned her sitting with a police sketch artist giving a detailed description of what he looked like. Making mistakes is definitely not allowed. He's mad as hell at himself because he was careless and he now has caused a ding in his plan."

"What description of the man did the young woman who was attacked give to the police?" a female officer in the front row asked.

"She thought him to be Caucasian, with blonde hair, possibly in his thirties, about six feet tall. Also, the assailant evidently has money."

"How do you know he has money?" she asked.

"When the assailant dropped to his knees after being pepper-sprayed, the young woman noticed yellow octagons on the bottom of his shoes. These are Danner hiking boots and they sell for over three hundred dollars. The police are currently searching all the shoe merchants in the area to find out if they recognize the description we have of the assailant."

A police officer in the back of the room raised his arm and asked, "Do we have any evidence left at the scene?"

"We haven't gone over all the evidence we've collected so far, but we do know he had a .32 caliber handgun with a possible silencer on it because no one has reported hearing any gunshots."

"Were there any other witnesses?" a uniformed officer asked.

"Yes, there was a teenaged boy on a bicycle who saw the car hit the young woman. He said the car was a beige or silver Honda. It was shiny and looked new. He didn't get a look at the license plates."

"Is this guy whacked out?" An officer from the back of the room asked while holding up his arm.

"It depends on what your definition of *whacked out* is. Is he crazy? No. He may be obsessed, but he is not crazy. I can understand why many of you think this guy must be insane. After all, what rational person could shoot and kill four young men and walk away? His mind may be evil, but he's not abnormal in the sense that he does have control of his decisions. He has to disregard the feelings of the victims to prove that he has control.

"Is he whacked out on drugs? No, I don't believe so because he must, at all times, keep his mind sharp. He's not on drugs or alcohol. He can't afford to make mistakes.

"On the other hand, he may be a man running away from something or perhaps he's wanted for some past crime he's committed. Someone just may be on his tail and now he will do anything to elude them. He has no respect for the law and he has to prove he is smarter and shrewder than any law enforcement agency.

"What we have here is a mass murderer and a psychopathic offender who some would say is an aggressive narcissist who has to restore his own sense of dominance; he has to feel the power."

"If he's so smart, doesn't he realize the consequences he'll have to face once he's caught?" a young FBI agent asked.

"The psychopath never thinks about the consequences of any of his actions. There's little if any, emotion reflected at the crime scene of mass murderers. He has an underlying reason for killing. We need to find out whom or what is pushing this guy to the edge."

Suddenly, Theo rushed up to where Hawk was standing and handed him a note. "Excuse me a moment," Hawk said to the audience.

"This better be good," Hawk said softly, annoyance clearly in his tone.

Hawk glanced at the note. '*FBI Agent O'Malley has positively identified Wes Blair and Kate Lee from photos from a surveillance video belonging to a local restaurant.*'

"Thanks, Theo." Hawk put the note in his pocket and Theo turned and walked to the back of the meeting room.

"Sorry about that. Well, that's all the information we currently have. Are there questions?"

No one replied.

"Should you come up with any questions, I'm available to answer them at any time. I ran off copies for all of you that cover the information I talked about today. Be sure to pick up a copy from the table in the back of the room. My cell number is on the sheet, so please feel free to call. Thank you."

Applause followed by mumbling and the scrape of chairs as people stood up and emptied the room.

CHAPTER

67

It was nine-thirty when Hawk walked into his office. When Emma heard him come in, she went through the lab doorway, dressed in a lab coat, Nitrile gloves, goggles on her head and a breathing mask hanging just below her chin.

The usual good-humored, cocky energy that she witnessed in Hawk yesterday had been replaced. Today he looked tired, the kind of tired that saps color from the face and reddens the eyes.

"You don't look like you rested last night, Hawk."

"I didn't," he said, walking toward her with a worried look.

"What's wrong?" Emma asked as her brows puckered with a look of concern that flickered in her violet eyes. "You seem anxious about something. Are there any new developments?"

"No, it's not about the cases."

Immediately, Emma's eyes filled with anxiety. "Then what?"

"Emma, we…" Hawk closed his eyes, his expression pained. "This is not good news," he said awkwardly, shaking his head.

Emma said nothing and just stared at Hawk. "And…?"

He didn't answer right away. He locked his eyes on hers, a muscle ticked in his clenched jaw before he said, "Wes is in D.C."

Emma's jaw dropped. Terror filled her eyes as she drew in a deep breath. The blood was gone from her face in an instant. Her features hardened as if she had been frozen. She just stood there, emotionally numb as fear, hate and remembered terror devoured her to the core of her being. She shook her head back and forth. The words make its mark on her consciousness, but she was at odds accepting the fact as reality. She went dizzy for a moment as she slumped toward Hawk.

Moments later, she stepped back, straightened her body, threw her hands in the air and burst out angrily, "My god, how did he know I was here? Just hearing his name makes me cringe. Where is he?"

"That I don't know," Hawk replied, his eyebrows pulled together in a scowl. His lips turned in on themselves as he rubbed his hand over his worried face.

"When did you find out he was here?"

"I just found out this morning," he said as he bit his lower lip.

"Did you see him? How did you find out?"

"When Theo heard about the mortgage fraud Wes was involved with, he contacted one of his friends in the FBI that works fraud. It seems this guy's wife spotted Wes and his girlfriend in the restaurant where she works. She took a photo of them sitting at the counter and sent it to her husband. As soon as he ID'd him, he called Theo."

"Where is Theo?"

"He'll be here shortly."

"I cannot believe it," she repeated. "Now what do I do?" she said removing her mask from her head and pulling her goggles off her head.

"You don't do anything. Just because he's here, doesn't necessarily mean he knows *you're* here. Where are the boys?"

"They're with Ellie and Ross. Does Uncle Ross know?"

"No, I wanted to tell you first. I'm about to call him now."

"Oh, I am so angry I could spit," Emma said with tears building up in her eyes.

"Come here, Em," Hawk said, holding his arms toward her. "No one's going to harm you or the boys," he said as he pushed a tissue into her hand and gathered her in his arms. She leaned against his shoulder and felt his warm breath in her hair. His lips kissed her briefly on her forehead. "Do you think I'd let someone hurt you or the boys? That will never happen, Emma."

Embracing him affectionately, she felt secure and safe in his arms. She had forgotten what it felt like to be watched over. She never felt protected while she was married to Wes. He was too self-absorbed to watch over anyone but himself.

Okay, I'm not going to panic, she thought to herself. *Right now, my life is more or less on an even keel and it needs to stay that way.*

"I would do anything to make you and the boys feel just a little bit safer," he murmured.

"I know you would, Hawk. I do feel safer when you're around."

A cell phone went off. They distanced themselves, wondering whose phone it was.

"Ah, it's mine, Hawk. Hello?"

"Hi Emma, it's Ellie."

"Hi, Ellie. How are the boys behaving?"

"Oh, they're outside with Ross playing ball. They're so much fun. I wanted to pass something by you. Have you got a minute?"

"Sure."

I wanted to know if you, the boys, and Hawk would be interested in going on a cruise to Bermuda in a couple of months. Ross and I were talking about it and thought it would be a great experience for all of us to go as a family."

"What a wonderful idea. It sounds great. The boys would love it. Let me talk with Hawk and see what he thinks. Not to change the subject, but Hawk just told me that Wes was spotted in D.C."

"What? Good God! Are you okay, honey? And here I am chattering to you about going on a cruise. I'm sorry, Emma."

"That's okay, Ellie. I'm in good hands. Hawk is standing right next to me."

"Okay, I'll let Ross know. I know he'll want to talk with Hawk later."

"I'm sure. Just let him know about it."

"I will. Bye, Emma."

Emma closed her cell phone with a snap. "That was Ellie. You won't have to call Ross. Ellie will let him know, but I'm sure he'll probably want to talk to you regardless. He'll call you."

"Fine," Hawk said. "How's our investigation coming along?"

"We'll have things wrapped up late this afternoon."

"Okay. Let's get together about five o'clock."

CHAPTER

68

"Good morning, may I help you?" the young woman asked when Wes and Kate walked into the Richardson Real Estate office.

"Yes," Kate responded. "We're looking for an apartment for perhaps a week or so. We would rather not stay in a hotel with all the commotion and noise so we were wondering if you knew of anything that might be available. We're looking for someplace where it's quiet and away from the maddening crowds."

"I understand. Come in, sit down and we'll see what we have. My name is Lois Preston," she said as she gestured to a small conference table.

"This is Wes Black, and I'm Kate Dell," Kate said as she led the way to the conference table and sat down. Wes slouched into the chair next to Kate.

Lois turned toward her desk to grab her briefcase. She placed it on the desk and reached inside to pull out a red ring-bound notebook. Flipping it open at one of the tabs, she snatched a brochure out of a folder.

"I think I have just what you need," she said as she pulled out a chair next to Kate. She smoothed her skirt as she sat down and handed Kate the brochure.

"From what you've described to me so far, I don't think an apartment or house is what you're looking for. You need something that's secure; where no one will have access. You don't need chambermaids coming and going.

I believe this will be much more suitable for you," she said as she pointed to the picture on the cover of the brochure—*Professional Apartments for professional people on the go.*

"This particular building was once a hotel and the new owners have turned it into full-service apartments catering to business people. You need a place to call your own without anyone bothering you. It's an office and a home combination. It has one bedroom, a den, a full bath and a half-bath, a kitchen, dining room, and living room. There's also a stacked washer and dryer in each unit, and a microwave. There's a pool on the bottom floor and a full-sized workout room. You don't have to leave the building if you care not to. You have access to the Internet, fax, a professional secretary is on the first floor, should you need one, and, of course, a telephone. If you don't have a computer, the office downstairs can rent you one for a week. It's up to you."

"That won't be necessary, we have our own computers."

"Now, I saved the best for last. The best feature and the most popular among the guests is the fact that there is a kitchen staff that will prepare your meals and deliver them to your apartment if you don't care to go out. There are menus in the apartment from which you can order breakfast, lunch, or dinner. As an added bonus, there's a rooftop access and many of the guests have had dinner served on the rooftop. The kitchen staff sets it all up. It's very romantic."

"That's quite different. Sounds wonderful," Kate said. "Perhaps we'll do that one evening."

"Is there some sort of lease attached to this?" Wes inquired.

"No, that's the sweetness of the deal. You can rent it by the week. If you would like a maid to come and clean for you, you just pick up the phone, name the time and she'll be there. It's your choice."

Kate handed the brochure to Wes. "It sounds like this is just what we've been looking for. What do you think?"

"Yeah, it certainly looks good. Are there any vacancies at the moment?"

"As a matter of fact, I was just over there earlier this morning, and yes, they do have two vacancies available. One unit is on the second floor and the other is on the fifth floor.

Wes turned to face Kate and asked, "Which floor would you like, Kate?"

"How about the fifth floor? It'll have a view." Wes nodded his head.

"Fine, I'll call and have them hold it for you. Oh, I almost forgot. They also have underground parking spaces for all the tenants."

"Perfect," Wes said.

"There's a security deposit of twenty-five hundred dollars and with a week's rent of forty-five hundred, that'll be $7,000 for the first week. Check out time is 11a.m. They would appreciate knowing two days in advance if you plan to stay another week. They usually have waiting lists."

"No problem," Wes said. He reached into his pocket and handed her seven thousand cash.

"I'll need you to fill out this packet," she said before she handed it to Wes. "It only takes a few minutes to fill out."

Wes grimaced at the packet and looked at Kate.

"I'll be glad to fill it out," Kate said as she gently took it from Wes' hands, grabbed a pen from her purse and quickly began to fill out the required information.

"Here's an enlarged map of D.C. I've marked the streets with a highlighter for you. This is where we are," she said, pointing to the 'X' on the map. This is where the

apartment building is; again pointing to another circled
'X.' It's only two blocks from here, so you shouldn't have
a problem finding the building."

Wes looked at the map for a few seconds and said,
"Thank you. We'll find it."

"Will you be going over there now?"

"Yes, we'd like to do that. Is it ready now?" Wes
asked.

"Yes, it is. I'll call and let them know you'll be
coming over. When you arrive, please check in at the front
desk. They'll be expecting you. Before they show you to
your apartment, they'll give you a short tour of the facility
to familiarize you with the layout of the building. If you
have any problems, here's my card. Feel free to call me."

"Thank you, Ms. Preston. You've been a great
help," Kate said, handing the paperwork to her.

"This is going to work out fine, don't you think?"
Wes asked as he unpacked his luggage.

"Yes, this is nice and it's quiet and best of all, it's
private."

"We can set up the computer in the den," Wes said.
"We need to work out how we're going to wire the money
from Panama to the Cook Islands."

"I can do that. We'll take a look after we settle in."

Wes was nervous because he didn't know where the
money was at any given time. Only Kate knew. She split
and routed, and rerouted the money as she saw fit. She was
familiar with foreign clients and understood foreign
markets, currencies, and banking—that was her specialty.
It was time he too knew how it was done.

"I'd like to see how you do that."

"You do? Why, don't you trust me?"

"Of course, I do, but I want to know what you
know, just in case something happens to either of us."

"Oh, there you go worrying again. Nothing is going to happen."

During the next few hours, Kate instructed Wes on how to move money safely from A to B. She showed him how to move it anywhere in the world and instructed him about offshore tax havens and the safest investments in which to put their money into. Kate scattered the money among three banks; one in the Grand Caymans, one in Brazil, and the third in the Cook Islands. She divided, dispersed and routed, giving Wes all the specifics.

"Is this safe? Can someone break into these accounts?" Wes asked.

"Yes," Kate said as she put a comforting hand on Wes' shoulder, "it's safe. Encryption is strictly about numbers and is based on asymmetric public key cryptography that allows the electronic transmission to be safe and viable."

Wes could almost pick up the scent of money as he transferred multiple funds to various accounts. After they absconded with the fourteen million dollars that belonged to the Russians and the six million the Russians had already paid them for their part in the fraud, they would have a full twenty million.

CHAPTER

69

The hour was a quarter past six in the morning when the driver stared through the windshield, singing along with a tune on the radio while he intermittently sipped his coffee. His cell phone jangled and he reached down, hit the speaker button and placed the phone in one of the cup holders.

"Burt," he said negotiating the curve in the road while he juggled his coffee.

What happened next transpired in seconds. His heart jumped, and he nearly dropped his coffee. "Arg!" he groaned when he slammed on the brake pedal. The car lurched to an absolute standstill several inches away from taillights right in front of him. Coffee spilled, the phone fell out of the cup holder. "What the..."

He had traveled this road five mornings a week for two years and had never seen any stopped vehicles in this area while en route to work. Suddenly, coming out of nowhere, blue flashers flickered in his rearview mirror. About sixty seconds ago, he would have sworn he had the road all to himself. He eased his car along the shoulder and hopped out to see what kind of situation had caused traffic to halt. He had walked down the road several hundred feet before he noticed a policeman. "Hey, what's going on?" he asked.

The police officer turned and said, "Sorry, sir. There's been an accident and it'll be another thirty minutes before we can open up the highway. Please return to your car, sir."

He waved his arm and walked back to his car.

Within minutes, tow trucks, police cars, and an ambulance arrived at the scene. A black van pulled up and several men climbed out, wearing blue jackets with FBI stenciled on the back in gold lettering.

A small cache of law enforcement officers quickly cordoned off the area with yellow tape that had the words CRIME SCENE—NO TRESPASSING printed on it. Others had cameras and were taking photos to record a pictorial view of what the scene looked like. Two-way police radios crackled and squawked, all communicating in garbled jargon while a heavy-duty tow truck with a hydraulic crane attempted to pull a car out of the water.

CHAPTER

70

The weather was clear and crisp, the sun was shining, and the blossoming cherry trees signified that the arrival of spring was here to brighten the city with pink flowers. Ross decided it was a perfect day to walk down to Union Station from his office to have lunch with his old friend, Bob Lucas. Ross did not usually take lunch breaks, but Bob had called him yesterday. Said he had something to tell him.

The Thunder Grill was a pleasant place that was favored at lunchtime by the many local office buildings and, of course, all the shoppers. It was one of their favorite restaurants and whenever they did meet for lunch, they always had the same meal—Texas Nachos made with beer simmered beef chili and melted cheese.

Ross' first stop was at the outdoor market to pick up some organic fruits and vegetables for Ellie. With shopping bag in hand, he crossed the expanse of the West Hall past the Center Café to the Thunder Grill.

From the small clearing immediately inside the entrance of the restaurant, Ross could see that the restaurant was, as always, extremely busy at one o'clock, the favored arrival time for at least half the lunch crowd. A small reservation desk was manned by a short, mustached man, who, at the moment, was talking on the telephone. Two women were waiting on a bench, huddled together, giggling.

Ross hesitated briefly as he scanned past the gleaming marble pillars to the dining room and spotted Bob sitting at a table on the far side of the restaurant that looked out to the mall. He was playing idly with the handle of his coffee mug.

He started through the maze of tables. Bob looked up, saw Ross and waved. He smiled warmly and his teeth caught a splash of light from the window.

Ross gave a wave back; one could always find Bob with his full head of graying hair, expertly barbered. He was dressed in a dark gray suit cut lean against his tall, slender frame. Pleased to see Ross, he shook his hand with vigor, demonstrating that there was an immediate connection between them.

"Great to see you, Bob. I hope I didn't keep you waiting."

"No, not at all," Bob responded.

Ross placed his shopping bag on the seat next to him, saying, "I had to pick up a few things for Ellie."

"How is Ellie doing?" Bob inquired.

"She's great. She just loves her job at Walter Reed."

Ross pulled out his chair and sat down. He looked directly at Bob, immediately noticing that Bob's thin, bony face looked drawn. His complexion was pale and there is a look of intense concentration in his eyes.

"Are you okay? You don't look well. Is something wrong?"

"I guess one could say something is wrong. I need to talk with someone."

"Start talking, buddy. I'm listening."

Bob looked at Ross for a moment before saying, "I'm dying, Ross. I'm fuckin' dying."

"What? What happened?" Ross asked, disbelieving what he just heard.

"I've got kidney cancer. I just found out two days ago."

"Oh, no, Bob. I'm so sorry to hear that. Will they be giving you any kind of treatments?"

"I don't want to go through all that chemo crap."

"What's the prognosis?"

"Oh, they rambled on and said anywhere between six months and two years. It depends on how fast it grows."

"You got any symptoms?"

"Not really… at least not right now. They say some are fast growing and some are not. So, we'll just wait and see. I'm so tired of all the poking and probing and biopsies. I don't want any more tests done."

"What prompted you to go to the doctor, if you didn't have any symptoms?"

"I had a backache. I don't usually have any back problems, but this one didn't go away."

"How's Judy taking this?" Ross asked.

Suddenly, they were interrupted by the young waiter. "May I get either of you something to drink?"

Bob quickly said, "I'll have Perrier water, please."

"And for you, sir," the waiter asked as he looked at Ross.

"I'll make it easy for you. I'll have the same."

"Two Perrier waters, coming up."

"Hold on a sec," Ross said to the waiter. "How's your appetite, Bob?"

"You know. It's actually pretty good, considering. Are we ready for those Nachos?"

"Yeah, bring em' on," Ross said. "Make that two Perrier waters and two orders of Nachos."

The waiter quickly turned after saying, "Yes, sir. "I'll get those right away."

"Where were we….Oh, yes, Judy. You know women. They want you to have all these tests done and go through chemo and radiation, or whatever the hell else they have. She's quite upset with me because I don't want any of it. I've explained it to her over and over again. I've seen men after they have chemo. Not a bright picture. I don't want any part of it."

"You should talk to Ellie," Ross said, knowing he was taking a chance that Bob would be angry with him too.

"I don't want to talk to anybody," Bob said as he nervously wiped his mouth with his napkin and put it down on the table in front of him. "I have been in front of more doctors and specialists and have heard more theories than I care to mention. I'm through with them all."

Ross could see the fear in his eyes. Fear of having all those treatments. Fear of being sick all the time and not being able to work. In a way, he couldn't blame him for feeling this way.

The waiter brought their food. Ross stared across the table at Bob the whole time the waiter was placing the plates down and filled their glasses with Perrier water. When he was gone, Ross spoke first.

"Look, all I'm saying is to have Ellie take a look at your medical report and then go and talk to her."

Bob didn't respond right away. He just stared at his plate of food and moved it around with his fork, but he did not eat anything.

"I guess it would make Judy happy. I really like Ellie. She's smart and to the point. I appreciate that in a doctor."

He then took the time to take his first bite of food.

Ross smiled and put his fork down. "I'll make a deal with you," he said. "After Ellie reads your medical reports, I'll go with you when you talk to her and find out what the best treatment would be. I don't want you to be alone in this."

"Thanks, Ross. This means a lot to me. I need another guy around for balance."

"Okay, consider it done."

"I heard your friend, Hawk is working on the case where four young men were killed in an alley," Bob said.

"Yes, he was called in by the police commissioner. He's a good man. Always seems to come up with the answers. He's been seeing my niece since she came back to D.C. and she's actually working for him now. You remember when they both studied forensics at GW?"

"Yes. As I recall, they were pretty close when they were in college—but just friends."

"Yes, they were, but Emma had to go off to California and marry that jerk."

"Ah, we all make mistakes. Don't you remember when you were young?"

"Yeah, don't remind me."

"How is Emma settling in with the boys?" Bob inquired.

"She's doing great and the boys are fantastic. Ellie and I are having fun with them. They're great kids and we're getting very attached to them. We've had them over for a sleepover a couple of times and they don't want to leave us. They are driving Emma crazy because Ellie has Violet, the dog and now they each want a dog. I just sit and laugh at Emma's reactions. She's a great mother and the boys aren't spoiled. Not until they come over to stay with Ellie and me… ha ha ha."

CHAPTER

71

After shopping for several hours in the mall, Kate slipped in Neuhaus Chocolatier to get some caramel chocolates. Wes was getting hungry, so he walked toward the Main Hall and noticed the Center Café.

He walked back and met up with Kate. "You getting hungry?" he asked.

"Are there any restaurants around here?"

Pointing toward the Main Hall, he said, "Yeah, there are several, right down there."

"Okay, let's stop."

When they walked down the aisle, Kate noticed a stairway leading to a balcony over the restaurant. "Hey, look at the upstairs. That's perfect. Let's sit up there."

Wes looked up. There was a second-floor rotunda all finished in dark mahogany wood with a curved stairway just above the Center Café bar and patio seating. It was lunchtime, and it was the perfect spot for people watching. They climbed the stairs admiring the architecture and statues. Perched high above, they were able to watch people run about trying to catch their trains. Patrons were already having lunch at several of the tables.

Kate placed her shopping bags on the seat near the railing and sat where she would have a clear view of the hall. Wes took the seat next to her so he too could see everything.

The table was set with glasses, napkins, condiments, and a menu. They scanned the menu for a minute or so, and by the time they decided, a waiter appeared who did not appear very friendly and seemed to be in a hurry. He quickly took their order: two Cokes, a smoked turkey wrap, and Pastrami Panini.

"This is a good spot for people watching, eh?" Kate said.

"It is just that," Wes responded, with a crooked smile. "We may just see what we're looking for."

"Oh, this place is too big to spot someone you know."

"One never knows, Katie, dear. One never knows."

Service was definitely not one of the strong points for this restaurant. It was twenty minutes before they got their drinks and forty minutes before they got their lunch, which turned out to be pretty bad at best. The pastrami was cold and the cheese wasn't melted. The wrap surrounding the smoked turkey was like cardboard. "This is horrible food," Kate muttered. "Is your sandwich any good?"

"Naw, it's bad too. Let's get out of here." Wes stood, staring at the bill: twenty-seven dollars. He dropped thirty dollars on the table. Kate grabbed her shopping bags. When they descended the stairs, Kate first, Wes suddenly grabbed her shoulder to stop her.

"What?" she said, turning to look at Wes.

"You're not going to believe this, but there's Emma's Uncle Ross."

"Where?"

Pointing his finger at him, he said, "See those two gray-headed men walking together?"

"Yes."

"Ross is on the right side."

"You mean the two guys who are now going out the door?"

"Yeah, let's go," Wes said, edging Kate down the stairs. "We've gotta follow them to see where they go."

"You go and follow them. I have an appointment to have my hair cut. I'll be in Cheri's Salon, right around the corner from here. It shouldn't take too long. I want to change the way I look."

"Okay, I'll meet you over there," Wes said as he hurried toward the door. Kate turned and walked down the aisle toward the salon.

"I made an appointment earlier today," Kate announced to the receptionist. "Kate Dell."

"Yes, have a seat Ms. Dell and Melanie will be right with you."

Kate turned to the row of chairs and before she sat down, she heard, "Ms. Dell?"

"Yes," Kate said as she turned around.

"I'm Melanie. Come this way, please. Kate followed the young girl down the aisle. She pointed to a chair and said, "That's my station." Kate put her packages down under the counter and she hopped up on the chair.

"What can I do for you?" Melanie asked while wrapping her neck with tissue and covering her shoulders with a colorful plastic hair styling cape.

"I want to change my hair-style. Something short, perhaps?"

"Okay. Do you need a shampoo or do you want me to just water spray it?"

"It's clean, so just spray it."

After thirty minutes, Kate looked in the mirror to see what the stylist had done. It was short on the sides and back and her hair was swept away from her forehead. She loved it. She no longer resembled the woman she'd been thirty minutes ago. There was nothing that anchored her face to her past life. *Wes probably won't even know me,* she thought with a smile.

CHAPTER

72

Ross and Bob were shaking hands by the time Wes stepped outside. Bob walked in the direction of the parking garage and Ross, with his shopping bag in hand, headed straight down 1st Street; a tree lined street with tall office buildings on both sides.

Wes pushed his sunglasses farther up on his nose so he could hide behind them as he carefully eased his way into the dense foot traffic, blending in as best he could. He took great care to keep Ross in sight while ensuring that he wasn't noticed. He *must* see where he goes.

When Ross approached the corner, he stopped abruptly. He unclipped his cell phone from his belt, stood for several minutes talking and then clipped his cell back on his belt. He crossed the street and headed toward the Union Center Plaza office building.

Wes was about to cross the street when a taxi suddenly pulled up alongside the curb and stopped directly in front of him. The cabbie, who looked like an immigrant from some Middle Eastern country, turned in his seat to collect the fare. The woman paid him and climbed out, running across the street and going to the same building as Ross.

When Ross grabbed the handle of the darkened glass door, he caught Wes' reflection in the glass. He did not turn to look back. He held the door open for the young lady who seemed to be in a hurry. Casually he walked into the building and once inside, he turned to look outside. Yes, it was Wes all right. "He wants to find me, well, come on and get me, you bastard," he said under his breath.

Ross walked directly to the reception desk to speak with Sal Martino, the security officer. "Sal, there's a guy outside... see that tall guy with the mop of blonde hair?" Ross said, pointing his finger at Wes.

"Yeah, I see him."

"He's probably going to come in here so would you please take a photo of him and call me on my cell if he gets in one of the elevators? Call me regardless and let me know what he does. I'll need to check the security cameras also. Would you relay the security camera out front and the one in the reception area up to my office so I can watch him?"

With one eye on the clock, Sal responded, "No problem."

"I'll need a copy of that photo also."

Sal nodded.

"Thanks, Sal."

"You got it, Mr. Griffin."

Ross walked briskly over toward the bank of elevators and pushed the button. When the doors slid open, Stella was stepping out. "Hey, Ross."

"Hi, Stella. Are you busy right now?" Ross asked her.

"No. Why?"

"You're just the one I need. Come with me," Ross said as he hurried her to the doorway of the lobby.

"I just learned that Emma's husband, Wes, is in town. He followed me here. Can you tail him and let me know what he does?"

"Sure, where is he?"

"The tall one with the blue jacket and blonde hair who's now crossing the street and heading toward this building."

"Yeah, that's him. Sure, I'll follow him. I've been waiting to meet up with this jerk."

"I've got to disappear. Thanks, Stella. Let me know what happens."

"Sure thing, Ross." Stella quickly walked over to the reception area, grabbed a magazine and sat down on one of the chairs.

Ross stepped inside the opened door of the elevator and pushed the button to the tenth floor. His company occupied the top two floors of the building; some thirty-seven thousand square feet of office space in a building that had a total of one hundred and ninety thousand square feet of space.

Wes crossed the street, stepped inside the lobby of the building, and immediately glanced toward the bank of elevators. Ross was gone. He walked across the gleaming slate floors to the directory to scan the names that could possibly be a security company. He found two names, *Global Security,* which occupied both the tenth and eleventh floors and *Protection Detail,* which was on the second floor, occupying Suite 201. *He's probably with Protection Detail,* he thought.

Before exiting the building, he turned and gave one last look at the lobby, not noticing Stella occupying one of the chairs partially obscured by a rubber plant. He crossed the street and headed toward the mall to meet up with Kate.

Stella was right behind him; *a tail on the tail,* she thought and smiled as she swept the area with the ease of someone in the habit of not only observing but also making accurate deductions from what she observed. After walking for several minutes, she noticed that he was stopped by a man. They exchanged conversation. She stopped and observed.

"Excuse me," a man shouted as he approached Wes on the sidewalk.

Wes stopped and looked at him. "Yes?"

"I'm looking for D Street."

"I don't know where it is," Wes said. "I'm a tourist in this city."

"Oh, sorry for the intrusion. Thanks anyway."

"That's okay," Wes replied.

"Oh, one more thing," the man said as Wes turned to walk away.

"What?" Wes said as he rolled his eyes.

"I know what you were involved with in San Jose, California."

Wes' eyes suddenly flashed toward the stranger. "What did you just say to me?"

"I know all about your mortgage scheme. You and your girlfriend."

"I don't know who you think I might be, but I don't know what you're talking about. Get outta my way and leave me alone," Wes said abruptly as he brushed past the stranger and walked away, still wondering how this stranger knew so much about him.

The stranger removed his sunglasses and studied Wes silently for a moment before saying loudly, "It would be in your best interest to listen to what I have to say."

With annoyance clearly in his voice, Wes whirled around in disbelief and said, "Or what?"

A flicker of a smile came into the stranger's eyes before saying, "You'll find out."

"What exactly is your game?" Wes asked, walking toward this man. "Are you trying to scare me? You have no idea who you are messing with and you don't know what you're talking about. Just exactly who are you anyway?"

"I'm a private investigator from California. Some Russian's hired me to find you and your girlfriend."

"What Russian's?" he demanded to know. "What are their names?"

With a suppressed smile and a playful edge to his voice, the stranger responded, "That's confidential. I'd rather not say."

"Exactly what is it you want?" Wes asked, suspiciously eyeing the stranger. "Money?"

"Bingo! That's exactly what I want. And from what I've heard, you have plenty of it."

"Drop dead, dickhead. You're never getting a dime. I don't know what you're talking about."

"You know exactly what I'm talking about. I've been on your tail since Las Vegas."

Wes shook his head, a tight smile on his face. "Las Vegas? I was not in Las Vegas. You have the wrong guy."

"Oh, I don't have the wrong guy at all. It's you that I saw in Vegas."

Wes smiled slightly in spite of his foul mood before asking defiantly, "Where in Vegas did you supposedly see me?"

"I spotted you in Harrah's. It was no great mystery finding you last night. I knew you were a gambler, so I took my chances that you'd go to Vegas when you left California. Turns out, I was right—you showed up. I also knew you gambled at Harrah's whenever you're in Las Vegas or Lake Tahoe. Actually, you were quite easy to locate."

"Look," Wes said, jabbing his index finger on the stranger's chest as if he were punctuating each of his words, "I've got some advice for you mister private detective or whoever the hell you are."

"Lose the attitude," the man shouted as he grabbed Wes' pointed finger and pushed it upward away from his chest.

Wes grabbed the front of the stranger's jacket with both hands and with eyes narrowed and teeth clenched, he said, "Don't tell me what to do and don't you *ever* touch me. Get your lame ass out of here or I will tear your fuckin' face off your head."

"Okay, okay," the man said when he watched Wes' eyes quickly turn red as the Devil's.

Wanting to smash his face, Wes glanced away from the man when he noticed several people staring at them. He instantly dropped his arms and the stranger straightened his jacket.

"Look, Blair, just stop pretending. You need me," the stranger said.

Wes' lanky six-foot frame leaned in next to the man, and he whispered, "I don't need you. If you value your life, go back to California and keep your goddamn mouth shut before I kill you. And that's not a threat. It's a promise. I *will* kill you if I see you again."

The man turned to walk away but suddenly swung his body backward in an attempt to knock Wes down. Wes ducked to the right, moved his leg out and watched the stranger make an impressive fall to the ground.

"If you want to make a war out of this, it's a battle you won't win. Don't mess with me," Wes yelled out as he watched the man get up and scurry away, but not before he flipped Wes off and disappeared into the crowd.

Wes spun around and hurriedly walked toward the mall without looking back. His mind consumed with how mad Kate was going to be. He and Kate had always been so careful, so thorough. With all our precautions, our disguises, our new ID's and this stranger somehow slipped through our defenses.

"I won't tell Kate about this guy," he muttered to himself. *I'm mad enough at myself right now. I don't want to listen to her ramble on about what a huge mistake I made going to Vegas. I just won't mention this incident with this stranger. She doesn't need to know.* "Yeah, I won't tell her," he says out loud. "What are the odds that our paths will cross again?"

He stopped abruptly for a brief moment and turned around; his eyes searched the street for a glimpse of the stranger. The man had disappeared. *Good, I scared him off,* he immediately thought to himself. *This is just a little burp. That stranger won't bother me again.*

Ross' phone was ringing when he got to his office. "Yes, Sal."

"Mr. Griffin, I just wanted to let you know that blonde guy who came into the lobby, looked at the elevators and then turned and walked over to the directory. He stood there for a few moments before he left the building. He looked like he was heading back toward the direction he came from."

"Thanks, Sal."

"I sent the video up to your office computer, and I'm sending his photo to you via e-mail. You should have it momentarily."

"That's great. You've been a huge help, Sal. Thanks."

"My pleasure, Mr. Griffin."

CHAPTER

73

Ross sank wearily into a leather chair in the study. Ellie was resting on the sofa reading the newspaper. "I had lunch with Bob Lucas today," he announced. "He told me he had kidney cancer."

"What?" Ellie said as she looked up from her newspaper. "Really? I didn't know."

"I told him I'd have you take a look at his medical records? He'd really like that," Ross said.

"I'd be happy to look at them. When did he find out?"

"A week ago. The doctors want him to have chemo and radiation, but he doesn't want any of it. Judy is having a fit over his decision not to have chemotherapy. He's pretty certain this is the end for him. I told him I'd ask you to look at this medical chart. He trusts you. If you tell him he should have chemo, he'd probably have it done."

"I'll make it a priority to look into it tomorrow as soon as I get to work. Do you know his doctor's name?"

"No, he didn't tell me. Do you need it? I can call him."

"No, I don't need his name. I'll find out when I look through his records."

"Thanks, Ellie. It'll mean a lot to Bob... and to me. Bob and I go way back. He's a good man, and I'd sure hate to lose him as a friend."

"There have been so many recent advances in diagnosis, surgical procedures, and treatment options. Since he's in the early stages, he needs to make the best choice about treatment so the odds will be in his favor. I'll go with him to one of the support groups at the hospital. He can learn a great deal by attending a meeting and talking with other cancer patients. Right now he's going through the shock phase. He's angry and frustrated that this has happened to him. It's a very difficult experience to go through."

"I'll be happy to go with him to any meetings. I'm glad I met with him today so he could vent how he feels. He felt better after we talked."

"That's good, Ross. The more support he gets from friends, the better he will handle the disease."

"I told him to call me anytime and I'd be there for him."

"I'm sure he appreciated that. Not to change the subject, but I have a wonderful idea," Ellie said.

"What's that?"

"Why don't we, when the boys have a break from school, take them to Disney World? Perhaps Emma and Hawk can join us. What do you think?"

"That's a very good idea. You do realize that Emma and Hawk are not a couple. You do know that, don't you?"

"Oh, it's just a matter of time. I've seen them together. They were made for each other. Emma's been through so much, she's just shy about getting into another relationship so quickly. They'll end up together. She just needs more time to adjust."

"She's a stubborn one when it comes to her personal life. She needs to be nudged."

"It must run in the family," Ellie said with a laugh.

"Why do you say that?"

"I guess because I always assumed that we'd get married one of these decades," Ellie said. "We're going to be the oldest living cohabitators in the world."

"That's not entirely true, Ellie. Your Uncle Al and Miss Vivian have been together for over twenty years and they don't marry because they don't want to lose their spouse's retirement funds or their social security benefits."

"Oh, yeah, like we'll need social security for our retirement," Ellie said as she reached over to throw one of the sofa pillows at Ross.

"If you may recall, I have asked you to marry me."

"You have? When?"

"Don't you remember back a few years when we flew to Las Vegas to attend your cousin's wedding, that I asked you if you wanted to get married at the Elvis Chapel? You just laughed at me. My feelings were deeply hurt."

"Oh, yes, I remember. The way I remember it, you didn't have any feelings that night because you had too much to drink and you were being silly."

"How was I being silly?"

"The Elvis Chapel? Come on now."

"Well, it seemed very romantic at the time."

A few quiet moments had passed before Ross spoke up. "Well, schweetheart, we can always go back to Vegas if you'd like." Ross smiled and his dimples winked. "What's going on that brought up this desire to get married? Do you really want to be married to me? You know what I do for a living, and you could be a widow tomorrow. One day, some idiot who has it out for me might just catch up with me."

"You're right Ross. With our busy schedules, we do just fine the way we are."

"Well, at least, the whole idea was pretty entertaining," Ross joked.

Ellie laughed and reached over to hold his hand, "I do love you, you big romantic goofball."

"I've got a ring in my pocket."

"You do not."

"Wanna bet me?"

Ellie tilted her head. "Show it to me."

"Oh, I don't think this would be a proper place to propose."

"Why not?" Ellie asked.

"A woman like you needs to be wooed and swept off her feet. You need to have moonlight, red roses, and fine wine."

With a loud chuckle, Ellie corrected Ross. "You should be saying a woman for you needs to be able to shoot a gun, be strong, and be able to stand on her own two feet."

"Hah!" Ross laughed. "You're absolutely right, my dear. She needs to be strong willed, decisive, and loving; all the wonderful characteristics you endure. When a man is pushing sixty years of living, he begins to look back on his life. Looking at his mistakes and thinking, if only I had that to do over if only I did this rather than that. However, when it comes to you, Ellie, I would not have done anything differently. You're the love of my life, and I'm a very rich man."

"We do have something special, don't we? While we are both committed to our professions, we never let our love for each other get in the way. I'm mad about you, Ross."

"I know, Ellie. We're pretty good together, aren't we?"

"That we are, Ross. That we are."

CHAPTER

74

Wes switched off his headlights before he turned into the parking structure. His eyes scanned the immense and eerily empty parking lot, illuminated by lamps that led along the walkway. He decided that the best vantage point would be against the rear wall—he would be able to see everyone that entered or exited. He pulled into a stall four cars away from a parked van.

He quietly slipped out of the car, only hearing the ticking of the engine as it cooled. He opened the rear door, got inside and slouched down in the rear seat. The space between the front and back seats barely accommodated his long legs. His chin was level with his knees, but he managed to slip his brown hairpiece and a black cap on his head. He grabbed the binoculars and nudged his body across the seat to straighten his legs.

Leaning back, he removed the lid from his coffee and opened the paper bag with two donuts inside. He sat in silence, noshing on his jelly donut and sipping coffee. Ten minutes passed. No sign of anyone yet.

Bored and tired, he shifted quietly, working out a cramp in his leg. He was not used to lengthy vigils. Surveillance work was not something he liked to do, but if he was going to find Emma and his boys, he had to know where Ross lived. His instincts told him he was in D.C.

and today he would follow him home and with any luck, find his boys. A single lucky break is all he needed.

WHAM! WHACK! A loud crash echoed through the parking garage.

"What the hell?" he yelled out spilling his coffee and suddenly finding himself holding a half-eaten donut with jelly droppings on his lap.

Like a flash of lightening, he bolted out the door, crouched down close to the front tire, and peered over the hood.

There was a young punk holding a baseball bat with his arms held high above his head ready to take another swing at the van.

Wes stood up and yelled, "Put that fuckin' bat down now!"

"What the fuck..." the astonished young man uttered. He threw the bat in the air, crossed the concrete like a cat, and disappeared in a flash.

Wes slipped back inside the car glad that it wasn't his car getting brutalized. He grabbed the box of Clean-Wipes to clean the jelly off his trousers and absorb the spilled coffee on his jacket. He was so intent on his cleaning that he hadn't noticed the arrival of a black Hummer that parked several rows in front of him. When he heard a door close, he slouched down in the seat for a few moments before he looked up and saw Ross walking toward the bank of elevators.

His cell phone vibrated. He snatched it up, flipped it open, and pressed it to his ear. "Yeah?" he said.

"It's six-thirty. Anything happening?" Kate asked.

"He just got here. He went inside the building."

"Are you going to wait there all day until he comes out?"

"Do you have another idea how to find my boys? You do realize that's why I'm here."

"Yes. I guess you have to wait and tail him. What kind of a car is he driving?"

"A black Hummer."

"Really? Well, at least you won't have trouble tailing him."

"Yeah, right. Are you coming down here later this afternoon?"

"Yes, I'll call you about three o'clock and see what's going on. I'll take a cab."

"Okay, I'll wait till I hear from you around three."

"Bye," Kate said.

Wes snapped the lid down, clipped the phone to his belt, and rested back in the seat, peering out the window. He was nervous, and he did not like feeling nervous. He was a man who liked to believe that he was in control. Now, there was a glitch. He screwed up. Kate must not find out that the Russians tailed him from Vegas.

Going to Las Vegas was a reckless, idiotic, potentially disastrous act. He made a mistake giving in to his impulses. That must not happen again. He cannot make any mistakes this time. He has to keep his mind on the plan. Track Emma down, kill her, and get his sons. He will have millions of dollars and his boys will get the best education money can buy. They will live in a big house with servants to wait on them... yes, the boys will have a great life with Kate and me living on an island.

Wes yawned several times trying to stay awake. It was hard sitting in a vehicle for several hours, with nothing happening. He decided to walk around for a few minutes. He stepped out of the car and tried to look like a man waiting to meet someone, pacing back and forth, looking at his watch. He forced himself to walk at the right speed, not too slow and not too fast. He mustn't draw attention to himself.

"Oh, shit," he murmured when he noticed activity at the elevators. He could hear voices and footsteps. Two men were walking in his direction. He couldn't see if either of them was Ross. His heart was pounding as the pair drew closer to him. They passed by him without so much as a curious glance. Wes took a deep breath and got back inside the car.

CHAPTER

75

"Good morning, Stella," a deep voice suddenly filled the quiet.

Stella jumped. "Oh, I didn't hear you come in, Ross."

"I'm sorry. I didn't mean to startle you," Ross said apologetically. He smiled at her, and instantly he could tell she was exhausted. "I see you pulled an all-nighter?"

"I did," she said. With a stack of papers in her hand, she waved them in the air. "There is just no way you're gonna believe what I found out! It just keeps getting better and better."

"Ah, so this is turning out to be a twister, eh?" Ross smiled. "Doesn't surprise me."

"Oh, but *this* will surprise you. You are thinking along the lines of a tropical storm. This, my dear Ross, is actually a hurricane—probably at the Category 3 level," Stella said in a state of excitement.

"I can't wait. Come down to my office. Let's see what you've got," Ross said as he led her toward the inner-office doorway.

"Sit, tell me everything," Ross said eagerly, gesturing with his arm for Stella to sit in the chair beside his desk.

"When I followed Wes after he left the building, some guy stopped him. I don't think Wes knew this guy, but the guy was persistent and kept after him until they actually got into a bit of a hands-on-hassle. The guy fell to the ground, and Wes walked away. I followed Wes to the mall where he met up with his girlfriend, Kate. I tailed them to their car, took photos of the car, Kate and Wes, and also got a shot of the guy who stopped Wes.

"This girlfriend of Wes' is a real piece of work. She's playing Wes and that poor sucker doesn't have a clue. We know Wes is wanted by the FBI, but they're not the only ones after him. I think we'll all just sit back and watch and see who gets him first. I'm going to enjoy this."

"What makes you say that?" Ross asked with a quizzical look on his face.

"Ah! Wes is messing with the wrong woman, that's what. Turns out she's the one who masterminded this whole embezzlement scheme. She's one shrewd little bitch."

"Am I to believe her face showed up on facial recon?"

"Oh, her face showed up all right, but her name is not Kate Lee."

"Is that right? Who is she?"

"She's Amanda Holmes. A gal who's had run-ins with the law since she was thirteen years old. She's a felon and did five years in prison for armed robbery and drug trafficking. She was released when she was twenty-five years old. Then she just magically dropped off the radar."

"Who's Kate Lee?"

"She took the identity of a woman named Kate Lee, who served in the U.S. Army and was killed in Iran in 1989."

"How did she pick this Kate Lee's name?"

"I wondered the same thing. I looked up her Army records and it turns out she and Amanda were school buddies all the way through high school. They lived near each other in Santa Ana, California."

"So she impersonated this Lee gal because she knew her and knew she was dead."

"Absolutely. Once she got out of prison, she just took the name of Kate Lee, relocated to San Jose and enrolled in college for a year taking only finance and accounting classes."

"So, with her new ID, they'd be no felony charges on her record and with her knowledge of finance, she was able to get a position in the bank. This *is* one shrewd woman," Ross said, shaking his head.

"She's been at the bank almost nine years now in various positions. Now, get ready for the real kicker!" Stella said with unconcealed delight.

"There's more?" Ross asked, his eyebrows shot up.

"Oh yeah, we're just getting started. Are you ready?"

Ross shook his head, "Go on."

"She married the assistant vice president of the bank."

Ross' eyebrows really shot up this time. "She married the assistant vice president of the bank?"

"She sure did. Nothing is going to stop this gal."

"So that's probably how she eventually became operations manager. This gal *is* smart. What's this poor sucker's name?"

"His name is Steve Daly. She never changed her name probably because of bank policy which states no married couples work together at the same bank."

"So, they evidently never told anyone they were married," Ross said, slowly standing up from his desk. "Wes evidently doesn't know any of this… unless the three of them are in this together."

"I don't believe so. Her husband is not wanted for bank fraud. The FBI is only after her and, of course, Wes."

"How about the stranger who Wes met up with? What did you find out about him?"

"Oh, yeah. This man's name is Dennis Perry. He put in twenty-five years on the police force in San Jose. After he had retired, he opened a PI office in San Jose, also hired a couple of guys to work for him. He married a younger woman, divorced her, and now has two college-aged boys to support. There was a police search done at his residence over a year ago. The police suspected he was involved in money laundering for the Russians. However, they did not find anything. He came up clean."

"So what we have here is Dennis Perry, who may be involved with the Russians as is Ms. Kate Lee and Wes Blair. What about the husband, Steve Daly? How does he fit into this scenario?" Ross asked as he paced the floor.

"I ran him and he's not even had a traffic ticket. Perhaps he never had any knowledge of what his wife was up to."

"He must have known something, Ross said. "Wes lived with Kate for several months before Emma left California."

"What? So they're a threesome?"

Ross paused a moment to let that statement sink in, then he said, "No, I don't believe that. We're missing something here. Perhaps they're separated. Was there a divorce?"

"I checked that also and didn't discover any divorce. The husband owns the condo that Wes and Kate were living in. I don't know where the husband lives. His driver's license address is the same address as the condo. Something doesn't make sense here."

"What about the car Wes and Kate were driving? Did you check the plates?"

"They're stolen plates. They must have picked them up in Arizona on their way to the east coast. The car is a 1999 Black Honda Civic."

"Let me think about this for a while. I'll go over it with Hawk and see what he thinks. He has an 'outside the box' kind of mind."

"I'm going to check further on the husband," Stella said. "Perhaps I'll find something on him if I dig a little deeper."

"I believe that's where the hang-up is. Let me know what you find out."

"I will do that," Stella said as she stood to exit the office. "I'll leave the photos with you. Perhaps Hawk will see something we didn't see."

"Thanks. You've done a great job, Stella."

"Anything I can do to put that guy away."

"Oh, by the way, Stella, please don't tell Emma anything about what we just discussed."

"I won't."

"Thanks."

CHAPTER

76

Dark clouds were rolling across the sky, with the sun ducking behind them and peeking out every so often; the air filling with moisture.

A distant rumble of thunder was heard when Hawk darted across the street with long brisk strides toward Matteo's Restaurant to enjoy his usual morning Espresso Sambuca.

When he pushed open the door, Matteo looked up and smiled. "You have a companion this morning, Mr. Hawk."

"I do? Is she beautiful?"

"Beautiful, no, but I've been told I'm quite handsome," a deep voice answered.

Hawk turned toward the voice. "Ross! What a pleasant surprise," he said with a welcoming smile. "What brings you out in my neighborhood so early?"

"Do you have to be somewhere?" Ross inquired.

"No, no. I'm on my way to the office. Come, let's sit at the back table," Hawk said, pointing toward a table in the corner.

Matteo followed right behind them with two Espresso Sambuca's.

"Thanks, Matteo."

Matteo gave Hawk the nod and salute before returning to the counter.

"I'd like to pass something by you," Ross said as he pulled out a chair. "You have such a sharp mind for the unusual or perhaps I should say you have a taste for unique analytical reasoning."

"I guess that's because I'm an odd duck," Hawk said with a laugh.

"I should be so odd. Anyway, Stella...You remember Stella?"

"Yes, I've met her a few times," Hawk responded, after taking a drink of his coffee. "Very bright, and I might add, also a beautiful woman."

"Yes, you're right on both counts," Ross smiled. "Well, after Wes tailed me to my office, I had Stella follow him. She saw him being stopped by a stranger on the street. She said Wes became extremely agitated at this stranger and began to rough him up a bit by grabbing his jacket and pushing him to the ground. I'm surprised that's all he did. I know all about Wes' temper. They talked for quite a while before they went separate ways. Didn't appear to be a very friendly parting. Before this stranger walked away, Stella got a photo of him. She continued to tail Wes to the Union Station Mall where he waited in front of a beauty parlor. He never went inside. He paced back and forth for about ten minutes before his girlfriend came out. From the body language, it didn't appear that he told her anything about meeting up with the stranger on the street."

"So why is Wes hiding this information from his girlfriend?" Hawk asked curiously.

"Exactly what I was wondering. Stella was able to get a photo of the girlfriend, Kate Lee, while she stood in front of the beauty parlor handing Wes several packages. She then followed them to the parking garage and took pictures of both the license plate and the car they were driving."

"I gather Stella ran both the stranger and Kate Lee through facial recon?"

"Yes, she did. Here are the pictures she took," Ross said as he placed them on the table. "This is where it gets fascinating."

"How so?" Hawk asked with a wry smile as he spread the pictures out on the table.

"Turns out, this girlfriend of Wes' is not Kate Lee. She's Amanda Holmes, a prior felon who spent five years in prison for armed robbery and drug trafficking."

"So, Miss Kate Lee and Miss Amanda Holmes are really one and the same person, and leading a double life; a real sweetheart. So, who is the real Kate Lee?" Hawk inquired.

"Originally, back in their high school years, Lee and Holmes were both school buddies. But after high school, Lee enlisted in the Army to be all that she could be. Sadly, she was killed in the Iran-Iraq war in 1989."

"So, Amanda becomes Kate Lee; very convenient and fortunate for Amanda."

"Yes, and a pretty smart move because there's no way she could ever work in a bank being a felon. After she was released from prison, she took Lee's identity, went to college for a year and took finance and accounting classes so she could land a job in a bank. Now, it gets even more interesting."

"I just bet it does," Hawk's eyebrows arched. "This gal is a dangerous, scheming, street-smart planner. She's no dummy; she knows where she's going and she knows how to get there."

"Here's the boom!" Ross said, his eyes twinkling with excitement. "She marries Steve Daly, the assistant V.P. of the bank."

"Hah!" Hawk said, slamming the flat of his hand loudly on the table. "The motives of women are so inscrutable. They never cease to amaze me."

"Ah, you're absolutely right. However, there's more. This is where it gets a little shady. They are all, and by all, I mean Kate, Wes, and the V.P. husband, working in the same bank at the same time. I don't know what's going on. She marries this V.P. yet she is having an affair with Wes, who is living with her in a condo that is owned by her husband. She never got a divorce from the guy. The husband is clean; no records. We don't believe Wes knows anything about this husband."

"Probably not."

"I doubt that they're a threesome, so one of them is in the dark," Ross added.

"I'd vote for Wes being in the dark. He's so egotistical that he would never think a woman would screw around on him. By screwing around, I don't mean sex, although he definitely thinks he's the best any woman has ever had. This girlfriend of his is pulling one over on the poor bastard and he doesn't have a clue. I'm beginning to like this. He deserves everything he gets."

"So how do you think this will play out?" Ross asked, raising the mug of coffee to his mouth. "Hey, this is pretty good coffee."

"Yes, it gets me going in the morning," Hawk said with a wink.

Sitting back in his chair, Hawk then asked, "Who is this stranger who stopped Wes on the street?"

"Oh, yes, the stranger. His name is Dennis Perry and it turns out he is a retired cop turned PI from San Jose, California. He's divorced, has two boys in college. A while back the police got a warrant to search his home and his office claiming he was somehow connected to a Russian money laundering scheme, but he managed to come out clean."

"Interesting guy, involved with foreign interests, eh? He's a long way from home, wouldn't you say? Evidently, someone is paying him well to travel this far away. I would say the Russians are behind him. He's the man you want to watch. He will do anything for money. He's got two boys in college and his wife probably got half his retirement since California is a fifty/fifty state."

"Good point," Ross said. "Stella also thought the stranger was working for the Russians and that they hired him to find Wes, so she checked rental cars at Dulles airport and found Dennis Perry's car was charged on a credit card belonging to Vladimir Kobzon."

"So, we now *know* Perry is working for the Russians," Hawk acknowledged. "So, we have the Russians who have hired Perry to find Wes and Kate because they evidently left California with a truckload of their money; I would guess somewhere between ten and twenty million dollars. The question is what is Perry going to do now? Will he report back to the Russians and let them know that he found Wes, or… is he going to try to extort money from Wes? Getting money is this man's ultimate goal, with two boys in college and an ex-wife to support."

"Since it didn't appear that Wes mentioned this meeting to Kate, he probably believes that by roughing him up a little and threatening him that he's chased him from the scene," Ross said.

"Exactly, Wes doesn't know that this stranger has a much larger scheme of his own. He wants money and plenty of it. This is his last hurrah. He is not going to disappear." Hawk stood, paced in circles for a few moments and then said, "I do have one remaining question."

"Only one?" Ross asked in astonishment. "What's that?"

Hawk sat back in his chair, a puzzled look on his face. "How did this man find Wes in D.C.? What made Dennis Perry come to D.C. to look for him?"

"That, I can't answer," Ross said, shrugging his shoulders. "Emma never told Wes that I moved to D.C. The last place he knew I was living was in Chicago."

"Yet, he found Wes here in D.C. Very strange," Hawk said, tapping his fingers on the table. After a few moments, Hawk said, "Well then, let's put this all together and see what we come up with. We'll start with what we know."

"We know that Wes' personal goal is to kill Emma and take the boys and run from the country," Ross said. "And we know Kate and Wes' goal is to run away from having to serve time in prison for bank fraud."

"Yes, but let's not forget Kate's personal goal—to have money and lots of it. She's thirty-eight years old; she doesn't want someone else's kids. She's playing Wes. Dennis Perry's goal is to have money and lots of it. The Russians want their stolen money back. If Perry tries to extort money from Wes, he may get a tidy sum of money, perhaps two million dollars. If he is just on a job for the Russians, he'll only get about twenty or thirty thousand," Hawk said.

"So, we have two persons who want money and lots of it. We have the Russians who want their portion of the money back. We have Wes, who only wants to kill his wife, take his two boys, and leave the country. What's wrong with this picture?" Hawk asked.

"Kate Lee's husband is not in the picture," Ross said. "We have no idea what he wants or what his part is in this, if any."

"Yes," Hawk said as he rose from the table and paced up and down the room. "That's the mystery we don't have an answer to at this moment. It is very probable that this man may fit into the scheme of things."

Hawk tapped a pen against his teeth, pondering these thoughts. He pulled out his chair and sat on it backward, hanging his arms over the backrest before saying, "Our next move is to have Stella find out everything about this husband, Steve Daly. He must, somehow, be involved."

"She's working on that, as we speak," Ross announced.

"Good. She needs to get some background on this guy. Find out what his friends and his enemies say about him. Talk to his co-workers. Look at his bank accounts and his tax returns. We need his life history. Where he went to school, what he majored in, how long he has been with the bank. Find out what romantic relationships he has had. Find out about his family, any siblings, talk to people in the condo where Wes and Kate were living. We need all the information she can get. He may well be the key we're looking for to solve this puzzle.

CHAPTER

77

At precisely 12:45 pm, Wes' cell phone vibrated. "Hi. Are you coming down now?" he asked.

"Yes. Anything going on?" Kate inquired.

"Nope. Haven't seen him..." he abruptly stopped talking. "Hold on a minute."

"What's happening?"

"Yes, it's him. He's heading toward his car... Emma is with him! I found her! I knew she was here. She's with him now and there's another guy with them. I've got to follow them. I'll call you later."

"Okay," Kate said and hung up.

He had no time to talk. He clipped his cell phone back on his belt and climbed over to the front seat. He jabbed the key into the ignition. As soon as the Hummer pulled forward, he started the engine, put his car in gear and pulled out into the street, keeping the Hummer in sight. After a few minutes, he saw them turn right at the light. He was about three hundred feet behind them when they made a left turn at the light.

When he reached the light, it turned red. "Damn it. I can't lose them now," he growled. He knew he couldn't get a traffic ticket either. He must be careful—both the FBI and the Russians were after him. He waited. When the green arrow glared, he quickly made the turn. No Hummer in sight. "Shit," he growled. "Goddamned son of a bitch!

"Damn it, I lost them." He continued driving, looking down all of the cross streets. They were gone.

Frustrated and angry, he turned the car around and headed back to the parking lot. *They'll come back here*, he thought. *They just went to lunch.*

He dialed Kate's cell. "I lost them. I'm driving back to the parking lot."

"You let them escape?" Kate yelled out.

"Don't yell at me," Wes snapped. "I didn't *let* them escape. I got stuck at a red light. I couldn't have missed them by more than a half a minute. Come on down now and bring something to eat. I'm starving."

"Okay, I'll be there in about half an hour."

Click. Wes abruptly ended the call. Nothing is working. Overcome with a feeling of hopelessness and a complete loss of power, he turned off the ignition and sat there with his head down, defeated, listening to the engine tick as it cooled. "Something positive needs to happen so I can get control back in my life," he mumbled to himself.

Silently he waited, seething with pent-up anger. "One lousy break, that's all I need," he murmured. The more he thought about it, the angrier he became. What was particularly frustrating was that the beginning of the plan worked perfectly. They drove cross-country without any hitches. He killed four men without any hitches. The problems started when that woman pepper sprayed him and she was able to get away from him.

"No," he suddenly said when his thoughts bounced back to the conversation he had with the stranger. *It was right after the stranger spoke to him. That's when he first felt a loss of power.*

Restless and scared out of his mind—he hated this debilitating feeling. With pressure mounting and time running out he knew he had to get a handle on the situation right now.

"No more screw-ups," he yelled out and slammed his fist on the steering wheel.

CHAPTER

78

A glance in the rearview mirror revealed Kate walking toward the car with several sacks of food in her hands. She gently tapped on the window and Wes unlocked the car, although he didn't bother to glance in her direction. "Get in," he said, glancing beyond her at the gathering of people standing by the elevator doors.

"Did they show up yet?" Kate asked. Her voice was low.

"No. It's been quiet. I'm sure they just went to lunch. They'll be back."

"I bought you your favorite lunch from a deli," she whispered. "Hot Pastrami on Rye."

"Well, thank you, Kate. It is my favorite sandwich."

"Here you go," she said as she handed him the wrapped sandwich which was still warm. "And here's extra deli mustard if you need it. I got you a Coke."

Wes held out his hand as she handed him his drink. "I'm so hungry. This surveillance crap is boring as hell. This waiting is driving me crazy."

"I know how you hate waiting, but the outcome is what you've been waiting for—your boys. Everything takes time. We'll be leaving the states before you know it. Just take deep breaths when you get nervous. It'll help you relax. You know where her uncle works and you've seen Emma so you know she's here. We're getting closer every day. Relax, Wes," Kate said as she rubbed his shoulders.

"You're absolutely right. But I shouldn't have lost them in traffic. If I knew the streets here, I wouldn't have lost them."

"They'll come back here. Don't worry about it. Stop blaming yourself. You need to stay focused."

"What have you been doing all morning?" Wes asked.

"I've been routing our money to different banks. I have to hide the money in fictitious corporate names."

"So it's all deposited?"

"Yes. All taken care of."

"You'll have to show me how you do that when we get back to the hotel."

"You want me to show you how I did it?"

"Yes. Is there a problem?"

"No. You just never wanted to know what I did with the money before."

"Well, we should both know, don't you think?" Wes said in a sarcastic tone.

"Sure, no problem," Kate said. However, that wasn't anywhere near what she was thinking. *Something's going on with him. He never showed any interest in how the money was transferred. What happened to make him suspicious?* she wondered.

Wes didn't know anything about trade law, but Kate had clients throughout South America, who were exporters to the U.S. and Canada. She specialized in trade law and several times a year she would travel there for bank business. She had a complete understanding of their banking practices, their currencies, and she had an excellent knowledge of foreign markets. She had the discretion to move the accounts as she saw fit.

Suddenly, Wes stopped eating in mid-chew, then swallowed hard. "Look, the Hummer is back. Let's see where he goes and who gets out. The windows are tinted so I don't have a good view of anyone inside."

They waited. The Hummer pulled into a space several rows in front of them. No one got out.

Several minutes later, the driver's door opened and Ross stepped out and walked toward the elevators.

"Damn it. He's alone. What the hell happened to Emma and the other guy?"

"I don't know. He must have driven them someplace and dropped them off."

"Now what do we do? Sit here and wait until he goes home tonight?"

"That's exactly what we do. That's the only way you'll find out where he lives."

"I hope he leaves work early so we can get this over with. I hate this waiting."

"It's almost three o'clock. It won't be long now," Kate said assuredly.

After watching for ten minutes, Kate said, "I have to go to the bathroom."

"Yeah, I've got to go too. Waiting for something to happen gives you nothing but distended bladders. I'll go between those parked cars in the back of the lot."

"Okay," Kate said. "I'll go when you come back. I'm going into the building to use the restroom."

"Be right back." Wes closed the car door quietly and walked to the back of the parking lot.

He was back in a minute. "Okay, you can go now. When you come back why don't you watch for an hour and wake me if you have to. I could sure use a nap."

"Okay. I'll be back in five minutes," Kate said. She got out of the car, hung her purse on her shoulder, and walked toward the elevator.

Wes watched as Kate entered the elevator and disappeared when the door closed.

CHAPTER

79

"You have a minute?" Stella asked Ross when he passed by her cubicle.

"I've always got time for you, Stella. Come on down to my office," he gestured with his arm. "You remember Hawk Shaw?"

"Yes. Hello, Hawk."

"Nice to see you again, Stella."

"Did you have any luck on the Daly guy?"

"Yes, as a matter of fact, we found out more than we bargained for," Stella said, as she followed both men down the corridor to Ross' office. She quickly sat in the chair next to his desk and waited until Ross sat in his chair. Hawk stood behind Ross.

"Who did you get in California to help you work on this?" Ross inquired.

"An old friend of mine, Mark Manza—he's a cop in San Francisco. He talked with several neighbors at the condo Daly owns and they reported that neither of them ever made any enemies at the condo. There were never any confrontations. Both he and Kate were pleasant enough, but never associated with any of the tenants personally. They were always cordial, very quiet, and kept to themselves.

"His bank account is only in his name. Nothing unusual in the account, just the basic payroll checks deposited electronically and the usual bills paid out. He makes one-hundred twenty-five thousand a year, but there's nothing extravagant in this man's life. He drives a Ford Escape. Oh, and he's an avid bowler and belongs to some bowling league in San Jose. He graduated high school in Long Beach, enrolled at San Diego state the next fall, majoring in finance and he received his M.B.A. He's been at the bank for eleven years.

"His parents are retired and living in Arizona. His sister, Ellen lives in San Jose, is single and works for IBM.

"Looks like an average middle-class family," Ross said.

"Middle class, yes. But I'm not thinking average," Stella added.

"Why do you say that?"

"Now it gets interesting. When Daly was in college, he did volunteer work. That's good, right?"

"Yes, that shows that the person is a good citizen helping others," Ross replied.

"Hah! Now get this—he was an activist in the Gay Liberation Movement."

"The guy is gay?" Ross said with a shocked look on his face.

"Yup, that's *his* secret."

"That's one hell of a secret," Hawk said. "That's why he doesn't live with Kate in the condo he owns."

"So why did he get married?" Ross asked.

"Yes, why did he get married?" Stella said with a smile. "Turns out he's putting up a happy front for *his family*. When my source spoke to his sister, she never acknowledged that he was gay. She thinks Kate her brother are living together. Once my source found this out, he never bothered questioning the parents. If the sister didn't know, then for sure the parents don't know."

"Well, that's not the secret I was expecting," Ross said.

"I know. So we can exclude him in this scheme. He's not involved with this fraud scenario. His record is clean—no arrests, not even a traffic ticket violation."

"So, it seems, he's the one in the dark," Hawk said. "He hasn't a clue what his wife is up to."

"Of course, he knows now and he's probably already sitting with a lawyer having his divorce papers drawn up," Ross said.

"There's more," Stella said with eyes widened. "Rumor has it that the current president of the bank is retiring after twenty-seven years. Daly's up for the presidency."

"So he doesn't want any marks against him should they delve into his personal life," Ross said.

"No, he doesn't. He might not get the position if they find out that he's gay. I don't think his divorce will affect him either way for the simple reason that no one at the bank knows that he's even married."

"Where did they get married?" Hawk asked.

"I don't know. Their passports show that they both went to the Yucatan together in 1997. They may have gotten married there which could mean that their marriage may not be recognized in the U.S.

"This would mean that he wouldn't have to file for divorce at all. No divorce filing, no record," Hawk eluded.

"Pretty clever on someone's part, wouldn't you say?" Ross declared. "One of them is aware of the laws."

"It's Daly," Stella said. "In college, his minor was law."

"This scenario is turning into something fascinating," Hawk said as he smiled slightly. "What we have is a P.I. who managed to locate both of them, but probably wants to extort money from them, since he hasn't turned them over to the Russians. The Russians want their money back now. The FBI wants them for skipping out on a $1M bail and bank fraud. The big question now is who will be the first to capture them? This just keeps getting better and better."

CHAPTER

80

Kate let Wes sleep. His over-anxious feelings wore him out. He was growing more depressed every day and his obsession with his boys had become annoying to her. She sat quietly in the front passenger seat and just stared out the window, occasionally using the binoculars. Oh, how she wanted to hop on the next plane to South America and get away with everything and from everyone. *We're spending too much time in this city.*

It was almost five-thirty by the time Ross emerged from the elevator. He unlocked the car with the remote, jumped in the front seat and he was on the road.

"Wes. Wake up. He's leaving." Wes jumped up and crawled into the front seat, keys in the ignition, he was ready to go.

"Okay, let's get this show on the road," Wes said. "Now, between the both of us, we shouldn't lose him, right?"

"We won't lose him now," Kate declared.

Wes followed at a non-threatening, non-suspicious distance as the Hummer turned left, to take the exit heading into Georgetown. "Ah, he probably lives in Georgetown near the water," Kate said.

"I don't know. He's only a security cop. The houses in Georgetown are high-end homes."

After ten minutes on the road, Ross exited and drove through a residential area. He made a right turn down a tree-lined street where the homes were red brick and quite large. When he turned into a driveway, the garage door rumbled open and the Hummer eased into the bay. The door immediately rolled shut, closing off any view from the street.

"Okay, now we know where he lives. This is great. My plan is back in motion. Now I feel like I have some control in my life. For a while, I thought I was losing everything. Boy, I feel good knowing where he lives. We're moving forward again, Kate."

"Yes, we are," Kate said as she kneaded Wes' shoulders trying to relax him.

CHAPTER

81

"I need to get out of here." Wes' words sounded urgent.

"Why, what's wrong?" Kate asked.

"I'm fidgety. I'm going down to the gym for a workout."

"Okay, I'm going to watch some TV."

Wes grabbed his keys, cell phone, and wallet and walked toward the door. "See you in about an hour."

"Have a good workout," Kate shouted.

Wes closed the door and took a deep breath in an effort to release the tension that was causing his mind to become scrambled by the afternoon's events. Still in a quandary not knowing where Emma and the boys lived, he was finding it impossible to process a new plan to get his boys.

He walked to the elevator and pushed the button to go down. Moments later, he was standing in the gym. He walked toward the men's locker room only to find it filled with steam and a stench of sweat and testosterone from the naked bodies of a dozen men drifting in and out of the showers. He glanced around in search for an empty locker to store his keys, phone, and wallet. There were no lockers available, so he quickly turned to leave only to bump into a bare-assed old man vigorously dragging a towel over his shoulders. He slipped his belongings in his pocket and walked out into the gym.

There were only two women conversing while they walked side-by-side on the treadmills. He walked over to the far side of the room toward the weight benches, his mind stilled jangled with dead ends. *Damn it. Until I find Emma, I will never get my boys back.*

He stopped in front of the incline weight lifting equipment, reinserted the selector pin and then sat on the bench and leaned his body back to begin his workout. When he looked up to grab the bar, eyes peered down at him.

It was the damn stranger! He had the same intense stare as he had yesterday.

Wes tried to catch his breath before he sprung up from the bench. "What the hell are you doing here? How did you get in this building?" he yelled out, his eyes glaring like that of a wild animal looking for a kill.

The man said nothing. Instead, he had a suppressed smile on his face.

"Oh, you think this is funny?" Wes said through clenched teeth.

"Oh, did I forget to tell you that I'm staying here? I thought it would be in my best interest to keep a close eye on you and your girlfriend. I'm on the seventh floor also— just a few doors
down from your apartment."

"So you're following me? Didn't I tell you I'd kill you if I saw you again? Leave me the fuck alone."

"Yes, as a matter of fact, you did. But after meeting up with you, I couldn't wait to match wits with you once again. I can't leave you alone. You have something I want."

"I don't have anything that belongs to you."

"Oh, but you do have something that belongs to my client. You do remember the Russians, don't you? I'm here to recover their money from you."

"I told you once, and I'm telling you again. You're not getting a fuckin' dime from me."

"I'm here to change your mind."

Wes cracked his neck and put his finger on the PI's chest. "You know what? You're really starting to itch my ass."

"Well, itch this! I'll just go and talk to your girlfriend, Kate. Have you told her that I'm here?"

Wes didn't respond. He worried what she would do if Perry showed up at their apartment. Then what? He'd have a lot of explaining to do. He doesn't even want to go there. She must never know he was spotted in Las Vegas and is now being tailed by the Russians. "None of your fuckin' business," Wes finally responded.

"Ah, so you haven't told her. Perhaps we should both go and talk to Kate."

"We're not going anywhere."

"If that's the way you want it," he said, looking up at the ceiling. "I'll just report back to the Russians that I located you and Amanda Holmes in D.C. I'm sure they'll take care of the rest."

"Who the hell is Amanda Holmes?" Wes asked with a puzzled look on his face.

"Oh, that's right. Her name is Kate Lee now. I keep forgetting."

Wes directed his gaze to the floor; his head was spinning in amazement. *Who the hell is this guy? How does this guy know Kate? Who is this Holmes girl?*

Extremely irritated by this stocky, gray-haired man with a robust jaw and hard eyes, he moved in closer to the stranger and asked, "Who the hell is Amanda Holmes?"

"You know her as Kate Lee. I know her as Amanda Holmes."

"What the hell does that mean?"

"She's actually an old friend of mine. After she had got out of prison, I contacted her."

"You don't know what you're talking about. Kate's never been in prison."

"I'm afraid it's you who doesn't know what you're talking about. I knew her back when she was Amanda Holmes. I was the arresting officer when she was twenty-two years old."

"What did you arrest her for?"

"Drug trafficking and armed robbery. It looks like little Miss Kate Lee didn't tell you much about her past."

"You're wrong. You don't know anything."

"Oh, I'm not wrong and I know everything there is to know about Kate. You see, she changed her name when she got out of prison. She actually stole her ID from her best friend who was killed while serving in the armed forces. I'm the one who introduced her to the Russians."

"Who are these Russians you keep bringing up? What are their names?"

"You don't need to know their names. Amanda… or I should say, Kate? She knows who they are."

Panic struck. Wes became silent. He didn't know what to do or where to turn. *What is going on here?*

"The way I see this, you have two choices to save both your asses. One, you give the Russians back the fourteen million dollars you took from them, or two, you give me one million dollars and I tell the Russians I never found you. I'll tell them you must have slipped out of the country."

"And, if I don't go along with this so-called scenario of yours?"

"Then you will leave me with no choice but to tell the Russians where you are, and that you refuse to give them back their money. They, in turn, will send a couple of their Russian assassins to get what belongs to them.

They will interrogate you until you give them their money and now, they will want their money plus all the money you have in any of your accounts. Do you have any idea how the Russians interrogate people?" the stranger asked with a smile.

"No."

"The Russian's are a violent breed specializing in the elimination and disposal of those they consider their enemies. They'll torture you first until you tell them where the money is, and after that they'll take you to one of their construction sites and drop you in fresh concrete where you will try to swim to stay afloat, but you can't move in fresh concrete so you will drown and your body will never be found. You'll be in the cement foundation of their next building project. I guess one could say you would become a *pillar of the community*," he said with a loud chuckle.

Wes' brain felt like it was detached from his body. He couldn't think. He didn't know what to say. He didn't know what to do. He felt as if he were caught in the middle of the ocean without a boat or paddle. Without thinking, he blurted out, "The money's not here. It's in some offshore account."

"In that case, they will have you wire the money to their account before they kill you."

"So either way, I'm a dead man. They get their money, and we're both dead."

"Why do you keep forgetting about the other option? Me."

"I didn't forget about you."

"My option is the safest and easiest way to get through this. Simply give me the million dollars and be done with it."

"Yeah, just like that, I'm going to hand you a million dollars."

"I can understand you being nervous discussing this with a total stranger, but right now, as I see it, I'm the only game in town when it comes to getting you off the hook. What do I need to do to prove that I can be trusted?"

"There's nothing you can do for me. I have no idea what you're talking about. Just leave me the hell alone," Wes muttered.

"You know, that line is really getting old. I know exactly what you and Kate are up to. I'm only here to get you out of a jam. I can solve all your problems."

"I don't have any problems," Wes said with determination. "Right now, you're my only problem. Leave me the fuck alone!"

"You have bigger problems than me."

"Problems with what?"

"The Russians want their money and being as ruthless as they are, they will get what belongs to them, one way or the other. They'll never stop looking for you."

"I'll take my chances."

"It's clear that we're not going to see eye to eye on this, but I feel I must warn you—you're in way over your head. However, if that's the way you want to play the game and you want things to get ugly, fine. I don't want your ass itching any more than it has to. I'm outta here, but you're ignoring the fact that I can guarantee that no one will come after you. Once I have the million dollars, I am gone and they'll think you already disappeared and left the country when I tell them that I never found you. It's much simpler and no one has to get hurt and no one has to die."

"Everyone wins, eh?" Wes said.

"Yes," the stranger said, shaking his head. "But if by some chance, you think you're smart enough and decide to take your chances and make a run for it, the Russians will be all over you. Not a good choice to make. I found you quickly enough."

Nervously clearing his throat, Wes asked, "How long before we have to let you know?"

"I have to report back to the Russians by midnight tonight. One way or the other."

CHAPTER

82

Wes heard the whirl of the elevator door opening. He stepped inside, nervously pressing the seven button and then the *close door* button. The elevator doors thumped shut and groaned as it crawled upward.

"Goddam Kate—she's a fuckin' felon!" he muttered to himself. "Who have I gotten myself mixed up with? She's Amanda Holmes? How could she lie to me? What's *her* plan? She must have a plan."

Suddenly the elevator slowed. He looked up and noticed the third-floor button lit up. He did not push the third-floor button. Someone was getting on. The elevator bounced to a stop. When the doors slid open, cigarette smoke filled the air. He heard someone talking. No one entered the elevator. He pressed the *close door* button several times before it shut. Once again, it crawled upward.

His nerves jittery, his mind jangled, and all he could think about was that Kate betrayed him. "She's been playing me all along," he muttered. *She never meant we'd have a life together; she meant she'd have a new life. I never should have trusted that fuckin' bitch. I'm going to grab her by her scrawny little neck and put a bullet in her fucking head and I'm going to enjoy watching her die. She thinks she's smarter than me. A fucking felon is what she is.*

She turned on me. Why must all women turn on me? This is precisely why I don't want any friends—they can never be trusted.

She was probably going to get rid of me before we left for South America. She doesn't want me or my boys. I never had any plans to take the Russians money. That was all her doing. She only wanted the cash. She's going to take all the money and make a run for it... or at least she was going to try. Now I will ruin her plans. She underestimated me if she thought I was a fool.

With so many unanswered questions and doubts rattling around in his head, he was unable to think clearly; *his* plan crumbled. He had carefully planned everything and now... it was all wrong. This PI stranger had forced him to change his course. As much as he wanted his boys, his conscience warned him that it would be a horrific mistake to follow his original plan now that everything had gone wrong.

He didn't like changes in his plan.

CHAPTER

83

When he exited the elevator, he looked both ways. No one in the corridor. No one must see him. He could feel his heart thumping the closer he came to the apartment. Battling to control his anger, he inserted the key card and pushed the door open.

He stood quietly in the darkened living room, his thoughts racing. *Damn that bitch. She said we'd have a life together. How could I have been so blind? I never should have trusted her.* He squirmed in agony from the pain that overwhelmed his body as he saw his life as nothing more than a series of bitter disappointments all caused by women. *They are the source of all my troubles. Damn them.*

He had to stop her. He must get control of his life. She is just another woman trying to wreck his life again. He must kill her and get out of the apartment before the Russians have a chance to catch up with him. He'll be safe once he makes it out the door. He must leave the country tonight if he expects to keep alive. He had only one thing left to do.

The bathroom door suddenly swung open, her figure outlined by the light. She was barefoot, only wearing the luxurious white hotel bathrobe, the logo embroidered in gold on the lapel. She walked into the living room and with her hand reached out to locate the light switch. He grabbed her arm and pulled her next to his body, his hot breath smothering her face. She smiled, but only for a split second after she caught the fire in his eyes. "What's the matter? What happened to you?" she asked when she saw his eyes wild and his breathing heavy.

"What's the matter? That's a good one. You! You're what's the matter, Amanda Holmes."

Instantly, Kate's heart raced, her stomach suddenly tied in knots. "Let me explain," she pleaded. She had gambled that he would never find out about her background.

Outrage reddened his face, violence roiled in his eyes, his lips compressed. Never before had she seen Wes in such a rage.

"Explain what? That you've been lying to me all these months? That you never wanted my boys."

She was silent, forcing her face not to give away the terror she felt as soon as he mentioned his boys. *Who has he been talking to? How did he find out about my name?*

Filled with hatred, he struck Kate across the side of her head. She went sailing across the room, hit the wall and fell to the floor. She staggered as she struggled to stand up.

"You know why I'm going to kill you?" he said, walking toward her. "It's not because you lied to me. It's because you never had any intentions of living with my boys. You're nothing more than a fucking liar."

He grabbed her by the hair, whipped her around and dragged her halfway across the room. He could hear her voice choking and breathless.

"No one messes with my sons," he screamed out when he dropped her.

She collapsed on the floor, blood dripping from her face. She struggled to her knees in an attempt to stand up, but she was dazed and lost her balance falling to the floor again. After a few seconds, she managed to roll groggily into a sitting position and leaned against an end table.

"What difference does it make what my name was," she mumbled in a throaty whisper.

"How about the fact that you never told me you were a felon?"

She was silent for a moment, and then looked up at him, "How do you know that? Who have you been talking with?"

"Nothing matters anymore, Kate. You've destroyed my life. You lied to me, and you broke up my marriage."

"Broke your marriage up? I never did any such thing," she protested. "Your marriage was well over when we met. After all I did for you... got you a job, made you a wealthy man, and now all you care about is that my name was once Amanda Holmes?"

"I don't care what your name was," he said as he stooped over her and dragged her into the bedroom by both her arms before dropping her at the foot of the bed. "You ruined my life." He reached into the nightstand drawer and grabbed his gun.

It was at that moment she feared she made a mistake; she *had* underestimated him. "You stupid asshole! Yes, I used you, you dumb moron. You and your precious sons. You can all go to hell."

He bent down, grabbed her head, and as she squirmed he yelled out, "Goodbye, Amanda Holmes, you lying little bitch!" He pulled the trigger. Blood splattered in the air. She was dead; one shot to the back of her head at close range left a massive exit wound on her forehead.

For a split second, he'd astonished himself. He'd never realized that he could be capable of murder. Sure, he killed those men in the alley, but his life was in danger. That was self-defense. *But this? This is cold-blooded murder.* He stood silently for a moment, breathing heavy, reorganizing his thoughts.

Carefully, he stepped over her body, walked into the bathroom, put the gun on the vanity counter and stripped off all his bloody clothes dropping them into a black trash bag. He headed for the shower, cranked up the hot water, and let the jets of water hit his face. The water rushed down his body encasing him in steam. He would now wash this day away and drown all the lies. Lies are like cancer cells that have invaded his body—every lie is multiplied as it fastens itself to a new host to ensure that every part of his being is infected. *I must rid my body of this invasion. My body will now be cleansed.* He turned the water off well before he was finished—the clock was ticking. He needs to rush to the airport and get out of D.C.

He toweled himself dry; grateful this endless day was almost over.

He put on a pair of black trousers and a black T-shirt and then combed his damp hair, leaving marks of the comb's teeth visible in it. He must move quickly before the stranger meets up with him.

He packed his suitcase, packed the computer, grabbed the carry-on bag filled with money, and got his passport. He put his black jacket on, hung the computer bag on his shoulder and grabbed his suitcase and carry-on bag. Lastly, he picked up the black trash bag.

He took one last look at the room before closing the door. They won't find Kate's body until the rent is due in another five days. "I'm outta here," he mumbled to himself as he closed the door. The elevator dinged just as he walked up to it. The doors opened and a couple stepped out and turned down the corridor without making eye contact.

Wes stepped in and pressed *garage*. Finally, he was on his way. He glanced at his watch: 7:15 p.m. All he needed to do now was drop his bloody clothes into the trash container in the garage, leave the car in the parking stall and walk out to the sidewalk to hail a taxi. He must get the hell away and focus strictly on survival since his attempt to kill Emma and get his sons now seemed remote.

With any luck at all, and knew he was due for some, he would get away without any hitches.

CHAPTER

84

The private investigator moved silently down the corridor toward their apartment. He knocked lightly on the door. No answer. He checked the time: 7:20 his watch read.

I know they're in there, he thought to himself. He took a credit card out of his wallet and carefully inserted it over the lock sliding the card tightly against the latch. He gently pushed the unresisting door open.

He stepped inside the darkened room, allowing the door to close. He heard no noise. He then pressed the light switch next to the door. Immediately, he saw Kate's body lying on the bloody floor. He went into the bedroom. No sign of Wes in the apartment. He checked the closet. No clothes belonging to a man. "Dammit! He's gone," he yelled out.

He hurried out of the apartment and hit the button beside the elevator. He immediately heard the whirl of the elevator as it began its journey down. Nervously, he checked his watch again. It was seven-twenty two. *Ding.* The door opened, then closed and within seconds, he stepped out into the garage. He spotted Wes' car, but there was no visible sign of Wes. "That jerk. He's making a run for it," he mumbled.

He ran to the street, scanned the pedestrians, cabs, and cars that flashed past him like a current. He leaped high to see over the crowds. Out of the corner of his eye, he noticed a man dressed in black sprinting down the other side of the street. He could see blond hair bobbing in an irregular field pattern through and around the pedestrians on the street. The dark figure, only about sixty feet away from him, instantly disappeared behind moving traffic. When the traffic passed, the dark figure was gone.

He stepped off the curb to cross the street, half-aware of someone coming up behind him. He started to whirl around, but the fierce blow to his back sent him flying headlong into the path of a moving bus. He tumbled into the gutter, fell to the ground, and landed on his hands and knees. The bus barreled toward him, the high-pitched screech, and the blare of its horn—in a split second, he realized that he was in its path. Air brakes hissed as it jolted to a stop.

Not realizing how close he came to death, he quickly scrambled to his feet and peered across the street. "Damn it! He got away. I've got to find him."

This one was worth serious money. I need those million dollars. Just maybe, by some ever so slight a chance—I will be able to convince Wes to give me the million dollars. There was still time.

But then, he thought, *if Wes had already gotten away, the Russians would probably kill him for allowing Wes to escape.* He grabbed his cell. He must alert the Russians that Wes had most likely made a run for it and was on his way to the airport. He also thought it best to tell them that Kate Lee was shot dead, and was probably murdered by Wes.

They informed him that they would immediately dispatch two of their men to the airport where he was to meet up with them. Together, they would find Wes if he was at the airport.

The PI turned and hurried back to the parking garage and jumped in his car. He slammed the car into gear and jammed his foot on the accelerator, driving down the street like a lunatic. He was unconcerned with speed.

Traffic suddenly became a snarl of cars. He cut in and out of traffic ignoring the horns blaring in angry protest.

He must find Wes. He needs that million dollars.

CHAPTER

85

The rain had started again—a drizzle that darkened the sky. Cursing the rain, he hunched his shoulders, pulled up the collar of his jacket, picked up his suitcase, computer bag, and carry- on and hailed a taxi.

Once inside the taxi he felt secure and began to relax. Though fatigued, he began to feel free again. He did not want to think of the past any longer—he had no time for the past.

As the taxi weaved through the streets toward the Reagan National Airport, he listened to the rhythmic swish of the windshield wipers while trying to weigh his chances of survival. His next move will be to fly somewhere in South America and stay for a few weeks before he goes on to Rarotonga. He must be certain that no one follows him to the Cook Islands.

He paid the driver, gathered his belongings, and made his way in the direction of the American Airlines check-in counter to see what flights they had to South America.

"Next," the young woman called out. Wes walked up to the counter. She smiled at him and asked, "How can I help you this evening?"

"Do you have any flights this evening that go to South America?"

"Any particular spot in South America?" she asked.

"Columbia."

"Bogota?"

"Yes, Bogota," Wes replied.

"Would that be one-way or round trip, sir?"

"Right now, I don't know when I'll be returning, so one-way."

"Let me check that for you, sir. One moment." She punched away at her keyboard and then looked up and said, "We have a flight to Bogota, Columbia, which leaves at eleven-fifty this evening and arrives in Bogota at seven-fifty three tomorrow morning. There's one stop in Miami, Florida with a change of planes."

"How long is the layover?"

"It's a two-hour layover, sir. You will have to go through customs in Miami."

"Okay."

She punched away on the keyboard and then said, "Unfortunately, it seems we only have first-class available."

"That's perfect. I'll take it," Wes said as he handed her his passport. "Thank you."

"All right, the price for a one-way ticket to Bogota, Columbia is one thousand eight hundred seventy five dollars, sir."

Wes retrieved his wallet from the inside pocket of his jacket and handed her nineteen hundred dollars cash.

She carefully counted it out. "Thank you," she said while waiting for the printer to print the boarding pass. "How many suitcases do you have?"

"Just one."

She punched another few keys and out popped a luggage ticket. She grabbed the suitcase, wrapped the ticket around the handle, picked it up and put it on the luggage carousel. "The plane will start to board at eleven-fifteen at Terminal B, Gate 76," she said as she handed him his boarding pass and passport. "Have a nice trip, Mr. Black."

"Thank you," Wes said, taking a big breath. *He is outta here.* He picked up his carry-on and computer case and looked around the area for Terminal B signage. He was finally on his way to freedom.

Suddenly, he was ravenously hungry. *There must be food courts somewhere along the way,* he thought. He kept walking and the first turn he made, the aroma of coffee in the air hit his nostrils. "Yes," he said softly to himself when he saw the neon lights, "Dunkin Donuts." He ordered a coffee and two donuts—that would tide him over until he got to Miami.

He checked his watch: eight-thirty-five. He sat at the long bar facing the walkway for a few minutes drinking his cup of coffee and eating his donuts. His mind kept wrestling back and forth. He needed to devise a new plan—a plan that he alone would come up with so he would get control of the situation. When women were in his life, he became a puppet, never quite feeling capable of navigating his own life. Now with Kate out of the way, he began to feel in control. He grabbed his coffee and started walking toward the security checkpoint.

He will start his life over again. He's healthy, strong, handsome, and now, wealthy. He smiled; he finally felt free and confident.

CHAPTER

86

A trip that should have taken thirty minutes took over an hour because of the rain and the traffic congestion. Frustrated, the P.I. pulled his car into the short-term parking lot, jumped out and dashed across the street to the terminal.

He stopped to study the monitors for all flights leaving this evening. *No, wait a second, these are domestic flights. Wes isn't staying in this country. He said the money was in an offshore account. That means he's going south. He's going to have to fly out of Florida or Dallas.*

He quickly scanned the schedule for flights to Dallas. Nothing going out late tonight. The last flight left at 7:45 p.m. He checked Miami flights. "Yes," he said softly. Miami flight out at 11:50 p.m. tonight on American Airlines. "That's the one. Terminal B, Gate 12," he mumbled to himself.

CHAPTER

87

With more than two hours before he could board the plane, Wes decided to walk around the mall. Within minutes, he spotted a Ben & Jerry's and stopped to get an ice cream cone. He sat alone on a stool and watched the passersby and gazed at several young children playing beside him. His boys—he missed them. They should be with him, he thought. He will come back and get them after he's settled in on the Cook Islands.

He finished his cone, threw his napkin into the trash bin and started to walk back toward Gate 76 when a young man holding a camera, stopped and asked, "Would you please take a picture of my family?"

Wes looked all around the area, then at the man and then at his family—a wife and two young boys. *It's just like the family I once had*, he thought. *I can have a family again, only this time, it'll be just my boys and me.* "Sure," he said with a smile.

The man handed Wes the camera and ran back to his family for the picture. Wes focused, pressed the button, and gave the camera back to the man.

"Thank you so much, sir. I really appreciate it," the man said.

"No problem," Wes responded as he turned to walk back toward his gate. He stopped at the News Express and bought a newspaper and some gum, which he slipped into the side pocket of his carry-on.

A few minutes later, the air became thick with chatter and laughter coming from Harry's Tap Room. The TV monitor was blaring. The baseball game was in the sixth inning and the Red Sox were leading six to two.

He went inside, put his carry-on and computer case on the floor, and grabbed his airline ticket from his jacket pocket before he hung it on the back of the stool. Resting his forearms on the bar, he stared at the ticket, and then sighed heavily, dreading the long trip he had ahead of him.

"What'll you have," the bartender asked.

"Jack on the rocks," he replied.

After an hour and three drinks later the edginess, he was feeling mollified. His body began to relax and he felt safe in the knowledge that he got away without being noticed. He sat daydreaming about the wealth that will now provide him the life he so deserved. He had enough money to last forever. Once he reaches Rarotonga, he would no longer have to look over his shoulder. His life will be changed. He won't be a run-of-the-mill individual. His money will put him in control of those who come in contact with him. He and his boys will live the good life, enjoying all the finer things life has to offer: designer clothes, satin sheets, and tutors and servants.

Unexpectedly, his daydreaming was interrupted—a feeling of pure panic pulsed through his body as if he was shell-shocked. "This can't be," he said as he winced in disbelief. His eyes must be playing a trick on him, he thought as he stared across the mall at a large gaggle of people walking rapidly toward various gates as if they were about to miss their flight.

The PI was walking among them! He was running down to the gates as if he too, was late for his flight.

"Oh, shit," he said aloud. *How did he find me? He got through security so he had to have bought a ticket. Where could he be going in such a hurry? He has probably already called the Russians. Goddammit, they will be here too. He is meeting up with*

the goddamn Russians! Damn it? Is anything ever going to go my
way

There was neither time nor a place to hide. He's got
to get out of here if he wants to be able to put his life back
together. His mind reacted; his heart pounded frantically,
and his insides tightened. "I must think," he muttered to
himself as he sprang from his seat, slipped his jacket on,
picked up his carry-on and computer case and headed
swiftly out of the bar. As he eased his way straight for the
exit the crowd soon swallowed him. His frantic gaze swept
the area for any sudden movements while his ears
searched for any unusual sounds. He could not get out of
the terminal fast enough, even though now he had no idea
where the hell he was going. Just far away from here. *I have
to think. Think.*

High on fear and excitement, he concentrated on
what he was going to do next. His mind quickly sifted
through all the possibilities, in an attempt to manipulate a
plan. He needed to do something that would confuse
them. Something that would throw them off track.
Something unexpected; something so staggering that it
would convince them that he already left the country. But
what?

"I'll leave and go back to the city," he muttered to
himself. No one will expect him to do that. His luggage is
gone. He'll stop by American Airlines and tell them he
can't leave until tomorrow. They'll hold his luggage in
Miami for him.

He walked up to the American Airlines counter and
said, "I need some help."

"Certainly, sir. What can I assist you with?"

"I purchased a ticket earlier this evening and I have
an emergency I have to take care of and I won't be able to
leave until tomorrow night. Would it be possible to change
my ticket for tomorrow?"

"Certainly, sir. Let me have your ticket and passport." She ran the ticket number through a scanner, punched in a few keys and the printer spit out a new passenger ticket for tomorrow evening.

"Here you are, sir," she said, handing him a new ticket and passport. "I've attached your claim ticket for your luggage to your new ticket and I've notified Miami to hold your luggage until you claim it. You can pick it up tomorrow in Miami in the claims department located in the baggage carousel area. You'll be transferring to Columbia so you will have to go through the International terminal in Miami for check-in."

"Thank you so much. You've been a great help."

"American Airlines is here to provide the best service for our customers, sir," she happily said with a smile.

"Yes, you certainly have accomplished that. Thanks again," he said, waving his ticket in the air, as he hurried toward the exit doors. Filled with anger and frustration, he tried to comprehend how the P.I. had tracked him down so soon.

Once outside, he hailed the first cab he saw and slipped inside unnoticed. "The Ritz-Carleton in downtown D.C.," he announced to the driver.

As the cab weaved through the streets, Wes had a vision, or more like a wide-awake dream. He saw his two sons. Adam was sitting on a swing being pushed by Lucas. Adam was yelling out, "Higher, higher!" Suddenly Lucas stopped pushing him. He walked around the path of the swing and a woman handed him a red Popsicle. Then she disappeared. She was gone with the vision.

"Where did she go?" Wes yelled out which caused the driver to glance at him in the rearview mirror. Wes ignored him and just stared out the window.

He squirmed uncomfortably in his seat, his thoughts, wrestling back and forth, trying to weigh his chances of survival. Whenever he focused on the immediate moment, he sensed an impending doom and started to envision his life in prison.

Anxiety filled him with fear; fear of being at the end of the line. He has no Kate, he has no Emma. Nothing he's done has turned out right. What should he do now? Questions still rattling around in his head; he's unable to think with any clarity.

He closed his eyes and rested his head on the headrest. At least, he got away from the airport without being seen. They'll be looking for him all over the airport. Whether or not the ploy will work was a crap shoot.

Moments later he straightened up his body. Something wasn't right—the vengeance he had pursued these past months—his plan for revenge. How can he leave the country without killing Emma? Everything became complicated when he arrived in D.C. and he had gotten off course.

His luck will change. Everything will be better once he leaves this god-awful place.

CHAPTER

88

Within the hour, the taxi driver pulled in front of the Ritz-Carleton and yelled out, "Ritz-Carlton."

Wes snapped back to the present. Struck by something he noticed as the driver opened the door, he hesitated. Something didn't look right. He grabbed his computer case and his carry-on and slowly stepped out. The street was dark; he saw a shadow move stealthily toward him. "Welcome to the Ritz-Carleton, sir," a man dressed in a navy blue uniform trimmed with gold braiding said. "I'll be happy to take your baggage, sir."

Wes frowned with annoyance, then said, "It's all right, I've got them," once he saw that it was the doorman.

Once inside, he felt the wealth displayed in the wood-paneled lobby, a giant marble fireplace, Oriental rugs and gray-streaked white marble floors. He immediately felt he was in his element. This is how he is supposed to live his life—enjoying the finer things in life. This is how he will live from now on.

"I would like a room for one night, but I'll need a late departure because my flight doesn't leave until eleven fifty tomorrow evening."

"Certainly, sir. What type of room would you like?" the clerk asked.

"What do you have available?"

"We have a Club Level, one bedroom on the fifth floor. We offer a never-ending flow of food and beverage throughout the day if that's something you would like. It also offers you transportation to the airport."

I'm not going out, so that will be perfect, he thought to himself. "Yes, the Club Level room, please," he responded.

"May I have a credit card and your passport, please?"

"Certainly," he said as he handed them to her. "I would like to pay cash for the time I'm here, but I realize you need a credit card to secure the room."

"That will be fine, Mr. Black. You can pay when you depart. I'll have you registered in a moment," she said as he watched her ruby-red fingernails glisten as she swiped his card.

He watched the clerk as she rifled through some paperwork below the counter for several minutes. He didn't like waiting. He fidgeted, shifting his weight from one foot to the other, constantly looking around as if he was waiting for someone. He became more intense, irritated by the long wait. His jaw tightened, and his anxiety was turning to anger. After a few frowning minutes, he gave the clerk a steady stare, hoping she would move faster. Finally, he asked, "Is there a problem?"

"No, sir. No problem. The printer was out of paper. Here is your card key. The bellboy will escort you to your suite."

Immediately he felt a heightened level of luxury when the bellhop opened the door to his suite. The living room was decorated in soothing colors. French doors opened to a spacious master bedroom with plush bedding. The master bath had a separate shower and Jacuzzi tub and plush white terry bathrobes and slippers. He tipped the bellhop, closed the door and turned the lock. Finally, he's alone—he took a deep breath of relief. He would take these hours to rest, knowing the PI and FBI were running in circles.

He took off his jacket, hung it over the nearest chair and reached for the TV remote control from the coffee table in front of the sofa. He turned the TV on and sat down on the sofa. The local news filled the screen.

Stomach growling, he realized he hadn't eaten anything substantial all day. He picked up the phone on the end table and rang room service. "Yes, I'll have a Porterhouse steak, medium-well, with a baked potato with butter, dinner salad with Italian dressing, apple pie for dessert and a large carafe of coffee. Thirty minutes? Thank you very much."

"Ah," he sighed, resting his head on the back of the sofa. "This is really nice," he murmured to himself.

He glanced at the television. There was no sound, but the tag on the photo being flashed on the screen read "Woman Found Dead In Upscale Apartment Building."

"That can't be," he muttered to himself. *They found Kate? There has to be a mistake. How could they find her so soon?* He clenched his hands into fists, trying to make sense of what he was reading. *Someone had to go into the room. But Who? Why would someone go inside the apartment?* He turned up the sound on the television.

The coverage was live. "Yes, there was a great deal of excitement at the Professional Apartment complex today," an attractive woman with a microphone said while standing in front of the building. "Police have reported that a woman was shot to death in her apartment early this evening."

Cutting to the anchor: "Charlene, do authorities have any indication who committed this crime?"

"Not at this point, Charlie. The Metropolitan Police are handling the case and are saying nothing more than it's under investigation." The image on the screen broke up in diagonal lines for a second before it switched back to the newsroom.

Wes got up from the sofa and began pacing, trying to figure out how this had happened. *I mustn't panic. No one knows I'm here. No need to get upset. Forget about it. I must focus my efforts on getting out of this goddamn country.*

However, he couldn't forget about it. He was full of confidence an hour ago, and now he felt virtually helpless. Such a change, such a suddenness, this can't happen. His mind cast about for explanations. What is happening to me? By now he should have been living in a huge home on a private beach sipping Malibu Red Mojito's in South America. Instead, the Russian's, the FBI, and that damn PI are hunting him down. His dream of living the good life was looking bleak.

He plopped down on the sofa, his head falling back, his eyes closed. He thought about the last several weeks that seemed to go according to the plan until that damn P.I. met up with him. *This guy has forced me to change my course. He screwed up everything. I shoved him three seconds too early… that bus should have killed him. Damn him.*

Moments later, he sprang up. "What does it matter who found her? Why am I interpreting this as a bad turn? I mustn't do this to myself."

I have to focus on a new plan—a plan that doesn't include Kate, he reminded himself as he sat back down on the sofa.

"Right on time," he said when he heard room service knock on the door. He opened the door and the waiter arrived with dinner on a rolling cart. He wheeled it next to the dining table and within a few moments, all the food was placed on the dining table. He tipped the server, closed the door and turned the lock.

CHAPTER

89

Wes awakened with a sudden start. The room was silent. He had blinked a few times before he glanced at the luminescent face of the clock on the nightstand. It was seven fifty-two. He got up, took a quick shower, toweled himself off, shaved, and dressed. He dragged his hands through his hair, scattering droplets of water on the mirror and countertop.

He picked up the phone and rang room service. "I'd like a large carafe of strong coffee, please. Also a Swiss cheese and avocado omelet with some whole wheat toast and lots of strawberry jam. Oh, and a large orange juice. Fifteen minutes? Thank you very much."

When he opened the heavy drapes in the living area, a shaft of piercing sunlight forced him to shield his face from the blinding early morning sun.

A fresh flow of air entered the room when he unlocked and opened the French doors. He felt a nip in the air and the coolness raised goose bumps on his skin. He stepped out onto the balcony, and thrust his hands in his pockets. He immediately heard horns honking, sirens blaring in the distance, and people yelling.

He glanced down the street at the congested traffic and crowded crosswalks with pedestrians busily moving in different directions. An immense building directly across the street had a uniformed doorman at the front entrance. "Must be an apartment building," he muttered to himself.

A knock on the door. He turned and went back inside to open the door. He was greeted with "Good morning, Mr. Black."

"Ah, come right in. Please set everything on the coffee table."

"Certainly, sir." The young waiter quickly placed the food on the table. "Would you like me to pour your coffee, sir?"

"Yes, please. Ah, that's perfect," Wes said, handing him a tip.

"Thank you, sir."

Wes followed the waiter to the door and said, "Thanks," before he closed and locked it.

He sat down and looked at the food. Earlier, when he ordered the food he had been ravenously hungry, but for some reason, he could only bring himself to take a few bites. Trying to devise a new plan had his stomach in a death grip.

Right now, he managed to escape from the Russians and the P.I. If he left the country tonight, he'd be free with millions of dollars to live the life he wanted. However, if he left the country, he would never be able to return to get his sons. At best, an awkward predicament to be in. He doesn't like the dilemma he's caught in.

His mind wandered as he sat and sipped his coffee. Thoughts of how he got to this point and how he's now going to hop on a plane to a place he's never been to without accomplishing what he came here to do—get his sons and kill his wife.

This whole scenario is stupid. What the hell am I doing? I want my boys. I can't leave without them. With certainty, I would be arrested if I ever tried to come back into the United States again. My boys deserve a better life and now that I have a lot of money I can send them to the best schools and have the best teachers for them. They'll love living on an island and being able to swim, go boating and catch fish. I can't let these bizarre circumstances change my plans.

I've got to scrape a plan together, reclaim my kids and flee to South America. This is why I drove cross country; to get my sons, and to kill Emma. She ruined my life and I don't want her ruining their lives. I hate the thought of them being with her. I've got to get them back. I know where Ross lives. The boys and Emma have to go over there at some point in time. I'll rent a car and go over there later this afternoon.

He smiled as he envisioned the wonderful life they would have together. All the thoughts he had buried deep in his mind had now begun to work their way to the surface. With the Russians' money, it felt like he'd won the lottery. He would not have to work, and he could do what he wanted when he wanted. He would disappear with his sons, like dust. Off to live the good life on the Cook Islands. No one would ever find them.

I'll be somebody on an island, he thought. No one will know me. I'm never going to get involved with another woman. When I want a woman, I'll go buy one and then get rid of her. Marriage is a prison that never will end well. Every woman I've known has screwed me over. It started with my mother. She allowed my father to beat the crap out of me while she watched, and did nothing to stop him.

I know I'll certainly be a better father than my father was. My father had made it very clear fifteen years ago, that I was not welcome. I've been able to put the fuck-up in the Navy behind me, but my father just couldn't manage to do that. He couldn't live with the fact that I spent two hundred and five days in the brig and was dishonorably discharged. He couldn't see that maybe, just maybe, that some of the strict military rules were mostly bullshit, and because of this he disowned his only child.

He picked up a slice of toast and smeared strawberry jam over the top. After he finished the toast, he drank the orange juice, he grabbed his coffee and walked over to the patio, watching people come and go from the building across the street. Limos and taxies sputtered along in front of the building's bright orange awning as they picked up and dropped off men, women, and children.

He noticed a black Jaguar pull up in front of the building and the doorman quickly ran up to the Jag to open the door for a young woman who had just exited the building. She jumped in the front seat and the doorman closed the door after her.

"Holy Hell," he shouted out. "Was that Emma? That sure looked like her," he muttered to himself. "Naw, it couldn't be. There's no way she could afford to live in a building like that. Naw. It's just someone who resembled her. Someone with a black Jag. Huh?"

"Do you rent cars from this hotel?" Wes asked.

"Yes, sir. We do," the girl behind the counter responded.

"Would it be possible for me to rent a car for the rest of the day and leave it at the airport?"

"Certainly, sir. We can take care of that for you. Let me get the forms. What type of car did you have in mind?"

"A four-door sedan should work well."

"Fine. What time would you like to pick it up?"

"About three o'clock."

"I'll need you to fill this out," she said, pushing a form and pen in front of him.

Not another fuckin' form, he thought. "You know, you took all that information when I signed in. Could you get it off my registration card? I have a few things I must do right now. I'll be back in about thirty minutes to sign the forms. Will that work for you?" he said as he slipped a Jackson under the paperwork.

"Oh. Yes, sir, I'll be happy to do that for you, Mr. Black."

"Thank you," he said as he walked toward the elevators, still holding on to his thought: *He has so much to offer his boys. He must get them today.*

CHAPTER

90

Ellie had just finished fixing potato salad for the barbecue. She had about ten minutes before everyone would be coming through the front door. She went into the dining room to check the table one last time. Balloons were tied to the chairs. The birthday cake Ross had delivered to her home was on the center of the table. She grabbed the punch bowl from the hutch and placed it at the end of the table. She placed the cups, silverware, napkins and plates beside the cake.

Before Ross left for work, he strung a banner across the room which read, 'Happy Birthday, Ellie.' She smiled when she looked at it and then turned to go back to the kitchen—the back door was not completely closed. *I know I closed that door.* Her chest tightened and for a moment she almost couldn't breathe with her heart pounding so hard. "I've got to call Ross," she murmured to herself as she reached into her pocket for her cell phone.

It was then that she saw it: the motion of a shadow behind her.

"Perhaps you can do that later," a gravelly voice said from behind her.

"Who are…"

A large hand quickly covered her mouth before she could say anything. The other hand grabbed her cell phone and threw it across the room. She wrenched her body in an attempt to get free, but the man was strong.

"Stop struggling," he yelled out. "Just shut up and do as I say if you value your life."

The gun. I've got to get that gun. It's only four feet away inside the end table drawer.

CHAPTER

91

Ross guided the Hummer to a stop in the driveway. Emma promptly opened the passenger door and jumped out to open the rear door to help the boys out of their car seats. They each cradled a wrapped present in their small hands. It was Ellie's birthday. They were both giggling and excited and could hardly wait to see her. As soon as their feet hit the pavement, they ran up the stairs to the front door and rang the doorbell. Ellie opened the door and grabbed them up in her arms smothering them with kisses before closing the door.

"I'm going to put the ice cream and pops in the freezer in the garage," Ross said.

"Okay," Emma said as she gathered her purse and camera. "Oh, here comes Hawk. I'll help him unload some of the things from his car."

Hawk pulled his car up next to the Hummer and stepped out holding a bag. "I'll go around back and drop off the charcoal and cooler full of drinks."

"You need any help? Emma asked.

"Yes, you can grab this bag?" Hawk said as he waved to Ross, who was coming out of the garage.

"Sure," Emma said, grabbing the bag. "See you inside the house."

Hawk pulled the cooler out from the trunk and placed the charcoal on top. He closed the trunk, picked up the cooler and walked down the path toward the backyard.

"Okay, let's go see the birthday girl," Ross said, climbing the three steps to the front door. Ross opened the front door and called out, "Where's that birthday girl?"

When Violet didn't come to the door, he immediately knew something was wrong. He heard a rushing noise behind him. Before he could turn, the blow from the gun's handle struck with a staggering force, coming out of nowhere. He'd been hit on the head a few times, but with no time to react, he crashed onto the floor in a heap. He gasped and tried to get up, but the blinding, agonizing pain in his head left him strengthless. His mind tried to grasp what had happened....but his body went slack.

Emma dropped the bag on the floor and ran to Ross' side in a disordered state of mind. She didn't know what had happened. When she spun around, she saw Wes. A tight knot of fear instantly filled her throat.

With an edge of panic in her voice, she yelled out, "Wes!" the name exploded from her like a curse. "Why did you do that?"

"Just shut up, you miserable bitch," Wes snapped, looking at her furiously as if she was a disobedient dog.

"Where are the boys? Where are they?" Emma yelled out in a panic.

"Don't get your panties in a knot. They're downstairs with Ellie."

"What are you doing here?" Emma asked as she stood up.

"I'm here to take what belongs to me."

"And what might that be? What is it you want?"

"What do I want? I want my boys. You ruined my life and now I want to ruin your life."

"You're the one who destroyed our lives, ruined our love. I see right through you—deep down through your demented brain and your vile heart. You were born with an "evil gene" ruining everything that you ever put your hands on. Now you want to ruin our son's lives? Why are you blaming me for your screw-ups?"

"Because you are the reason for my screw-ups; always telling me what to do and how to do it. Now I'm telling you what I'm going to do. I've been searching for you for weeks, and I'm not about to leave without finishing the job I started months ago. I should have killed you in California when I had the chance. I told you I'd kill you if you ever took my boys away from me? Well, my sweet little wife, your time is up. Now it's my turn to take away everything that's dear to you, just like you took everything away from me."

"I never took anything away from you. The boys are my sons. You haven't been a father to them."

"I'll be a father to them now. When I'm finished here, the boys won't have any relatives—just me. I'm going to kill all of you so they'll be no family left. This may not have worked out like I planned, but the end result is the same. You'll all be dead."

Ross groaned as thoughts spun violently in his head. He clutched his head, trying to grasp where he was or what had happened. His eyes struggled to come into focus. The side of his face lay on the cold tiles and when he tried to lift his head up from the floor, a shock-like pain pulsed through the back of his head.

He had a sudden flash of memory— *I walked up a few stairs carrying packages inside the house. I remember going inside, then something heavy hit me on the back of my head and I went down. Before I blacked out, I heard Emma scream.*

Emma knelt down next to him. "Your head is bleeding. Are you all right, Uncle Ross?"

"Yes, Em, I'm okay," he mumbled. "Are you okay, Em?"

"I'm fine," she responded.

"What happened?" Ross glanced upward. "Oh, it's *you*," he said, with contempt in his voice. "I might have known."

"Yes, old man, it's your so-called *son-in-law*," he laughed as he walked toward them. With lightning speed, he grabbed Emma by the hair and pulled her up against him. He closed his right arm around her neck while his left hand jammed the barrel of a handgun into the back of her head. "Say good-bye to your niece, old man."

Emma felt the blunt metal of the gun pressed against the back of her head. Her heart pounded, her stomach was in a knot, her vocal cords were frozen with fear; she couldn't speak. Adrenaline raced through her body—she flailed her arms around trying to get a grasp of Wes' hair, but he squeezed his right arm tightly around her shoulders to hold her where he wanted her. "You scared now, Emma? Your big shot uncle can't save you."

"Yeow!" Wes screamed out as a sharp rivet of pain shot through his forearm. His eyes opened wide as he watched the blood pouring out of his throbbing arm. "You fucking bitch," he screamed out. "That's the second time you bit me, you little fucker." Fused with hatred and pain, he struck Emma across the side of her mouth. She felt her lip split, felt the blood dribble down her chin.

He grabbed her and snapped his arm around her throat, squeezing her like a boa constrictor. She felt his heart thumping against her back.

"Don't even think about doing that again," he shouted, yanking her head farther back and pushing the gun harder against the back of her head. She couldn't turn her head. She shifted her eyes toward Ross.

In an attempt to get Wes' mind off Emma, Ross said, "You're real tough, Wes. Who'd you pick on while you were in the brig? There weren't any women and children around."

Wes' eyes narrowed and his jaw dropped. Inflamed, he breathed heavily through an open mouth as he tightened his arm around Emma. "Shut the fuck up, old man," he snarled.

"So now you just kill everyone who gets in your way?" Ross said.

"That's right. Anyone who wants to get in my way. The four men in the alley who tried to attack Kate and me are dead. It was self-defense."

"You killed those four men?" Emma asked.

"Yes. They came after me with a baseball bat and a knife demanding us to give them our wallets and jewelry. One of them wanted Kate. It was kill them before they killed us. They weren't getting anything from me."

"Where is your girlfriend, Kate?" Is she waiting in the car for you? Ross asked.

"No. She's dead. I had to kill her—served the bitch right. She got me mixed up with the Russians and then if that wasn't bad enough, she had the audacity to lie to me. She's a fucking felon."

Hawk climbed the cedar stairs to the large deck. He slid the glass door open and yelled out, "Emma," as he stepped inside. Instinctively he stopped. There was a forbidding quiet to this home—too quiet for a birthday party. He could feel trouble's breath trembling on the back of his neck. He left the door open for a possible means of escape in case things got crazy and he needed an easy exit.

He stood motionless, listening for any movement as his efficient eyes took in every detail. The only thing he heard was his heart pounding. With a growing sense of dread, he moved quietly through the kitchen. He caught a brief look at Emma's face—eyes filled with fear, tears slithered down her cheeks. A man, whose eyes were smiling, had one arm tightly wrapped around Emma's neck while the other arm held a gun to the back of her head.

Hawk reacted in milliseconds when a hundred percent adrenaline flooded his veins. With lightning swiftness, he jerked his gun from his shoulder holster, leveled it, and fixed the man's head in his sight before he yelled out defiantly, "Kill her and I kill you. Let her go right now because this will not end well for you," he demanded. "Right now! Drop the gun! Do it, or I'll blow you straight to Hell!"

Wes retreated a step, dragging Emma with him. "Why would I want to do that?" Wes yelled out as his arm snaked tighter around Emma's neck.

Eye to eye, Hawk said, "If you harm one hair on her head, I'll kill you where you stand. Let her go now."

Wes stared at the intruder. "You must be the notorious wonder boy—Major Hawk Shaw!"

"That would be me," Hawk said firmly with his gun aimed.

"Well, ain't this my lucky day," he said with a snicker. "I got me a real-life wonder boy NCIS agent. Now, we finally meet. I've had to live all these years hearing about you," Wes said, with a smirk on his face. "Over the years, I've developed a hateful and intense dislike for you."

Enraged, Hawk's cold eyes stared at him as he conjured up a mental list of reasons he despised this gutless wonder. What he really disliked at the moment was the smirk on his face—he would love to personally remove it. He had no compunction about killing Wes. He would not lose a second's sleep over it.

"Is that right?" Hawk said calmly, keeping his rage under control.

"Yes, indeedy. I know all about the infamous Major Hawk Shaw," he said as his grin widened.

Hawk smiled, trying to figure out what this guy thought he knew about him. "Must have been the wrong information you heard about me."

"How's that?" Wes chuckled.

"When I told you to let her go *now*, I meant, let her go *now*."

Wes laughed out loudly while strengthening his grip on Emma. "So, you're a man of your word, are you?"

Finding it hard to believe that Wes found this situation something to laugh at, Hawk answered, "That's right. I am a man of my word."

Wes had an instant to look stupefied when the last thing he saw were the words that formed on Hawk's lips a millisecond before Hawk pulled back the hammer and squeezed the trigger.

POP!

A scarlet spray of blood burst into the still air when the bullet crushed through Wes's forehead. A cry of pain had vibrated the air before blood dribbled out from his mouth. His body instantly flexed back as if suspended in midair before he spun around dragging Emma down with him as he dropped dead to the floor, his life pumping out on the tiles. His gun clattered as it slid across the ceramic tiles, stopping when it slammed against the wall.

In seconds, stillness filled the air. Emma's heart stopped momentarily before she screamed as she struggled to dislodge herself from his body. Her hair and body doused with blood, she looked up at Hawk and saw the wisp of smoke rising from his gun.

Hawk moved swiftly across the room toward Emma's trembling body. "Are you all right?" he asked, looking at her blood-flecked face.

Yes, she nodded, her voice too shaky to speak. She wrapped her arms around Hawk's neck so he could lift her up.

She stood, staring down at the body. Her reaction was one of passivity—she felt no remorse, no victory—she saw her mistake lying lifeless on the floor—the death of a man filled with hatred and bitterness—a man who had changed her life forever. In one way she felt defeated, even though it was his life that came to a dead end.

It would be a long time before she fully understood *her mistake.*

A few moments later, a hoarse voice uttered, "You done good, Hawk. No, you done *great,*" Ross said as he lay on the floor with his gun in his hand. "If you didn't shoot that bastard, I would have," he said waving his gun. "Love that suppressor you have. We can still hear now."

Emma immediately turned toward her uncle, "Oh, Uncle Ross, are you okay?" she asked as she and Hawk bent down to help him stand up.

"I'm better than okay now that that bastard is dead," he said. "It's over, Em. You and the boys no longer have to live in fear."

With Hawk's help, Ross got to his feet, but he was dizzy. "You should sit quietly for a while," Hawk said as he guided him to a chair.

Ross sat down heavily on the chair, rubbing his neck.

"Are you in a lot of pain, Uncle Ross?

"I've got a hell of a headache, he replied. "Emma, do you think I could have an ice pack?"

"I'll get you one right now," Emma said as she ran to the freezer to grab a package of frozen peas and a towel.

"Wes confessed that he killed the four guys in the alley when they came after him with a knife and a baseball bat."

"What?" Hawk said, not quite believing what Ross just said.

"Yup, that's what he told Emma and me. He also killed his girlfriend Kate because he found out that she was a felon."

"Christ what a night," Hawk said.

"You got that right," Ross agreed.

"Your head is bleeding," Emma said as she put the wrapped peas on his head. "Hold this. We've got to....where's Ellie?" Emma exclaimed. "Oh, my God, where's Ellie?! Where are the boys?"

"The boys are downstairs with Ellie," Ross said.

Hawk raced downstairs. He found Ellie sitting on the floor in the corner of the den, tears rolling down her cheeks. "I'm so sorry," she uttered in a weak hoarse voice.

"There's nothing to be sorry about, Ellie," Hawk said. "Everyone's fine."

"I felt so helpless. There wasn't anything I could do. He said he would kill everyone if I made any noise. I feel so bad that I was unable to do anything. If only I could have reached the gun. I would have killed him."

"You're traumatized, Ellie. You're human and not even you can endure trauma and keep on going as if nothing happened," Hawk said. "Put your arms around my neck and I'll lift you up."

She stretched her arms up around his neck and kept saying, "I'm so sorry," over and over again, her voice muffled against his chest when he lifted her.

"You just did what he asked you to do, Ellie. Everyone is fine."

Emma came running down the stairs in a nervous flutter. "Where are the boys? Ross said they were with down here. Oh God, where are the boys? Uncle Ross, the boys aren't here!" she screamed. "Are you okay, Ellie?"

"Yes, I'm okay and the boys are perfectly fine. They're hiding with Violet in the back bedroom under the bed. I told them to not make a sound until I came and got them. Are you okay, Emma? You've got blood all over you."

"Yes, I'm all right."

"How's Ross?"

"He's got a head wound. You need to take a look at him," Emma said.

Ellie reached for her medical bag and headed toward the stairway, shouting, "I'm coming Ross."

"Do you think the boys heard the gunshot, Hawk? They mustn't see any of this."

"They were in the back bedroom at the other end of the house so I don't think they heard much. Good thing this house is big. I'll take care of everything. You need to clean yourself up before you see the boys. You've got blood all over you."

"Oh, dear Lord," she said, looking down at her clothes. I'll jump in the shower and grab something out of Ellie's closet. It'll only take me two minutes," she said as she ran to the closet.

Hawk speed dialed Police Chief Morris.

"Hawk? What's going on?" the captain asked.

"I think I've got your mass murderer. He's here in Ross' home—he's dead."

"Who killed him?"

"I did. I'll need your people to come as soon as possible and get the body out of the house."

"I'll get on it right now. I'll be down in about ten minutes to get the details."

"See you then."

Emma covered her lips with a "shhhh" motion signaling Hawk not to make a sound. She slowly opened the bedroom door, singing in her usual off-note fashion, *"Hide and seek, hide and seek, where or where are you hiding seek? Here I come, here I come. I'm looking for my boys for fun. Hide and seek, hide and seek. Ready or not, here I come."*

Violet scooted herself out from under the bed and the boy's giggling instantly gave their hiding place away. "I see you," Emma said, bending down to look under the bed. She grabbed Adam's arms to wrestle him out. He wriggled and shrieked. Violet jumped up and down and barked in excitement.

"I see you, Lucas," Hawk said from the other side of the bed. He grabbed both his feet with one arm and dragged his wiggly body out and raised him over his head as he screamed and giggled.

With the boys' screaming and giggling and the dog barking, it was sheer music to Emma and Hawk's ears.

CHAPTER

92

A quartet of patrol cars, blue and red lights flashing like beacons in the night, were parked along the street blocking the entrance to the house. Two ambulances and a fire truck were parked ahead of the police cars. A white van with the dreadful words MEDICAL EXAMINER printed in black letters across the side parked in the driveway. Several officers had placed a yellow police tape across the front lawn and were standing there blocking people from entering.

Curious neighbors, pressing against one another, talking and pointing, were gathered on someone's front lawn directly across the street. They looked both scared and excited. Several news teams from local TV channels were reporting live from outside the perimeter of the crime scene tape. The street was crawling with media as they swooped in like buzzards. The reporters were elbowing one another out of the way in an attempt to be the first to try and stick a microphone in someone's face—anyone who would talk to them.

The night was alive with radio chatter when Police Chief Morris stepped out of his car and walked briskly toward the house, not giving the media any chance to close in on him. He approached a cluster of police officers who were standing in a tight group, some smoking cigarettes, and several others writing comments on their clipboards.

"Anyone know where I can find Hawk Shaw?" the chief asked.

One officer turned and pointed toward the house and said, "He's inside the house, chief."

A cluster of men stood by the front door when the door opened abruptly, and someone shouted, "Step aside, please." The men immediately separated to let the paramedics hustle a gurney through the door. Chief Morris glanced at the man lying on the gurney—it was Ross. Ellie was rushing beside them, shouting orders to clear the walkway. "Everyone step aside, please."

"Hi, Ellie, what happened to Ross?"

"Oh, Chief Morris. I wasn't aware you were here yet. Ross sustained a head injury and we're taking him to the hospital. He may have a concussion."

"Where are you taking him?"

"We're going to Medstar."

"I'll come down and see you there."

"Okay," Ellie responded. "See you later."

The house was crammed with uniformed cops, crime scene techs, men from the FBI and homicide detectives. Chief Morris walked cautiously through the room past the yellow chalk outline where the body had fallen. He saw the blood stained carpet and an accumulation of scattered medical debris littered on the floor as the crime scene techs collected evidence. Brief flashes of light dazzled the area as the police photographer took photos of the blood sprays on the walls and ceiling.

Hawk immediately waved his arm and the chief walked toward him. "Hi Hawk. Is Ross going to be okay?"

"Yes, he should be fine. Just a bump on the head and we both know that's not his first one. I was just giving the ME information on what happened, but we're finished here. Why don't we step out to the patio and get out of the way so these people can do their jobs."

"Sure. Lead the way. I see that some members of the forensics team are still here," Chief Morris stated.

"They just have a few things left and they'll be leaving shortly," Hawk said, gesturing with an extended right arm toward the door leading to the patio. Hawk followed the chief outside and immediately the noise level was subdued once Hawk closed the door.

"You've already given your statement to the police?"

"Yes, I have."

"Did they take your gun?"

"Yes, they have it."

"So tell me what happened here?" the chief asked.

Hawk, with a half smile that started on one side of his mouth and never quite got to the other side, said, "You're not gonna believe this."

"Why not?"

"The man I shot, Wes Blair, was the person who killed the four young men in the alley."

"How did you find that out?"

"He told Emma and Ross that he killed them because they were attacking him and his girlfriend when they cut through an alley to get to their hotel."

"That's unbelievable?"

"I told you that you wouldn't believe it. And, he also shot his girlfriend, the woman that was found dead in the apartment building. This guy was on a killing spree and he came over here to kill Ross and Emma."

"Why would he want to kill Ross and Emma?"

"This Wes Blair was Emma's abusive husband from California and his one goal in life was to kill Emma for leaving California with his two sons.

For several moments, Chief Morris was silent. After taking a deep breath, he said, "Wow, you've had some day, Hawk."

Hawk shook his head looking pensively at the moon. "If only I knew sooner that it was Blair."

CHAPTER

93

Many weeks later

Emma relaxed, feeling peaceful and comfortable on the sofa as she listened to soft music fill the air. She sipped her wine, closed her eyes, and let out a deep breath. She had fantasized about this moment—the day when she would no longer have to live with fear—the day when she can finally answer to her real name.

She's Emma Griffin once again and her boys are Lucas and Adam Griffin. In spite of all the pain she had suffered in the past, she was blessed with two wonderful boys, which proved that something good could come out of a bad situation. Life was good.

The shrill sound of the phone startled her for a moment. She quickly sat up, reached for the receiver and said, "Hello."

"Hi. What are you doing?"

"I'm in bed watching a movie."

He pictured her in bed and wondered what she was wearing. He imagined her in a little lacy teddy with a thong. No, she's got two boys who probably go into her bedroom. She probably has on a flannel nightgown.

"What are you wearing?" he asked in a soft sexy voice.

"Who is this?" she said loudly. "Is this an obscene phone call?"

Laughter roared out on the other end of the line. "You're good. How many obscene phone calls have you received? You sound very experienced."

"Actually, I've only heard about them," she responded, pushing her hair away from her face. "I never have gotten one… until now."

Heaving breathing and sighs. "So, tell me what you're wearing," he said in a whisper.

"Pajamas," she responded as she swallowed a laugh, puckering her lips to quell any sound.

"No, don't tell me that. I have you pictured in a little pink teddy with a thong."

A loud laugh burst out of her. "Is that right?"

"You've ruined my fantasy. Why didn't you just tell me you slept nude. Just humor me a little."

"I'm sorry. Who is this?" She could almost hear his smile on the phone.

"Very funny… very funny. The reason I called was to let you know that I have an assignment out of town."

"Oh," she said sadly, surprised by his announcement. "This is rather sudden, isn't it?"

"Yes, I'm afraid it is, but I just received the call a few minutes ago."

"Where are you going?"

"To the Middle East."

"You call that out of town? When are you leaving?"

"Later tonight."

"How long will you be gone?"

"For about two weeks."

After a long pause, she said, "Be careful, Hawk."

"I will. You take good care of yourself and the boys."

"I will do just that."

"I'll call you when I get back," he said softly. "Love you, Emma. Have you given any more thought about us?"

"No. I mean yes, I've given it quite a lot of thought. I need more time."

"I understand, Emma. We'll talk next time we meet."

"Yes, we'll definitely do that. Love you, Hawk. We'll all miss you."

"By the way...."

"Yes..." Emma said.

"In case you're wondering, I sleep naked as a baby."

Emma looked at the phone and broke out into laughter. It felt fun to be flirted with over the phone. Hawk had a way to make her laugh.

He hung up before she could say good-bye. She held the phone tightly before putting it back on the cradle. Ending the call so abruptly made her feel strange. How could she let him go off to the Middle East feeling rejected? What did she just do? Men like Hawk only come around once in a lifetime. Why is she afraid to become attached to another man?

It's just too soon, she thought. *Too soon. I must do this to protect myself from more heartache.*

Bzzzz. Bzzzz... the doorbell rang.

"Who could that be at this hour of the night," she muttered to herself as she walked toward the door. She pulled open the door. Hawk was standing alone with one of his hands tucked into a pocket of his black jeans, and the other hand anchored the scarred leather tan jacket he had slung over one shoulder. She immediately saw in his face that he had something definite to say to her.

Laughing out loud, she said, "You called me from the hallway? What are you doing here?"

A slow, dangerous smile curved his mouth, and without saying a word, he stepped inside, hooked his jacket on the tree stand, and closed the door. He swept her off her feet, into his arms and spun her around several times before saying, "I just wanted to come over and officially say goodbye."

Emma was giggling. "You already did that on the phone."

"Aren't you happy to see me?"

"Don't I look happy to see you?"

He smiled at her and gently lowered her feet to the floor before he locked his arms around her waist and started dancing....and singing softly in her ear... *"Are you lonesome tonight... Do you miss me tonight... are you sorry we'll be drifting apart..."*

"You are such a romantic...."

"Yes, I am when it involves you."

"Does this mean you're not going to the Middle East?"

"No, I'm still going. I just couldn't leave without seeing you before I left. I thought I'd come by to talk about us."

Emma's eyes opened wide. "Ah, that's why you said, *next time we meet*. You tricked me, Hawk Shaw."

"Kind of looks that way, doesn't it?"

"I told you I needed more time to think this through."

"When a woman says that she needs more time to think it over, it's obvious that she has already thought it over. Is this decision that difficult?" Hawk asked, frowning.

When her eyes met his she could see the disappointment on his face. But in seconds, a slow smile spread from one side of his mouth to the other.

"Well, *I've* made a decision," he said pointedly.

"Oh, what decision have you made?"

"I've decided that I want to be around more. This will be my last assignment out of the country."

"That's great news, Hawk."

"I thought you'd like my decision."

Emma stood on her toes, pressed her mouth against his neck and whispered, "You knew I wanted to hear that."

"Emma, you are an amazing woman, and there is no chance that I'd ever find a woman like you. I can't imagine ever trying to live my life without you. I want to start a new life with you and the boys. There are trips to go on, ball games to go to with the boys, and late-night dinners with the love of my life... my one and only."

Emma became quiet when she saw a few rare tears brimming in Hawk's eyes after he made this announcement.

"I realize you're afraid of having a relationship again, Emma," he said uneasily. "I once felt the same way, but you've changed all that. For the first time in my life, I feel I have something to give back to a woman, and I want that woman to be you."

"I know you love me, but I'm just not sure about marriage right now, Hawk. We've been friends for a long time and it's not the relationship part I'm concerned with. What I'm most afraid of is losing you, Hawk. What if you left me, or died, or were killed while doing your job? Where would I be then? Alone. I can't handle any more grief."

His hands cradled the back of her head and he said, "Emma, there isn't the slightest chance I'd ever leave you. I'm never going to harm you. Uncertainty is in everyone's life. Logically, the only thing I'm certain of is right now is being here with you. I love the woman you've become. I love everything about you... I've loved you from the first day we met."

Emma's eyes focused on his face, calculating, considering. "You know, lately, I've been asking myself something. *Am I happier when I'm alone, or am I happier when I'm with Hawk?*"

He gave her a curious look. "And what, pray tell, was your answer to yourself?"

Emma laughed and ultimately gave up trying to keep any distance from him as she launched herself at his chest and wrapped her arms around his neck. She looked up into his eyes, and softly said, "I don't like talking to myself and I especially don't like getting answers back from my…"

"Sshhh," he said as he put a finger to her lips. With a surging wave of relief, Hawk wrapped both arms around her waist, pressing her body tight against his. At first, he kissed her lightly. She didn't resist, so he kissed her boldly, just so there would be no question about how he felt about her.

Weak in his arms, she moaned. *It shouldn't feel this good… he makes me feel so wonderful,* she told herself. *It feels so natural, so right and his depthless love for me means everything.*

When he finally lifted his head, he said, "So you'll marry me?"

Their eyes locked. "Yes, and I hope you know what you're getting into, Mr. Shaw."

Emma saw an outburst of relief flare in Hawk's eyes followed by a slow smile that spread from one side of his mouth to the other. "I'll take my chances, Emma. You know I love a good challenge."

Before another second passed, he caressed her face with both hands and ran his thumbs over her lips before he wrapped his arms around her—their mouths met in a fierce kiss—a kiss that was meant to last every minute of every day they'd be apart.

Moments later, he glanced at his watch, dropped his arms, and with a sigh of regret, he looked into her eyes, wishing he could do the romantic thing like in the movies and whisk her off to an island. "I guess that will have to hold you until I get back," he said firmly. "I've got a plane to catch."

Emma watched him walk away, unhook his jacket from the tree stand, and open the door. He turned, flashed a huge smile, waved a small salute of farewell, and strolled out the door.

Now, there is a time *after* him, and that is the *big difference* in her life.

Made in the USA
Coppell, TX
03 February 2023

12117895R00277